LOVE IS A
REBELLIOUS
BIRD

LOVE IS A REBELLIOUS BIRD

A Novel

ELAYNE KLASSON

SHE WRITES PRESS

Published 2019
Printed in the United States of America
ISBN: 978-1-63152-604-6
ISBN:. 978-1-63152-605-3
Library of Congress Control Number: 2019906961

For information, address:
She Writes Press
1569 Solano Ave #546
Berkeley, CA 94707

She Writes Press is a division of SparkPoint Studio, LLC.

This is a work of fiction. Names, characters, places, and incidents either are the
product of the author's imagination or are used fictitiously. Any resemblance
is coincidental.

To David and Bill,
mensches both

Love is a rebellious bird
that nobody can tame,
and you call him quite in vain
if it suits him not to come.

Nothing helps, neither threat nor prayer.
One man talks well, the other's mum;
it's the other one that I prefer.
He's silent but I like his looks.

Love! Love! Love!

Love is a gypsy's child,
it has never, ever, known a law;
Love me not, then I love you;
If I love you, you'd best beware!

The bird you thought you had caught
beat its wings and flew away . . .
Love stays away, you wait and wait;
when least expected, there it is!

"The Habanera"
Excerpted from *Carmen*, 1872, by Georges Bizet

1
Beauty

Over seventy, I am considered by most of the world and for most of history, an old woman. I find that all of those things said about getting old are true. I walk by the mirror and am startled to see the reflection of my mother, who died long ago. It is not an unpleasant image. My mother was a reasonably attractive woman—with well-chiseled Russian features. I inherited her fine skin and narrow face. She was a fashionable, well-groomed woman for almost her entire life. Unfortunately, toward the end, she lost most of her memory and allowed bits of dropped food to remain on her clothes. She looked up when I came to visit her at the assisted living facility in suburban Skokie, her once-lively eyes having now taken on a blankness, and said, "Where the hell am I?"

I am terrified of this confusion I saw in my mother at the end. So now, before the memories are lost, and while curiosity still flickers in my eyes, I am trying to make sense of what I did with my life. You see, I have these two essential questions. Who is it we love and why have we loved these people? For me, it was always you, Elliot. Even now, more than sixty years later, with the evidence at last completely gathered, that fact remains unshakable. I do not know if you will hear this story, and if you do, how you will react, but I present it in its entirety and swear, just as in the courts of law you knew so well, that it is truth as I know it. Volumes have been written of such an enduring and obsessive love as mine. Sometimes you and I even discussed them: Nabokov and his Lolita, for example, being the gold standard. But wasn't it usually a man's obsession we read of? Women are more pragmatic. We get on with life. We search for the appropriate sperm to unite with our eggs, which are, after all, numbered and won't (unless stored in a freezer somewhere) wait around unfertilized forever. We get married, have children, maybe get a divorce or two, and, actuarial odds being what they are, become widowed.

Certainly there is pragmatism in my story as well; I may have acted foolishly, but I am not wholly without reason. By many, I was even regarded as a sensible person. I appeared to live life fully, marrying, having children, working in a profession known to help others. But the true tale is one of a passion consuming, painful, and, ultimately, unsuitable. Why you, Elliot? I asked myself again and again. Yes, I am a stubborn woman. But surely, sixty years of unwavering love could not be mere tenacity. As I puzzled over this question, I tried to examine the components of this love for you. I began, of course, with your beauty.

Love is like an economic transaction; we reach more easily for someone in our own range: social, financial, or educational. Race used to be a factor, although in recent times, it is less of a deal breaker. Beauty of the partners is usually part of the equation. A very beautiful woman may jump several strata in social, economic, or educational standing. However, a less attractive woman will rarely be found with a beautiful man (barring some exceptional attributes of money or standing of the female).

There was a relative inequity here. You, Elliot, the boy, were very beautiful and the girl, me, was spoken of as cute. Neither plain nor ravishing. Nice regular features, the nose perhaps a bit on the long side. Small stature, medium build. Thick, dark hair that could not make up its mind whether to be curly or straight. Frustrated by this hair that refused to behave, I kept it rather short, the so-called pixie cut contributing to the impression of cuteness. Clear brown eyes and, my best feature, a wide, ready smile. I was complimented often on my smile. "Judith is such fun," people would say. The smile made people assume that I was happy, but I'm not so sure about that. It was just my smile.

I am not saying that there was a shocking disparity in our looks, yours and mine, one in which passersby might turn their heads and wonder what on earth you saw in me, but the generally agreed-upon opinion was that you, Elliot, possessed unusual attractiveness. You had no awkward phase, no blemishes, pre-, during, or post-adolescence. You almost always had a dash of color high on your cheekbones, looking as if you'd just come rushing in from outdoors. And you had grand hair, just the right weight so that it settled on your forehead and then was flicked from your eyes with that careless toss of the head. Later, people would call that tousled mane Kennedy hair. Your eyes were dark and heavily lashed, the full lips ready with a self-deprecating smile which showed your even white teeth, never marred by the metal braces found on almost all Jewish children of that time and place. (This information can be verified by anyone growing up in that particular neighborhood of Chicago, West Rogers Park, in the mid-1950s.)

Let me further describe you. Once, in my twenties, I was visiting Boston and found myself with an afternoon unplanned. I walked through the Boston Museum of Fine Arts, browsing the galleries. Suddenly, I stopped dead in my tracks. There, painted by El Greco in 1609 and placed inside a lavishly gilded frame, was a young man. The young man in the portrait was Fray Hortensio Félix Paravicino, a seventeenth-century friar. You, my dear Elliot, were then twenty-five, studying for the New York bar exam and making your first stab at being a proper Jewish husband. No friar. Yet, I saw your face in that of the elegant Paravicino. His broad forehead spoke of his intelligence, while his narrow nose and full lips were those of a poet. El Greco must have been a little in love with fine young Hortensio.

How else could he have painted the boy so luminously? Mind you, I'm over seventy, and my knowledge of the digital is not as comprehensive as it might be, but with the Internet, I found Fray Paravicino in just a few clicks and I still concur with my assessment of so many years ago. You, so like that boy painted by El Greco, were undeniably beautiful. Your remarkable face, your long, well-shaped limbs, lovely shoulders, and slim waist, stirred everyone: your mother, father, your two brothers, all of us, even as children.

And me? No resemblance to any famous portraits. However, once you wrote that you'd seen Liza Minnelli in performance at Carnegie Hall. "You look just like her!" you told me. Liza Minnelli. Ugh. Who wants to look like Liza Minnelli?

The first time I saw you was the morning I transferred to Pratt Elementary School. I was ten when we moved to our north side neighborhood, a more prosperous community in Chicago than the one we'd come from farther south in Logan Square. On that first day of fifth grade, my mother accompanied me for the eight-block walk to the new school.

"Nervous?" she asked, going at a maddeningly slow pace in her high heels.

I walked backward to see her face as well as to slow down. I thought about it. "No," I said. "Just excited. Everything's different here. Nicer."

"Good," she said. "It's good you like new things. It's good you're not afraid." Then she spit three times into a tissue and used it to smooth down my hair. This gesture was an efficient combination of wishing me luck and tidying me. The fancy new neighborhood would do little to change my mother.

We entered the school office. With amazing nonchalance, she signed a few papers, presented my birth certificate, then gave me a quick kiss and walked out the door. My mother never lingered. Mrs. Zimmer, the principal, a likable lady who I would see only at school assemblies and graduation from eighth grade nearly four years later, guided me through the deserted corridors, her hand resting lightly on my shoulder.

"You'll like Miss Schaffer," Mrs. Zimmer said. "You're a smart girl. I saw that from the report cards your mother brought. Sometimes children find Miss Schaffer strict, but you'll get a fine education from her." *Oh, dear,* I thought. *A strict teacher.* I began to worry. I'd coasted through school up until then.

Miss Schaffer was a frightening sight at first glance, looking more like a Japanese geisha than a middle-aged American schoolteacher. Her lips were painted a bright scarlet, her face heavily powdered. I remember her hair, dyed vivid orange, and lacquered straight back from her forehead. The tension was relieved when a girl in the back row, a long stick of a girl, jumped out of her seat and waved her arms.

"Judith, Judith. Remember me? It's Roberta!"

The principal had left the room. Miss Schaffer narrowed her eyes as she peered back at Roberta. "Miss Feingold, if you don't wish to stay inside at recess today, you will sit down immediately and quiet yourself."

But Roberta, a child of irrepressible enthusiasm, could not do that. Roberta lived on the same block as my aunt Gussie, who was my mother's twin sister. Aunt Gussie and Roberta's mother were good friends, regular mah-jongg partners, and I'd visited the Feingold house several times. Roberta had already been told by my aunt that I would be transferring to Pratt Elementary and she hopped up and down with excitement.

"But I *know* Judith," Roberta wailed to Miss Schaffer. "I could show her around. Be her New Student Buddy."

"Sit down, Roberta. We'll pick her Buddy later. And it will certainly be someone who can set a better example for our new student."

"I told you I knew the new girl," Roberta said in a loud whisper to the child on her left. "She's a really good dancer."

Bless Roberta Feingold. Her recommendation got me invited to the weekend slumber parties that were social currency for preteen girls. We danced with each other in carpeted and paneled basements, some larger than the whole apartment my father had persuaded my mother to move to, which was at the fringe of this affluent Chicago neighborhood, barely inside its "good" school district. I didn't often host the slumber parties, but was regularly included in these Saturday nights of pizza delivery and practicing dance moves we'd seen on *American Bandstand*.

On that first day at the new school, I obediently sat down in the seat Miss Schaffer indicated. I knew that I had a lot to learn. An only child of aging parents, I was long used to watching people, well attuned to social cues. My eyes darted around the classroom and the well-dressed fifth graders. I tingled with excitement and felt no nostalgia whatsoever for the dingy old neighborhood. Tucking my gray poodle skirt under me, I barely heard Miss Schaffer give instructions for the history lesson. Instead, I watched the classroom clock, slowly creeping minute by minute toward the really important part of the day—recess. There I would meet these exotic new people. Luckily, boisterous Roberta would serve as my unofficial and capable guide.

Recess went well. Roberta and I did a little dance demonstration on the asphalt, my skirt twirling outward. The other girls nodded appreciatively. These girls would populate my world for years to come. However, it wasn't until after recess that the day's truly significant event occurred. We'd settled back in our seats, giving up the fresh fall air of the playground for the stale classroom atmosphere. Miss Schaffer had just told us to take out our math books when the door opened and the recess monitor, a plump, grandmotherly type, came in, leading, almost dragging, you by your upper arm.

"This one's been fighting again. It took two of us to separate them. They were around the side of the school. The other boy is in the principal's office already," the monitor said.

"That's fine," Miss Schaffer replied frostily. "Leave him here. I'll deal with it."

I hadn't noticed you before recess. I had been too busy looking at the girls, assessing their outfits, comparing myself to them. But now, every eye was on you, a tall, lanky boy, standing in front of the class. It was theater. You were extraordinary looking that day, dressed all in white. What fifth-grade boy dresses all in white? The others wore dungarees or dark slacks. But you wore a dress shirt, long-sleeved and crisply collared. Your pants, now dusty, had also been white, a thin black belt snaking through the belt loops. However, a long tear in your trousers revealed a bloody gash. Blood dripped down your leg and your white cotton slacks were turning red from absorbing it. Certainly it must have hurt; the cut was deep. But you showed no pain. Stoically, your hands at your side, you gazed somewhere off into the distance, seemingly not registering Miss Schaffer or the class. No one giggled or whispered; we sat silent and still, the seconds ticking by.

At last, Miss Schaffer spoke, her voice a low growl, filled with disgust.

"No wonder your mother landed in the mental hospital again. You drove her there, Elliot. You would make anyone go crazy."

I think we all gasped. I know I did, and the noise seemed very loud, as if it had come from the inhalations of all thirty children. Finally, your composure broke. You cried out some animal sound. I'd like to think you said, "You bitch," to our teacher, but I think it was just a wordless cry. Then you turned and ran from the room, fiercely slamming the door as you left.

I don't know where you went that day, whether you ran home, or to the nurse's office, or back out to the deserted playground. But your pain and sorrow were obvious. Miss Schaffer was such a formidable opponent, looming over you with her size and power, and her cruelty knew no bounds. She hated almost all children, I suspect, but you, that particular day with your leg streaming blood, aroused her greatest fury.

In the coming years, I watched you master the skills needed to achieve success in school and beyond. Your intelligence was obvious and you emulated your brothers, working hard and accumulating accomplishments. You stopped getting into fights, and learned to smile sweetly at teachers, becoming everyone's favorite. How did you do that? I wondered. As an adult, your success bypassed everyone else's sitting in that classroom. But back then, in fifth grade, your sorrow was too raw. You were the youngest of three boys, and your mother had been in mental hospitals much of your childhood. Your brothers were older when she first got sick; they had memories of a more intact woman. A toddler when she first became ill, you received so much less from her than did Phillip or Jeffrey. She was either away, in a series of hospitals, or home, sadly pacing the rooms of your apartment, not at all present for a small boy who yearned for mothering. You missed her so fiercely and could not have understood what took her away for such long absences.

Before you ran from the classroom, blood dripping in your path, I stared wide-eyed at the beautiful boy in front of me. Of course, I had already fallen in love. It took root sixty years ago, and yet I can still summon the moment and feel the lurching of my heart. Stupid, isn't it? Are you smiling at my foolishness? It doesn't matter. I know I am not the only one who felt that way about you. Probably even Miss Schaffer, in spite of her venom, was a little infatuated herself.

Your brothers possessed none of your dramatic beauty. They were serious boys, studious and impressive in their accomplishments. Phillip was then an eighth grader, and Jeffrey went to the all-boys technical high school in Chicago. It was a public school that held a rigorous entrance exam, and Phillip had already been admitted for the fall. I soon learned who Phillip was and saw him occasionally around school, a bulky bear of a boy who participated in debate competitions and was president of the eighth-grade class. Jeffrey, at sixteen, had already won citywide science fairs and usually had his beaky nose and thick eyeglasses in a chemistry book. All three of you Pine brothers were tall, but only you wore your height gracefully, while Phillip lumbered and Jeffrey stood awkwardly, hunching his shoulders forward, shifting his weight from foot to foot.

My father had waged a long campaign persuading my mother to move, talking about how much better the schools were farther north in Chicago, specifically in the West Rogers Park area of the city. (Saying the schools were better was one of the codes for it being a Jewish neighborhood.) He had to convince her to give up the large, high-ceilinged apartment she loved, as well as the old, familiar neighborhood, a rich stew of Poles and Greeks and Lithuanians.

"You'll see, Judith will finally be challenged. She'll be with a different type of child," my father argued.

"She's fine where she is," my mother answered curtly, busily chopping carrots. "Those new buildings have no dining rooms. Only a skimpy square off the kitchen. A dining *area* they call it, not even a real room. No space for our table. Where will we put the family at the holidays? And where will I shop? Everyone drives out there."

Again and again she repeated her objections. It was the first time I heard them argue, and it went on for weeks, frightening me. My usually agreeable father persisted. "So, two, three times a year we'll set up a table in the living room," he said. "The High Holidays, Thanksgiving, Passover. And I'll drive you to the stores on weekends. For a little inconvenience, we'll be in a good, safe neighborhood."

The apartments Dad dragged us to on the weekends were indeed small and boxy, no trims or cornices like we had in the old place. My father kept using the word modern, but the most exciting feature he could find was sliding mirrored doors on closets. He slid the doors back and forth on their tracks, as if they were clever pieces of machinery. My mother sniffed. Sliding mirrored doors did not impress her.

She did not drive a car then, or ever. Moving meant she would give up the pleasure of visiting neighborhood stores and chatting with her friends at the butcher or in the greengrocers. She correctly envisioned her life as a prisoner during the week, waiting for my father to take her on weekends to shop in the new neighborhood. But she finally capitulated, my father's desire to see me educated in a better school winning out. When my parents signed the lease on an apartment in the swanky West Rogers Park neighborhood of Budlong Woods, they were exhausted by the battle, and school had already started several weeks earlier. I'd answered my mother's question honestly—I wasn't nervous about the move. Even back then, I loved an adventure. I'd spent the summer before riding my bicycle in increasingly wider concentric circles around the old neighborhood. Farther and farther I went, thrilled at the space I could put between myself and home, welcoming new sights and unknown territory.

In that first year in the new school, I'd watched you from a distance. Then sixth grade brought us closer. Two important things happened. First, in that Jewish neighborhood of privilege, it was the beginning of parties and boyfriends, children pairing up. You were precocious in that regard, one of the first to have a girlfriend. You chose, or were chosen by, Rochelle Bennett. Rochelle was perfect, yet also sweet. Everyone loved Rochelle. She was already quite curvaceous, one of the first of us to wear a bra. (By the time I got a bra, I had to resort to stuffing Kleenex in the cups and lived in fear of seeing a wadded-up tissue left behind as I exited the floor at school dances.) You and Rochelle made an ideal couple, our own royalty. No one could be jealous, because everyone realized the appropriateness of you two being together. I entered the royal court as the girlfriend of Steven—a good friend of yours back then. Because of our stature, it was Steven's and my destiny to be paired up. Although Steven was terrific at sports, he was very short and would not get his full height until well into high school. Since I was so petite, I became his girlfriend. Short with short. Beautiful with beautiful. We all hung out together, a loosely defined group of around twenty kids. Just as my family's apartment was on the edge of the good neighborhood, I was on the edge of that crowd of popular kids. You were at its center.

The all-girl slumber parties now included boys for a few hours—although most parents insisted that the doors to the basement rec rooms be kept ajar. By the end of sixth grade, kissing games began. They happened on the deserted playground where we gathered on spring nights, or in the homes of the more permissive, or distracted, parents. I didn't much like kissing Steven. In fact, it gave me a queasy feeling in my gut. I worried, too, about how my Kleenex-stuffed bra felt against Steven's chest. However, you and Rochelle seemed entirely delighted by the kissing. You boldly held hands at movies and later, when Rochelle undressed at the slumber parties, it was obvious that she needed no Kleenex to fill the cups of her bra.

Besides being at the same parties, you noticed me because we were often in competition for the same academic prizes. In sixth grade, there were two classrooms. We'd both been placed with Mrs. Aron. It was clear that the smart kids were with Mrs. Aron. And Rochelle? She was in the other one. After a year of being terrorized by Miss Schaffer, it felt like landing in heaven to be assigned to Mrs. Aron, known to be one of the best teachers in the school.

She spoke French like a native, and taught French as part of our curriculum. Each month, she invited the top students in her French class to a delightful French buffet. She prepared a sumptuous meal at home and brought it to school, teaching us the French words for all that we ate: savory *poulets à la diable*, crispy baguettes, and heavenly, smooth crème brûlées, which she explained were burned on top on purpose. You and I excelled in Mrs. Aron's class, although your accent was far superior to my own, and we were always invited to the French luncheons. I loved the checkered tablecloths and candle that she placed over desks pushed together. Somehow she managed to turn that sixth-grade classroom into a bistro, with Edith Piaf record-ings playing softly in the background.

The competition between us that year culminated with our shared love of reading. In a contest Mrs. Aron devised, students each had their name printed on a paper rocket ship. When a student completed a book, he or she would write a report in their reading log and hand it in, and if the report was approved, their rocket ship would move upward another level in space. We were all excited about space travel in those years, and Mrs. Aron had covered a board in shiny blue alu-minum paper and glittery stars. The student closest to the moon at the end of the year would be the winner. You and I soon left the others far behind. One week, your rocket might creep ahead; another, I'd triumphantly move my ship farther into outer space. The contest was to conclude at the end of May. On the Friday of the long Memorial Day weekend, we both left Pratt Elementary laden with books from the school library. That Tuesday, I excitedly watched Mrs. Aron place my rocket ship onto the surface of the moon. Yours was just inches behind, but you might as well have been in another galaxy. I was the clear winner. At the awards assembly on the last day of school, I was called to the front of the auditorium, and Mrs. Aron hugged me and with great ceremony presented me with my prize: a lovely book about women adventurers. She'd inscribed it, "Judith, may your dreams take you to the moon. Fondly, Sylvia Aron."

After the assembly, you were waiting for me. "How do you do it?" you asked. "I never saw anyone who could read as fast as you. I've watched you flip the pages so quickly, I can't believe you're taking in the words. But then you write your reports and Mrs. Aron loves them. Says they are perfect. Is there a secret to reading so fast?"

"I don't know," I said, and shrugged. "I've always read quickly. My dad's a fast reader, too. You should see him turn the pages of books he's reading." My heart was pounding as I tried for a casual tone.

You shook your beautiful head and stared at me, as if still trying to figure out my secret. "Well, you beat me," you finally said and sighed. It might have been the first competition you lost. "Your rocket beat mine fair and square. So from now on, Judith, I'm going to call you Rocket." You pushed open the school's heavy front door for me. "Come on, Rocky, I'll walk you home," you said, and smiled at me.

The admiration on your face filled me with pleasure. I laughed as we left Pratt Elementary together and walked the eight blocks to my apartment building, one of the few times I was happy to live so far from the school. Your family's apartment was in the opposite direction, but we walked slowly, chattering about the books we were going to read that summer and whatever else came into our heads. We had all the time in the world. It was summer vacation and you had given me a nickname—a ridiculous nickname, but still, a badge of honor. This recognition was a prize greater even than dear Mrs. Aron's had been.

That year was a taste of things to come. Your nickname from sixth grade stuck, in private you always called me Rocket, sometimes Rocky. For the rest of our lives, our relationship was a cocktail mix of rivalry and loyalty—shaken with a strong dose of passion and resentment.

2

Consolation

Your father, Max Pine, was a purveyor of kosher meats on Chicago's north side. By the early 1960s, his company had six or seven delivery trucks, all of them white, with "Pine's Meats" painted in green on their sides. A tall, clean pine tree was incorporated into each green *P*. These trucks were seen in alleyways behind kosher butchers in the Jewish neighborhoods of West Rogers Park, and later into Skokie, the first of the northern suburbs where the Jews eventually began to drift. I sometimes saw men wearing thick, insulated gloves unloading slabs of meat from trucks into freezers in the shops our mothers frequented. Everyone I knew kept kosher in those days; they even perpetuated the myth that kosher meat tasted better. It didn't, of course; at least not the way steaks were cooked in our homes back then, overdone and chewy, with a faint taste of soap in the meat. I learned what good steak tasted like only when I moved to California a decade later and tried, along with fine filet, still pink at the center, other once-unavailable or forbidden delicacies: avocados, artichokes, shrimp, clams, and bacon, especially bacon. To this day, I am filled with wonder as I remember my first taste of that delight—a BLT: crispy and salty, moist and sweet, all in one bite.

Your family was slightly more affluent than my own. Although Pine's Meats was a small, family-owned business, run by your dad, along with your uncle Lou, over the years, we saw the number of

Pine's meat trucks increase. The business supported both families comfortably, each with several kids to put through college. However, though you rarely mentioned it, your family had an additional burden: the private sanitariums and doctors required by your mother. Your father worked hard for his family. As in most households of that time and place, there was reverential guilt toward our fathers. The men of the neighborhood, including your dad and my own, worked at back-breaking jobs. It would take another generation before the Jews we knew no longer toiled at this kind of labor and became professionals: doctors, lawyers, academics.

My father, along with two cousins, owned an army-navy surplus store: three floors of dusty cots and tents and work boots. None of the mothers, including my own, were employed outside the home. They stayed in their houses cooking and cleaning, perhaps getting together a few afternoons a week for card parties and mah-jongg. When the men arrived at the end of the day, they were greeted with a drink, usually a whiskey, neat, and the promise of quiet. Kids knew that they should stay out of Dad's way until dinner was served. You could see the fatigue on those men; they didn't hide it as they trudged up the stairs, and we respected it. I find my grandchildren oddly lacking in respect for their parents' labors. In fact, parents today seem apologetic for being tired after a hard day earning a living. They feel they should be always available, on call for the children. Ah, but that's me being cranky. Maybe it's better this way, maybe their kids will appreciate their parents' availability. (I doubt it. But we'll see.)

Once I ate dinner at your home. We were in high school, both of us sixteen years old and ardent members of a Jewish youth group. Your brothers had also been in this group, a Zionist organization. We met weekly in the basement of our local synagogue and pretended to be pioneers. There, we danced energetic Israeli dances, kicking high into the air, and singing heroic songs, like we were settlers of the holy land. We organized car washes and bake sales to raise money, which was sent to help the brave Israelis who were, we were told, making a Garden of Eden in the desert.

You were a rising star in the American Zionist Youth, impressively making your way up the organizational ladder. First, you became the local chapter head of AZY, then the Chicago area president, and now, you were preparing your candidacy for regional. At the Midwest Regional meeting, to be held later that month at the Hilton in Chicago's loop, hundreds of Jewish kids would listen to campaign speeches by ambitious young teenagers from communities much like our own in Cleveland, Detroit, or Milwaukee. They would scream and cheer for their candidate and then elect new leaders.

I was at the Pine house almost every afternoon because you had mistaken my lovelorn eyes for devotion to the cause of Israel. You'd appointed me your campaign manager, and we spent days with magic markers and poster boards. I'm ashamed to admit that, despite our fervor, we came up with nothing better than "Pine Is Fine," but I copied the same straight pine tree onto posters for the delegates to wave up and down as was seen on the white trucks plying our neighborhood with brisket and flanken.

The sun had already gone down one late fall afternoon when your mother stood in the shadows of the doorway to your room. We were busy making banners and placards. I remember that Mrs. Pine had the habit of standing very still when she entered a room, waiting until she was noticed. I looked up and saw her first. You were still working, your head down and talking a mile a minute, as you always did.

"I think we'll get the delegates from Indiana," you, ever the politician, said. "South Bend and Hammond at least. No problem there. They really have a leadership vacuum and besides, all those Indiana kids know me from summer camp. But I'm not so sure about Ohio. What do you think about that curly-haired girl from Cincinnati? Nancy something or other? Man, those Jewish kids from Cincinnati sure are organized."

Your mother was tall and had the palest skin. With her elegant features and long limbs and torso, you resembled her. That day, she was wearing a clean white apron tied over a dark green housedress that buttoned down the front. The dress hung on her, much too large for her slim frame. She stood still, her hands at her sides, listening and watching her youngest son with the same adoration I imagined was on my own face. Then her eyes moved to mine and she gave me a small smile.

"Judith," she said softly and shyly, "it's nearly time for dinner. Why don't you call your mother and ask her if you can eat with us? One of the boys will drive you home later."

My heart began to beat quickly. Although you and I had often done school or youth group projects together, I'd never before eaten dinner with the Pine family. You still had an off and on romance with Rochelle Bennett, who also was in the youth group, and seemed to get prettier every year. These dynamics were tricky, since Rochelle and I had become friends—close enough for me to have heard intimate details of her relationship with you.

"Elliot likes to French kiss," Rochelle had confided as we refreshed our lipstick in front of the mirror in the girls' bathroom. "He knows how to do it good, too."

Of course, when Rochelle spoke to me this way, I never allowed myself to appear to be coveting you. That would be laughable. After all, you two were the King and Queen Judith, instead, I settled for less glamorous boys, such as Jordan, my current boyfriend. Jordan was an intellectual who wore thick glasses and expertly played the accordion. (Although today accordion playing has become somewhat of a joke, I remember that back then it was played by many kids, especially those whose families couldn't afford a piano.) Jordan and I had become so inseparable that when our temple youth group sat on the floor in a circle and sang the old spiritual "Swing Low, Sweet Chariot" and got to the line "I looked over Jordan, and what did I see," everyone gleefully shouted in unison, "Judith!"

I also hesitated at the dinner invitation because I didn't want to make more of a burden for your mother. By this time, it was common knowledge that Mrs. Pine was not well, although none of us had a name for her sickness. But she *had* invited me to dinner, so I supposed it would be okay.

You lifted the stencil from the poster we were working on. "Hi, Mom. I didn't see you standing there. But that'd be great. We can keep working on the posters after dinner. Okay, Rocket?"

"You're sure, Mrs. Pine? Is there enough?" I asked.

"One thing you can be sure of, Judith, there's always enough meat in this house." And with a little smile, she was gone.

At dinner, I watched everything carefully, excited to see how your family ate their meal. My own house was too quiet. There was uninteresting conversation with long silences in between sentences. I felt pressure to fill those silences at home and usually wished I had more accomplishments to speak of at the table, as this is what made my parents more pleased than anything else I could say. Dinner at the Pine house was different, a big, rowdy affair, with three large sons (both your brothers, Jeffrey and Phillip, were by then at the University of Chicago in Hyde Park and often came home for a meal) and your even larger father. Mr. Pine was the biggest and bulkiest man I knew. He wore a white T-shirt to the table and had massive forearms and a broad forehead. His thick, curly hair made his already large head, huge. Your mother set a plate of well-done roast beef and a bowl of steaming whole potatoes boiled in their skins, in front of your father. She didn't completely sit down, but rather perched on the edge of her chair. Suddenly, she took a sharp breath in and said, "oh" softly and went quickly back to the kitchen. She returned with an oven mitt on her hand and carrying a cookie sheet of hot rolls. The rolls were almost, but not quite burned.

The conversation continued, everyone, except your mother and me, weighing in about your upcoming election. Suddenly, Mr. Pine stopped speaking and put down his knife and fork. He stared at your mother and there was an ominous silence for a few seconds before he spoke.

"No greens?" he asked, his eyes scanning the table as if he might have missed them. "No greens tonight, Helen?" he repeated.

She flinched as if he'd struck her. "Oh my goodness. I'm sorry, Max. I'd been feeling I'd forgotten something all afternoon. I couldn't think what it was, but I felt so unsettled. Judith, please forgive me. I didn't make a vegetable. Or even a salad." She put a hand up to her mouth, covering it.

All three of you boys spoke at once, interrupting one another.

"Mom," Phillip said, "I can cut up some lettuce."

Jeffrey broke in, "This is fine, Mom. Fine. You know I hate vegetables. Don't worry about it."

Phillip tried to finish his idea. "You want me to go to the kitchen and cut some lettuce?"

You reached for the breadbasket and, stuffing a roll into your mouth, mumbled, "Good rolls, Mom. Like the rolls a lot."

"Oh, Elliot," your mother answered tiredly. "Don't talk with your mouth full. They're just packaged rolls from the supermarket. And nearly burned at that."

"Well, I like potatoes, Mrs. Pine," I said cheerfully. "I wish my mom made potatoes more often," I said, digging a big forkful from my plate.

"Call me Helen, dear," your mom said, and stood up, smoothing back her hair. You had your mother's dark, shiny hair. She wore it long, unlike most of the other mothers, including my own, who had their hair cut short, then set in curlers once a week at the beauty parlor. They wrapped their heads in toilet paper at night, so that the lacquered helmets wouldn't get mussed. Your mother's hair fell to her shoulders, but it was parted severely in the center and pulled tightly back behind her ears with bobby pins. Her hair might have been pretty, had it been loose around her face, but the bobby pins flattened it, pulling the skin taut at the sides of her face. She was such a tall, angular woman, her elbows and clavicle prominent, the skin stretched tight over them as well.

Standing stiffly behind her chair, your mother gave me another of her small, shy smiles. "You're a lovely girl. I've enjoyed having a girl at the table, Judith. All these booming male voices every night. It tires me. They're quite loud, aren't they?" She untied the apron from around her waist and placed it over the back of her chair. "Now don't you get stuck doing the dishes, dear. Just leave them in the kitchen. I'm going to lie down for a little bit. I like to do the dishes later, when I can't sleep. It gives me something to do. I'll be very angry if I see you've done those dishes, Judith. You and Elliot just work on the posters tonight. That's what's important."

She left the dining room, and you followed her with your eyes as she shuffled soundlessly down the hallway in her slippers. We heard the bedroom door open and shut. At the table, everyone was quiet. The only sounds were our knives and forks clinking against the china.

Slowly, you and your brothers wound up the conversation again. You spoke about Chicago's mayor, Richard Daley, politics of one sort or another always being a prime topic in your family.

"Do you think Dick Daley can be re-elected?" Jeffrey asked, wiping his mouth after taking a long drink of water. "Despite all the scandals?"

"Sure," Phillip answered. "The Democratic machine still has plenty more good years left in it. Scandals don't hurt Daley."

Then your father spoke, interrupting his sons. "It's good that she gets reminded about the greens," he said gruffly. "You boys *need* a balanced diet, with all you do. Those treatments of hers, they played hell with her memory this time. She specifically told me she *wants* to be reminded when she forgets things." He placed his large hands on either side of his empty plate, clenching the edge of the table tightly.

"I'll make a list for her," burly Phillip said softly. "I'll write every-thing she has to do for dinner on a paper and I'll stick it up on the refrigerator."

We finished eating. You were the first to stand and you began to clear the table. There was a swinging door from the dining room into the kitchen, and when you went through it, the door swung shut behind you. Then we heard a long whistle. "Will you have a look at this," you called and came back out through the swinging door, care-fully carrying a beautiful pie with both your hands. You set it down right in front of your father. We all stared at it, the perfection of the strands of dough on the top crust woven over and under one another, the juice oozing lushly through the lattice.

"Peach," your father said, after he leaned over to smell it. He pursed his lips. "She knows it's our favorite. You like peach, Judy?" he asked me.

I saw your mother just once more while we were in high school. It was a couple of months later, the following January. Not surprisingly, you had won your election, making a thrilling speech about support-ing the young State of Israel, inspiring everyone who listened. Your voice, even then, was mellifluous and there was not a sound when you spoke, even in a room full of antsy teenagers. At sixteen you became the Midwest Regional president of American Zionist Youth. Still a boy, you wore a suit and tie and got on planes to far-off places like Kansas City and Omaha, Nebraska. You even carried a briefcase, for God's sake. You attended national conferences and conventions and eventually were appointed the youth delegate for some promi-nent adult Jewish organizations. High school must have seemed tame on Monday morning for a kid who'd been treated like a celebrity on the previous weekend. You were like a rock star for Jewish girls in ten states. Handsome and charming, you could work a room with remarkable aplomb; and you had that hair that you tossed off your forehead or raked your fingers through casually. You remembered the name of every person you met during that year when you were regional president, and would speak that person's name while looking them in the eye, a remarkable quality for a teenager and one you later found useful in your illustrious law career.

A few weeks after the election, your parents threw a victory party. The apartment was packed with teenagers, parents, and local Jewish leaders. Everyone took off their winter coats and piled them on top of the bed in your parents' room. After I unzipped my own bulky parka, I stood in front of the oval mirror above your parents' maple dresser. I didn't see how I was going to face this party. Yesterday, my skin had betrayed me. There was a red circle, about the size of a half dollar, extending from my cheek to lower jaw. I wondered if people might think it was a hickey; Rochelle had once come to school with a hickey on her neck and no one seemed to think any less of her. She was nonchalant about the evidence of her passion, proud of this proof of your ardor, not even bothering to cover it with makeup or to pull up her collar.

But my mark was *not* a hickey. On the contrary, it was the disgusting symptom of a fungal infection and just a bit too high on my neck to cover with a collar. I'd been babysitting children who had a cat. The cat was one of those creepy felines that slinks up and rubs against you if you stay still. After I put the kids to bed, the cat pushed itself under my palm, trying to get me to pet it, desperate for human touch. I was watching television and nodding off when I'd felt the cat nuzzle up against my face and neck. Ugh. The cat had ringworm, which left behind an angry, itchy circle. I was enormously lucky, the dermatologist said. If the ringworm had been on my scalp, I'd have had to shave my head in order to treat it. *Why me?* Stuck with this stigmata and I didn't even like cats.

I walked down the hallway to the kitchen, the ringworm side of my face to the wall. There was your mother, pouring water into an industrial-sized coffee percolator. She swung around, her sad eyes suddenly brightening. She seemed enormously pleased to see me, as if all evening she'd been waiting for me to arrive.

"Judith, I'm so glad you came. I was just thinking about you. I don't think Elliot could have won without you. You must be the hardest-working girl in the entire organization. Come here and let me hug you. I'm so proud of all you did to get him elected."

"Be careful, Mrs. Pine," I said and pointed to my cheek. I lowered my voice to a whisper. "Ringworm. It might be contagious. I'm not sure. Doesn't it look awful?" I asked. "I feel like a leper."

"Oh, you poor girl," she said. "It must itch. But Judith, I didn't even notice it. That sweater you're wearing. It's a perfect green with your dark hair. Apple green, I'd call it. That's all I see—how lovely you're looking tonight in that nice sweater. I didn't see the ringworm at all." She enveloped me in a warm hug.

My own mother had flinched when she'd seen me go out the door that night. "Are you sure you ought to be going out in public with that thing on your face?" she'd asked.

Your mother made me feel better and we stayed together in the kitchen all that night. It was warm and smelled deliciously of coffee and rugelach and brownies. She made the night tolerable. I know you mentioned me when you gave your thank you speech. I heard you call my name, but I didn't leave the kitchen and walk through the swinging door. Mrs. Pine glanced over at me, but I shrugged my shoulders. She nodded and went back to scraping and washing dessert plates. I dried, then put them away in the cabinets. The two of us kept a nice rhythm going. After the plates were done, we took a break and she poured me a mug of steaming coffee and I added cream and two heaping spoonsful of sugar. Side by side, we leaned against the counter and ate the flaky rugelach which we held over napkins, speaking comfortably to each other. At ten o'clock, when I could hear the party breaking up, I went into the Pines' bedroom and extracted my parka with its fur-lined hood from the rest of the coats piled on the bed. I pulled the zipper all the way to the top, so that it covered my neck and part of my face when I said my goodbyes. You were off in a corner, talking to some important-looking men with yarmulkes on their heads.

Later that year, several of us from youth group were asked to be counselors at the big Jewish camp near Oconomowoc, Wisconsin. The camp was called Avodah, the Hebrew word for work, indicating that the camp was like a workers' collective in Israel; we weren't actually supposed to be having fun. Instead, we were to be serious of purpose and to sweat and create like settlers in Israel were doing.

To my surprise, that summer I discovered I loved the outdoors. My parents had done little to show me the joys of nature; never once had I been camping. You couldn't blame them; their own immigrant lives had been full of such threat and insecurity that staying in the city seemed safer, more predictable to them. Who knew what lurked in the woods of America? Russia's woods had been dangerous enough, and there they *knew* their enemies: wolves, Cossacks, and anti-Semites.

By then, Rochelle was tiring of youth group and hadn't gone off to summer camp with the rest of us. She was starting to meet college boys through her older sister, and had begun a job at a steak house in downtown Chicago. (Here I would like it noted that another of my mother's prophesies has come true: back then when I bemoaned my own lack of breasts, she'd tried to reassure me by saying, "You'll see. Those girls with their big chests and movie star looks, they'll burn out early." My dear, annoying mother was, as usual, right. At our recent high school reunion, I saw Rochelle. Her skin was leathery and tough, that of a lifelong smoker; and her breasts, though still impressively large, sagged, no longer possessing the perky upward tilt of her youth. I apologize, Elliot, for I am not proud of my lack of charity on the issue of Rochelle, but it was reassuring to see that the years have spared none of us, not even Rochelle.)

That August at Camp Avodah, I was seventeen, and after we got off the bus from Chicago, I blissfully found myself assigned to a cabin in a lush pine forest. I'd had no idea that nature could make me so happy. I gazed up at the vast Wisconsin sky. The blanket of stars overhead was a miraculous new invention to me. After I'd gotten my campers settled that first night, I pulled on a sweatshirt and headed back outside. There was an all-staff meeting scheduled for ten thirty that night. Junior counselors had been assigned to patrol the cabins in shifts, making sure the children were safe and asleep. Everyone else was to report to the meeting with the camp director. You and I met on the way to the dining hall.

"How's your group?" you asked, waiting for me to join you on the path.

"Sweet girls. Eight-year-olds, most away from home for the first time. A few sniffles, but I think they're going to be okay. I love it here, Elliot," I added.

"Me too. It's cool that you came this summer. Avodah is my favorite spot anywhere. I count down the months until it's time to come back. Can you believe all this?" you asked, and waved your arm across the night sky I'd just been staring at with wonder. You and the sky made me breathless. "Come with me, I want to show you something." You fished a small flashlight from your back pocket and shined it on the ground in front of us, then ducked and took my hand, guiding me into the thick trees. There was a pillow of pine needles under our feet. We sat on the soft ground and you turned off the flashlight. Above us, there was an opening in the trees, a window. I looked up, marveling at the stars, more than I had ever before seen.

There, among the fragrant pines of the Wisconsin woods, you

kissed me for the first time, putting your hand under my head as we lay on the soft earth. Our kisses became deeper and longer. The little opening in the woods became the whole world and nothing besides that spot existed for me. For how many years had I imagined kissing you like this? I'd listened to Rochelle describe your embraces, then dreamed it was me. Only this was better than I'd imagined. We were in a place of beauty that I'd not known existed until this very day and I was enveloped in your arms. I stopped thinking about the time, or the meeting, or anything else besides your lips and the moist, humid air surrounding us, laced with its ever-present piney smell. You slid your hands under my shirt, cupping my breasts gently, and I felt myself lean into your hands. Then, abruptly, you stopped, sat up, and shined your flashlight onto the face of your watch. I covered my eyes, the light from even that small beam shocking me.

"What?" I asked.

"We've got to go," you said urgently. "Right now. Leonard hates it when anyone shows up late for staff meeting. He goes apeshit when people walk in after he's started." You reached down and pulled me from the ground. We hurriedly rearranged our clothes, brushing off our jeans, and then you took my hand and we ran toward the cafeteria. It was the only building in the campground ablaze with lights, and these lights muted the star-filled sky.

Two important things marked our late entrance to the meeting. First, you and I established on that first night of camp that we'd become a couple. The other girls' eyes met and brows were raised. It was a formal announcement of our new status. By entering that dining hall late and together, with a few stray leaves stuck to our sweatshirts, news of our romance was broadcast loud and clear. I floated into the meeting, cruelly ignoring poor Jordan, my clueless accordion player boyfriend, who'd been saving a spot for me beside him.

The second occurrence that marked that night was that I did

arouse the anger of Leonard Chover, the camp's director. Leonard was probably a decade older than the rest of us and was a real stickler for rules. He was a doctoral student at the University of Chicago. When he wasn't at camp, he was doing research at the Orthogenic School in Hyde Park. This esteemed school, led by the famous German child psychiatrist, Bruno Bettelheim, treated children with severe emotional needs. Leonard, himself, wanted to work with emotionally disturbed children when he became Dr. Chover. That night, he marked me as a troublemaker, someone he'd have to keep an eye on.

"I believe I called this meeting for ten thirty," Leonard said and squinted at me sternly under his thick, bushy eyebrows. "Was there some difficulty in your cabin? What did you say your name was?" I felt his disapproval directed solely toward me. You, Elliot, obviously, had special status with Leonard.

"Judith Sherman. Everybody in my cabin is fine. I have the eight-year-olds. A little homesickness, but it all seems normal." Every set of eyes was upon me. I shrugged and sat on the floor, trying to disappear into the crowd.

"You've already missed a lot of information, Judith. It's Elliot's third summer here. He knows the rules, the routine. But I hope your lateness is not an indication of a casual attitude. I insist that my staff take its work with children very seriously. We have a huge responsibility and I don't tolerate casual attitudes. I also don't consider home sickness to be at all trivial. Everything that happens to these children can be cause for later trauma."

At that, I choked back a laugh, but then saw a small frown on your face. Fortunately, Leonard had turned from me and continued his lecture, speaking on and on about abandonment and childhood separation issues. Attachment disorders and other crap like that. Almost every night, he got us together in the cafeteria, asking us to "process" (that was his favorite word) the children's interactions of that day. He talked about our suburban Jewish campers as if they were the fragile and emotionally wounded kids he worked with at the Orthogenic School. This psychological jargon was completely new to me and made no sense. I sat on the floor with the other counselors, ready to scream, desperate for Leonard to release us back into the beautiful evening, staring at the big dining hall clock and wondering how much time you and I could steal under the trees before we had to rush back to our cabins and the children.

One night, as Leonard was analyzing whether little Rosalyn Goldstein, a dramatic twelve-year-old from Highland Park, was really making a veiled suicide attempt when she refused to swim back to shore from the deep part of the lake, I caught you glancing in my direction. I rolled my eyes, sure you agreed with me about Leonard's tediousness.

When we were released, I pushed open one of the screen doors to leave the dining hall and muttered to you, "God, I can't believe how long he talked tonight. Leonard goes later and later each meeting. And he's so serious all the time. This is summer camp, isn't it?"

"I don't know, Rocky. Leonard can teach us things. Don't forget, he knows a lot about kids. We have to be sensitive to their issues. You know, being away from home, some of them for the first time."

I looked up at you with surprise. "I guess. But now it's midnight and you and I haven't had a minute together in two days. I just wish we had more time together," I said. "I never see you." I heard my voice. I was whining. How quickly we'd gotten to this—me asking for more than you were willing to give. Your lips tightened. I saw your displeasure.

You rubbed your eyes. "Believe me, I'm tired, too, Judith. And I still have to finish the program for Friday night's service before I can turn in." To my dismay, you picked up your pace and joined a group of counselors who were walking ahead of us and laughing at something, leaving me behind. You didn't wait for me and walk me back to my cabin, as you usually did. The precious moments I had become accustomed to at the end of the day, when you pushed me up against a tree and we kissed feverishly, would not happen that night. I watched you go farther up the path with the others, then I noticed Jordan. His eyes also followed the laughing group before he turned to me with a look of commiseration.

"Elliot's a big deal here," Jordan said. "He's been coming to Avodah forever."

I looked at Jordan. "Yeah, I know. But thanks, Jordie," I said, and we smiled at each other helplessly.

That was our first fight—me asking you for more than you gave.

Another important dollop of wisdom my mother had dished out was that a couple's first fight would inevitably be the same fight they'd be having until the end. I'd heard her say this to her lady friends: "You should have paid good attention to your first fight. Then decided whether you were willing to keep having it. Because you will—you'll have that same argument over and over."

Despite that tense beginning early in the session, there were other nights with you, hours under the stars that made me crazy with desire and love. One evening, very late, we sat on a patch of grass near the lake, leaning our backs against a stack of silver canoes. On the side of each canoe, the words "Camp Avodah" had been stenciled in shiny red paint. You balled up your sweatshirt and placed it behind my back, then put your arm protectively around me. We watched the moon rise over the lake, its reflection a perfect circle on the still water below. You brushed your lips softly along my neck. Even though the Wisconsin night was warm and humid, I shivered. I still shiver at the memory. The words came into my mind with great clarity: *this is what love feels like.* This is it, this exact sensation sitting by the lake with Elliot. This Is Love. I have never forgotten that night or those words. Yet when I saw you in the daytime, I understood that I was to keep it light, make no demands. It surprises me that at only seventeen, I already knew those two things—what love feels like and how I must not kill it with demands. My love for you was already bundled together with restrictions.

Two weeks later, we rode the camp bus back to Chicago. I made sure that I was jovial and sang every Avodah song energetically with the children and other counselors. I was expert at the hand and body motions that went with the silly camp songs and I was a popular song leader. I learned that I was not to complain. You liked me to be cheerful and you liked it when I was funny. When we arrived back in the city after our weeks in Wisconsin, I gathered my sleeping bag and duffel from the pile at the bus stop and scanned the crowd for my parents. I gave you a quick smile and wave. No longing stares, no desperation. I would not park myself by the telephone when we got home. I had other projects. College applications, for example. There was much to do.

Later that night, the phone did ring. I was sorting through my camp clothes before tossing them into the hamper. Everything was covered in dust. I'd been shaking the dust from my clothes into my duffle bag, so the camp dirt wouldn't fall onto the carpet, making work for my mother, who was always obsessively cleaning. When I heard the phone, I got up and stood in the doorway of my room, listening.

"Yes, it's me. Hi, Rose. No, no, I didn't hear a thing. What's the matter? Rose, why are you crying? What's going on?"

I walked into the kitchen. My mother was slumped down on the small chair she kept next to the telephone. She'd gotten very pale. Rose was the synagogue secretary, and a good friend of my mother's.

"Oh, my God," my mom said. I immediately felt a premonition of dread, and had the feeling that this news was going to be more than I would know how to handle. "Terrible. Just awful. Yes, of course I'll tell Judith. Thank you for calling."

She looked up at me, and although this was a rarity, I saw tears falling. "Judith, that was Rose. From the Temple. She was calling to let us know bad news. Helen Pine has killed herself. That poor, unhappy woman committed suicide. And those poor sons. You'll have to go over there and see Elliot." Then, seeing my stricken expression, she added softly, "Not now. Maybe tomorrow." She reached up for my hand and I stood looking down at her, frozen.

It was then, when your grief for your mother was still so fresh, that we discovered an important part of our relationship: consolation. I gave you whatever solace I could and I discovered something surprising about myself: I was actually quite good at consolation. Maybe that's why I became a social worker. Your grief didn't scare me half as much as I expected. In the weeks and months that followed your mother's death, I was able to fill some terrible hole for you. Your father and brothers walked around the apartment aimlessly, trying to avoid each other, yet caroming off one another like pieces in an air hockey game, while you and I spent hours together quietly in your room.

We sat on your narrow bed. Someone made the bed each day, pulling your blue corduroy spread neatly up and over the blanket and pillow. It must have been your aunt, your uncle Lou's wife, who tidied your room and kept the rest of the house in order. I'd heard she'd made it her habit to stop by the apartment each morning, even stocking the refrigerator. I also came every day, even after senior year began. We shut the door behind us and spoke softly to each other in that stifling hot bedroom. You opened the window, but few breezes stirred the sheer white curtains that muggy summer and fall.

"Do you think she planned it before I left for camp?" you agonized again and again. Mrs. Pine had killed herself late in the night before the day we returned from Wisconsin. It was said your father found her hanging when he went into the bathroom early that morning. She was often absent from their bed in the mornings, in another room, unable to sleep, so he hadn't been alarmed when he woke and didn't see her sleeping beside him.

"Or," you asked, "do you think it was just a spontaneous decision?" You kept dwelling on the significance of the timing of her death. What did it mean that she had hung herself the night before you arrived home? Was it a message to you in particular? Had you failed her in some way? What could you, or any of them, have done differently?

"Thank God you're here, Rocky," you told me over and over, your beautiful orator's voice now husky and strangled sounding. "I think of her body down the hall, hanging right there in the bathroom." You covered your eyes. "It's so awful to think of her that way. Why the hell won't my father move out of here? What does he think about when he goes into the bathroom? I've started peeing out the window just so I don't have to go in there at night." I almost smiled at the image, then brushed back your thick hair from your forehead.

I let you talk. You'd always been a talker. Sometimes one or the other of your brothers arrived home in the afternoon, driving north from their rooms on the University of Chicago campus. When they were there, we heard music coming from the bedroom they shared. We knew it was Jeffrey when we heard jazz, and that it was Phillip if the music was classical. Phillip particularly favored Bach. I couldn't decide which was more grating, the jazz without recognizable pattern or the overly organized Bach. You seemed not to hear the records. I suppose you'd grown up with this constant music, so you paid no attention to it.

Once your brother Phillip knocked on the door. "Elliot," he called. "Leonard Chover's on the phone. He says he's written you several letters, but you haven't answered. He wants to talk to you."

"Not now," you said. "Tell him I'll call him later."

"You ought to talk to him," Phillip said through the door, more softly. "Leonard really cares about you."

"I will," you answered. "Soon. I promise."

You stared at the pile of letters on your desk. "He recites all this psychological bullshit to me. He says he understands. But he knows shit," you said, and swept the letters to the ground.

I rubbed my palm over the corduroy spread and looked at the posters covering the walls. Pictures of Israel and happy workers with tanned faces, wearing shorts and sandals. I listened to you talk. There were no answers, but the talking seemed to comfort you, to give some relief. Soon, we began to lie down together on the bed, but didn't touch, a narrow space between us that seemed disrespectful to cross. Finally, one day, you stopped mid-sentence, then got up and took a sip from one of the cans of fizzy soda on your desk. We both loved sodas, though back then we called it "pop." Grape was our favorite. When you came back to the bed, you pulled me close and I could smell the sweet sticky flavor on your breath. We embraced and wrapped ourselves around one another. I remember that in those sultry summer afternoons, in the tiny back bedroom that was yours, we created a private world that seemed as much ours as the opening in the trees in Wisconsin had been.

"Do you have to leave now?" you asked, whenever I stood to go home. "Is it time already?"

We were never interrupted in that room, except once. Your father must have come home early and we hadn't heard him. There was no music, so your brothers weren't visiting. Your father couldn't have known we were there; he usually arrived after I'd left. He walked into your room, carrying a pile of laundry. We were dressed, although our clothes were in disarray. You were on top of me, moving rhythmically, faster and faster, our limbs intertwined. Dry humping was the crude expression they used back then, but what we did gave us such pleasure and release. We were moaning and breathing heavily and didn't hear your father until he had come into the room. Then we flew apart.

"Sorry, sorry," Mr. Pine mumbled as he backed out the door, still carrying the clean laundry. He closed the door behind him. Never again would that man bellow at his sons or order them around in the old way. His wife's suicide had left him permanently apologetic.

Although we kept our clothes on in those afternoons, we took extraordinary comfort from each other's bodies. You rubbed up and down on me, over and over, and my tight jeans touched me in a way that made me gasp. Even with my clothes on, I had orgasms. Of course, I was so naïve back then, I didn't know what word to use to explain what was happening to my body. But we clutched each other and held one another and rubbed each other raw.

At home, by myself, I sometimes felt moments of shame. Was I exploiting your grief in order to be close to you, to make you love me in return? Was I using your mother's death to do this? Maybe a little. But I also knew that in the months following her suicide, whenever the time came for me to leave, you got a panicked expression on your face. In those late summer afternoons before school started, and then throughout our senior year of high school, your need was clear. I'd walk the eight blocks separating our parents' apartments with a terrible ache in my gut, hating to leave you alone in that house.

Thirty years later, when I too was faced by a sorrow that almost felled me, you were the first person I called. I was sitting on our velvet couch that Sunday morning, having been up all night. As the sun rose over the California hills framed by my front windows, I phoned you in New York. There were others I might have called. My husband and I had many friends. Maybe it was because it was three hours later across country, and I knew you'd be awake. Others, closer by, might still be sleeping. But I think the real reason I phoned you was because I needed to say these words to the right person. If I told the wrong person, I might be fated to a reaction that I didn't want or couldn't live up to. It would be the one I remembered. There would be no foolish words from Elliot. No empty sympathy.

I needed to tell someone that Walt, my second husband, had been diagnosed the day before with a cancer so terrible that the doctors did not think they could cure it. My youngest was still small, my marriage to Walt, my rock.

"I don't know if I can get through this," I said. "How will I manage?"

You listened until I was through and then said, simply, "You will. I promise you will."

"How can you know that?" I asked.

"I know. You'll do this better than anyone I can think of. I'm certain of it. You're Rocket, remember?"

"Elliot, I'm so scared," I said softly, the tears falling again. "The kids."

"Remember that night at my parents' apartment?" you asked. "That crazy victory party? Regional president of American Zionist Youth. You'd have thought I was elected president of the United States."

"Of course I remember," I said. "I didn't think you realized I was at that party. I stayed in the kitchen the whole evening. We never said a word to each other."

"You're right, I probably didn't see you at the party. I was so full of myself. But afterward, my mother spoke about you. She hadn't been talking much, she was shutting down by then. Getting quieter and quieter. It was less than a year until she . . ."

"I know. I remember," I said. "The next summer."

"She told me you were with her in the kitchen that night. She asked if I realized how much you'd helped me. She was kind of pissed off at me because she didn't think I appreciated all you'd done. And she told me she loved your smile." You paused. "Me too, I've always loved your smile, too."

"She was such a kind woman, your mother. I wish I'd spent more time with her," I said.

"Yeah," you agreed, "we all did. But she said you were good for her. You brought life into the kitchen. She said she liked it whenever you were around helping on the campaign. That fucking campaign. But the thing I really remember is, my mother said you were brave."

"Brave?" I repeated.

"Yeah, at first I thought it was a strange thing to say. I'd never used that word about you. Brave. You were just always there, getting the job done. But my mother saw it. And later I knew what she meant."

We spoke until the sun was fully in the sky, and somehow, by the time I hung up the phone, I was ready to go up to Walt, my sick husband, and care for him. You had convinced me to believe your mother a bit. Whatever else you'd done in the intervening years, and whatever you would do in the years to come, that morning you consoled me.

3

Magic

After we graduated from high school, you went to Brown. You'd been awarded a substantial scholarship for young Jewish leaders. I enrolled at Michigan. I'd dreamed of Berkeley, or schools on either coast, where the political activism of the times was beginning to heat up, but Michigan was what I could afford, and it was a fine school, I could not argue that. In the dorm, I was assigned to live with two other girls, Caroline and Audrey, who'd come to Ann Arbor together from Squirrel Hill, one of the wealthy suburbs of Pittsburgh. Caroline was from a family of old money and Audrey's father wrote a nationally syndicated column on chess. I was in awe of both girls' self-confidence. I suppose coming to school with a best friend made you more secure. But the crowded dorm room seemed built for two, not three, and I wondered if they were disappointed when they discovered they had a third roommate. In the lobby, each of us in the dormitory were assigned a cubicle with frosted glass at the front, unlocked with a small, silver key that I preciously guarded. I became a sickening slave to the mail. Day after day, I ran to my mailbox, sometimes even checking several times a day, as if I did not know the precise time that mail reached our boxes. There'd usually be something from the family, or a few punchy notes from friends at schools across the country, but because there was no letter from you, these gave me little cheer. I was desperate to see your writing, yours alone. You always used a fountain pen with deep blue ink. That, and your firm, broad scrawl, gave whatever you wrote gravitas.

Even though I knew that it was not smart to pursue you this way, I deluged you with letters, in the beginning, sometimes three or four times a week. I told myself that mail going to and from Providence might take a long time. So I kept writing—long intense letters in which I told you every detail about being a freshman at Michigan, as well as embarrassing pages of sheer emotion. I reminisced about the year before, about the oh-so-unique love that we'd found. For it did seem unique to me, a meeting of our spirits and bodies and minds. An eighteen-year-old can be so arrogant about her own feelings, sure she is the center of the greatest drama since Romeo and Juliet. But in the year following your mother's death, our senior year of high school, we'd spent every available moment together. It wasn't only the consolation, although that was how it started. We told each other our dreams. You were still obsessed with politics, and through you, I became more aware of the world. We both imagined travel, though I had no clear idea how that would happen. Perhaps, I could find work that took me to remote places of the earth where I could help people. What about the newly created Peace Corps?

"You'll do it, Judith. I know you will. You'll see things," you encouraged me.

"I hope so, Elliot," I said, wishing I knew what my future looked like, hoping it would be exciting. Always, my parents had stressed safety, fear of the outside world. I craved experiences, adventure. Their fearfulness felt stifling.

That last year of high school had brought us so close, I wasn't prepared for silence once we were at college. Eventually, however, I admitted that mail from Providence to Ann Arbor could not possibly be taking so long. You simply weren't answering. I pictured my love letters piling up in your room, stale and stagnant, the emotion in them overripened like smelly cheese. I pictured you checking your own cubicle in your lobby, perhaps a wooden block of letter-boxes, the Brown lobby a fancier Ivy League version of my own modern, state-supported dormitory. Only I imagined that rather than rifling through your mail with anticipation, instead you felt a wash of pity and guilt as you saw yet another postmark from Ann Arbor.

All through high school and your days as regional president of the Jewish youth group, you regularly received notes from smitten girls. You told me about them, groaning that it was such a chore to answer them. I saw those pink envelopes, like petals carelessly dropped from a bouquet, scattered on the desk in your bedroom. I peeked at them when you left the room, though I never went so far as to open an envelope and read the letter inside. I saw they were written in girlish hands, some embellishing the dots on the *i*'s of both Elliot and Pine with little hearts. Pathetic, I thought. Those silly girls chasing after Elliot were pathetic. Now I was one of them.

By mid-October I finally told myself that whatever we'd had in the year after Helen Pine's death was over. Then, soon after I'd given up hope, I finally received a letter from you—a thick envelope with the familiar deep blue script. I felt as happy as when I'd raced to collect the mail at home and found thick acceptance envelopes from good schools. But that first letter was merely newsy, with absolutely no reference to our romance of the year before, and I realized that our relationship had been given a significant makeover. You did not want to sever the connection between us; you wanted to keep our friend-ship intact. So, you ignored the heated letters I'd sent and answered instead in a charming, witty, but decidedly unromantic tone. You told me about your classes, quoting lines of literature. You wrote amusing character sketches of the people you met. You included details you knew I'd appreciate—about the authors we'd loved and discovered together, the kinds of people we'd both found tiresome. Occasionally, you'd speak of events from our shared past, but made no mention of the relationship we'd come to after your mother's death. When we'd left for college that previous August, there had been passion and intensity. Elliot. I did not fabricate this. Every single weekend there were dates ending in fogged car windows. Our shared confidences were true memories of that year. But when you wrote to me from Providence, it was as if we both understood that what we now had was friendship, albeit a deep and important friendship.

How foolish I felt after reading that first letter. We'd never really discussed what we would be to each other after we went away to school, that important conversation when people say: "We're both going away, so we need to be free to meet other people, but I want you always to be in my life." I'd expected that conversation and of course I would have agreed to the new terms, any terms at all, really. But the words were never said. And although I would have agreed, I also knew that what I felt toward you was not friendship. I loved you as passionately as I had since we were children and you'd come hurtling into our fifth-grade classroom with your bloody leg staining your white trousers. Finally, after your mother's suicide, you'd reciprocated that love. During that terrible time when your grief was still new, our friendship had changed. Her death had given us a closeness I do not know would have happened otherwise.

But despite your grief, we were, after all, teenagers—brimming with life and curiosity. How could it be otherwise? It was nature. On weekends, we began double-dating with your brother Phillip, who was then a junior at the University of Chicago. He had his own car, a luxury few of us in high school possessed. Still a bear of a guy, Phillip squeezed himself into the front seat of a turquoise Oldsmobile, a big lumbering car that had been retired by your father, Max, who regularly bought himself a new Oldsmobile every two years. The steering wheel of the Olds cut into Phillip's incipient gut; it looked terribly uncomfortable, but he refused to slide the seat backward, toward me, where I sat behind him in my customary spot in the back with you.

"Phillip," I said each time I got into the Olds, "it's okay if you move your seat back. I've got loads of room back here. Honestly."

"No, I'm fine, Judith, you relax," he'd say, sucking in his belly.

I felt terrible about making Phillip uncomfortable. All three of you Pine brothers had impeccable manners. But along with courtesy, there was a note of condescension in Phillip's voice. I wondered if perhaps in his eyes I was too ordinary, less brilliant than he expected for his younger brother. Phillip's girls were exceptional types. They'd published poetry or played violin in a professional string quartet. Despite his good manners, I felt disturbingly ill-at-ease in the company of Phillip and his University of Chicago dates. Was there anything special about me? I could think of nothing. I was smart enough, cute enough, well liked enough, but in no way distinctive.

Phillip's current girlfriend was Diane, a fellow student at the university, whose family, like Phillip's, lived locally. After you collected me from my parents' apartment, Phillip would ride alone in the front seat, like he was our chauffeur. He'd fiddle with the radio dial until he found a piece of classical music he liked, and then silently he'd turn onto the Outer Drive, the four-lane expressway with sparkling, luxury apartment buildings to the west, and dark, brooding Lake Michigan to the east. Phillip drove like someone's father, carefully and considerately. He never braked suddenly, but took each turn on the expressway smoothly and competently. Once, just once, I'd have liked to see Phillip speed. Or get a ticket. But, of course, neither happened.

Diane's family lived in one of those glittering Lake Shore Drive apartments. Usually, Phillip would leave us in the car, the motor running to keep the heat on, while he dashed into the apartment building and brought Diane down. But one evening, as he drove along the lake, he told us that Diane's family had asked why he kept us waiting in the car. They'd invited us up to their apartment before we went to the movies. They wanted to meet Phillip's kid brother—and his girlfriend, of course.

"Great," you said. "I'd love to. Right, Judith?" you added.

I mumbled something pleasant, but immediately felt my stomach clench. All these Saturday nights going to the movies, getting the delicious deep-dish pizza we all liked, or going to hear a group on Chicago's near north side, where there was a burgeoning folk music scene, had made me acutely self-conscious. I was a high school girl with neither the sophistication nor experience of Diane. I constantly fretted about how well I stood up to the comparison in your and your brother Phillip's eyes. Diane herself was a folk singer, a tall, willowy young woman with a blond, waiflike haircut. She'd already performed in clubs in Hyde Park.

"Hey, Judith," Phillip said with a laugh as he drove. "You really have the *shpilkes* back there. You haven't stopped tapping the bottom of my seat with your feet since you got in. Everything okay?"

You laughed along with your brother. A real guffaw. I froze. My body was always betraying me; the nerves I felt had transferred into a nervous rat-a-tat drumming under Phillip's seat. But Elliot, you betrayed me as well, loudly laughing with Phillip while I put my hands on my thighs and willed my legs to stay still.

"No, I'm fine," I said. "Maybe just a little cold."

Phillip courteously cranked up the heat and drove the rest of the way humming to the music on the radio. He found a parking spot on a side street off Lakeshore Drive and we pulled on our hats and gloves to face the cold Chicago night. The wind off the lake left piles of trash swirling in front of us. It was at least ten degrees colder in this part of the city than it was in our own neighborhood, farther to the west.

Your brother walked nonchalantly past the doorman, who recognized him and tipped his hat. "Hi, Artie, how's it going?" Phillip asked.

"Great, young fella. Come on in where it's warm. I'll call Miss Diane and tell her you're on your way up," the uniformed man said as he held open the heavy glass door.

"Thanks, Artie," Phillip replied, at home even with this magical ritual of doormen. You and I scurried inside behind the hulking Phillip. We took the elevator to the twentieth floor, where there were only two apartments, one to the right and one to the left.

Diane opened the door before we knocked and gave Phillip a small peck on his cheek.

"Come on in, you guys. My parents are dying to meet your brother, Phillip. You too, Judith. Let me take your coats."

The Bergmans were waiting for us in the living room, which had heavily draped windows facing the lake as well as elegantly carved furniture. There were Persian rugs and a baby grand piano topped with silver-framed family pictures. I have since come to know many such apartments. I have even lived in some myself, and I know now that there is a checklist for apartments of cultured Jewish city dwellers, with only a few variations: paintings, Persian rugs, parquet wooden floors, antiques. The Bergmans' apartment was the home of musicians, so there were three music stands set up in front of three empty chairs. But when I was ushered through the door on the twentieth floor of one of the most desirable addresses in Chicago, it was the first of its genre I had ever been inside.

I saw how Phillip had provided his younger brother with much useful guidance. Three years older, Phillip possessed social graces and confidence that I could only gawk at. You subtly received a cue from Phillip and responded, perhaps a beat behind your older brother, with absolute correctness, and with a flair all your own. Deftly taking a cracker and instantly placing a napkin underneath it so that no crumbs fell, sitting back comfortably on the couch with an ease of possession, commenting on the art. It was an eyeful to watch Phillip initiate an action, then have you echo it. There was absolute elegance and even musicality to your duet. Perhaps you had done this your entire lives. My own actions that night in the lakefront apartment were clunky and unharmonious. I spilled crumbs, sat at the edge of the couch, and recognized none of the artists discussed. I contributed little to the conversation.

Mercifully, we stayed at the Bergmans' only a short time, and even more mercifully, we went to a movie nearby where I felt no more responsibility to speak or respond. I know now that all teenagers are awkward and worried, second-guessing their every move as they desperately watch themselves and obsess about what others see. It was you Pine brothers and your poise, not my own insecure fumbling, which was the exception. At the time, though, Phillip paralyzed me and your subtle mimicry of your brother made my fragile confidence disintegrate, just as flour for my mother's cakes drifted through a sieve.

That winter and spring of our senior year, we went on regular dates. You no longer needed to ask me out for the coming weekend—it was assumed we'd be together. "What are we doing?" replaced "Would you like to go out on Saturday?" Occasionally, you were able to borrow your father's car and then we went alone, not in the back seat as Phillip's passengers. When we were by ourselves, no matter the weather, we ended up at the lakefront. You would find a dark spot to park in and then turn off the engine. Our kisses became longer and you explored my body with greater boldness. You gently touched me first under my clothes, reaching inside my bra, under my skirts, or into my jeans, eventually feeling under the elastic of my underpants. I held my breath, loving you so much, accepting all that you did, aching for it, but hesitant to explore on my own.

Finally one night, after we were gasping for breath and, despite the cold weather, dripping with sweat, you put your fingers farther underneath that elastic. I was wearing a skirt, long since pushed up around my waist. You had been stroking my thighs until I actually felt something unhinge in my brain, a click, and then something opened up inside my head as well as my lower body. I arched my back and moaned as you slipped a finger into my vagina. Your finger, first one and then two, explored deeper inside me, while with your other hand, you took my hand and put it on top of the bulge in your pants. I slowly began to unzip your trousers, thinking that if I moved very slowly, it would seem as if the zipper was descending on its own, not because of any action of mine. As your fingers began to probe deeper, with greater urgency within me, there was a horrifying, loud rapping on the windows. The windows were rolled all the way up and were completely fogged over. My first thought was that it was the sadistic killer we were all warned about, the one who preyed on couples parked in darkened spots along the lake. I jerked my head around to see if the door was locked.

"Open up in there, you two," said a deep voice, and there was more knocking. It was, I realized, a policeman. He was rapping on the window with his nightstick, and then he shined his flashlight right into the car, illuminating my skirt hiked up around my waist and Elliot's undone zipper.

"Yes, sir," Elliot gasped. "Okay. Yes. Right away."

The driver's seat was reclined almost all the way back, and Elliot tried to zip his pants and raise the seat at the same time. I slid over to my side of the car and fumbled with my own buttons, trying to yank my bra down over my breasts.

"Pull down that window," the cop demanded. "Right now." I saw that he wasn't alone. Another officer with a shiny Chicago Police Department badge was behind the first. I hated Chicago policemen—every kid in the city, black or white, did. The cops were unpredictable and cruel, and our parents warned us never to get in their way. My father, a modest and principled man, had even been forced to bribe the driver's license examiner after I failed my driver's test twice. Bribes were a way of life in Chicago in those days, but I certainly didn't know the protocol for late night taps on the car window and didn't know if Elliot did either.

"How's it going in there, young man?" the policeman asked, a smirk now on his face, the flashlight trained on me alone. He slowly shined the light up and down from my face to my bare legs.

"Okay, sir. We were just going home," you answered with amazing aplomb and smoothed back your hair. You tried to smile at the policeman.

"How about I see your driver's license?" the officer said. You dug in your wallet and handed it to the policeman, who studied it, then passed it to his buddy.

"You kids are awfully young to be out here at this hour. This isn't such a safe neighborhood, you know. Lots of unsavory folks prowling the paths along the lake here at night."

"Right. You're right. I think we ought to get home now," you said.

"What would your mother think, young man? What would she say if I gave her a little call right now and told her what her sweet baby boy was up to out here? With this pretty little girl?" the policeman asked, a lascivious grin on his face as he looked at me.

There was a long silence. You took a deep breath in and looked ahead over the steering wheel into the black night.

"He doesn't have a mother," I finally said, almost whispering in the dark. "She died. Last summer."

The policeman swung his flashlight back to Elliot, shining it in his eyes, making Elliot blink hard. "Well, that's a tough break, kid. That's a sad story. You better get this young lady home right now." He handed Elliot back his driver's license. "We'll stay here and watch while you turn this car around and get back on the Outer Drive. How about that?"

"Yeah. I will. Thanks, sir. I'll do that."

On the way home, we said little. Finally, when we got to my house, you turned to me. "I wish you hadn't told him about my mother. It sounded cheap. Like we were using her being dead to get out of trouble."

"Yeah. I know," I said. "But he frightened me. I just wanted to get us out of there."

"I'm sorry it happened," you said and pulled me close. "I don't think he was going to do anything, though. Just trying to scare us. Embarrass us. I don't know."

Sex was like that for us that year. We both desperately wanted to do it, but there were so many prohibitions for good girls. Our high school had been divided into fast girls and good girls. Those who went all the way, sluts, and those who did not. It seems so silly now. There we were, at seventeen, as sexual as we'd ever again be in our lives, our bodies wanting each other so desperately, but we were not supposed to act on it. The night of the policeman surprising us in the car stirred up my feelings of shame. I told myself I had no business doing what I'd done and certainly no business wanting it as badly as I did.

That night, after the frightening rap on our windows by the policeman, I combed my hair in the car and smoothed my clothes as best I could. There was nowhere to park, so I got out of the car in front of my building, and trudged dejectedly up the stairs. When I unlocked the front door of our apartment, I found my father sitting close to the light of the lamp on an end table, his feet up on an ottoman, reading a paper. Other than the one table lamp, the living room was dark. He was reading the *Manchester Guardian*. I don't know where he first got the idea, but he maintained all his life that the *Guardian* was the one truly unbiased paper in the world. He subscribed to the Sunday edition, receiving it on the next Friday in a wrapper covered with stamps from England, its news old, but still immensely satisfying to him. The paper was thin, parchment-like, not at all like the paper used by the Chicago papers: the *Sun Times* or the *Tribune* or the *Daily News*. He read every word of the *Guardian* on Friday evenings, staying up late into the night. I think reading a paper that came all the way from England made him feel that he was different, more intellectual than the other men we knew. And he was, even though he'd never traveled and was just a shopkeeper. He was a voracious reader, an autodidact; and his politics were liberal and thoughtful. As I walked into the living room and saw him comfortably sprawled out on the couch, his glasses perched low on his nose and his smile welcoming me home, I decided to speak to him about what I was feeling. Speaking to my mother about sex was out of the question. She would have made a huge fuss if I even mentioned the word. But my warm and gentle father, the kindest and most intelligent man I knew, perhaps I could broach the subject to him.

"Hi, sweetheart, did you have a good time?" he asked. "Come on over here," he said and patted the couch beside him.

"Yeah, it was fun. We went to hear some music. Near the university," I lied.

"I hope you brought some money with you. I don't like how you run around without money in your purse. What if you got stuck somewhere? That's not a good neighborhood."

"No, I took money. But there's something else. I wanted to talk to you about something else," I said and sat down next to him. He had a particular smell, my father, stale pipe smoke along with an overwhelming scent of Listerine mouthwash. He went through bottles of mouthwash each week.

My father folded the soft sheets of the newspaper, carefully along the creases. "Sure, honey. Anything the matter?"

"No, but I was wondering. About you and Mom. She wasn't that young when you married. I wondered what you would have thought of her if she hadn't been, you know, a virgin, when you married. If she'd done it before she met you."

The words were difficult to say. My father and I had never before had a discussion that dealt with any bodily functions, let alone sex. The warm glow of the lamplight as I came in the door, watching him as he comfortably read the paper in his pajamas, must have deluded me into thinking that my father was not who he was and that we could have this conversation that he was not equipped to have.

There was a long silence as my father reached down and slipped his bare, calloused feet back into his slippers, probably both stalling for time as well as reducing the intimacy that I'd forced upon us. Once his slippers were on, he sat up straight on the couch and stared ahead.

"I can't imagine what made you think that your mother's age when we got married had anything to do with anything," he said.

"Dad, she was twenty-six. Wasn't that old back then for a woman to get married? She must have had other boyfriends before you."

"Maybe she was on the older side. Not old. But that had nothing to do with her decision to be a good woman. Your mother always was a good woman. Someone I could *respect*," he said, and removed his reading glasses.

"But Dad, why would it have made any difference to you if she had slept with someone before marriage? Even, for example"—and here I took a deep breath—"you."

"Judith, I don't know what's gotten into you tonight." He began to crack his knuckles, which he did whenever he was feeling strongly about something, pulling each knobby finger until it made a satisfying pop. "I told you how I respected your mother." He was getting angry, a rare occurrence.

"I understand that," I said. "Of course you respect Mom. But would sleeping with her before you got married have changed anything? Why would that have affected if you respected her or not?"

For the first time that I ever remembered, my father raised his voice. "Of course it would have changed things," he said and looked more outraged with every word he spoke. "I never would have married a woman I did not respect. And any respectable woman saves herself for marriage. What's the matter with you? You know all this.

Why are you asking me these questions?" He picked up his paper and unfolded it with a lot of noise.

"Now go to bed before we wake your mother, Judith. This conversation would kill her," he said. And as I walked away, he added, "I certainly hope you haven't already done something with that Elliot. Something that would make us ashamed."

"No, Dad. I haven't done anything wrong," I said, defeated.

I didn't ask any more questions. My father picked up his reading glasses and disappeared behind the *Guardian*. I slunk off to bed.

In the months to come, we never stopped our exhausting routine of arousing each other, but always stopped short of intercourse. I loved the feelings of your fingers searching my body, finding places that made me shiver and moan, and yet I kept hearing my father's distraught voice from that night, confirmation that if I had sex with you, I would be crossing over into territory so dangerous that I might spend a lifetime regretting it.

As the time approached when we were to go away to our separate schools, I became even more powerfully conflicted. Some days it seemed that sleeping with you before we went off to college would be the right thing to do. I'd plan it and think about it, but could never find the courage to initiate it. And I would have to initiate it, as you were convinced that because I wasn't one of the fast girls, you were supposed to stop.

Away at Michigan those first weeks, I wondered if perhaps the reason that I wasn't hearing from Elliot was because I hadn't been brave enough to have sex with him. Everyone was experimenting with sex. It wasn't like high school with lines drawn between those who did it and those who did not. In the bigger world of college, virginity increasingly seemed an oddity. Caroline and Audrey, my roommates in the dorm triple room, had come to Michigan, like me, as virgins. When we discovered this, we laughingly wondered if there was some way the administration grouped us. Were there virgin rooms versus non-virgin rooms? But soon, tall, confident Caroline and beautiful blond Audrey both had boyfriends, and we began endless discussions about whether to go all the way or not. This would seem unbearably boring to young people today, to think that this subject caused so many hours of debate and discussion, but we were on the far side of the cusp of the sexual revolution. Finally, one night, I was nearly asleep, but I woke up completely when the door to our room opened and shut and I heard Caroline and Audrey begin to whisper on their side of the room.

"I did it," I heard Caroline exultantly whisper.

I sat up in bed, looking in the darkness toward where the other two were sitting on Audrey's bed. "No you don't. You've got to tell *both* of us," I said. "Turn on the light."

And Caroline described how she and her boyfriend, an upper-classman who majored in engineering and had his own apartment, had had sex that night. He'd had a condom ready in his nightstand drawer, she said with feigned casualness. I was so jealous I could barely stand it. Even though she downplayed the importance of her announcement, I heard the triumph and excitement in her voice. Caroline immediately seemed more mature, and, of course, we saw her in our dorm room less and less. We covered for her, even signing her in at night so that she could stay at her boyfriend's. Within the month, Audrey began sleeping with her boyfriend as well, a boy with long hair who followed her adoringly everywhere on campus. Soon I was alone in that room most evenings. A single in a room for three. I slept by myself and imagined that all the other girls I saw in classes, on the quad, or in the library were having happy, exuberant sex with their boyfriends, while I went back to my lonely single.

I could not, for the life of me, figure out what use this virgin-ity thing had now. My father's advice came to seem irrelevant and quaint, and besides, he was hundreds of miles away from Ann Arbor. I began to detest my virginity. It became an unattractive burden. I did not, however, want to have sex with anyone besides Elliot. After all that deferred passion, it seemed absurd to lose my virginity with anyone less significant than the great love of my life, Elliot. Now, more than half a century later, an old woman, I regret few things in my life. But I do regret not sleeping with you, Elliot, that summer before we went to college. I regretted it back then and I tried to blame my father, but since I listened to very little other advice either of my parents gave, why had I so desperately clung to this particular advice? I decided that during that winter break, in December, I would stop all this virginity nonsense and tell Elliot that the time had come for us to maturely express our emotions. I rehearsed the conversation again and again.

Within a day of coming home for the December vacation, I called you. I plunged in headlong. The time for hesitation and reticence was long past.

"Elliot, when can you come over? I'm dying to see you. Weren't we other people when we went away to school last September? I've never changed so much in so short a time."

"Yeah, I know exactly what you mean," you said. "We thought we knew so much when we went away. But it's a much bigger world out there, isn't it?"

"Let's go for coffee tomorrow. And catch up," I said, with whatever seductiveness I could muster, knowing that on a weekday afternoon there was a greater chance that we could be alone at his house. With his father at work, and his brothers no longer living at home, the sprawling apartment would be empty.

"Yeah. That'd be great. I'll pick you up around noon. I'm really wiped out, still on East Coast time," you said.

I finally fell asleep that night, in my girl's virginal bed, wondering if I'd be feeling differently the next night. I hoped for two things: first, that my father, more finely attuned to my moods than anyone else on earth, would be preoccupied when he came home for dinner that night, and second, that my mother wouldn't keep Elliot too long when he came for me. I feared that her endless questions and prying would spoil any chance of romance for the afternoon. I could imagine her saying, "Elliot, tell me about your classes. Elliot, tell me how your brothers are doing. Elliot, do you want some milk and homemade rugelach?" When she started talking to my friends, she never stopped.

But luck was with me when it came to my mother that day. Although she looked disappointed, she had already made plans for mah-jongg and lunch with her friends and would not be home when Elliot arrived.

However, for an hour before she left, she made my nerves even more jangled by sitting on the bed and questioning me about everything I planned to wear. She inspected each thing that I pulled out of my drawers—even the bra and panties I gathered to take with me into the bathroom. She almost managed to dampen my own romantic anticipation with her hovering. When I came out of the bathroom and put on a nice pair of charcoal gray slacks and a pale gray V-neck sweater, she made a face.

"Those are nice slacks, Judith," she said in the Russian accent I could barely detect, but that others commented on. ("Where's your mother from?" people asked me immediately after they met her.) Then she sniffed loudly, always the sign that came was to follow. "Quality material. But a little tight. That dorm food has settled somewhere around your *tuchus*. Exactly where my weight goes as well." She patted her own backside. "Besides, you have a panty line."

"Jesus, Mom. Somehow I've managed to get myself dressed every day these past few months. I don't know how I did it all by myself, but I did."

"No need to be rude, Miss College Girl. I see what my eyes see," she said firmly. "And they see tight." She crossed her arms in front of her chest and pursed her lips.

"What do you expect me to do about it?" I asked, my voice rising. "Go on a diet right now?" She made me crazy; I felt as if I was suffocating in this house.

"Of course not, Judith. There's no need to get huffy. That's what panty girdles are for. You pull one on, and you get a nice, smooth look. Believe me."

I didn't think I had the will to argue with her, so I opened my underwear drawer where there were several panty girdles, white, black, and beige, and took off my slacks. Then I stepped into the black one, and fiercely tugged it up around my hips. It tortuously encased my entire midsection and extended almost to my knees. The satin panel over the abdomen was so tight, I could no longer breathe adequately; but I must admit that when I turned and inspected myself in the mirror, I saw a much smoother profile in both back and front.

"Now, maybe you'll listen to me once in a while," said my mother with satisfaction. Then she looked at her watch. "Okay, I have to hurry and put my face on. The cab will be here any minute."

The day was an especially cold one, the sky a drab, midwestern gray, and the sleet was turning to snow. After my mother closed the door, I stood at the front window and looked at the scene below: the stark red brick apartment buildings that lined my street, the trees, planted at regular intervals, which became barren sticks in winter. It was strangely quiet, and when the occasional car went by, it crawled clumsily past, its tires wrapped in bulky chains, the chains slicing into the ice. A cab stopped in front of our building and my mother appeared below on the street, her head wrapped in a babushka to preserve her hairdo from the still-falling snow, but her feet fashionable in short, black boots trimmed in Persian lamb, so in vogue that year. She walked carefully and slowly across the icy sidewalk. When she reached for the door of the waiting yellow cab, she turned and gave a jaunty wave up at me as I stood watching from the upstairs window. How did she know I was there, watching? I wondered.

You arrived at noon. I almost wished my mother had been at home chattering and asking questions. It would have diffused my shocked silence about the transformation you'd undergone. You didn't look anything like the boy who had left Budlong Woods for Brown only a few months earlier. You must not have cut your hair since the summer. And it was greasy and scraggly, without its usual luster. You also had the beginnings of a beard. More shocking were your clothes. You'd always been turned out neat and tidily. In high school, you looked like a rising executive. When we became a couple, I self-consciously got rid of the frivolous, faddish pre-Elliot outfits in my closet and replaced them with severe and businesslike clothes as well—ironed button-down shirts and coordinating cardigans and blazers. I guess that's why I chose the charcoal gray pants and sweater to wear that day.

But you no longer looked businesslike. Your meticulous dress had metamorphized into that of a wizard. Despite the gloomy winter weather outside, your clothes were bright and mismatched. Under an orange hooded parka, you wore a peacock blue T-shirt. Your jeans were striped, like those of a train engineer. They fit tight through the thighs, had rips in both knees, and then flared out widely at the bottom. Below your jeans, you wore high-topped sneakers which were a vivid shade of purple. Until I saw them, I hadn't imagined that sneakers came in purple. Most remarkable of all, you were carrying a purse. And you seemed not at all shy about it. The purse was a fantastic mélange of fabrics patchworked together. You wore it over your left shoulder, where it crossed your body, then rested low on your right hip. Tiny mirrors were sewn onto the patchwork. I stood in the doorway hypnotized as you climbed the stairs. We gave each other a quick kiss of hello and I shut the door behind you. I saw then that the mirrors on your bag sprayed reflections of light all over my parents' somber green couch, the chairs, as well as the beige walls. Each time you moved, the mirrors magically shifted and reflected yet other patterns, like a kaleidoscope. Our living room was transformed by these twinkling patterns, and I turned from you, watching the sparkles, unable to take my eyes from the magical lights the purse cast on my parents' bland curtains and furniture.

"Love the purse," I said. "I mean it. I love it. I want it."

You laughed. "This girl I know at school makes them," you answered. "I'll see if I can get her to make one for you. Each bag comes out differently, though."

"*You* look different," I said, staring. "You should have warned me."

"Yeah, the first thing my dad said to me yesterday when I got off the plane was, 'Get a haircut.' He's barely said anything to me since." You looked at me. "You look the same." He saw my face fall and then quickly added, as he stroked my cheek, "No, no that's a good thing. You look great. But your hair is longer. I like it that way a lot."

We went to our favorite hot dog stand on Petersen Avenue, nothing like it in Ann Arbor or Providence, we agreed. I was so nervous I couldn't eat, so you finished mine as well. Then we went back to your house. You turned the key in the lock and we walked through the familiar and empty apartment back to your bedroom. It looked exactly the same, the Israeli posters, the neatly made-up bed. Seeing your bright clothing and long hair had made me expect that the room would be different, too. But the only change was the duffel bag at the foot of your bed, colorful wrinkled clothes spilling out it.

I sat on the bed, while you stood searching through a stack of albums on your desk.

"Here, you have to hear this," you said, finally

You put on a single. It was "Eight Days a Week." This was the first time I'd ever heard the Beatles. Then you played "Twist and Shout." I tried to smile enthusiastically, but I wasn't as excited by the music as you were. I suppose, when you think about it, hearing the Beatles for the first time is as big an event as losing one's virginity. You'll always remember where you were when it happened and who you were with.

But I was preoccupied with my other mission, and it would be several months before I realized what genius I was being exposed to. When you finally joined me on the bed, you started to talk about the music. You were rambling, so I took a deep breath and interrupted.

"Elliot, one of the things I wanted to tell you today was that I've thought about the whole virginity thing. When I got to Michigan, I kept thinking back to how we always stopped." I couldn't meet your eyes. I was so scared, but kept talking. "I don't want us to stop anymore." My heart was pounding as I said this. "It's stupid that we stop."

You shrugged and said, "Okay," as if what I'd said was so obvious it didn't bear discussing. You sat beside me on the bed and started kissing me, but then hesitated and looked hard at me. "Wait, you're still a virgin?" you asked.

I nodded, for the first time realizing that, of course, you were not.

"Wow," you said and then we leaned back on the bed.

I should have taken it off before we left my house, but I had liked the smooth shape the panty girdle gave me under the gray pants too much. Elliot, do you remember how you struggled to get the damn thing off me, pulling and tugging and, finally successful, throwing it to the floor? It seemed to have taken forever. The offending garment lay next to your glittering mirrored patchwork bag. We stared as the elastic curled up on itself, the girdle resembling a large squashed cockroach.

The romance had evaporated. You began to laugh. We looked at the floor, at the ridiculous heap of our mismatched clothing: my heather gray sweater and your torn train conductor's jeans, your purple sneakers and my gray flannel trousers. They were all tangled together, but the contrast represented the enormous chasm between us. This time, it was the black panty girdle that came between us.

You were still laughing. You couldn't seem to stop. You were laughing so hard, tears were flowing. I stared at you, depressed. Was my panty girdle really all that funny?

"Sorry," you said. "Sorry. I got stoned before I picked you up. That thing looks so weird, it just set me off," you said, and pointed to the panty girdle and started laughing again. "I smoked the last of it. Sorry. I wish I had more, but I had to get rid of it. I didn't want my father to find it. He would go nuts. Probably pull me out of school. But I'm still totally high. Have you tried pot?" you asked, still smiling, but more in control and looking at me with interest.

I shook my head.

"It's amazing. You have to try it. We'll have to try it together. Sometime."

Pot, another new experience I hadn't yet had. I couldn't keep up. And instead of losing my virginity that afternoon, my carefully planned deflowerment, we lay back on his narrow bed and talked about school, our classes, what we were reading. Just like always. There were long silences, when you were absorbed in the music. Talking softly on that narrow bed, curled up together, was reminiscent of the summer before, but different. Because you'd told me about the pot, I felt awkward. Sometimes, in the middle of the conversation, you would jump up and change the record, saying, "You gotta hear this," or dig through your duffle to find a book and then read me a passage. "Isn't that beautiful?" you'd ask. I tried to act normal, to react as I had always reacted, but I wasn't sure when I was supposed to be quiet and listen or when I should keep chatting. I felt left behind, unsure of how to behave with you now.

A more experienced girl might have tried to have sex again, wouldn't have let the first failure deter her. It would have been as simple as reaching down and touching you gently beneath your white briefs. I could still see a bulge there. But, at that age, I couldn't do it, could not be the one to initiate it. I was too afraid of rejection. You had decided that our body parts would not fit together any better than the pile of clothes on the floor and I didn't know how to change that. Occasionally, you got so lost in the music, it seemed you didn't even know I was there. Your eyes would close and your head would rock up and down in time to the beat. How would I answer Audrey's and Caroline's questions back at school? They'd known about my plan to have sex with you. I'd have to lie or admit what happened. Eventually, we heard Mr. Pine in the kitchen, and smelled meat sizzling in a pan.

We sat up, gave each other rueful smiles. "Maybe next time," you said, and we quickly dressed, me stuffing the offending black panty girdle into my purse. The magic was gone.

I finished the vacation in Chicago in a terrible funk. I barely went out, until it was time to pile into a junky Plymouth with four other people to make the drive back to Ann Arbor. At school, I started to pay more attention to my classes, reading late at night. I decided that I would stop worrying about boys, and focus on being an intellectual. I wore less makeup, acquired several black turtlenecks, and had endless cups of coffee with people I met in classes, even some professors. About a month after I returned from the winter break, I was invited to a party where I smoked pot for the first time, getting lost in my own reverie of music.

In the dead of February, a terrible time of year in Ann Arbor, the gray winter feeling endless and the lovely crunch of leaves underfoot from autumn almost impossible to remember, I came in from my morning seminar in comparative literature and took out my small silver key to check for mail. Inside the cubicle, I found a bonanza. There were several letters and a small notice printed on yellow paper. We all knew that those yellow notices informed us that there was a package to collect from the dorm office. For me, this usually meant a package containing red coffee tins stuffed with homemade cookies or brownies, sent from my mother. My birthday was the next day, February fourteenth. I loved having my birthday on Valentine's Day. Besides seeming very romantic, people were more likely to remember it. Perhaps there was a package from my aunt Gussie, something sent from the wonderful jewelry store where she worked. I did love receiving presents.

When I presented my yellow ticket to friendly Mrs. Gelfman in the office, she brought out not one, but three boxes. "Quite a haul, my dear," she said and smiled. "Valentine's Day. Somebody loves you."

"It's my birthday, too," I told her. "Valentine's Day *and* my birthday."

I looked at the return addresses and saw, with a shock, that one was from Providence. Audrey and Caroline would be in class, so I took the packages upstairs so that I could be alone. First I opened the care package sent by my parents. Inside, in addition to the sweets packed in coffee tins, there was a generous check. My mother's brownies were still soft and the room became thick with their chocolaty smell. There were chocolate chip cookies, most of them intact. And there was also the round loaf of date and nut bread that was one of my mother's baked specialties in another, smaller, tin can. This bread was brown and dense, delicious when sliced thin and spread with cream cheese. Aunt Gussie hadn't failed me, either, sending a small package containing a pair of gypsy hoop earrings, real gold. I ran to the mirror and tried them on. I thought that with my short hair, the hoops made me look elegant, yet Bohemian. With unusual patience, I'd saved the best for last, the box from Providence with my name, and the word "Rocket" written in parentheses after it, scrawled in the familiar blue fountain pen. I unwrapped the package slowly, prolonging the pleasure. Inside was a patchwork bag, the fabrics easily as colorful as and covered with even more mirrors than the one you had worn over your shoulder at the holidays. It was the same design, though the strap was a bit shorter, so that it fell to my hip at exactly the right place. "Happy Valentine's Day and Happy Birthday," the note on top of the purse read. "Sorry I was such a jerk in Chicago. We'll make up for it someday. I promise." The sparkles from the bag reflected on the walls and beds of the little room, brightening the Ann Arbor gloom.

4

Insanity

The line between sanity and insanity has become blurred as I aged. There were those times in my thirties when I was so exhausted at the end of a long day and the children refused to cooperate and get ready for bed, that I shouted vile things, becoming so enraged that I shook and could not see straight. In short, I acted insane, full of misplaced rage for my innocent children. Later, when I finally got them to sleep and could do what I had wanted to do since I'd come in the door from an exhausting day of listening to other people's problems—turn on the television and eat a bowl of ice cream by myself, curled up on the couch—I'd think about the awful things I'd said. "You never leave me alone," I shrieked with absolute venom to the twins. "Can I never, ever get a moment's peace?" To this day these words make me cringe and I am ashamed.

A few years later, there was the day when their father came to get things out of the garage, boxes I'd retrieved from the storage unit and hadn't yet had a chance to go through.

"Open the garage, Judith," he said. "A lot of things in there are mine."

Seth had all the money in the world back then, while I was broke, scraping by paycheck to paycheck from my county social worker job. I was seething with the unfairness of it all. What right did he have to go through the boxes of kitchen dishes and cooking implements?

These were *my* things. He could afford new spatulas and bowls and mixers. And so, when he wouldn't leave, I got a knife from the kitchen. Waving the knife, I stood in front of the house and shouted, "No, I'm not opening the fucking garage door. Just get the hell out of here." Spittle flew from my mouth. I am sure I had never looked less attractive.

"You're crazy, Judith. Insane," Seth said with disgust, and slammed his car door and drove off with tires squealing.

He was right, of course. I was insane. Worse, and I'm not positive, because the front door was closed, but it's possible that Evan and Miriam were peeking around the living room curtain and heard me threaten their father with a knife.

However, when I was nineteen, long before my marriage and divorce from Seth, before I'd experienced the exhaustion of being a single parent, or bouts of mad jealousy because of this husband who left me for a younger woman, I believed there was a clear division between sane and crazy. I had much to learn back then about the thin divide separating sanity from craziness. This education began the summer after we returned from our first years away at college.

You phoned soon after you arrived home from Brown, sounding depressed. "I'm working for my father this summer," you said. "Ten long weeks. Max has this ironclad rule that at some point, everyone in the family has to put in time at Pine's Meats. To see where the money comes from, I guess. I told him I'd planned to use the summer to write."

"What did your father say?" I asked.

"He laughed. Said the discussion was over."

Your experimentation with the incipient hippie life at Brown, which I'd seen the previous winter, was still in bloom. In another year or two, your interest in politics would resurface. You'd realize that in order to change the world, you would likely need to attend law school. Faculty and more experienced friends suggested that when applying to a top-tier law school, shorter hair and a drug-free profile might be the wiser course. You listened. The suits and briefcase of your AZA days would be dusted off. But that summer, at nineteen, you were not yet looking at the long view. You were full of discovery and the thrilling new life you'd found on the East Coast. This exciting new life, however, was apparently not impressing your father.

It was like that for me as well. No matter how much we felt changed by our first year away at school, the world we'd left behind in Chicago continued just as it had been before we left. It's that way when you're young. You cannot believe that those back home can ignore the seismic changes you've undergone. You wonder if they are blind and deaf.

"What will you do for your father?" I asked, thinking your father might put you in the air- conditioned office of Pine's Meats, where you could put to use that perfect score on the math section of the SATs, while assisting the company's aged bookkeeper.

"I'm not sure. But whatever it is, it's sure to be a ballbuster," you answered. "That's what my brothers and cousins all said about their summers at the meat company. There's no way out of it. My dad and uncle are getting old. One's got bum knees, the other has back trouble. I'm sure I'll be hauling ass. Probably lifting carcasses off and on trucks, that kind of shit."

Some of our more privileged classmates from college went off to family summer homes, places with wisteria arbors and cool evening breezes. Some traveled through Europe. But in our world, summer vacations meant summer jobs. We were expected to spend two months working hard and put money in the bank for the coming year. Even though they had saved for our college expenses their whole lives, neither Max, nor my own parents, understood summers of indolence.

"When you get an education, you can pay for your own trips," had been my mother's response when I'd suggested riding through

France and Italy on a Eurail pass with my roommates Caroline and Audrey. Traveling abroad was not to be an option.

"So what're you doing this summer, Rocket?"

"I've got a job at a psychiatric hospital," I answered. "It's not such a bad place, actually. Part of Northwestern's med center downtown."

"Yeah," you said. "I know the place." I felt stupid for not realizing that, of course, you did. There was a long silence as we both thought about your mother, Helen, who had been in and out of every mental hospital in Illinois during your childhood.

"Have you decided to major in psychology?" you finally asked, changing the subject.

"Something like that. Social work, I think. For now, I'm just an aide. They call me a psych tech. I start on Monday."

"We're both going to need some diversion," you said. "Me from frozen carcasses, you from the patients."

We made a plan to go to the beach the following Saturday, after we'd both finished our first week of work. That June, there had been a terrible heat wave in Chicago and temperatures reached into the triple digits, with the humidity equally high. Rain would have been a blessing, but instead, day after day, there was hot, sticky weather, with more predicted all week. Like everyone else in the city, we knew that the only relief to be found was at the beaches along Lake Michigan.

Unlike you, I was actually looking forward to my job. As soon as I'd returned home, I'd gone to a hospital supply store and purchased two crisp white uniforms, as well as a pair of nurse's shoes, also white, lace-ups with thick spongy soles. I'd shortened the uniforms, which nipped in flatteringly at the waist, as much as I dared. My stockings, although white, had a glistening sheen to them.

My father would drive me to the hospital each day as it was on the way to the army-navy surplus store he owned farther south on Wabash, just past the Loop. Though excited, I was nervous and unsure of how I was supposed to behave around mental patients. When I looked in the mirror that first Monday before we left the house, I gave myself a pep talk. With my white uniform and shoes, I thought I could pass for a real health care provider, not a little girl dressing up for Halloween. I glanced down at my dress and shiny stockings and gleaming white shoes approvingly. Cute, but still professional, I told myself. I'd be fine.

The week began well. By Wednesday, I was telling anecdotes about work to my parents as we sat around the dinner table. I spoke about "my" patients. Imagine my arrogance—a lowly psychiatric technician, the bottom rung in the ladder of mental health workers at the hospital, who'd had no more than two introductory courses in psychology at the University of Michigan, yet spouting insufferably to my family and friends about the diagnoses and pathology of the men and women on that ward.

The teaching hospital was modern and progressive, a five-story structure that faced the lake. There were attractive flower arrangements set into recessed alcoves in the lobby and, on the lawn, a metal fountain containing swans shooting streams of water high into the air. A dark green awning covered the walkway leading to the entrance. It looked more like the expensive apartment buildings located farther to the north on Lake Shore Drive than the mental hospital it was.

Soon after I arrived on the ward each morning, my job was to accompany about ten patients onto the elevator and go to the occupational therapy clinic one floor below. During the day, the patients were exposed to a wide range of activities and therapies: music, psychodrama, expressive dance. The occupational therapy clinic resembled a cheery, well-equipped home economics classroom from high school. There were tables, with vises attached to the sides. Patients worked at these tables on craft projects of their choosing, although the therapist subtly guided their choices.

The occupational therapist, a small woman with dark bangs

and a serious demeanor, had informed me that it was necessary for the activity to be properly therapeutic, not just diversional. It was theorized that repressed anger caused the despondency seen in the depressed patients. So, they were encouraged to externalize this anger. For these patients, I would set up blocks of clay. The occupational therapist showed me how the patients were to wedge and pound and energetically strike the clay with their fists in order to get rid of the air bubbles. Most of the time, however, the men and women merely stared balefully at the red lump I'd placed before them, moving their fingers aimlessly through the muck. I went from one group to another, smashing the clay, trying to vigorously demonstrate what the occupational therapist had showed me. The patients ignored my efforts or moved back from the table uncomfortably.

Disorganized schizophrenic patients were given sorting tasks, putting nails and screws into appropriate plastic trays, or sorting the tiles by color. It was thought that repetitive jobs helped patients with schizophrenia order their disordered thoughts. Some were even given a toothbrush and asked to scrub the grout in the kitchen area. I blithely supervised these tasks and chirped words of encouragement as I moved among the patients.

Very early in the morning, even before I'd arrived at work, other treatments had been administered: electric shock therapy, insulin coma therapy. Modern psychotherapeutic medications were still being developed. Lithium, to treat bipolar disorders, was in the earliest stages of research. Although some patients received drugs, the side effects of drugs in those days were problematic. Instead, the hospital offered electric shock treatments. And, for the sickest patients, those who had not responded to anything else, high doses of insulin, high enough to induce a coma, were injected.

When I came onto the unit at eight in the morning, it was apparent which patients were receiving which treatment. Those who'd had the dangerously high doses of insulin injected that morning needed close observation. Their names were written on a chalkboard in the nurse's station. Glasses of orange juice were kept ready, orange juice being the quickest way to get sugar into the pancreas. While we were down in the occupational therapy room, I had the task of watching for symptoms of insulin overdose. The head nurse told me that these patients might get pale or their skin might become clammy. If that happened, I was to hurry to them with a glass of juice and make sure they ingested it before they passed out.

Other patients, the ones who'd received a massive jolt of electricity earlier that morning, had a vague, confused look. Short-term memory loss was typical in these. Their eyes had a blank, vacant expression, and they would sometimes lose their way in the hospital corridors, not remembering which room was their own. I would gently guide them to where they needed to go, or remind them of the day's schedule.

After morning activities and lunch, a community meeting was convened in the large, sunny dayroom. Another of my tasks was to set up chairs in a circle for the twenty-five or so patients on the ward, and then go around to each room, reminding people it was time for group. Few of the patients wanted to go to the community meeting. Most turned their faces to the wall.

"Come on, Mr. Nerebaum, time for the community meeting," I'd say to one elderly man who always took his pants off when he got into bed and lay in boxer shorts with the fly disconcertingly agape. "Let's get dressed now."

"Girlie," Mr. Nerebaum replied, "why can't you let an old man have some peace and quiet? I'm resting, can't you see?"

The treatment philosophy of the unit was called "milieu therapy." Patients, or residents, as they were sometimes called, were encouraged to discuss the day's events in the group. It was felt that the experience of living and working and creating together would duplicate life on the outside; the patients would learn from their daily experiences on the ward. But most people, except the manic patients or those hallucinating, did not want to talk. Neither to each other nor to the staff.

The chief psychiatrist of the unit, Dr. Albanese, felt quite strongly about these daily community meetings. *Everyone* was supposed to attend. Staff and patients alike were encouraged to speak up and to get to know one another. The nurses, doctors, therapists, even lowly psychiatric technicians like myself, were to participate and discuss our observations of the unit at the meeting.

I have no real recollection of what I said in those community meetings that first week. But I do know that the white uniform and spongy white shoes actually convinced me that I knew something about mental hospitals and the patients hospitalized in them. I'd always felt, and actually still do, that dressing the part is half the battle. When I took up tennis, I got a fabulous new tennis skirt; when I started to ride horses, nothing but proper English boots would do. In truth, I knew next to nothing about mental illness. I'd studied the classifications at school and I supposed I recognized that the schizophrenics might hear or see hallucinations or that the manic-depressives would have mood alterations, but I knew precious little about how such people might best be approached.

On Friday of that first week, I helped gather the twenty-five residents for the usual community meeting. I found an empty chair next to a very quiet middle-aged woman who had been admitted a few days earlier. So far, Mrs. Gideon rarely responded to any of the staff and usually sat by herself at meals, keeping her head down and eating little. Her complexion was pale and her short brown hair unwashed and combed straight back. Mrs. Gideon didn't care to get dressed in the mornings, and I knew that another psychiatric technician had the job of getting her out of her robe and into street clothes. This task took upward of an hour.

I decided that I would try to draw her out at the meeting. Soon after the group started, I spoke up. "Mrs. Gideon, is there something you'd like to share with the group today?"

She ignored me, staring down into her coffee cup.

"Mrs. Gideon, we're interested in getting to know you. Please, tell us something about yourself. Anything at all." I smiled encouragingly at her.

Again, Mrs. Gideon did not respond.

I decided to let her know how much I was interested in getting to know her, so I got up from my seat and kneeled down right in front of her in the circle.

"Mrs. Gideon"—I touched her arm gently—"we haven't had a chance to learn anything at all about you. Can you share something about what brings you here?" I thought I asked this in a kind, therapeutic voice.

Mrs. Gideon raised her eyes and stared down into my face. I probably looked like a pesky child to her. She lifted her cup, the coffee still steaming from the percolator always brewing in the dayroom, and flung its contents at me, soaking through the front of my crisp white dress. I jumped up and gasped, the hot coffee running down the uniform I was so proud of, burning my skin underneath.

While I ran off to the staff bathroom to clean up, I saw two male psychiatric technicians take Mrs. Gideon by each arm and walk her toward her room. She clung to the empty cup by its handle, but walked cooperatively along with them.

What was I to make of that hot coffee flung at me? Other staff members tried to console me in the nurses' bathroom as they helped sponge off my uniform, but I heard little. I was furious and humiliated at the same time.

"Don't you think she should pay for my uniform if it's ruined?" I later asked another technician as we were leaving the ward at the end of our shift and riding down together in the elevator. "I mean, don't you think there should be consequences?"

The other technician, an older black man who had worked at the hospital for many years, shrugged his shoulders and looked bored. "What are you going to do? Send her a bill?"

I stared at him and then down at my coffee-stained dress, so fresh and clean at the beginning of the day. "I don't know," I said. "I just don't think she should get away with this. It sends the wrong message."

"Try some baking soda when you wash it. It'll come out. And if it doesn't, so what? Wear it anyway. Who cares?" He went out the door and I watched him turn and walk toward the subway station on Rush.

The next morning, Saturday, you rang the bell to my parents' apartment promptly at ten. I was waiting, humming with excitement, the coffee cup incident tamped far down in my brain. I hurried down the stairs to meet you, so that you wouldn't come up and get involved in one of my mother's long-winded inquisitions: "What are you studying, Elliot? Tell me about your roommates. Are there many Jewish people at Brown?"

It had been six months since our aborted lovemaking at winter vacation. We hadn't seen each other since then, but I'd thought of you almost constantly and was full of regrets. You'd jumped right into college life at Brown, changing and growing, absorbing it all, obviously trying the drugs, sex, and rock and roll of the time. I had taken it more slowly at Ann Arbor, where there was less wildness to be had. I *was* interested and drawn to what little I saw of the developing protest movement there, and by the time I left Michigan, four years later, I was sitting in and demonstrating—but these activities took a little longer to find on the big midwestern campus.

When I opened the door to my apartment building that morning and stepped out into the already bright day, I saw that you were more beautiful than ever. You wore a too-short, raggedy T-shirt, and I could see the muscles of your abdomen and the beginning of the thin line of hair that began at your navel and descended into your well-washed jeans. That dark, thin line fascinated me. I was unable to look away, imagining your nakedness under the jeans, wanting to touch you. Does that shock you, Elliot? Or did you feel the heat coming from me? I forced myself to look up, then stared at your profile as you drove us toward the beach. You looked far more exotic now than you had in high school with your long, dark hair and straight nose and full lips. You looked Italian or Greek, perhaps, and more man than boy. You drove east toward Morse Avenue, the beach we'd gone to every summer of our lives.

The beaches of Lake Michigan would certainly be packed after the sweltering temperatures of the week before, but salvation would be found in the cool water. Thousands might be crowded together on the sand up and down Chicago's lakeshore, but any time we got too sunbaked, we could run into the refreshing lake, which was always deliciously cold, no matter the temperature of the air. The day promised both relief and pleasure. You and I would have hours and hours together. I desperately wanted you to see that I was no longer the naïve college girl of the previous December. You asked about Michigan. More cautious than you, I had still been meeting people and having my own adventures at Ann Arbor. I told you some of that.

We found a good parking spot, always a good omen. I'd brought cold drinks in a cooler, and we unpacked that and a blanket from the trunk of your father's latest Oldsmobile. I'd also methodically dripped a few drops of iodine into a bottle of baby oil and shaken it vigorously before putting it into my beach bag. Baby oil and iodine. the recipe we all used back then to toast our skin into flattering tans.

"How was your first week?" I asked as we walked from the grass toward the sand, each holding one handle of the cooler.

"Every bit as horrible as I expected. The smell of raw meat is so disgusting. You have no idea. I'm thinking of becoming a vegetarian.

But I don't want to talk about it. I have a present for you. A wonderful surprise for the day."

"I hate surprises," I said. "You know I hate surprises. Just tell me."

"Something special that I brought back from Providence. I'll show it to you on the beach. You'll like it, though, Judith, I promise. Now tell me about your job. About the hospital. It's great that you're doing something meaningful this summer."

I shrugged. "I don't know what I'm doing. It's as if we're supposed to know the right things to say, but they keep secret what those things might be. I hate how my voice sounds when I try to talk to the patients. Fake cheerful. I hate how I hover."

You smiled at me. "Just talk to them normally," you said. "Like you would to anyone. You'll be great, I know you will."

I wasn't ready to tell you about Mrs. Gideon and the coffee yet. Maybe later, when we were lying side by side in the sun. I did want to tell someone.

We threaded our way through the people, blankets already dotting the sand. Then we found a spot just the right distance from the breaking waves and put down the cooler. We faced one another, shaking out our own blanket, watching the turquoise plaid make a parachute as it drifted slowly to the ground. There was no breeze that morning. I took off my shorts and shirt and stood shyly in front of you wearing my red bikini that was on its first outing into the world. Your eyes widened as you looked at me.

"Wow," you said appreciatively. "This semester has certainly agreed with you."

Even I, the grand inquisitor and chief torturer when it came to my own body, had to agree that it was looking its best. I'd lost weight that spring and my skin was smooth and firm. I was bursting with energy as we stood together on that beach and I drank in the look in your eyes. Finally, my breasts had come into their own and their fullness now provided balance for my hips. I was healthy and young and unblemished. I would never have used the word beautiful to describe myself, but that June, I was ripe as only a nineteen-year-old girl can be and I reveled in this man's appreciation.

You reached into the cooler and took out two grape sodas. The soda, always our favorite, was bottled right in Chicago, in a factory that was visible from the expressway near our houses. We both said we missed it while we'd been away. The day was so familiar: the crowded beach, the feel of the thick Chicago summer air, the sweating, cold bottles we held in our hands while we looked out at the huge expanse of water.

"Remember what Leonard used to say when we were at camp?" you asked.

"Don't remind me of Leonard," I said. "That man was nuts."

"No, really, sometimes he said some good things. He said that young people like to look at the lake because its endlessness makes them feel less guilty. The bigness and the constant waves makes you put things in perspective." Then you reached into your jeans' pocket and pulled out a piece of paper. Carefully, you peeled a small square of cellophane off the paper and handed it to me.

"Put it on your tongue and let it dissolve."

"What'll happen?" I asked

"It's an experience I can't really describe. Lots of old crap in your brain disappears and you see things in a different light. When I tried it, that's what happened. I thought about my parents and how it was in my house growing up. But I saw them in a new way, as real people. I saw how they had suffered and I forgave them. Honestly, I wouldn't give you anything that wasn't good stuff." You put your other hand on my shoulder and smiled, then continued. "At school, when I first tried it, I thought about how I wanted to share this with you. At the lake. At our beach. We've shared so much. Last summer and before that. You saw me at my lowest back then and you were always there. I wanted to do this with you, Rocket. More than anyone I could think of."

I stared down at what you had put in my palm. It was invisible, not even a pill to swallow. Ingesting something invisible seemed harmless. We were both kneeling on the scratchy turquoise blanket, surrounded by people everywhere. I took the tab of cellophane and placed it on my tongue and we locked eyes while I waited for it to dissolve. You smiled at me, a sweet and loving smile. Did I want to show you that I trusted you? Sure, that was part of it. But more than that, I wanted you to see that I was not the same girl of the previous December. You needed to know that I now took risks, no longer someone who held back.

We sat together on the sand, your arm protectively around me, watching the water, and the people jumping over and then diving into the slow, languorous waves of Lake Michigan. I listened to fragments of conversation around us—mothers warning their children to be careful, couples who exchanged tender words, others arguing. At the beach, no one bothers to whisper or even to lower their voices; the conversations swirled around us in all directions. I reached into my bag for the sticky baby oil, tinged reddish brown with iodine. You took the bottle from my hands and unscrewed the top. Without saying a word, you began to rub the oil into my skin, first the shoulders and then into the shoulder blades, reaching under the tie of my bathing suit with your fingers. You rubbed the oil in tenderly and thoroughly. I'd never felt so close to you or so in love with you. My back felt as if it had no bones at all in it, and I arched underneath your fingers and allowed myself to sway gently with your hands as they rubbed oil into my skin. I inhaled deeply, smelling the baby oil and iodine. Even today, I can close my eyes and still smell that sweet, clean smell.

I felt your fingers as they went lower, slowly caressing the small of my back. But then, through my lovesick haze, I slowly became aware that something was strangely different. The sounds all around us, the conversations of families and couples, the gentle droning of the waves lapping up and down the beach, the music from the transistor radios—all were drowned out by an insistent buzzing. At first, this buzzing was merely annoying, something you wanted to swat away like a fly, then it became louder.

I looked up. Above me was a propeller airplane. Shockingly, it was dropping lower and lower to the ground, the roar overhead getting alarmingly close. As I cupped my hands over my eyes to shield them from the sun, I stared at the plane and then gasped. Things were being dropped from the plane. Red and purple and orange bits rained down on us. As they dropped, they looked like streaks of fire, maybe even bombs.

You remember the times we were in. Beneath all of our calm in the early sixties, the daily going about our business, there was also awareness of the war going on across the world in Southeast Asia. The boys of our neighborhood, the boys you and I knew, were all safely ensconced in school. But no one on a college campus anywhere in America could ignore Viet Nam. On the evening news, sanitized as it was, dreadful scenes of horror and bombing were aired. Buddhist monks were immolating themselves. I hadn't yet joined any organized peace movement, but I know it was there for me, under the surface, the sorrow and fear of the war was going on across the world and the knowledge that death was occurring that very moment, for both the unlucky soldiers and villagers.

And, in the drug-induced emotions that were beginning to attack the synapses of my brain, the plane overhead was dropping something terrible. Something frightening. Soon screams erupted on the beach. People began to run, seemingly all in one direction, away from the water, and as they ran, there was wild shrieking and shouting. I hunkered down onto the blanket and put my hands over my head. The people running across the beach tried to go around me, but some stepped very close to my head, running across our turquoise blanket. As I huddled closer and closer to the ground, flattening myself on the scratchy wool, all I could see were dozens of feet—large, small—all running through the sand.

Finally, the drone of the airplane got fainter. It began to climb from its perilously low altitude, and disappeared into the cloudless blue sky. I cautiously lifted my head and, as I looked around, saw that the beach was littered with the red, orange, pink, fiery things.

I was crying uncontrollably. "Elliot, stop, stop them." I was sobbing. "Make it stop!" My nose was running, the mascara running into my eyes, blinding and burning me.

"Judith, it's okay," you said. "You're okay, Rocket. Talk to me."

I could not speak; I could not stop shaking.

You sat next to me and held me tenderly, whispering comforting words. But I could not be comforted. We had been bombed. I shut my eyes and didn't want to look around, afraid that I'd see the bodies and body parts that were undoubtedly strewn on the beach.

How many were dead? I wondered. How had we been spared?

Eventually, as I realized that the beach was resuming its normal sounds, I stopped weeping. People around us were talking again, music was coming from transistor radios, and I could even hear the lapping of waves once more.

"What was it?" I asked, when I finally lifted my head and looked into your face.

"Look," you said gently. "They were dropping these on the beach." You held a pair of bright orange underpants up to my face. I touched them. Tiny underpants. They were made of paper, each with a thin strip of elastic around the legs and waist. The paper looked like the stuff doctor's masks were made of, sturdy paper, but disposable.

"You're very high," you said. "It was the acid making you see crazy stuff." Then you reached behind me and picked up two more pairs of underpants, one yellow, a bit bigger than the first, and one shocking pink, a larger size still.

"See," you said. "Underpants. Ladies underpants. They were

dropping them from an airplane as a promotion. Look over there." You pointed to our left. "They're still filming. I think it's a commercial for television."

"Why were people running? Why were they screaming?" I asked.

"They were running to get the paper pants. You know how people are when there's free stuff. They go nuts. The camera was filming them as they ran to get the paper underpants."

And there, where you pointed, were two men behind huge movie cameras. They aimed their cameras at people who were doing silly things with the underpants: pulling them on over their bathing suits, wriggling their hips, one man even tugging a pair down over his head like a hat.

I stared at the paper pants you held in your hands, touching them wondrously. "I thought we were being attacked. I thought the planes were dropping bombs."

"Yeah, I know. You were having a really bad trip. I'm so sorry. You're going to be all right, though. Drink some pop," you said. "Or some water. You need liquid."

"No," I said. "I feel like I'm going to throw up." I took the paper underpants away from Elliot, but as quickly as I'd begun to cry, I started to laugh. I couldn't stop laughing. I rolled around the sand and gasped and shrieked for what seemed like hours. My stomach hurt from laughing. I clutched the bare skin of my abdomen and my jaw felt as if it was going to slip out of joint. But I could not stop laughing.

At first you laughed along with me. "Yeah, I know," you said. "That was insane. Dropping paper underpants on the beach." You rolled on the sand, holding me and laughing with me. But then you, who must have had a better grip on reality than I did, looked around and realized that people were watching us, that the conversations around us had stopped. You stood up.

"Hey," you said, and reached down and pulled me to my feet. "Let's go for a walk. We should walk."

I look back on that day and I realize how far gone I must have been. Usually I was preoccupied with my appearance, especially so with you. Yet, that afternoon I allowed myself to be pulled from the sand, and as we walked, my nose was still running and snot was dripping into my mouth. Mascara smudged into my eyes. Sand was caked in my hair, on my back, underneath my bathing suit. And I didn't care about any of it. Instead, I felt euphorically happy that there were no dead bodies on the beach, relieved that no body parts were strewn around us, and that the airplane had not dropped bombs on us that sunny day in Chicago. Most of all, I felt joy that you and I were together again, holding hands, our feet skimming the water's edge.

We walked a very long time, traveling back and forth along the entire length of Morse Avenue Beach many times. I felt for you the purest love I had ever felt for another human being. And then, as I looked up and down the beach, I felt this same pure love for every single person sitting or lying or swimming before us. Everyone seemed joined together in the humanity of that beach, everyone trying to get a bit of fresh air, a bit of coolness from the lake that democratically ran north and south along Chicago's eastern perimeter—there for anyone and everyone in that large, teeming city who wanted it. I wished everyone on that beach would always be as happy as they were that day. I felt grateful to be alive, on that beach, in that city, safe and in love with this man I could only see as flawless.

That Saturday, we stayed at the beach until very late. The sun had set and we were among the last people left on the sand, but you didn't want to bring me home until you were sure I was no longer in a hallucinatory state. You did an admirable job of looking after me, especially since you had also put an LSD tab under your own tongue that morning. Somehow, I don't exactly know how these things work, your responsible self, the boy who had never really had a childhood, but had had to look after himself and then help his mentally ill mother, triumphed over the potent chemical we'd both swallowed.

The next day, on Sunday, you called to make sure I was okay. Other than a small headache and a bit of a sunburn on my back, I felt fine. I was no longer as euphoric as I'd been when we walked, but neither was I frightened or having flashbacks about the war coming to Chicago. I thanked you for calling, hoped your second week at work would go better than the first.

We saw each other only once more that summer, two days later on Tuesday when you took me to Burt's Delicatessen. The restaurant was on a corner near my parents' brick apartment building and we walked there in the twilight. You had your arm around me protectively again as we walked, treating me as if I was still having a bad trip. We ordered coffee and plates of the lush blueberry pie we both always ordered.

"You're really okay?" you asked. "Back to normal?" You peered into my eyes.

"Yes," I said. "I'm fine, honestly. No flashbacks, or whatever they're called."

Then you took a sip of black coffee and said, "Well I'm getting out of here. Tomorrow. This job at Pine's Meats, it's going to make me lose my mind."

"How can you leave?" I asked, puzzled.

"I heard from a friend back at Brown yesterday. He's a research assistant for the sociology department. He told me that another faculty member in the department needs an assistant. He got a big grant. I called the professor and it's something really interesting. He's researching voting patterns in college students. I can help with interviews and then collate data. If he likes my work this summer, the job will continue this fall. Even my dad can't argue with that, a job for the fall. And doing serious research, something that'll look good on my record."

"Wow, Elliot," I said. "You did it. You escaped loading frozen meat."

"Yeah. Thank God. No more frozen sides of beef," you agreed and shuddered. "Can you believe my luck?"

"That's so great," I said, and put my hand on yours. Rotten luck for me, was what I was thinking. Not fair. My summer in Chicago suddenly became less exciting. I knew I wasn't enough to keep you there.

The next day, wearing my white uniform and thick-soled white shoes, I returned to my job at the psychiatric hospital. My mother had soaked the uniform in baking soda on Saturday while you and I were at the beach, and the stains were almost, but not quite, erased. At first, Mrs. Gideon and I warily avoided each other in the community meeting, circling around one another, finding chairs on opposite sides of the circle. Eventually, however, we sat closer together. I stopped seeing the patients as people different than myself. In all the years I worked as a social worker, I never again told amusing dinner table stories about them.

5

Renunciation

Your fountain pen, its thick nub filled with blue ink, was a lifelong affectation I admired, yet admittedly found pretentious. And until email took the place of paper and pen, I waited for those letters written, savoring each. You wrote infrequently, only a few times a year, but the letters were witty and rambling, each one a thick seven or eight pages that I read and reread. Surprisingly, you also continued to remember my Valentine's Day–Birthday. I received a present from you every year. You never forgot. They arrived wherever I was living, on or just before February fourteenth. The gifts were never throwaways, didn't seem to have been bought by a wife or a secretary. They were thoughtful gifts and were, to me, evidence of how thoroughly you knew me and knew what would give me pleasure. Sometimes the parcel contained a book, perhaps a volume of that year's Nobel prize winner: poetry by Neruda in 1971, a first edition of an early I.B. Singer novel in 1978. Because you knew that I loved monkeys of all sorts, I received several pieces of jewelry with monkey designs, also small monkeys carved in soapstone or wood. Once you sent me a page of the script from a movie you knew I liked, and had had the lead actor sign it. You moved in circles where that sort of thing was possible. I did not and I had it framed.

I have done a great deal of winnowing down my possessions, but I still keep all of your letters, a half century of them, as well as most of the gifts, even the little monkeys. The letters are stuffed rather inelegantly into several manila folders. Near the letters, there is a wine-colored leather box, about four by six inches, lined in satin and embossed with gold leaf on its top. In that box, I have three pictures. One is a faded newspaper photo. You are sixteen and wear a V-necked sweater and preppy button-down collared shirt. Although the picture was shot in black and white, I still remember that sweater as it was, deep rust colored and very soft. The clipping announces your election as president of the Midwest Region of the American Zionist Youth. You are described as the youngest son of Max and Helen Pine. Reading her name still gives me a pang. The memory of a suicide always does that; it isn't like reading of someone who died a more timely death. The article lists your accomplishments, a list particularly impressive in one so young. I treasure this picture, the shy and unassuming smile, the serious, dark eyes. How the camera loved you. That photograph is how I always picture you. In the second photo, we are side by side on prom night, high school is nearly over, and we are eighteen. It is almost a year since your mother has been gone, and there is a nascent smile on your face. Your arm is around my waist (so tiny back then). You are wearing a white-jacketed tuxedo, ill-fitting, too big in the shoulders for your narrow frame. It was rented from the neighborhood wedding shop on Lincoln Avenue. The rush before prom made the clerks a bit sloppy. I am a head shorter than you and my gown is lovely—white bodice, with a long black skirt. The matching black and white of your tuxedo and my dress is striking. We are in front of the drawn living room drapes at my parents' apartment. How proud I was that night. I felt like a queen: off to prom with the boy of my dreams, one of the most popular boys in our class, and surely the most handsome. Who could have imagined it? Certainly not me.

The last picture I keep in that wine-colored box shows us in front of a grimy building far uptown in Manhattan. This time our arms are looped around one another's shoulders, buddy style. The building is in Washington Heights, where you'd recently moved with your young wife, Laurie. We no longer match as nicely as we had in that prom picture. Once again we have become unavailable to one another. A passerby, maybe a Columbia student, likely took the picture on that sunny July day.

We were twenty-six. I'd just returned from a wild ride of a journey, going nearly around the world with Seth, my then boyfriend, later husband. You'd recently graduated from Harvard Law and were holed up in a box of an apartment studying for the New York State Bar. We were young, still being formed, but even so, it surprised me when I saw how we had changed from the last time we'd seen one another. Perhaps this is why I needed to record the day, flagging down some stranger to snap our picture with the camera I often wore looped around my neck in those days. By the time that picture was taken on a blistering hot summer in New York, we had changed roles. I was now a world traveler, the collector of adventures, while you spent your days tethered to your desk studying dutifully.

You can see a lot in that photograph. You are wearing rumpled khakis and need a haircut, and there are bags under your eyes. For once in your life, you look terrible—pale, unsmiling, and haggard. I, on the other hand, am radiant. I wear a long hippie skirt made from the printed Indian fabric we favored back then in clothing and even bedspreads. Over the skirt, I have on an embroidered Indian blouse of the thinnest, sheerest white cotton. The sleeves are rolled up above my elbows and the top buttons opened to reveal the swell of breast of a tanned and healthy woman in her mid-twenties. My dark hair is long and thick then, gathered back to reveal large silver earrings. What is going on here? Why do you look so miserable, while I appear so joyously full of life?

The answer is that after you'd graduated from Brown, with honors, and been awarded a Fulbright to study in England, you'd returned to your college girlfriend, who'd waited for you. Only one

year of comparative freedom before you stepped back on the tread-
mill of gathering accomplishments. You married Laurie Wasserman
just before you started your first year of Harvard Law. Laurie was
a serious girl, Jewish of course (you had not yet begun your fasci-
nation with sexy blond shiksas). You told me you met in a seminar
on French playwrights. You and I read *Cyrano de Bergerac* together
when we were in high school—we'd both loved it. I'd swooned when
you'd quoted, a bit loosely, a line from *Cyrano*: "And what is a kiss?
A rosy dot on the 'i' of loving." I wonder if you recited those words
to Laurie? I hope not. That was *my* quote, but it's a good one and I'd
understand the temptation to use it again.

 With several acceptances in hand, you added another jewel to
your crown and decided on Harvard Law. Ever a planner, you told me
later that you'd researched where clerks to Supreme Court justices
attended law school. The vast majority went to Harvard, and that
informed your decision. I'd received an invitation to your wedding,
but my boyfriend Seth and I were in Los Angeles, working and saving
for our travels and I declined, sending a present picked from your
and Laurie's lengthy wedding registry. The wedding sounded as if it
had been a splashy affair at the Plaza.

 Even though Laurie came from wealth, for the three years you
studied law, Laurie used her degree in museum studies and worked
hard to support you. She was employed in the education department
of the Boston Museum of Science. You found a flat in Cambridge, and
she put in long hours at the museum, riding the T in both directions.
As soon as you graduated from Harvard Law, you moved back to
New York, to Washington Heights. Laurie again rode packed trains,
this time to her job at the Museum of Natural History on the Upper
West Side. She was a confirmed New Yorker and never liked Boston.
The whole time you were at Harvard, she'd lobbied mightily for eventual relocation to New York where she could be close to her family
and Zabars and all those other things Manhattanites seem to think

they cannot live without. That miserably hot summer, recorded in the photograph kept in that wine-colored leather box, you were spending ten hours a day preparing for the bar and, supposedly, looking for a job in the city. As soon as you opened the door, I saw, even smelled, your unhappiness. The rumpled clothes, the tired eyes, a dingy shirt that had an unwashed odor to it, this was not the Elliot I was used to.

Now I was passing through New York with Seth. I phoned you and you suggested I come the very next day, a Tuesday afternoon, that fact important as I later discovered. In the stifling heat, I took the subway uptown, then rode the elevator to your twelfth-floor flat. There wasn't much to see in the neat, sparsely furnished apartment; Laurie was evidently an immaculate housekeeper. You certainly had never been known for your neatness. I noticed a large wedding photo in a silver frame on the coffee table. You and Laurie were at the bottom of a curved stairway, and rising grandly above, one per step, were eight bridesmaids, each dressed identically in a long peach-colored dress. My eye went to the only other sign of Laurie in the place, a peach cardigan of almost the same color as the bridesmaids' dresses, folded carefully over the sofa arm. Under the window, on the desk where you worked, several large legal volumes were open. It was the only messy corner of the apartment.

I'd made my way west several years earlier, going to LA for a social work internship. There I met Seth. Although he was a small, compact man, he had the biggest personality in any room. Dazzlingly bright, he wanted to be a doctor. He took his medical school entrance exams and scored high enough to assure a place at a good medical school, but decided that what he really wanted was to see the world. He got a deferment from medical school. Sure, the University of Southern California obligingly said, after seeing his fine test scores, he could take some time off. Travel was a good thing. They'd admit him later. To my astonishment, he asked me to join him.

Apparently, all one had to do was ask. This was an important lesson I learned from Seth. Sometimes all you have to do is ask. Back then, if it had been me, I would have been so grateful for that letter of admission, I would never have pressed my luck to ask for a deferment. I'd have taken what was offered and been happy with it. Now I'm different. I learned a few things from Seth—as well as from life. Now I ask for special treatment all the time. I humiliate my children in restaurants when I pester the waiters for substitutions even though the menu clearly says, "No Substitutions." I ask landlords for special favors: new carpets, fresh paint, more towel racks. And, when traveling, I never *ever* settle for the first hotel room I am shown.

You took me on a tour of the apartment near Columbia, a very brief tour, showing me the small narrow place you shared with Laurie. I looked out the kitchen window at the view: sooty bricks of the building next door. On the counter, there was a plate with a sandwich on it. A small bag of potato chips and a bunch of grapes were placed neatly with the sandwich, a folded napkin beside the plate. The kitchen was positively scrubbed. There wasn't even a glass drying next to the sink. I eyed the thick sandwich, made on healthy whole wheat bread.

"Laurie fixes me lunch every morning before she leaves for work," you explained when you saw me staring at the plate, then shrugged. You had the unshaved, glassy-eyed look of someone who spent too much time staring at books. Nowadays people look like that when they've been staring at a computer screen for too long. "She knows I sometimes forget to eat," you said.

"She doesn't leave it in a Spider-Man lunchbox?" I asked, then realized how I sounded. "Actually," I added, "it looks delicious. It's nice that she does that for you, leaves you lunch."

You shrugged again. "Take it if you like. I'm not hungry. I'm way too wound up. I'll make us coffee. Then you tell me about India. And everywhere else you've been around the world."

"No, don't bother," I said.

"It's no bother. I make two pots a day and drink it all myself. Look at this," you said and held your hands out in front of me, palms down. They had a slight, but perceptible tremor. "I'm a caffeinated wreck. Do you have any idea what the failure rate is for first-time takers of the bar in New York? Thank God, it'll soon be over." You closed your eyes and exhaled deeply. "Okay, enough. Tell me about your travels. Please get me out of my own head and this bar exam obsession. And sit down." You motioned to the couch, removing Laurie's sweater and putting it on the desk, still carefully folded. "Tell me where you went. Every single place."

I sat and ticked off each country with one finger of my right hand. "Let's see. Fiji. Tahiti. New Zealand. Australia. Indonesia." Then I went to the left hand and took a breath. "Singapore. Malaysia. Then Thailand. Burma and India. By the way, when we got to India, I picked up the birthday present you sent. I can't believe you remembered."

"The gift made it?" you asked.

"Yeah. It was waiting at American Express," I answered. "I take that leather journal everywhere with me. It's beautiful."

"I can't believe you actually got it. I just took a guess and sent it to Calcutta, hoping you'd catch up to it. Then, after India?"

"Turkey. We got robbed in Istanbul. Somebody sliced the pockets off the sides of our backpacks."

"What?" you asked incredulously.

"Yeah. Gross. Didn't even notice it until we slid the packs off our shoulders," I said.

"You didn't get hurt?"

I shook my head. "They must have used a machete, a nice, clean cut. Amazing, right? But funny."

"Christ," you said. "I think Laurie would have gone nuts."

"Then," I went on, "we ended in Europe. The Greek islands, up through the Balkans, then to Western Europe. We went as far north as Wales and flew home from London. We landed in New York only a few days ago."

"All that," you said, and shook your head. "It is amazing. I want to go to those places. I'd love to see Asia."

"You will. And you had your Fulbright to England. You traveled afterward, right? It's not as if you've never been anywhere."

"Only a little in England. But Laurie was waiting. The wedding"— you grimaced and made a small wave toward the picture on the coffee table—"and then law school right after. Anyway, I mostly studied when I was over there. What you did was completely different. Two years. Even more, wasn't it? No agenda, no itinerary." You stared at me, as if seeing me for the first time, and said, "Wow, Judith, you look great. Fantastic." You went to the kitchen and poured the coffee. "Tell me about everything. And Scott. What's he like? Where is he today? He didn't want to meet me?"

"Seth," I corrected. "Not Scott. He's with his cousin, where we're staying. It's unreal being back in the States, Elliot. Everything moves so fast. So much noise. We both feel shell-shocked."

"What was your favorite place?" you asked.

"I loved the South Pacific the most. We actually lived in a grass shack in Fiji. Down the Rewa River. I'd look around and wonder at being in such an exotic place. To wake up in a jungle. I could never have imagined it."

"The South Pacific." You stared at me again with that look of discovering me.

"There's this mosquito repellant," I told you. "They used it everywhere. A green coil. Lion Brand Coils, they're called. You light one end and it burns slowly through the night until in the morning there's nothing left but a snake-shaped ash. They work well, mosquitoes hate them. I can still see that ember burning at the end—like a cigarette left burning in an ashtray. They probably fried my brain—those Lion Brand things. God knows what's in them. I've never seen them sold here. But there was always that ember when I'd wake up during the night."

You said, "Tell me about somewhere else. I want to hear about another place." I felt like Scheherazade.

"Malaysia," I answered immediately. "The island of Penang. The beaches had the softest sand. So different from our beaches near Lake Michigan. Tea grows on terraces in the hills. And monkeys everywhere."

"Monkeys?"

I nodded. "Once we were hiking through a forest of tea and we saw a beautiful woman sleeping on top of a wooden plank. There was an umbrella rigged up beside her to shield her from the sun. We didn't wake her, just walked by. Later, I asked someone why a young girl would be sleeping outside like that, in the daytime, on a bare plank. They told me that at night, someone has to stay outside to guard the tea. To scare away the monkeys. Otherwise the monkeys might destroy the crop. She must have fallen asleep in the morning, exhausted after lying out there, awake all night warding off monkeys from the tea." I laughed. "I'm talking too much, Elliot. Sorry. You shouldn't have started me."

You still stared at me. "No," you said. "I want to hear. I'm living vicariously, I want to know everything." You cocked your head and asked, "Like what did you eat? You were always such a fussy eater."

"I was?" I was amazed that you knew that fact about me. I thought only my mother and father knew how picky an eater I was. When we'd been on dates together, I used to pretend that I liked everything. "Curries," I answered. "I've become an aficionada of curries. They're different everywhere. Red. Green. Yellow. One time, at a roadside restaurant in Penang, I pointed to something on the menu. It turned out to be the very hottest curry they had, but I didn't know. The owner shook his head, tried to warn me off it, but I stuck with my order. When I ate it, my eyes streamed with tears and I gasped, sweat poured from my forehead. Seth was astonished. All the local people in the restaurant were staring and laughing, but I finished it.

Spooned up every bit. It was painful, yet the most delicious thing I've ever tasted."

"Travel agreed with you," you said. "I can see it. You look as if you were made for it. And you were gone for so long. Over two years. I can't even get Laurie to agree to go to Mexico for two weeks after I take the bar. She wants to go out to the Hamptons with her family. As usual."

"I liked everything about traveling," I agreed. "Maybe not the smelly toilets, but everything else. The accomplishment of figuring it out. Where to sleep. What to eat. Each place had its secrets. Meeting other travelers and looking at maps by candlelight. Following with your finger to see where someone has been and where they're going next. Then, just like that, changing your plans, and deciding to go there with them. Seth's really spontaneous. I felt such satisfaction when we navigated through the challenges."

"Like what?" you asked, your eyes never leaving my face. "Tell me what kind of challenges?"

I loved the attention you were lavishing on me. Your apartment was so quiet. I was surprised that any place in the middle of the city could be so still. The windows were shut tight against the heat and all I could hear was the soft hum of the air conditioner unit. I was glad you were asking me these questions, that you seemed truly interested and that Seth wasn't with me. Seth, the master storyteller. Even if I started telling a story, Seth would take it over. He was admittedly wonderful at it. People in the room would stop their own conversations and listen. But now, it was just me, alone with you in that quiet, spotless apartment.

"Once, when we were in Indonesia," I told you, "the military junta confiscated all the airplanes. A coup was threatened. We'd come from northern Australia, Darwin, to the island of Timor and we were stuck. No way to fly from there and get to Singapore, where we were headed. I talked to some locals and I found there was a ferry to the next island. Flores. So we hopped, ferry by ferry, through the islands, each one more beautiful, more lush than the one before it. The ferries were just floating barges. Flat, no seats. So we had to stand the whole way, balancing our backpacks, falling against people and their animals and their baskets of fruit. When we finally got to Jakarta, we were so proud of ourselves—like we were astronauts landing on the moon. People said we wouldn't make it, that we'd have to turn back to Australia."

"You made it, though," you said, then called me by our old nickname. "You got yourself where you needed to go, Rocky." As you studied me, I could almost hear you asking yourself if you'd made a mistake and underestimated me. I became embarrassed and picked up my coffee cup.

"I haven't been called that in a long time," I said, and shrugged. "I guess I'm persistent." *Like with you*, I thought. *Never giving up on you*. Flustered, I kept talking. "I kept looking for boats and eventually we got there. To Bali. Once I start out on a path, I don't like turning back. But it was Seth who dreamed up the trip. I never imagined that I'd actually get to those places. You know how much I wanted to travel around the world. I'd never been anywhere. You did have that time in England. You know what I mean."

"Yeah, England," you said dismissively. "But it wasn't monkeys and hopping ferries to Bali or fighting for food or whatever. Nothing like what you did. The most exciting thing that happened to me was when I got picked up by some actors from the Royal Shakespeare Company. I was hitchhiking near Bristol."

"You love Shakespeare," I said.

"I know. This actor was driving an ancient Morris Minor with his girlfriend. They stopped for me."

"What were they like?"

"They were really funny," Elliot answered, almost grimly. "It was the best part of the trip. That whole afternoon I was doubled up with laughter in the back seat. They did voices, characters. He and his girlfriend tried to get me to go with them, to keep traveling with them. They said they were going to kidnap me. But I went back to Cambridge." You shrugged. "Like the good boy that I am."

"Then you came home and married Laurie," I said. "After England. I got your wedding announcement and I was surprised."

"Why surprised?"

"I didn't expect you'd marry young," I answered. "I imagined you'd be the fifty-year-old bachelor. Lots and lots of girls first."

"Ah, Rocket," you said. "Who knows anything? All I know are torts and constitutional law."

"That's a lot," I said.

You refilled our coffee mugs, rubbing your neck. I'd never seen you so exhausted, so beaten down and old looking. Your posture had changed and your shoulders slumped forward. Here I was, exhilarated from travel to exotic places, having nearly circled the globe. In all those years before, when we were in high school, I was the one who'd watched enviously while you were having experiences: flying around the country as a teenager, speaking to crowds in hotel ballrooms, practically running a summer camp. I was the audience, on the periphery of your accomplishments, nervously dipping my toe into the water, while you dove in confidently. At Michigan, I felt so backward and provincial. You were the sophisticated one on the East Coast. Now it was different. You were listening and admiring. Oh, I must admit, I savored the moment.

Of course, I knew much of what happened was because of Seth. Life ratcheted up once he entered my world. After Michigan, I'd gone to Los Angeles for that internship in social work. A friend from school, a boy who'd transferred to UCLA, suggested that I phone Seth. (Much later, after Seth and I were married, I found a letter about me from this same boy. I wasn't snooping, it was tucked into a book on our shelf. He'd written Seth that if he wanted to meet a girl with "a big rack," he should check me out. A big rack! I was devastated when I read that letter. I thought he'd . . . oh hell, never mind; who needs to hear my pious outrage? It was fraternity boy talk and we were all of twenty-two. What did I expect?

But then Seth makes such an easy target. I've done very little honest talk about him, neither to myself or others in my life. I've drawn him in the harshest of lights—my evil first husband. He fathered my twins, Miriam and Evan, and, of course, that could be enough to redeem him right there. However, he left me for another woman, a much younger woman, and he'd been a womanizer for all of our relationship. That makes him the villain, right? That's what I always claimed. Well, the truth is not that simple. I can't forgive or forget the infidelity. Yet, my deepest self knows it wasn't love that bound me to Seth. It was the tantalizing life raft he gave me. I leaped when he offered a chance to travel—the dream I'd always had, but not yet envisioned how to make happen. In those days, it seemed impossible for a girl alone to have the kind of adventures Seth promised. This offer of travel, backpack strapped on, crammed with maps, but no itinerary, was tantalizing beyond belief. Perhaps Seth sensed that I didn't love him absolutely and without qualifications. He probably realized that I had used him as a way into a bigger world. Maybe that even had something to do with those other girls, maybe he wanted to feel love greater than what I gave. He looked confident, Seth did. But underneath, he so desperately needed the approval of women. You could see it in the way he performed for women—how much he needed conquests. Oh, Elliot, I am getting old. Feeling sorry for that bastard of a first husband of mine. Shame on me.

Before Seth, I knew what waited for me. If I returned to Chicago after college, life would be no different than it had been before I'd left. As much as I hate giving Seth credit for anything, I know I'd not be the person I am today if our paths hadn't crossed. The grand around-the-world journey, his impetuousness, his creative spark—it changed my life. It is also true that there was terrible yawning pain, pain that lasted nearly the entire time we were together. Sometimes it was like being on the inside of a washing machine; the adventure full of chaos and frenzy. I got bruised and eventually I wanted the emotional highs to stop, because devastating lows always followed. Yet, with the distance of years, I remember less of the hurt from all that buffeting and see more clearly how the experiences with Seth gave me resilience and even wisdom.

"What will you and Seth do now?" you asked that afternoon in New York. "Another National Geographic–worthy journey?" You pursed your lips in a small smile.

Oh, I definitely liked this. You were jealous, hanging on to my every word. "Seth is planning to start medical school now. Maybe, when he's finished, we'll travel more. And," I added casually, "we're thinking of getting married." I pulled a wisp of hair back behind my ear. "Do you recommend it?"

You looked shocked. "Marriage? Sure, yeah. If that's what you want. But your stories, those postcards you sent from everywhere. You have no idea how much I looked forward to seeing where you went next. Envied your experiences. Why marriage? Why stop the adventure?"

"Oh, we'll travel again," I replied airily. "Seth never wants to stop that. We'll go back overseas and help people. Poor people. Maybe"—I hesitated again for dramatic effect—"maybe even have a kid. We met lots of people traveling with children. Seth loves kids. He's great with them. Do you and Laurie think about children?"

You laughed a short bark of a laugh. It wasn't a kind sound. "Laurie does. She thinks about babies nonstop. She's on a real campaign about it."

"So, what's the problem?" I asked.

"Judith, what isn't a problem? Every damn thing with us is a problem."

I put down my coffee cup. "What's wrong, Elliot? Tell me."

You sighed and gestured again toward the photograph on the low table. "Even at the wedding, I had concerns. Laurie's a sweet, giving person. She tries so hard. She wants us to be happy more than anything. But I see it all laid out in front of me. I'll get a job with some firm here in the city. Her father knows everyone. We'll stay here a while. Until we have our second kid. Then we'll move to the suburbs—to Connecticut or some town near her family in New Jersey. I'll have an ungodly commute into the city and Laurie will stay home with the kids."

"What's so bad with that scenario?" I asked.

"I hear you talk, and it makes me think about the other things I always wanted," you said. "Like making a difference somewhere. Maybe travel."

"So do it," I said.

You sighed. "Laurie hates traveling. We actually did go to Jamaica. On our honeymoon, to an all-inclusive resort. They practically lock people in, so you never even see a Jamaican—except the people working at the resort. And she refused to leave the place, said it scared her and she was afraid of getting sick. I'd like to go back again, to really see it. You traveled the right way."

"What about politics? You always wanted to go into politics and change the world," I said.

"I still think about it. Maybe someday. But not yet. Now I just want to stop for a while," you said. "I have this fear of getting stuck in the wrong life."

"What do you want instead?"

"I'm not sure. Write, maybe. I want a bigger life than Laurie sees us having." You looked at the pile on your desk and grimaced. Then you lowered your voice. "Listen, don't mention this to anyone, but I did apply for a Supreme Court clerkship. One of my professors at Harvard recommended me. I'll hear soon. But I doubt it'll happen. It's a crazy pipe dream."

"The Supreme Court. Whoa. You're kidding! That's certainly big."

"It's such a long shot, I didn't even mention it to Laurie. She's so happy to be back in New York, she won't want to leave, not even for Washington." You paused. "Judith, I made a mistake marrying so young. We don't want any of the same things. Whatever the next step is, I can't see it being with Laurie."

"Then why did you do it?" I asked. I had never seen you so unhappy with where you were in life. "Why did you get married?"

"For one thing, I've realized how susceptible I am to parental pressure. You know me—keep the grown-ups happy. Wasn't I always doing that? I acted like I was forty when I was sixteen. Remember the suit and the briefcase?" You finally smiled a little.

"You did impress the grown-ups," I said. "You impressed everybody."

"Every weekend, we go to Laurie's parents' summer place in Bridgehampton. It's beautiful there. An estate. I used to think I wanted that kind of life. Big, happy family. Her older sisters always come out as well. Three of them. All married, with kids. The longer Laurie and I were together, the more they looked at me expectantly. Waiting for the announcement. The hints they dropped. Honestly, it was intense. When I told them I was going to England, it was clear I was supposed to give her a ring before I left. Her father even asked if I needed money for a ring. I actually like the guy. He's in extermination. He keeps mentioning how perfect it would be to have an in-house lawyer."

"Extermination? Like the mafia?" I asked.

"No, no, of course not." You laughed. "Bugs. They kill bugs. Cockroaches. Rodents, too."

I shuddered. I absolutely hate cockroaches, though I saw my share of them in Asia.

"Hugely successful. No shortage of bugs in New York City. He's got all the big contracts. His three sons-in-law all work for the company.

They talk as if I've decided to join them already. Pretty soon they'll start asking when we're going to start a family."

"Oh, Elliot," I said and of course I felt sorry for you. I leaned over to put my hand on yours.

Instead, you pulled me from the couch and we ended up embracing. It felt as it always had. I inhaled your smell, which, if the truth be known, was a bit stale that day: the wrinkled shirt and lack of fresh air in the apartment. Yet, even stale, it was still your familiar smell. I don't think Seth's embraces ever did this to me, made me feel so woozy and fluttery. Damn, from the beginning I'd kept asking myself if what I felt for Seth was love, and here was my answer. This was love. Once again, you and I were kissing. Your tongue explored mine, and I felt your hands rising up my back, under the flimsy Indian shirt. Your touch on my clammy skin felt electric. Yet, after a minute or two, I stopped and pushed you away.

It was agony. I was having trouble breathing. I wanted you so much. I knew I was wet with desire and that I mustn't let you touch me between my legs. I faced you and stared into your eyes. "What's going on here?" I asked. "Tell me."

It could have turned out differently that afternoon. If you'd said the right words. My imagination was running wild, and seeing you in this sad, sterile apartment, I wanted to believe that you felt what I felt. You might have said, Judith, we should be together, living the life we're supposed to be living. I should never have let you go."

But, alas, you did not give such an answer, did not tell me that you regretted letting me go. You made no such declarations. If you had, then before rushing downtown for my backpack and sleeping bag, I'd have allowed what the blood pulsing through my chest, head, and the more sexual areas of my body was urging me to do. On the contrary, you didn't speak at all, but began to kiss me again, holding the back of my head and weaving your fingers lightly through my hair in the way you knew I adored. You gathered my long skirt in your other hand

and began to explore beneath it. And I moved away, smoothing the wrinkles from my cool Indian hippie skirt. I knew that nothing was different and that I would regret staying that afternoon. It wasn't me you wanted, it was diversion. Pushing away from you took every bit of strength I had. Did you know that?

I walked past the coffee table, and looked again at that wedding picture with the bridesmaids draped down the stairway of the Plaza. Where would we be today if instead of you proposing to your college sweetheart, you'd married me? Would we have been happy together? Laurie could not possibly understand you as I did. The bond you and I had could not be replicated. How would Laurie know what it was like sitting at the dinner table with your mother, her specific sadness as she realized she was forgetting things, yet the graciousness that never slipped from her? Laurie had never even met dear Helen Pine. How could Laurie know the sorrow in you that year after your mother died? The hours we lay together on your narrow bed and spoke about the important things, like why people chose to live or die. How we both wanted our lives to be different from our parents' lives. Had she seen the way the muscles around your eyes twitch when you try to keep the tears from falling? Or the way you looked as a little boy, when the raw wound of your mother's illness was exposed by our horrid fifth-grade teacher before you ran from the classroom? No one besides me had that with you.

I looked out that window of the apartment you shared with Laurie, and I also considered that for three years I'd been joined to another man. We were talking about marriage, even having a baby together. Seth loved babies. I had no doubt that he'd make a stupendous father. He was happily looking forward to having a child, perhaps even more than I was. Was that nothing? Seth was a firecracker, popping and exploding when you least expected it. Hadn't he taken me to the exotic places I'd dreamed of going? But, as I stared out the window, I doubted whether I'd ever feel for Seth what I felt for you.

How sad that made me. Despite Seth's joyfulness, I never felt at home with him. His happy, unworried face still felt like a stranger's face to me. He was like the spicy curries I'd tried in Asia. The taste of those curries was jarring and exciting and I was proud that I'd been brave enough to try them, but they were not what I wanted for a lifetime. I looked over at you, your serious face, your intelligent eyes watching me. Your long, lithe sensuality. You were what I always wanted. But I was not at all sure you wanted me, Elliot.

"It's no good, Laurie and me," you said. "Talking about it today has made it more clear. I always get clarity when I talk to you, Judith."

"Clarity?" I asked.

"I was too young. Laurie was too young. The marriage was a mistake. We need to face our mistake and end it before more damage is done. Before we have kids. I see you and what you've been doing, and I know my marriage isn't working. You are so full of life, you shine with it. I want to feel that kind of energy in my life."

I wasn't nearly as brave as you thought. I'd just trailed along with Seth. The backpacks, the mummy sleeping bags that zipped together, the maps of Asia that had been folded and refolded so many times that the creases were beginning to split open—all had been initiated by Seth. I was the sidekick. Sure I'd always dreamed of travel, but if I was honest, I would have admitted that I'd have been more than satisfied to be sharing this apartment in grimy Washington Heights with you, Elliot. I looked more wise than I felt. It was clearly a sorry mismatch—Laurie was a nice, but ordinary girl and I wanted to scream, "Me! You should have chosen me, Elliot!" Yet you gave me no such encouragement.

During that summer you studied for the bar, you had one foot out the door of your marriage. Yet you stopped short of any declaration to me. And I was smart enough to realize that if I had indeed married you, I might now be your keeper. You'd be chafing and pushing against your confinement with me. If I'd been the one you had chosen, you might well be telling someone else what a mistake you'd made—how the marriage you were in was all wrong. I turned to you, and saw that you were pensively twisting your wedding ring around your finger.

"Give it time, Elliot," I said. "Talk to her."

"I've missed you, Judith," you said and then came to the window where I stood. "Don't stay away so long. Let's always be there for each other. Let's be in each other's lives even when we're old and in a nursing home. Promise me."

I leaned up and kissed you. I put all of my love into that kiss, and when I finally took a breath, I said firmly, "I will always be there, even when we're old. I promise. But right now, I'm going to go. It's late. I told Seth I'd be back for dinner. And Laurie will be home soon, won't she?"

"No, she works late on Tuesdays. I thought I told you when you phoned. Until eight. She has her staff meeting today." You looked over at me hopefully. "So, you don't have to leave. You could stay. She won't be home for hours. We have so much more to catch up on, Judith."

"No, you didn't tell me she worked late."

You were miserable and needed me. What a drug that need of yours has always been. But I replayed in my mind what you'd just said: "She works late on Tuesdays. She won't be home for hours." You'd invited me to your apartment not on any day, but on a Tuesday, when your wife worked late. As that thought wormed its way into my consciousness, I said to myself, *Oh, God. He's planned this.* The part of my brain that had been screaming, *Sex! Now! I want sex with this man right now, on the carpet!* was replaced by the thought that you'd calculated this afternoon tryst. You'd been so sure that we'd end up in bed together, even after all these years, that you made sure I visited on a Tuesday. Hubris. I pushed away from you stiffly and answered, "I really have to get back. Seth's waiting for me."

We rode down in the elevator in silence. I didn't second-guess my decision; for once I felt strong and smart. Even though I sensed you watching me, I didn't turn to you, just stared at the descending numbers of the floors. It was outside your building, as we stood saying goodbye, that I must have stopped someone and handed over my camera to take the picture that I still keep in the wine-colored box. There it is—the sun beginning to set and New York lit up radiantly from behind. Some felt that Manhattan was dirty back then, full of cigarette butts and candy wrappers and worse, but I had come from Calcutta. New York looked pristine, even beautiful. I kissed you, more lightly this time, on the lips, and gave you a little smile

"Write me," I said, my hand on your shoulder. "Tell me how you did on the bar. I know you'll pass. You'll do more than pass. You'll probably clerk for the Supreme Court."

"Your eyes. They're so bright. I'd forgotten." You gave another pursed smile, a look of regret.

The afternoon had cooled and the air was so fresh, I could not think of going down into the subway and pushing and being pushed against sweaty bodies heading home after work. Instead, without looking back, for I knew you still stood there watching, I sashayed toward downtown, walking the nearly fifty blocks to where Seth and I were staying. I had a long stride back then and covered the distance in no time. I ran up the three flights to Seth's cousin's apartment. I could hear the party that was already in progress behind the closed door. Wherever Seth was, in Los Angeles, Singapore, Melbourne, a party would soon materialize. Sometimes the parties were unwanted, but that afternoon, I was pleased to hear the merriment inside.

I put on my best smile when walking through that door. I stood for a moment and watched the people who'd crowded into the apartment: young people sitting on big cushions on the floor, wrapped in embraces, swaying to the music. The stereo was very loud and a haze of marijuana was mixed with the cigarette smoke. Six or seven partiers were dancing in a circle, hands clasped, coming together, and then moving back out again, laughing and carefully avoiding the people sprawled on the floor. Like a folk dance—as if there was a maypole in the center of the living room—they moved together and then apart. A Moody Blues record was playing, and it sounded, indeed, like an English country dance. "Tuesday Afternoon," the song is called, and I shook my head and laughed because that was the name of the song and it *was* a Tuesday afternoon. It's such a lovely song, I can sing it even now.

Seth sat at the far end of the room, swaying to the music, knees folded akimbo, smiling up at the circle of dancers. When he saw me in the doorway, he quickly stood and came to me, covering my eyes and cheeks and neck lightly with kisses, then kissing me deeply on the mouth.

"Glad you're back," he said. "Have fun?"

My lips, I realized, were bruised from kissing you earlier in the afternoon. Seth's kisses were on top of your kisses, and this secret made me feel joyously alive.

6

Deceit

You, Elliot, went on to do great things—ever more impressive things. Across the country in California, I received updates about you. You could never be accused of bragging. Your humility was real and charming. From friends I learned of your accomplishments. When you were chosen chair of the *Harvard Law Review*, you didn't even mention it. And the news of your appointment as a clerk to the Supreme Court—working for one of our country's most widely respected judges—came from my father. He read about it in the *Northside Jewish Bulletin*. Even my mother was impressed, told me everyone at temple was talking about it and what a shame it was that Helen Pine had not lived to see her son so honored. Later, in another phone call, my mother asked if I'd heard the news about Elliot Pine and his young wife. Someone in the neighborhood had told her they'd gotten a divorce.

"After only three years," my mother said, "doesn't seem like they gave it much effort. But nobody asked me." She sighed one of her unending sighs.

"Yes," I answered. "He told me."

"Why a divorce? After only three years."

"He said they weren't a good fit," I replied, trying to sound casual.

"Not a good fit," my mother snorted. "Is a wife a winter coat? That's the way young people are these days. If something doesn't work out, just return it to the store—even if it's a bit used."

"Mom," I tried to explain, "it's better they found out earlier, rather than later. At least there were no kids." But my mother's attitude toward divorce was fixed and unyielding and I gave up.

I'd have thought that an appointment as clerk to a Supreme Court justice was an honor anyone would recognize. But you wrote me that Laurie hadn't seen it that way. It had been the final blow to your marriage. She understood what the clerkship would mean to your future, but it was not a future she wanted. Washington, the Supreme Court, politics—her dreams were of a more modest sort, and she resented that her husband had not even discussed the possibility of a move to Washington with her. She angrily said that she'd waited long enough and now she'd hoped to start a family. She wanted to be settled and had imagined giving her parents more grandchildren to share the Hampton weekends with. When she realized that your ambitions were more outsized than the Hamptons, you grew further apart and could not breach the distance. From what I gathered, you separated on friendly terms. Laurie soon found a more suitable husband, an ear, nose, and throat specialist, and started a family.

You clerked to a Supreme Court justice universally revered as both a scholar and an athlete. When young, this judge had had an illustrious career in basketball. He'd been an All-American in college and, before attending law school, had a brief career playing professional basketball. He was an intellect of the best kind—one with the common touch. Everyone recognized the judge's name and this glamour and esteem rubbed off on you. You were the subject of a glowing feature in Brown University's *Alumni Magazine*, forwarded to me by a friend who'd gone to Brown for graduate school. She remembered that I knew Elliot Pine. Was my interest in you to be permanently recognized by all the people who shared our histories? Or was it simply newsworthy that one of the old crowd had reached such illustrious heights as a clerk at the United States Supreme Court?

I'll always remember one story you told me about this judge, a story that you were inordinately delighted by, and simply could not keep to yourself. During your final interview for the clerkship, the judge demonstrated an interesting vetting process. A moment or two after you entered his august chambers, the judge glanced up from his papers. He took off his reading glasses, looking you up and down.

"Son, you've got some serious height on you," the judge said. "What's your shoe size?"

You were completely baffled by this question but managed to respond. "Twelve medium, sir."

"Good. Now go ask my secretary for some shoes and get rid of the tie and coat. I'll meet you at the court. Let's see what you can do."

You became even more confused and your face must have reflected this.

"Young man, I am not talking about the Court with a capital *C*. I mean the highest court in the land, the *basketball* court at the top of this building. Betty will direct you. You look like a person who knows his way around a basketball court. Am I correct? Good. I'll see you up there in ten minutes." And the judge stood, peeled the black robe from his lanky frame, and hung it on a clothes tree behind his desk. Then he kneeled to unlace his wingtips.

You walked back out to the reception area and were shown a closet stacked with boxes of new or nearly new sneakers in almost every size, up to and including fifteens. Betty took your jacket and tie, newly bought for the interview, and hung them in another closet. She walked you out to the corridor and pointed you toward a stairway.

"Go up three flights and make a left. Then out the door. You'll see the court. I'll let the security guard know you're coming, so you can warm up before the judge gets there." She'd raised her eyebrows and looked at you significantly. "You'd better hurry. *He* never needs warming up."

The judge, who was at least thirty years your senior, ran you ragged around the court. You said you soaked through your new white dress shirt, but when you snuck a look over to the judge, you saw that the gray-haired man had not even broken a sweat.

"Thank God," you said, "for the hours of hoops my brothers and I shot in the alley behind the apartment. And those endless defense sessions our asshole coach in high school put us through, because I must have held my own. After twenty minutes of brutal one-on-one, the judge finally scooped up the ball. 'Okay, Pine, you'll do.'"

"I swear, Rocket," you told me later, with your usual modesty, "until I received the official letter on Supreme Court stationery, I didn't know which court he meant that I'd do on—the basketball or the Supreme. He never even asked about my résumé. Not one question. Only my shoe size."

The judge meant both courts. Long days of research and legal analysis, broken up by lunch hours filled with intensely competitive basketball games. You clerked for the scholar-athlete for four years, and he grew fond of you, though not as fond as you were of him. Afterward, you were in demand by top law firms all around the country. You became an associate with one of the most prominent practices in New York—a large firm with clients around the globe. Soon, because of decisions you'd researched while working for the Supreme Court, you became a specialist in antitrust law. You told me you did nothing but work, barely sleeping; that was the way with new associates—they were expected to be workhorses. Once the new hires put in their time, it would be worth it, you were told. But that hardly mattered—you loved the work and the intensity. You loved the adrenalin rush you got knowing the importance of the cases you worked on.

By then, Seth and I had settled back in Los Angeles. We had a small wedding, families and just a few close friends, and Seth finally began medical school. He traveled to Watts each day, to the University of

Southern California, while I worked as a social worker at a private psychiatric hospital in Westwood. We rented a little bungalow in Echo Park, and each night, after our exhausting commutes on the LA freeways, I cooked us dinner. We ate at a table we'd made from a door rescued from a construction site, then sanded and painted a bright orange. We lived on memories of our around-the-world travels. We tried to hang on to those memories of when we'd been unencumbered by jobs and schedules and each day had been an exotic surprise, but spoke of that time only to each other, as we'd learned the painful lesson of returned travelers. Unless they've been there themselves, nobody really wants to listen to other people's travel stories. If they haven't themselves traveled, the exotic stories, even the pictures, will be met with uninterested silence. If they *have* traveled, they'll wonder why it takes you so long to finish your story, wanting instead to chime in with their own experiences. In those early years, Seth and my shared bond of our grand overseas adventure was instrumental in keeping us together. Late at night, after he finished studying and I'd cleaned the kitchen, we'd lay in the dark, remembering with wonder how we floated down the Rewa River in Micronesia or hitchhiked between jungle villages in Malaysia. We remembered the beautiful sleeping woman who guarded tea plants from marauding monkeys. We talked to remind ourselves that it had truly happened. It was real. We'd done these things together.

The problems began not long after we married. Although I tried to restrain myself from asking too many questions, I had a sinking feeling in my gut that Seth was unable to resist the temptation of adoring nurses and student nurses. I didn't like the jokes I heard from Seth and his friends about those too-available nurses. In the mornings, for he left much earlier than I did, I watched him preen as he got ready to leave for the hospital. He'd squint in the mirror as he combed back his hair, cursing his already-receding hairline. His need to be adored—always and without reservation—increased along with my growing failure to provide him with this adoration. It played a part in the demise of our marriage. There was good reason for Seth's need, and although I knew this, adoration was getting harder to fake, much like repeated faked orgasms get more and more tedious. More than once, my husband had told me about his mother's obvious preference for his older brother. This neglect by his mother was a devastating fact of Seth's childhood, and I thought it was a large part of his need for constant and lavish appreciation by women.

Soon after we met, Seth's mother died of the ovarian cancer she'd been sick with for several years. I never even met her. Seth went back to Phoenix for the service. A few days after the funeral, he and his father and his older brother, Alex, went to the bank to open the safety deposit box his mother had maintained. As they looked through the contents, all three squirmed uncomfortably. They lifted out piece after piece of memorabilia. None of it was Seth's. All belonged to his brother. Things as mundane as report cards and kindergarten art projects were carefully preserved in the safety deposit box. But everything was Alex's. Their mom had even carefully wrapped two graduation cap tassels in white tissue paper, but the school colors revealed that both belonged to Alex—one from high school, the other college. It was as if she'd had only one son. Why is it like that in some families? Why an obvious preference for one child over another for no apparent reason? When I saw Seth's face after he returned from Phoenix, and he told me about his mother's safety deposit box, I was glad I was an only child. He grieved for her death as well as her life-long abandonment of him.

But still, even though I understood it, I grew impatient with Seth's ways. I watched him at parties, flirting with women, loudly clamoring for attention, and it began to repel me. His need for approval seemed fed only by new conquests. I drew away from him. Our once-enthusiastic lovemaking became quieter, my responses more muted.

And though I was married and knew it was inappropriate, I

waited with outsized anticipation for those thick letters from you, still written with the old-fashioned blue fountain pen. I'd run to the mailbox, just as I'd done when I was in college. In your letters, you chatted about high-minded matters—literature, art, the fine points of politics. I read and reread those letters and saved them, along with all the ones that had come before. We sent poems and quotes from books back and forth. Seth was a man of action, brash and adventurous, smart, but not an intellectual. He was a thrill seeker, but every time I watched a foreign film that moved me (and made Seth fidget in his seat), I wished you were there with me—and often framed an imaginary conversation with you in my head. From time to time, I found myself turning away from small, compact Seth in bed, regulating my breathing and pretending sleep. His beard was rough, his chest was hairy, and there was something indefinable about his smell that I began to find unappealing. Always, God help me, I compared the two of you. When Seth was in his second year of medical school (admittedly a difficult time) and my birthday came, he completely forgot it. Only when he saw the gift with the brown wrapping paper folded neatly beside it on our dresser, did he remember.

"Shit," he said and smacked his forehead. "It's today, isn't it?"

"It is," I replied with fake cheer. "And Valentine's Day, too. You get to forget two for the price of one."

"What did Mr. Wonderful send you?" Seth asked. "He never forgets, does he?"

"A necklace," I said. "Kind of old-fashioned."

Seth nodded and was asleep in moments, not even asking to look at it.

I got up and went into the kitchen, taking the box with me. You'd sent a cameo, a woman's raised face in profile on a coral background. The note, which I'd carefully hidden away before Seth returned home, said, "I walked past an antique jewelry store on DuPont Circle and saw this in the window. I think she looks like you, the same profile. I hope when you wear it, you'll know how special you are."

I love old jewelry. I always have. I like to imagine the woman who might have worn the piece before me. The lady in this cameo had a long, straight nose. Did she look like me? Sometimes people say I have a classical Roman nose. I've never particularly liked my nose, though now, I barely see myself. But as a child, I used to scotch tape it at night, pulling the tip up toward the bridge, hoping it would develop an upward tilt while I slept. I looked carefully at the cameo you sent from Washington. I rubbed my index finger up and down the length of my nose. Was it an elegant Roman nose? I hoped so.

Poor Seth. Forgetting my birthday *and* Valentine's Day, on a year when I received this perfect gift from you. When I finally went to bed, I turned away from my husband. He hadn't a chance.

But I kept hearing my mother's comment about you and Laurie. "Doesn't seem like they gave it much effort." I was the one with determination, the woman who wouldn't turn back when there were no planes out of Indonesia, but hunted for ferryboats to take us island to island. Somehow, I would find a way to navigate Seth and me from island to island in our marriage. I would not give up.

In a while, I began to find evidence of his infidelities: a phone number scrawled on a napkin and left in a pocket, an unexplained call that he'd end abruptly when I came into the room. He started out denying my accusations, said my suspicions were poisoning our marriage. He called me paranoid. So, like betrayed women everywhere, I questioned my own sanity. Perhaps I *was* the jealous harridan he accused me of being. Why could I not trust Seth? I didn't trust my own instincts; I was confused. Our fights were acrimonious, dramatic, and tear-filled. Surprisingly, it was Seth who was more the crier. I was exhausted, but I couldn't cry. Instead, I became unpleasantly hardened.

Not even two years after we married, I discovered something

devastating, something that could not be explained away by Seth's excuses. On a day he didn't expect me to drive his car, I found a letter he'd left on the front seat. In this letter, a woman sorrowfully asked Seth for money for an abortion. She was begging. These were the days, the very brutal days, before abortion was legalized. Women who had unwanted pregnancies were faced with dreadful alternatives. I cannot even abide hearing the foolish arguments now of right-to-lifers. The poor child who wrote the letter, and that is what she seems to me now, a child, told my husband that she was at least eight weeks pregnant. If he could find the money, she'd go to Puerto Rico immediately, where a friend of hers had a contact who, supposedly, could do the job in a clean and safe way. However, if Seth could not come up with the sum required to go to Puerto Rico, and it was a large sum, perhaps he could help her find someone locally in Los Angeles. There was no blame or threat. It was a desperate plea. She was frightened and didn't know where to turn. I was sick then, and I'm sick now thinking back on it.

After reading the letter, I set the table in the kitchen. At Seth's place, instead of a plate, I propped up the letter. He would see it as soon as he came in. I waited in the bedroom, working on a needlepoint pillow I'd started, jabbing the silver needle in and out quickly. When I heard him come through the back door into the kitchen, I listened for his steps, my stitches becoming more and more tight.

There was a long silence until finally I saw Seth standing in the doorway. He looked truly stricken. This time he didn't even attempt to lie. "Judith, so help me God, I don't understand why I hurt you this way. I am so sorry you had to find that letter. I'm so sorry," he said and his voice caught. I could see he was beginning to tear up.

I stared at him. How foolish he looked. Tears running down his cheeks. I resumed stabbing at my needlepoint with the metal needle. I pulled the stitches so tight the canvas puckered beneath my fingers, but still I said nothing.

"She wasn't worth it," Seth said, wiping his eyes. "Just someone who works in the clinic. I hardly know her and now she's gone and gotten pregnant. All those girls are on the prowl for med students. You should see how they throw themselves at us."

When he came toward me, I threw my work down on the desk and moved backward in the room. Finally I was up against our bedroom wall, still staring dry-eyed at him.

"Listen, Seth, she's got the real problem," I finally said. "Not you or me. What do you plan to do? How're you going to help her?"

He went to the edge of the bed and sat and put his head in his hands. He began to sob for real. "Judith, I am so sorry," he said between gasps for air. "I don't know what to do. I feel like such a scumbag. I want to start a family with you. She's a bimbo."

My voice never rose during this discussion. Instead I watched him coldly: his tears, his shaking shoulders. Many times in my life I've wished I had the gift for tears that Seth has. He's always been quite the crier. At happy or sad times, he mists up. Other people find it appealing. He cried at our daughter's wedding while he made the toast; he cried when our grandchildren were born. People think him sensitive because of it. They think he's got a tender heart. Maybe he does. It would be nice to cry once in a while, as Seth seems so able to do, to breathe deeply and sob. It would be cleansing, I think. And maybe people would stop assuming things about me, that I'm so strong and tough. I get colder and more silent in these situations. For the life of me, I cannot cry.

"I'll tell you what you'll do, Seth," I said in a low, hard voice. "You'll get her the best and the safest abortion money can buy. Take out a student loan or ask your father, but get her the money she needs. You do your research. Talk to people at the medical school. Somebody will know someone. You haven't got a lot of time, so start today. And let her know she's not alone, that you'll go with her wherever she has to go. You'll drive her there and you'll wait for her until it's over. And

then afterward, when you tell me it's done, we'll talk. Not until then."
I pushed past him and went into the kitchen for the car keys. I drove
to Griffith Park and walked the trails and didn't go home until the
sun was setting and the park was closing. Then I got in the shower
and tried to scrub off the filth I felt covering me.

For about a year after that, Seth was a model husband and I was a
model wife. My mother once told me, "Treat him like a prince, and
he'll treat you like a princess." I tried.

I think we were both terrified by the thought of the marriage
ending, of being divorced so soon after we'd married, so we were
careful with one another. I'd looked into the abyss of leaving him
and couldn't abide what I saw. No one I knew, in my family or circle
of friends, except of course, you, Elliot, had gotten divorced. I'd be
the first. And so I made a vow to myself to be more the wife that Seth
needed. I'd keep him from wandering. I'd devote myself to him.

This was an age of advice books for women on how to please their
man. If they roamed, we were at fault. The ones on women's liberation came later. In those years, we worked at making ourselves more
appealing to men. I found articles on how to spice up the bedroom,
how to look and act more sexy. One author suggested a wife greet her
man wrapped in nothing but clear plastic wrap and a big red bow. I
didn't go that far; I couldn't figure out how to wind the plastic wrap
around me without help, but I did visit Frederick's of Hollywood and
invested in racy lingerie. I cooked meals for Seth that were worthy
of a magazine spread, each including a main dish, a vegetable, and a
starch. I got up early before work and started these meals—lasagna,
beef stroganoff, complicated recipes I'd cut from the newspaper. On
weekends I baked my own bread, our little bungalow filling with a
warm, yeasty smell that almost convinced us we were happy.

Seth, for his part, came home directly after classes and the clinic.

He called when he was going to be late and complimented me on my lasagna. Then he began to talk about our having a child. The time seemed right, even a bit late. We were twenty-eight and Seth was entering his last year of medical school. He adored children. He planned on becoming a pediatrician.

Although I was flattered by his desire to begin a family with me, I was less sure it was a good decision. I loved my job and was getting more skilled as a social worker. I found I had a real gift for group work. I'd learned a lot since those days when I'd been an aide in a psychiatric hospital in Chicago and faced off with angry and depressed Mrs. Gideon who had thrown a cup of hot coffee at me. My work, I knew, required years and years of practice before one became excellent. Of course I was also worried about the marriage. Even though we were fighting less, I asked myself many times if what I felt for Seth was indeed love. Or was I just scared to leave?

What made it more complicated was that I could not stop thinking about you, Elliot. You were always in my head. I was sensible enough to realize that although I idolized you, we'd never had a real, flesh and blood relationship. We'd never lived together. Yet I could not stop seeing your intelligent warm eyes, remembering your vast knowledge of books and music that crept into our every conversation. I remembered how you really listened to my thoughts and ideas as no one else, except perhaps my father, ever had. I thought about these sweet, sensitive gifts you sent each year on my birthday. Most of all I remembered how your touch had made me light-headed. That wasn't real love, was it? It was a fantasy. But still, it seemed as if I shouldn't have these thoughts about you. I should have those feelings for Seth.

By Thanksgiving, when Seth was in his senior year of medical school in Los Angeles, I was pregnant. The maternal urge proved stronger than my doubts. We discussed options for Seth's pediatric residency. We weighed which parts of the country would be best to raise a child in, spending hours looking at maps and discussing urban versus rural, north versus south, culturally diverse versus homogeneity. Poring over maps together felt like the old days. The whole world was ours and soon we'd embark on another adventure—the single best thing we did together.

However, a bit of heredity made things more complicated. When I'd first met Seth, we discovered we had an unusual fact in common—an interesting coincidence.

"Do you have many relatives in Phoenix?" I'd asked when we were exchanging family histories. "Other than your parents?"

"Just one aunt and uncle," he'd answered. "They have two kids. My cousins and my brother, Alex, and I were raised all together. My aunt Lena is my mom's identical twin. They were very close. Sometimes, when we were kids, I'd run to her, not my mom, when I got hurt. Like they were interchangeable. But not exactly, because I'm pretty sure Aunt Lena liked me more than my mom did. She was actually nicer to me."

I stared at him. "Your mother was a twin? *My* mother is a twin, too. My aunt Gussie is her identical twin," I said, and then laughed. "That's so strange. Well, we'd better not get married. I've been told that twins run in families, but that it skips a generation. With both of our mothers being twins, that would be our destiny."

And so it was. Within two months of my pregnancy, a pregnancy marked by severe nausea and violent throwing up almost all day every day, the doctor informed us we were expecting twins. And, I don't care what anyone says, having twins is infinitely more stressful and complicated than having two single children. Two for one. Ha. Get it over with quickly. Ha. Only one pregnancy and you've got your family complete. Ha. At twenty weeks, my pregnancy was deemed high risk, and I was ordered on bed rest. I had to leave my job and stay at home, recumbent, my belly a huge mound rising in front of me. In our innocence, before we realized twins were coming, we'd planned on taking our new baby to Europe that summer. Seth had been dreaming of the trip all during medical school, a way to repeat the two years of blissful wandering we'd had before we married. He optimistically thought we could travel before we settled down somewhere and he began his pediatric residency.

"Man, it's easy when they're little," Seth said to me and everyone we knew. "People all around the world, in Indonesia and Thailand and Fiji, everybody in those countries we traveled to center their lives on children. We never heard crying kids anywhere we visited, did we, Judith? People just tie their babies into a pack, hoist them onto their backs, and the kid becomes part of them."

"A newborn, Seth?" I asked. I wanted to, but just couldn't see it.

"Of course. That's when they're most portable," he'd replied. "It'll be easy."

People we knew who actually had children would stare at us incredulously when they heard our plans.

"You want to travel abroad with an infant?" one friend asked. "Jesus, I couldn't manage getting out of the house for two months after we had our baby. We had no clean clothes and I couldn't even find time to go to the Laundromat."

Seth maintained that it all came down to attitude and flexibility. He said to me in the privacy of our bedroom, "Spoiled Americans. That's what our friends are. They forget how natural it is to have a baby. They overanalyze everything. You just have to get organized." And if anyone could have carried this off, it was my ex-husband. But that was before the doctor heard two heartbeats and I was diagnosed with a high-risk pregnancy.

"I guess we won't be going to Greece this summer," were the first words out of Seth's mouth when we left the doctor's office that sunny day in December. We had just learned the news and I was in shock. Seth walked quickly through the parking lot, got into the car before me, and slammed the door. Then he must have realized that I was still far behind him, so he reached over and opened the passenger door from inside. He didn't look at me, just stared straight ahead while we drove home. You could see those Greek islands dissolving before his eyes. No more Mykonos. No more Santorini.

The trip was impossible because I was carrying twins, and I felt that somehow I'd failed him. My high-risk pregnancy made Seth's brightest dream—to travel again—impossible. It was the dream that had kept him going through the sleepless nights of medical school. Yet traveling with newborn twins was beyond what even indefatigable Seth could envision.

Miriam and Evan were born at Cedars-Sinai in Los Angeles that spring. I didn't want to give birth at LA County Hospital, where Seth worked and where all his medical school buddies might want to scrub in. Fortunately my job provided good insurance. The twins were beautiful babies and surprisingly healthy, even though they arrived five weeks early. But the time after they were born was more difficult than I'd imagined. My mother came for the first two weeks, and was enormously helpful, but our tiny house made her visit stressful, and I couldn't ask her to stay longer. I felt as if I'd become a burden to Seth, an incompetent one at that. I was tired and overwhelmed and completely unavailable to my husband. I barely noticed him in the haze of diapers and feedings. Seth loved those babies, but not the time and attention they took. He tried to help, but I could see how itchy he was for diversion. He chafed at the constant domesticity and took up new hobbies, getting certified as a scuba diver, then disappearing on weekends for dives in Mexico. I was relieved to see him go. I could feel his resentment when he was at home helping with Miriam and Evan. We weren't a cool couple traipsing the world with a baby in a pack, as he'd imagined. We were boring and homebound, and I had little energy for anything besides the babies. Travel seemed laughable. When the babies were a few months old, I discovered there was an organization for mothers of twins. One morning, with great effort, I packed up the twins and all the necessary equipment, and attended a meeting.

"They're your first, aren't they?" one particularly lovely woman said as she settled her own two into a porta-crib.

Her blond hair was artfully pulled behind her ears with a wide headband, her clothes pressed, and her children were quiet. How did she manage it? I was completely exhausted and knew that soon we had to start preparing for our move to Northern California, where Seth would begin his residency. How did anyone get anything done with twins?

"Yes," I answered, desperately patting Evan's back so he would burp before I picked up Miriam, who was taking the deep breaths I knew would soon develop into a wail. "Does it show?" I tried to smile, smelling the coffee percolating and desperately wanting a cup.

"No," the attractive blond woman said kindly. "It's just that when twins come first, before you've had a chance to practice with another, single baby, it all seems harder. It's a cruel twist of nature to make twins a woman's first crack at raising kids."

"Yeah," I admitted. "I don't know what the hell I'm doing."

"It'll get better," she said. "You'll get the hang of it. They're more resilient than you think."

It did get better—at least with the babies. We loaded the U-Haul and rented an old, rambling house in Oakland. Seth began his internship and then residency at Children's Hospital. We made a life. I was busy with Evan and Miriam and made friends I'd have for the rest of my life, Marnie and Rachel, women who had children the same ages as my twins. But, within a few short years, my husband's unexplained late nights began again. When the children were five, after nine years of marriage, we divorced. It was the end of a chapter that I am only now, as an old woman, recovered from, the bitterness and bile no longer rising in my throat when I think of Seth.

They say that it takes twice as long as a marriage lasts to get over it. But I am a persistent sort. I dwell on things and I did not bounce back easily. For years, I alternated between blaming Seth and then myself.

Every glitch that the children had: a poor grade, disappointment with a boyfriend, Miriam's seriousness, even Evan's later experimentation with drugs, I attributed to the failed marriage. Their father, on the contrary, lived happily in the present. Seth married three more times, and had four more children. He loved each of those children extravagantly, I will give him that; and though all his wives were young and pretty, as far as I could see, the IQ of each decreased at least twenty points with every successive marriage.

Our daughter, Miriam, now in her early forties, and always one with a sharp tongue, told me that she'd recently asked her father what on earth he found to discuss with his newest wife, a gorgeous girl he'd met at the gym who was several years younger than Miriam herself.

"Oh, sweetheart," Seth said, and looked up from the monster motorcycle he was tinkering with in his garage, "I've tried smart. Your mother is a very smart woman. But Mimi, I figured out that smart doesn't really work for me."

So if I was so smart, why, at thirty-six, when Seth and I had been divorced for two years, did I find myself in a closet, in the dark behind a closed door in a hotel in Union Square? Pushed there by none other than you, my darling Elliot.

You were in town because the prestigious New York law firm you worked for had assigned you to the biggest case of your career, defending a high-tech giant in an antitrust suit. You were the junior attorney on the team, an associate among partners, but it was an enormous case, and you were there because of your expertise in antitrust law. Within days of learning you'd been selected for the defense team, you phoned me with the news.

"Finally, Judith. We'll be able to see each other regularly. This case means I'll be coming to San Francisco every six weeks or so," you said. "When I heard I was on the team, I couldn't believe my good luck. Not only the importance of the case—I realize what a great opportunity this is—but it'll bring me to California often. Often. In your backyard, practically. The case is so complicated, depositions are bound to go on forever. We'll need a lot of technology experts."

I'd be seeing Elliot regularly. I was divorced. He was divorced. My mind raced ahead of itself with the possibilities. We made plans for the weekend following the first days of depositions. I walked around with a goofy smile. I found myself unable to stop daydreaming, even as I spoke to clients. Usually I prided myself on my unwavering attention to the children and adults who came into my office at Child Protective Services. Now I kept staring at the clock, counting the hours and days until you'd arrive in San Francisco. In phone calls, you told me it was the same for you.

One of the only positives I'd discovered about divorce was that children are nicely taken care of by their dad on alternate weekends. (It was such a great perk, I wondered why intact marriages didn't also have such a clause.) My ex-husband now had a new live-in girl-friend. I knew she wanted to marry Seth and that she understood that the twins were part of the package. Both kids were nuts about ani-mals, and Evan was particularly partial to cats. I'm allergic to cats, but as soon as this girlfriend became a regular fixture in Seth's life, she appeared at my ex-husband's house with a velvety, gray kitten she said she'd conveniently "found" near the dental office where she worked. There was no trouble getting Evan to visit his dad after that. Miriam could not be bought quite so cheaply, but Seth enrolled her in riding lessons, something she'd longed for but I'd told her we could not afford. After that, she had her bags packed and riding boots at the door well before her father arrived.

To get ready for my weekend with you, I did as much maintenance as a single mother on a social worker's salary could afford. My hair was styled; I waxed, polished, and scrubbed. I drove across the Bay Bridge from Oakland, and by the time I arrived in San Francisco, the tiredness from work as well as the loneliness of my life was gone. Arriving at the hotel, I felt like another woman—a supremely worldly one. I easily learned how it was done. The valet, in his red velvet get-up and gold epaulets, reached out and I handed him the keys to my car. I smiled and nodded, then walked briskly through the lobby in my high heels and short skirt. Men eyed me appreciatively. I'm sure that the anticipation of seeing you, Elliot, gave me a sexy glow. It's like that for women. When one man desires you, it shows. You become more desirable to others.

Yet there was this ridiculous, somewhat embarrassing situation: although we were thirty-six years old, you and I had still not slept together. Ever. There had been more kisses than I could count in those intervening years—passionate, steamy embraces. We had touched and fondled each other until we were crazy with desire. But, to put it bluntly, the relationship had not been consummated. I will summarize. We were either too young; I was too concerned about virginity; or, one or both of us were in other relationships. Now, at thirty-six, neither of us was married. The long wait would be over. I shopped for a black negligee and, with my heart pounding, wrapped it in soft tissue and packed it in my overnight bag.

After a wonderful meal at a French restaurant, ordering knowingly off the menu as if we were students of Mrs. Aron again, we walked back to your hotel on Union Square. As the elevator took us up, I gazed at our reflection in the mirrored cubicle. I liked seeing the grown man and woman we'd become, a couple that was finally going to spend the night together. You unlocked the door and I saw your large, elegant room. The furniture was mahogany and stately. It was a suite, with a couch and separate sitting area, so we could sit comfortably and chat without jumping right into bed. But I thought of little else and kept sneaking looks at the thick duvet and pillows piled on the bed. You were the man by which I had measured all other loves. When I dreamed of you, I knew it would be a good dream. I would wake with pleasure, my body alive, then feel the terrible let-down as I realized it had been a dream, not real at all. Now, we were finally together sitting on a silk shantung settee in a hotel room. We'd brought a bottle of wine up from the restaurant, a good red that easily cost over a hundred dollars and that you'd ordered carelessly and put on your expense account. I unfastened my shoes, then kicked them off, stunning high heels with ankle straps, which had cost me a good chunk of a month's child support check from Seth. They were the most beautiful shoes I'd ever owned. Fuck-me shoes, my girlfriend Marnie had called them when we went shopping.

You turned my head toward you and looked at me with those dark brown eyes. "I've been looking forward to seeing you ever since I found I'd be coming out here, Rocket," you said. "Between depositions, even during depositions, I thought about you. I want to know everything you do all week. I want to picture your life."

"My weeks are all the same." I shrugged. "They're not exciting. I take care of my kids. I get ready for work, then go to my office at the county building," I said.

"What you do is exciting." You put your finger under my chin and raised my face so we were looking at each other. "Your work is important. You do vital things for people who need you. Tell me about your office," you said. "Let me picture it."

"You know the kind of building—a Soviet-style concrete block. For eight hours a day I listen to people in trouble, help them prop up their lives. Then I get the twins from daycare and make dinner. Sometimes it's spaghetti. Sometimes it's chicken. Usually it's white. They like food that's white." You must have been used to talking to important people about important subjects. Yet you said you wanted to see my life as it was and you seemed fascinated by it, listening attentively to everything I said. You were always a good listener.

"God, the twins must be so big by now. How old?"

"They're seven," I answered. "Miriam's a head taller than Evan. He hates that. I keep telling him he'll catch up."

"I'll bet they're smart. They'd have to be—you're their mother. Do they like to read yet?"

"They are smart. And creative. Both of them, but in different areas. But Evan struggles in school. He's disorganized, reading hasn't come easily to him. Miriam's the opposite. She's so organized, it's frightening."

"Like you," you said.

"Like me." I took a photo from my purse and showed you.

You studied the picture, then looked up at me as you handed the photograph back. "Jesus, what beautiful kids we'd make, wouldn't we?"

I couldn't answer. Did you know how many times I'd thought the same thing?

Then you asked, "So what are the evenings like? What do you do?"

"After dinner, the twins have their baths. I always read to them. I sit on one of their beds and Miriam and Evan sit on either side of me. They listen to every word of every story and then they wrap their arms around my neck and give me these enormous hugs. Both of them, in their soft cotton pajamas, both squeezing me at once, practically knocking me over. They smell delicious. I usually stay until they're asleep."

"You never go out at night? Get a sitter and get out by yourself?"

"Not very often," I admitted. "Seth has them every other weekend. Sometimes I have a night out with the girls, but usually I'm too tired." I looked at you then, suddenly shy. "But this week, after I've gotten into bed, I've stayed awake thinking about you. I pull the thought of you out of a drawer I keep in my mind. I imagined being here, sitting beside you, just as we are right now." I looked down at my hands. "It's exactly as I imagined."

"We would have had beautiful children together, wouldn't we?"

you repeated, tipping my head back and softly kissing my eyes. "I always thought we would. Beautiful, smart children."

These were heady words, delicious words. "I suppose," I said, smiling. "Maybe. But haven't there always been a few things in the way? Like being married to other people. Or you in New York and me out here," I added.

You reached behind me and slowly began to unzip my dress. With my hands shaking, I reached for your belt. I don't think I'd ever felt so excited, even when we were teenagers with hormones raging and the windows of the parked car steamy.

We stood and as my dress slipped down to the floor, you bent to kiss my exposed shoulder. Your thick hair brushed against my neck and I put my head down into it and inhaled. Your hair smelled wonderful, as it always had, fresh and clean, with an addition of some new musky fragrance.

Then there was a loud, aggressive knock on the door. We froze. Jesus. I thought about the policemen that night in Chicago. Pounding on our window as we caressed each other in the parked car. I stared at you in confusion. You put your finger to your lips. "Sh," you said softly.

"Who could it be?" I whispered.

You shrugged your shoulders, then turned toward the door and said loudly, "Yes? What is it?"

"Hey, Pine. You in there? Open up."

I heard the raucous laughter of several men outside in the hall. They sounded drunk.

"Yeah. Okay, just a sec. Gimme a sec," you said. You put your finger to your lips again and spoke softly into my ear. I could barely hear you. "Come with me. I'll get rid of them. Lawyers from the team. Assholes."

You grabbed my arm and yanked me forward, just as Miss Schaffer had done in the fifth grade when we did something wrong, and dragged me toward the closet. You were shirtless and held your pants up, unzipped and with the belt unfastened, with the other hand.

"Be right there," you called loudly to the men on the other side of the door, zipping your pants and reaching for a shirt.

I heard more laughter, and then everything grew dark and the sounds fainter as you shut the closet door, me inside, astonished. *Why?* I wondered. *Why does he need to put me in the closet? I'm a perfectly respectable-looking woman. He could introduce me to anyone. Why is he hiding me?* I was there alone in the dark for what seemed a long time. I pulled my dress up over my shoulder and gingerly tried to zip it without hitting the hangers and making them clang together. I smoothed my hair, knowing that, despite this humiliation, I needed to exit the closet with as much dignity as possible, whenever it was you finally let me out of there.

There was talking, but I could not make out the words. At last, I heard the door to your room shut firmly and the closet door opened. You stood there, staring at me apologetically, an ashamed, rueful look on your face. Finally, you took my hand and gently guided me out into the room.

"I'm not accustomed to being pushed into a closet, Elliot. That was a first."

"I am so sorry, Judith. That was awful and I am so sorry," you said, trying to reach for my other hand.

I refused to let you take it. "Why couldn't I meet your buddies?" I asked, smoothing out the skirt of my cocktail dress, the beautiful black dress bought especially for this weekend.

You sat back down on the couch and put your head in your hands. I sat as far away as I could, crossing my legs, fighting for dignity.

"I work closely with these guys," you said.

"Yes? And?"

"And"—you swallowed and hesitated—"I've been seeing a paralegal from our office. She's very sweet. But it's nothing serious. Ever since this case began, I've been working late, crazy long hours. She works the night shift."

"There's a night shift for paralegals?" I asked.

"Yeah. The work is intense, so they hire a whole crew of people during the evenings to help the lawyers. These guys on the team, they know we're involved, the paralegal and me. I've even brought her to some parties from the firm. So, you see, it looks sleazy that I'm in a hotel room with another woman."

"It is sleazy," I said and wondered how I got to be the other woman. My own marriage had floundered because of other women. I'd vowed I'd never put myself in that position.

"Judith, you can't compare yourself with this girl. Compared to us, that doesn't even seem real. I just couldn't explain it to those guys. Our history. How you and I have known each other all our lives. What you mean to me. They've all had a few drinks. They'd have made comments or given you looks. And when we get back to New York, there'd be this nasty undercurrent. I'm sorry, I panicked."

"What's her name?" I asked. "The paralegal."

"It's not important."

"Yes, it is. It's important to me."

"Meredith," you said, and your head dipped even lower. "She's young and naïve and going through a hard time. She works the night shift so she can stay home days with her kid. He's still small. A baby really."

"Your fancy law firm sounds like a sweatshop. Around-the-clock paralegals."

"It is like a sweatshop, you're right. The associates constantly have to prove themselves. I collapse when I finally get home after midnight. Then I get up a few hours later and do it again. You have no idea how much I was looking forward to getting away, to seeing you. We keep a brutal schedule at the office, especially now, on this case. But if it goes well, some people have told me I could make partner. It would be some kind of record, as young as I am. It's that big a case."

"What's this got to do with Meredith?"

"I never see anyone outside the firm. There's no time. She's there late, working with me, so sometimes, after we finish, we go and get something to eat. She understands the craziness right now—until this case goes to trial. I feel like an asshole about it, but somehow, we slipped into a fairly inappropriate affair. It's a cliché, isn't it?"

"Maybe. But I guess I'm a cliché, too," I said. "Divorced, lonely woman. Waiting for you to get into town."

"Judith. You're no cliché. All these years. We've shared everything. You know everything about me. You're the person who gets me most of all. You can't imagine how I was looking forward to seeing you. And, being with you. Finally." You touched my arm tentatively. "God, I want you, Rocket."

I looked out toward Union Square, just below us. It was early November, but San Francisco was brightly lit and decorated for the holidays. There was a giant Christmas tree in the plaza, and this year, for the first time, a huge menorah. I thought that the smartest thing I could do would be to get my coat, walk out, and drive home. But I didn't. The kids were at their father's house. My place would be dark and lonely. I had a negligee in my overnight bag, and the unexplored sex between us was too powerful to walk away from. I looked down at you on the silk couch.

"Please, Judith," you begged. "Let's see what happens between us. I promise I won't lie to you anymore. Give us a chance at least."

At this point, I would like to describe the wonderful night of romance that happened between us that night in November. I wish I could report that the passion was so overwhelming, our lives were changed forever. But, alas, that is not what happened. Not then.

The passion was there, but you, poor Elliot, your body failed you. For hours, we touched and caressed. We were no strangers to this touching. For years, in high school and even college, we had participated in such frenzied hours of touching, then stopped short. It was the times: I was conflicted back then. Now, with our arousal so high, both of us flushed and sweaty and tired, but with nothing to hold us back, it was clear that consummation was still not to be.

"It's happened before," you finally said, rolling over in the bed. "But only when it's been with someone incredibly important. I'm so sorry."

I wanted to ask if it happened with Meredith, but I just sighed and wished I hadn't given up smoking back when I was pregnant with the twins. It would be heavenly to light up and inhale deeply now.

"It's almost funny, right? We've wanted this for such a long time, and now that we can . . ."

You made many more visits to California. The depositions went on for months. And of course, finally, there was sex. After that first disastrous weekend, we took time and rediscovered each other's bodies, the bodies that we'd rubbed and teased and aroused so many years earlier. Foreplay had been going on since we were sixteen. You were the boy I'd loved since childhood, as well as the brilliant man with tired lines around his eyes and strong, hard muscles that I could not stop stroking. I saw all of you, the vulnerable ten-year-old boy and the accomplished man in his thirties. All of these Elliots were at last, unbelievably, in bed with me. Physically, I felt a freedom with you that I'd never felt before. I felt you truly knew me and I you.

These times together became like mini honeymoons. The rest of your team began staying at a hotel in the financial district, closer to the offices they used. You told them that you worked better at the Union Square hotel and insisted on staying there, even paying your own bill instead of putting it on your expense account. We hid ourselves away from the world those weekends, eating good food and drinking lovely wines. We were what we had always been: friends who could talk about anything. Only now we were lovers as well. I shut my mind to Meredith's existence and this was made easier because, after that first night, you didn't mention her again. "Just someone in the office," you'd said then, reducing her to a convenient diversion. And I didn't ask more.

You talked about the case and about the government and corporate lawyers you faced at long conference tables. I talked about my week at the County Social Services Department where I tried to find homes for children who had nowhere to go and about the sad parade of poor people coming in and out of my office. Our worlds could not have been more different and yet we gave each other our full and undivided attention, both of us interested in and finding value in what the other was doing.

The antitrust case you were working on was huge. It consumed you. It was going to make or break one of the biggest technology corporations in America. Although you started on the case as a relatively junior member of the legal team, gradually you were given greater responsibility in gathering evidence and taking depositions. The experience clerking at the Supreme Court with antitrust cases gave you the advantage of having analyzed both the government's as well as corporate arguments in similar suits. You became invaluable to your firm's big firm of the California tech giant.

This case stretched on for eighteen months. You flew from New York to Northern California at least once, sometimes twice, a month. It was a grueling schedule, but you seemed to thrive on the pace, always enthusiastic about the work, even when you'd taken a red-eye from New York, going straight to JFK on Wednesday after having worked a full day in Manhattan. You'd be in San Francisco several days, working hellish hours, before I arrived on Friday evenings. For a single mother raising twins, these weekends in San Francisco were exciting breaks from ordinary life. I no longer stared bleakly at the growing pile of dirty school and soccer clothes, at the stack of bills that never got completely paid, or at empty weekends when Seth had the children. Instead, I circled the dates of your visits on my calendar and cheerfully got Miriam and Evan ready to go to their father's house. This was the love affair I'd dreamed about. Even better. This boy I'd loved had grown into an exciting and brilliant man, one who always seemed delighted to see me.

We couldn't get enough of each other, now that we were finally together. "It's so wonderful," you said over and over. "You're so wonderful. Now, at this time in our lives, it's as if we've never been apart."

In our room, after we'd made love, I'd ask about the case. Your work fascinated me. I suppose being close to such power was exciting for me to hear about. Your firm represented the richest companies in the world. I don't remember feeling critical of the work you did. It seemed glamorous. But sometimes, not often, I would remember back to what we used to talk about in Chicago. You'd once been so passionate about social justice, about helping the underdogs. Back then in our Jewish youth group, we had sung songs of change. Our hearts were bursting with compassion for the poor and those without a voice. Yet you told me that the year before, you had successfully defended a multinational corporation accused of starving third world babies through its aggressive marketing of prepared formula, instead of mother's milk. Public health advocates were outraged that uneducated women in Africa had been swayed by clever advertising to switch from breastfeeding to the less safe and nutritious cans of formula. Your team had helped this company avoid paying out huge damages to poor women. What about this current antitrust suit? Could it really be good for our country and the economy to allow a few corporate giants to gobble up the competition? I asked you questions tentatively, wanting to learn from your explanations, waiting for you to make it right.

You were not defensive about your choices. Clerking for the

athlete-judge had convinced you that in order to be a successful lawyer, your job was not to take moral positions, but to provide the best legal advice possible. You had reverence for the law and the law became your god. You studied every possible argument and precedent and gave your clients, whoever they were, your very best. Sometimes when we were not together, I worried about those articles I'd read condemning the producers of baby formula, accusing them of causing the deaths of thousands of African infants from intestinal disease because of dirty water, the only water available, which mothers used to mix formula, instead of staying with breast milk. Usually, though, I put those stories from my mind, thinking that the issues must be more complicated than the newspaper accounts were describing. The press simplified issues.

I believed that you were incapable of representing truly bad guys. There was something so pure about your description of the cases, past and present. I listened to your voice and your accounts of the depositions. In your voice and telling, it did not seem possible that the clients you represented could be anything but world leaders concerned with the greater good. Of course there was a great deal of wealth in your world. You were beginning to make big money and to act like someone with money. I noticed how you took luxury for granted, the monogrammed shirts, the hotel and restaurants, the enormous tips doled out so casually.

When February arrived that year, you realized you'd be in California on the fourteenth. "It's your birthday the next weekend I come out there," you said. You never once forgot. "Is there somewhere special you'd like to go?"

"You've already taken me to so many special places," I answered. "I've never eaten in so many terrific restaurants."

"Yeah," you said. "But what else would you like to do? What are your favorite places? Somewhere you'd like to go with Evan and Miriam?"

I closed my eyes and thought for a while. "I wish we could go down the coast," I finally replied. "We love driving through Big Sur. Such a beautiful ride, green-blue ocean on one side, the mountains on the other. My favorite part is just past San Luis Obispo. San Simeon, where Hearst Castle is. The hills there are golden in summer, lush green in winter. There are sycamore groves along the rivers and then the live oaks, lone trees with huge, gnarly branches at the tops of hills, like you see in cowboy movies. We should go there, Elliot. You've never met the kids. Miriam would show you how to ride a horse and you could be a cowboy."

"I'd like to be a cowboy." You laughed. "I wish the firm didn't always keep me on such a tight leash." Then you added, "Maybe someday, though."

That next weekend, you handed me an envelope at dinner. "Happy Birthday. And Happy Valentine's Day to my valentine."

Inside the envelope was a gift certificate for a week at a guest ranch. It was outside Solvang, in the central coast region, not far from the area I'd spoken to him about. The gift certificate was for three people. I looked up, puzzled.

"Three?" I asked.

"One of my clients owns this place. This ranch. He's always talking about it. When you said it was your favorite part of California, I thought about it. There are cottages and horses and a lake with fishing. He says it's a kid's paradise and they'll love it. They have a hay ride and a small farm with baby animals. I thought maybe you and the kids could go during their spring vacation. Could you get the time off?"

"Me and the kids?" I asked, trying not to let my disappointment show. "You wouldn't come?"

"I doubt I could get away. But, listen, I'd be so happy thinking of you and the twins having a great week there. You'd tell me all about it and show me pictures. Do you have a movie camera? I'll get you one. Make a movie of all of you on horseback," you said.

"Elliot, how could I accept such an expensive gift from you? These dude ranch places cost a fortune."

"I'm telling you, Judith, my client made all the arrangements. He said he'd been wanting to say thank you for some extra work I did for him. I'm just passing on the gift to you. Please let me. I'll treat him to something when he's in New York. Tickets for a Broadway show, maybe. He's so rich, it's nothing to him, I promise you."

It would be a dream week for the kids, I knew that. Of course, I wished he'd made arrangements for something that he and I could do, a romantic getaway, but this seemed almost as wonderful. I imagined how excited Miriam and Evan would be. And he made it sound as if it was nothing, just like two tickets to a Broadway show. How could I turn it down? So, I accepted this gift and the kids and I went to the ranch outside Solvang. We had a taste of luxury that week, the special sort of luxury where rich people pretend to be roughing it. The cottages were furnished in designer plaids, wood laid perfectly in the fireplace, so that one match was all it took to start a cozy fire. The barn was immaculate and the horses so well trained, anyone sitting on their backs looked like an expert. Miriam called them "push-button" horses, but she was in heaven. All the riding she wanted. The trail rides, led by friendly but laconic cowboys, took us through country so magnificent, we did indeed feel we were starring in a cowboy movie.

Evan caught trout and bass in the well-stocked lake, and the ranch's chef cleaned and served them to us at dinner. In the sunny afternoons, the children swam with other guests' kids, and I read books beside the pool, uninterrupted by any responsibility. At night, there were family activities organized by the staff: line dancing, cowboy poetry readings, talks by naturalists. The most popular evening, as far as I could tell, was bingo. At this event, wealthy guests bought bingo cards for a dollar each, lining up as many as five cards in front of them. At the beginning of the night, the winner of each game got a T-shirt with the ranch logo. Later in the evening, the prizes became increasingly exciting—pots of cash, based on the money collected from the guests when they bought the cards. I learned that rich people can be very competitive bingo players, their eyes focused intensely on their multiple cards as they scanned for the number called. Idle chitchat was not allowed. These rich people wanted to win. However, one night, eight-year-old Evan won the last game, loudly calling out "Bingo!" and waiting breathlessly while the pretty young staff member checked his card and verified his win. He received a pot of nearly two hundred dollars. He was rich. For the rest of the week, everyone on the ranch said, "Congrats, buddy," when they saw Evan and he glowed.

When we checked out after the glorious week, I asked if the owner was on the property. I wanted to say thank you in person and tell him how the children had loved the place. The desk clerk looked at me, puzzled.

"The owner? There isn't really an owner," she said. "We're part of a large corporation. Based in Boston. They have a lot of properties. Resorts all over the world."

"Thanks," I said, and saw that you now lived in a world where giving gifts such as a week at an elegant dude ranch was merely a small token. You had wanted to give me this present and concocted the story about knowing the owner. I was very naïve about your world, as well as the cases you defended. Unfortunately, these were not the only things I was naïve about.

We had many idyllic weekends during those months you worked in San Francisco. Our time together that year was lovely, so uncomplicated. Until one beautiful Friday evening the next December, a warm and clear night, when you took me to a restaurant on the water. We'd begun to think of it as "our" restaurant, the staff recognizing us and giving us special treatment. We were taken to a window table. "No fog," our waiter said. "You and your lovely lady can have the perfect table for the perfect view." You smiled and looked out at the glittering lights outlining the Bay Bridge. I knew the case was drawing to a close and I knew we were both thinking about it.

"What a city," you said. "You've taught me to appreciate San Francisco. I love New York, but it's so much more livable out here. We've had a good time here, haven't we?"

When we got back to our room after that waterfront dinner, we made love and I remember thinking that all those years of waiting for you made our lovemaking now even more delicious. My eyes were beginning to close, when I sensed you leaning on one elbow and looking down at me with a serious expression.

"What?" I asked. "You look sad."

"We need to talk," you said quietly. "About Meredith."

Meredith. How shocking to hear you speak her name out loud after over a year. Why had she entered our room? I was immediately awake, my heart pounding.

"What do we have to talk about?" I asked, the sex and the red wine no longer making me drowsy. I switched on the bedside table lamp; you shielded your eyes from the sudden light.

"There's something about Meredith I haven't told you."

Meredith. Would you stop repeating her name? I had allowed myself to form no real picture of her. She was a weak, poorly defined image, a faint, insignificant presence in your life. She ran to the copier. She spoke quietly and did your bidding. She was forgettable and I had forgotten her.

"Okay," I said. "What about her?" *Please*, I said to myself. *Let him tell me she quit, left her job as a paralegal at the firm and went somewhere far away.*

"She's been sick," you said and swallowed. "She had cancer once, a few years ago when she was really young. Before I knew her. And she had to have a hysterectomy. Now the cancer is back. She's really ill."

You began to stroke my head. "Judith, I feel so terrible for her.

It's a tragedy. She has a little kid. She and her ex-husband adopted him when she couldn't have children. The dad is a real loser. He did drugs heavily. Now he's in jail and she's alone. Sick, with a small child she lives for." You looked out the window and then back at me. "Honestly, Rocket, I didn't think all of this would happen between us." You swept your hand across the room to encompass, I suppose, "all of this."

"What did you think would happen?" I asked in a whisper.

"I thought it was great, of course. That we reconnected. We were such good friends back then. I love being with you. We've always meant so much to each other. But I didn't expect to feel these feelings for you." You kissed me softly on the forehead, then over my eyes.

"I never didn't feel this way for you," I said and sat up. "It's always been the same for me. I've loved you ever since we were children. You must have known that." My hands were beginning to tremble and I was having a hard time getting the words out. I had never spoken honestly with you about what I felt and it frightened me. In the rules of our relationship, it was an unsaid agreement that I not talk about my love for you.

You winced. "No. What we have has always seemed outside of normal day-to-day life. When we're together, it's something separate and special between us alone," you said and at first you spoke hesitantly. "When we would spend hours in my room, after my mother died, it was our own secret space. The same as this room is now. Ours alone. There's no one else. Afterward, we go back to real life."

"This is real to me, Elliot," I said.

"I know, I know. But you have to remember that time in New York, when I was studying for the bar?" I saw you become more sure of what you wanted to say now, warming to your own words. You were constructing your legal argument and it was starting to coalesce. "After you and Seth traveled. You were completely strong. So independent. I think I was intimidated by you. When I watched you walk away that day back to Seth, I knew he was everything I wasn't. Fun, spontaneous. He was your real life. Not me."

"Meredith doesn't know about me, does she? She doesn't even know I exist, does she?" I asked, already knowing the answer.

"Judith, come on. She isn't like you. She's not tough and capable like you. Especially now that she's sick. Of course I've told her about you, what a good friend you've always been. I've told her I've visited you here. She knows you're important to me."

"But not that we've stayed together here in your hotel room. And that we're sleeping together," I said and made you meet my eyes.

"No, not that I've slept with you," you admitted, sighing.

Meredith was not the pale shadow of a girl you dallied with and took out to drinks after work in New York. Meredith was real. You reached to the floor and pulled your T-shirt over your head. "Judith, please understand. I have to help her. She's got no money. No insurance. She's going to have to stop working and have more surgery. She's really sick. And she's alone." You pushed the hair back from your eyes and looked out the window.

I lay back on the pillow, wanting to tell you just how wrong you were. How much I had always longed for you. I wished I could cry and fall apart in your arms. But I knew what role I was to play. I was the faithful friend. I was to support, not need you. So I scraped the spilled milk of my feelings back into the bottle. I would understand and go on with my own life, my real life, just as you'd said.

You came to San Francisco only a few more times, now staying where the other lawyers stayed, the hotel in the financial district. The verdict was announced and it was a huge win. You won the case for the important Silicon Valley firm, defeating the government's antitrust suit. Your name was in the news and I saw you being interviewed on Sunday morning talk shows. On your last visit here, you took me to a restaurant in Sausalito for a congratulatory meal.

"You'll find someone, Judith," you said that night. "How could you not? Someone as smart as you, as alive as you. Someone will be part of your life out here. I know it."

It was crazy, but I wasn't angry with you. Our friendship, amazingly, remained intact. We continued to speak on the phone about our lives and work. About the twins. Except now, every conversation ended with me asking about Meredith. How had her latest surgery gone? Did they get all the cancer? Had it spread? I even began to ask about Meredith's little boy. He had a name as well. Matthew. He was only three years old. How could I not care?

Eventually you married Meredith, maintaining that the reason was so that she and Matthew could be added to your excellent health insurance coverage. What else could you do? She had no one else.

Once more, you did not choose me. You gave your love to another woman. And, of course, I asked myself the question that any sane person would be asking. Why, after you'd treated me the way you did, did I stay around in your life? I had no easy answers, but one night, after the twins were asleep, I lay awake and remembered an incident that had happened to me as a little girl in Chicago when I was in kindergarten. Suddenly the memory took on a powerful significance. Growing up an only child, my parents had taken great pride in me—in my health and my cleverness. I was living proof that their misery in the old country was over. The bastard Russians hadn't managed to annihilate them. They'd made it to America. They had a lively, bright-eyed child to prove their existence. People even stopped my mother on the street in the old neighborhood to admire me when we were out walking.

"She looks just like Elizabeth Taylor," old ladies said and lifted my chin to study me. "A little Elizabeth Taylor with that thick dark hair. You should get her a screen test."

My mother never complimented me, or anyone else, directly. But

I could see how proud of me she was on those outings. Even when we were going on simple errands in the neighborhood, she brushed my long, shiny dark hair and dressed me in full-skirted dresses, bleaching and starching the white collars, ironing the full skirts. Somehow, she, an immigrant from an insignificant shtetl in Russia, had come to Chicago and produced this healthy American child. A child who people even said looked like one of the most popular child stars of the day.

My father treated me as his confidant, always sharing his pleasure in books, discussing politics while I sat near him on the couch as he puffed on his pipe. He'd put down his ever-present newspaper or book and tell me about what he'd been reading. I inhaled his liberal and generous view of the world, along with the sweet smell of his pipe tobacco. I felt loved in that house. It was only when I first ventured out of the house and into the neighborhood public school, that I learned how people were ranked and how a caste system for children is created from a very early age.

In the large, sunny kindergarten room, children were seated at square, wooden tables. Two boys and two girls sat at my table, one at each side of the square. Our small chairs were of the same blond wood as the little tables. I don't remember the teacher, or much of anything else about the room, except those light tables on a sea of green linoleum. The table became the site of my daily torture.

We'd hang our coats on low hooks in a cloakroom and in winter, sit on the floor to pull off our galoshes. Then, we'd troop to those square tables. Coloring, the first activity of the day, was my torment. At our table, one girl and one boy were the upper caste, and the other boy and I were the untouchables. Literally we were untouchable. The other little girl had golden ringlets, with barrettes that each day matched her dress. The boy, the favored boy, was robust and well groomed. He also had blond hair, a comb brought through his still-wet hair so that the teeth marks still showed. The girl with ringlets was in charge.

The other boy, the unacceptable one, was somewhat dirty. No one had taken care dressing him and his clothes were rumpled and mismatched. He also had the unfortunate habit of picking his nose and then, disgustingly, eating his snot. He was dreadful, and I certainly would not have chosen to align myself with this child. However, Miss Ringlets and her major domo, the neatly combed blond boy, decided that he and I were to be equally shunned and tormented.

All four of us would work quietly, heads bent over our coloring projects. The two favored children would pleasantly pass crayons back and forth between themselves, but never share them with us, clutching them when one of us untouchables would reach for a color they'd just been using—as if we would contaminate the crayon for later use. The judging came after the drawings were complete.

Miss Ringlets would look at the blond boy's paper and say, "Oh, beautiful."

The blond boy would look over at his superior, Miss Ringlets, and know what was expected. He'd say, "Yours is beautiful, too." He would stretch out the word *beautiful* to four syllables. Be-u-ti-ful.

Then the little girl would look over at the messy boy's paper. "Pee-yew," she'd say and both blond children would hold their noses distastefully. And the whole routine would get repeated as my work was considered—including the nose pinching.

They actually did consider the drawings each day. It wasn't an automatic response. I know this because one day, one miraculous day, I drew a scene of children holding colorful umbrellas and walking over puddles. I carefully circled each raindrop with a black line. Somehow, this drawing was different and the two judges looked at it with raised eyebrows. Miss Ringlets said with surprise, "That's beautiful!" And, her fellow torturer agreed. "Yes, that's beautiful," he said, using all four syllables of the word and nodding his head up and down vigorously.

The messy child got his usual, "Pee-yew."

I, usually an untouchable, was shocked. In a way, that one day of affirmation made the following days of disparagement more painful. The messy child never seemed to mind. At least the disparaging comments didn't seem to register with him. He scribbled on his paper with abandon, seemingly with no plan. When he finished, he stared out the window until the teacher released us from the tables and we were allowed to move to wherever we were going next—circle time for stories, the bathroom, outside for recess—I don't remember where. I only remember the square tables and how carefully I tried to draw a picture that might win the approval of the other two.

What was that cruelty based on? My mother, whenever subjected to a slight or snub in the old neighborhood, would darkly mutter, "Anti-Semite!" If I had complained to her, she would certainly have accused Miss Ringlets and Mr. Perfect Hair of being Jew haters. That would have been that. This was, after all, before the time when we moved to the Jewish neighborhood. Most of the children at the first school had Polish or Lithuanian surnames. It was the early fifties and there probably were a fair number of Jew-haters in that school. But I don't know what caused the rankings at the square kindergarten table. I did, however, grasp that I was not one of the favored ones. I was an outcast and I fear that all of those "pee-yews" may have made me more accepting of second-rate treatment.

Or perhaps it was that you could do no wrong, Elliot. I accepted your verdict, as I had that of the ringleted girl. Someday, if I worked diligently and persistently, perhaps the word *beautiful* might be mine. I might be the chosen one.

7

Serendipity

Meredith's cancer spread and you took care of her devotedly. Despite your claims that you'd married Meredith only to help her with health insurance, there was tenderness in your description of the day you'd married. It had been in your garden in Beacon, the town on the Hudson where you now lived. You married under a wisteria trellis, which Meredith had lovingly planted when she was still able to work in her garden. The garden was her greatest pleasure.

"A wisteria trellis," I wondered out loud. "Mmm. A stand-in for a chuppah?"

"Come on, Judith," you had answered with a laugh. "Only you, or maybe my mother, if she were alive, would think that. *Not* a chuppah. I'm not into Judaism anymore. It doesn't seem relevant right now. Just a trellis," you said with finality. "A pretty archway for the flowers Meredith loves."

I sniffed, then realized I sounded like my mother and hoped the noise hadn't carried over the phone wires across country. *Okay, call it a trellis*, I thought. *Let Elliot take his gentle gentile, the blond-haired blue-eyed girl who was sick with cancer, as his second bride.* I couldn't begin to understand it. The cancer inside this young woman was a stubborn one, and Meredith had looked unequal to the fight.

I'd met her only once, on the melancholy trip you took shortly before you married. A pre-honeymoon, you told me. You wanted to show Meredith the redwoods before . . . and although your words trailed off, I heard them anyway. Before it was . . . too late. Meredith had endured multiple surgeries, chemo, then radiation. There was nothing else left to do. You traveled while she could.

Matthew was with you on the trip, and the three of you came to my house in Berkeley for dinner. We sat around the big table I'd refinished with care, and the six of us crowded closely together on the wooden benches: Meredith and Elliot and four-year-old Matthew, as well as the twins and me. It was cozy and cheerful in my kitchen with its bleached pine planks and the bright oranges and yellows I'd painted the walls. Meredith looked up at me as I ladled the fragrant chicken soup into her bowl. She was so thin and frail, she looked like the anorexic girls I'd worked with on psychiatric wards. I could not help but stare at the bones of her clavicle jutting through her skin, and her arms, almost skeletal, resting on the table. I glanced down at my own fleshy arms. Perhaps, a very small case of cancer, I thought. The cancer diet was always a successful one, the ultimate no-fail diet. Second only to the divorce diet. But no, I had never been sickly in my whole life. Besides, wishing for cancer, even a little case of it, was a morbid, ungrateful thought that I immediately suppressed and hoped would never reach the ears of God or whoever doled out fatal illnesses. Anyway, the divorce diet had been short-lived. Slowly, all of those pounds shed after the split up had found their way back on my frame.

Meredith brought the soup spoon to her nose, inhaling deeply but, as far as I could see, ingesting none of it.

"I love the smell of homemade matzo ball soup," she said with a sweet smile. "The steam is making me warm for the first time since we arrived." She shivered and you took off your jacket and draped it over her thin shoulders. "Sorry," she said. "This fog really gets me. I can't get warm."

"They say that about San Francisco summers," I answered and

spooned a matzo dumpling into Evan's bowl, filtering out the carrots and celery, which would ruin any chance of getting the soup into him. He was a picky eater and thin and small for his age. Miriam held up two fingers, signaling me that she wanted two matzo balls, and I nodded. No such problems with Miriam, who was a hearty eater and remained a head taller than her twin brother. "Summer is the coldest time of year here," I said. "Colder than the winter." I wanted to add, *Remember, Elliot? How clear it was when we were together in San Francisco?* but I didn't. Instead, I smiled at Meredith. "August is the worst," I told her. "The fog and mist hardly ever lift. But when we go south, toward Santa Cruz, you'll see the sun. I promise it'll be warmer."

Matthew ate all that was in his bowl, then asked for more carrots, please. He was a polite child, though with his dark skin and eyes, resembled his mother not at all. Meredith had explained earlier that Matthew was biracial. He had been given up for adoption by a Puerto Rican mother and a father who was possibly, or probably, black. Not biologically related to her or her deadbeat ex-husband.

How did she get a four-year-old to eat vegetables, one who liked them so much he picked them out of his soup and ate them with relish?

"It's lovely that you'll take us to the redwoods, Judith," Meredith said in her soft, wispy voice. "I've always wanted to see them. The oldest living things on earth." She closed her eyes.

There was an uncomfortable silence. Oldest and living. Bad words coming from a very young person with a terminal disease. I sat down across from Meredith and studied her, the frail wrist that seemed not even strong enough to hold a soup spoon. She wore a filmy white dress that was too loose and looked as if it belonged to an older, larger sister. I could still see her prettiness, though; it hadn't completely disappeared with her illness. Her features were flawless: wide, set-apart eyes and a small nose and mouth. I could stare and stare at her delicate face. Someone should paint her, I thought.

"What's that lip gloss you're wearing?" I finally asked. "It has wonderful shine." The stain was a glimmery, honeyed color, a color I had been searching for forever.

"Oh." She laughed. "Just drugstore lip gloss." She leaned down and reached into her purse and took out the tube, passing it across the table to me. "Here you take it. Maybe a few dollars at the most. Nice, though. It stays on for hours and hours."

I studied it, shaking my head at how much money I'd spent on expensive lipsticks and glosses at Nordstrom. And, here it was, a drugstore brand casually taken from Meredith's purse. "Modern Mica," the label read. It was the absolute perfect color and shine.

On our visit to the redwoods, I led us on an easy loop through the trees, one that I knew Meredith and little Matthew could manage. Evan and Miriam walked ahead with Matthew, and I was proud of how one or the other took the little boy's hand when the trail grew uneven. They played with him in the hollows of the enormous redwoods, finding and hiding behind burls of wood, which jutted out from the huge trunks and were, I can think of no other metaphor, like cancerous growths on the trees. Matthew stared up at nine-year-old Miriam and Evan adoringly. The twins had sometimes mentioned to me how they wished they had a younger brother or sister. Would that ever happen? I wondered. Afterward, we rode the narrow-gage railroad, our loud ride through the redwoods, stopping and getting out at a grove of trees that the engineer said was called The Cathedral. He added that it was a popular spot for couples to get married in.

"You could get married right here," I whispered to Meredith and looked up into the trees, the sunlight filtered through the branches as if it were, indeed, coming through stained glass. The crowd had suddenly hushed, just as if they were inside a cathedral. "It's so pretty. You wouldn't have to wait until you got back to New York. Think of the effort you'd save."

You and Meredith smiled at one another and you took her thin hand in yours. I walked off and left you alone, going toward the front of the crowd where the three children stood next to the conductor, listening to his radio announcer voice. It was becoming an impossible visit, but it would soon be over. How could I hate Meredith, someone who was so deathly ill? Besides being so sick, she was also very sweet. And perhaps not as naïve as Elliot had thought. Sometimes when she was looking at me, I was sure that she knew about us, that the secrecy about our weekends in San Francisco had been unnecessary. Her gaze remained friendly, yet it was steady and penetrating, seeming to know all.

You and Meredith did not accept my suggestion to marry in the redwoods, but said your vows soon after you returned to New York, in the garden under that trellis. It was just as Meredith had planned. The leaves were beginning to change color and it must have been beautiful. But within the year, Meredith was gone, buried in the little cemetery in your town along the Hudson. Her death, not so long after your wedding, was a hard death. There had been a lot of pain, you said, and though she grieved at leaving Matthew, she wanted it to be over.

In the weeks after her funeral, you phoned me often from the house near the Hudson River. Once again, I found myself listening to your grief, consoling you through the awful period of aloneness, just as I had after your mother's death. Although you'd never been a drinker, now I heard the clinking of ice cubes against glass as we spoke.

Without your knowledge, while her mind was still clear, Meredith completed paperwork assuring that her older sister, Renata, would receive primary custody of Matthew. Renata already had two kids, close in age to their cousin Matthew. She and her husband lived farther upstate in New York. Their house was small, but there was land and woods and they could give the boy a family. On their land, they raised goats, and made goat soap and goat cheese which they sold at farmers' markets. They had a big, sloppy Australian shepherd that Matthew adored. Renata and Meredith had lost their own mother early to the same cancer that killed Meredith, and she was sure that the bad decisions she'd made in her life (namely, the disastrous first marriage to a junkie) occurred because she'd been deprived of her mother during her formative years. She'd had less time to absorb her mother's sound judgment and guidance. By comparison, her older sister, Renata, was more wise and settled. You and Meredith were alike in that—you'd both lost your mothers young. Meredith hoped that Matthew would have the mothering he needed by growing up in Renata's home. Although Renata and her husband were poor, at the time just getting by in the goat soap and cheese business, Meredith was sure Renata would be an excellent mother to Matthew, perhaps even better than she herself had been. And, with your generosity, Meredith had set up a trust fund for Matthew. His future would be well taken care of. Of course, Meredith stipulated, Elliot should be free to visit whenever he wanted, every weekend if he liked.

Meredith's decision to put Matthew in the custody of her sister devastated you. You told me you suspected that Meredith and her sister had been concocting this plan for some time, but you learned of it only after her death.

"Elliot Pine has been the best stepfather a child could want," Meredith had written, "and his love of Matthew is not in question. However, his demanding work schedule and commute to the city would be incompatible with single fatherhood. My hope is that Elliot will remain active in Matthew's life, but my sister, Renata, and her husband, Jake, are the most able to assume full-time custody of my son." (Meredith's first husband, now in prison for selling cocaine, had terminated his parental rights.)

Losing Matthew so soon after Meredith died made the house even more desolate. You had tried hard to be a good father to the boy. It seemed to you that you'd failed an important test you didn't even know you were taking and did not understand how Meredith had deemed you unworthy of caring for her precious child. You thought of contesting her will, but when Matthew ran from your car after you brought him to Renata and Jake's place, excited to see his cousins and the dog and the farm animals, you gave up on that idea. For months after Meredith's death, you rattled around alone in the house, trying to maintain the garden and making frequent trips up the Hudson to visit Matthew.

A bit more than a year after Meredith's death, I arranged to go to New York, a Thanksgiving trip for me and the twins. For Jewish children, watching the Macy's parade on television is a non-threatening, non-Christian way to imbibe holiday spirit. No baby Jesus or even Ave Maria. Just marching bands and colorful floats and Santa Claus at the end. Just as I had done as a child in Chicago, the children would get up early on Thanksgiving morning and, while I cooked, watch the parade on television from start to finish. Evan loved the floats and the fantastic balloon characters, while Miriam adored the horses prancing in rhythm. I scheduled the trip so that we could watch the holiday parade in person, and I did my research, thoroughly, as usual, and found a very nice hotel on the west side right along the parade route.

The trip across country with the eleven-year-olds had gone well. What a pleasure it was to travel with them now, each able to carry their own backpack of things they wanted for the plane, me finally no longer responsible for crayons and books and snack crackers. It was bitter cold when we walked out the doors of JFK and the children squealed when they felt the first gust of freezing air, huddling around me as I found a cab to take us into the city. They didn't complain, though. The cold was part of the adventure.

There was also real pleasure for me in avoiding the holiday back home. If it was Seth's year for Thanksgiving (holidays and birthdays with the twins had been carefully and equitably distributed in the divorce settlement), I attended someone else's dinner without the children. However, this meant certain loneliness. I felt their absence acutely. The chatter around the table and the abundance of food felt hollow without Miriam and Evan, my family, at my side.

The years when I did have the children for the holiday weren't much better. I drove myself mercilessly, feeling that as a single parent I needed to incorporate every tradition that would make the holiday memorable for the twins. Perhaps I needed to do it to excess in order to make up for the fact that no father was at the table to carve the big, golden bird. So, on the days preceding the dinner, I dragged two long folding tables in from the garage. I placed white, freshly ironed cloths on them and set up to twenty-five places, a number that completely filled the narrow living room. It felt important to fill the house to overflowing and to pile the coats on my bed, just as my parents had done in their apartment in Chicago on holidays.

I'd prepare far too many of the recipes I'd encountered on super-market magazine racks—cranberry biscuits from scratch, green bean casseroles that were not sullied by canned soup filler, fragrant orange and apricot and almond stuffing for the turkey, and perfect *x*'s carved into the chestnuts before roasting. Afterward, at midnight, when I was alone in the kitchen, and exhaustion filled me as I rinsed glass after glass, I wondered whether the effort had been worth it. Would the children remember, in years to come, that their turkey had been preservative-free? I doubted it. I wished for someone to be at my side as I cleaned up in the now empty and messy house that I'd spent days cleaning. I didn't want help with the dishes. I just wanted someone there to talk about the evening. Had there been enough side dishes? Was the turkey moist enough? What about the seating arrangement? Did everyone have someone to speak to? Oh, how I wanted to process the evening with a partner. And then, I wanted to fall into bed with that someone and have exhausted, thankful sex. It was done, I'd made another elaborate holiday meal, and now it was time for me—to be stroked and appreciated and caressed into sleep.

I am embarrassed to confess how many times I did allow some not very appropriate man, a guest at the dinner, to stay after the Thanksgiving celebration. Ostensibly, it was to help me clean up. But the real reason was to push away the loneliness and exhaustion. These men were not allowed to stay the night, of course. They could not be there when the children awoke. And, I rarely saw them again.

It would be a different Thanksgiving for this year. Honestly, I told myself, it wasn't to console a lonely Elliot Pine. When Evan had been very small, he'd called the city Une Nork. That was how we always referred to it—even decades later when Evan lived there himself and his sister, Miriam, had children of her own. We're going to Une Nork, the twins excitedly told their friends and their dad. To see the big parade and, maybe, snow. They were too old to believe in Santa Claus, but there was still a thrill as they thought about Santa at the end of the parade, the elves throwing out candy to the crowds gathered on either side of the street.

My parents were disappointed when they learned that I was going to take the children across country on a plane, but not bring them to Chicago for the holiday. I suppose it was a little selfish of me. There was no question that they were getting old—my mother's Russian accent seeming to reassert itself more than I remembered and my father spending increasing hours reading at his spot on the couch, paying less attention to both his wife and the world around him. I would visit them with the twins soon, I promised them and myself. But not this Thanksgiving.

We spent the day in front of our hotel. The music of the flutes, the sunshine reflecting off the tubas—everything was laid out before us almost close enough to touch. When we got cold, we'd run inside and ride the elevator up to our room on the eleventh floor. We'd warm ourselves a bit, watching the parade from our window so we didn't miss anything, then go back down again to the street. We had cups of delicious cocoa all day, followed by bags of warm chestnuts and peanuts. For dinner, instead of turkey, we had chicken noodle soup and bacon, lettuce, and tomato sandwiches from the hotel coffee shop. It was perfect, a memorable day, just as I'd hoped. The kids would not forget it.

Later that night, when they had well and truly fallen asleep, I studied their eleven-year-old faces in the stream of moonlight coming through the hotel room window. Serious Miriam, her need to organize and direct was as powerful as my own. She had thick brown braids and a splash of freckles across her nose. She looked like a child of the American prairie, just like one of the characters in the Little House series she adored. Tomorrow, we'd go skating at Rockefeller Center. But first, I promised her we'd look at the horses at the Central Park stables. Miriam was a sensible and efficient girl, never shirking a chore or a responsibility. She always drove herself hard, my daughter did. I was glad that there was this one thing, her passion for horses, that made her so euphorically happy. Within ten feet of a horse, she softened and visibly released her tense shoulders. The worry wrinkle between her brows relaxed.

Evan, on the other hand, was all nerves and feelings. He was disorganized and unfocused. Week after week, I found unfinished homework at the bottom of his backpack, some problems penciled in, but never removed from its hiding place. Evan was clearly bright, but because his work was often missing, he brought home low Cs or even Ds. The parade had been exciting for Evan, but the homeless people outside our hotel and the beggars who leaped out at red lights when we'd come by taxi from JFK had affected my sensitive boy. Occasionally, he got upset stomachs from tension, and I hoped this would not be a night when he woke with one. In the moonlight, I pulled the blanket over his sleeping frame, watching as his fingers and legs twitched, the nerve endings still firing and reacting to the day's excitement. He was five inches shorter and twenty pounds lighter than Miriam. Were there ever twins less similar?

When I organized the trip, I hadn't wanted to appear pushy. Was it too soon after everything you'd been through? Meredith's prolonged illness and excruciating death? Then losing Matthew as well. But I needn't have worried. When I called to tell you of my plans to bring the children east over Thanksgiving—okay, perhaps harboring just a few thoughts of cooking for you and rescuing you from a lonely holiday—you told me you were thrilled. What a wonderful idea, you said. Maybe there'd be snow. There was sometimes snow in New York in November. Had Evan and Miriam ever seen snow? Then, after a brief hesitation, you told me you had news. You'd met someone. You were at the beginning of a new relationship with a woman. "Now you two can meet," you said. "You're going to love her. She's fantastic."

Lillian ran a gallery on the main street of Beacon. One Saturday, still carrying a cup of coffee you'd picked up down the street, you wandered into the gallery for no particular reason. While you were staring at the art, not really seeing any of it, she came up behind you and took the paper cup out of your hands.

"No eating or drinking in the gallery, please," she'd said in her precise diction. "Everyone thinks they won't spill, but you would be surprised how many accidents do happen. I'll keep your cup up front for you." And she walked away holding the still-steaming cup.

You turned and stared after her as she walked off with your coffee. You told me you had never seen anyone so extraordinary looking. She had long, almost black hair that cascaded in unruly curls down her back, and she was wearing a short, puffy skirt, like a ballerina's tutu, with purple tights under it. From the back, with her tiny frame, you might have thought she was a very young girl. But her face was not that of a young girl. She was beautiful, but obviously not young. You walked to the front of the gallery, following the trail of steaming coffee. Later, you said that you'd always associate the smell of strong coffee with Lillian. It was a fortuitous association, as one of your great obsessions, much more than wine or hard liquor, is coffee. You could talk blends and roasts until I wanted to take you by the neck and throttle you.

"Shut up about coffee," I once screamed during one of your endless lectures on the stuff. "Enough. Coffee is coffee and the only thing that makes it tolerable is two cubes of sugar and a healthy dose of cream." I, myself, have always been a tea person, but of course, Lillian loves coffee and brought her own Gaggia Classic espresso maker to the relationship. (You reported this to me with reverence. "A Gaggia," you repeated, as if talking about shares in a gold mine.)

I looked at my watch. It was ten o'clock. Too late to phone you. I'd wait until the morning. Tonight I would enjoy the stillness of our room and listen to the soft breathing of my children as I looked out at the street below, quiet except for street sweepers still clearing away the debris from the crowded parade route. I tried to imagine your home in the Hudson Valley, a longish train ride from the city. I still thought of you as a city person, and couldn't picture you anywhere else. I almost couldn't picture you at all. We hadn't been alone since the day after the verdict was announced in Circuit Court, decided in favor of your client. At our celebratory dinner in San Francisco, at the old place on the water, you were jubilant about your victory, but there had also been regretful looks. You said you'd always wonder what might have happened between us if things with Meredith had been different.

"No different, Elliot," I'd answered.

"Don't say that, Judith," you said. "How can you know what might have happened?"

"I think I do, Elliot." I put one hand over yours and with the other picked up my cup and finished the last drops of coffee. I had a long drive across the Bay Bridge back to Berkeley. On the way home, it occurred to me that I was an addict. An Elliot addict. I told myself that if I ever hoped to kick my habit, I would have to stop re-addicting myself with these visits. I knew then that I was a junkie and was appropriately disgusted with myself. I also knew enough about addiction to realize that I would have to be ever-vigilant if I did not want to face a relapse. Relapse happens more often than not, I'd learned in graduate social work school.

Now, a year after Meredith's death, had anything changed? You were in a house somewhere up the Hudson with yet another woman. I should not have been surprised. Elliot Pine would not be alone long—I must have known that. Lillian was five years older than you. Five years! Back then, at forty, a woman being five years older than a man sounded like a huge gap. My goodness, that made her well into her forties. She was middle-aged, probably couldn't even have children anymore. You sang her praises in conversation after conversation. Lillian was independent and accomplished. She had turned a little frame shop into one of the most successful art galleries on the Hudson. She hadn't much formal education past high school, but she was practical, efficient. It drove me crazy. Obviously, the woman had bewitched you.

In the morning, when I finally phoned your house, your new girl-friend answered on the first ring. I tried for a breezy, natural tone, but I heard myself sounding stiff and awkward.

"Hello," I said. "Uh, you must be Lillian."

"This is Lilly. May I help you?" Not Lillian, as you had written. Lilly. And she had an accent. Was it French? You also had not mentioned this.

"Ah, Lilly. Sorry, I thought it was Lillian." I spoke softly into the telephone on the nightstand, stretching the cord as far as it would go, almost to the bathroom, hoping not to wake the kids quite yet. "This is Judith. Elliot's school friend from Chicago. Did he mention I'd be in town?" I asked. "With my twins?"

"Oh, yes. Certainly he did," she said, warmer now. "Of course he spoke about you, Judith. I'm so pleased you've called. And Elliot will be, too. I'll get him for you now. You two can make plans. I look forward to meeting you and the children very soon."

She was efficient and confident. And with a sexy French accent.

You picked up the phone. "Rocket! You're here."

I caught my breath. As soon as I heard it, your deep, resonant voice always made me tremble. When I planned this trip, I'd imagined it quite differently. I thought we would spend time together, have fun taking the kids around the city. I hadn't expected that you would be with a woman. Already. Perhaps I'd opened a small window of hope that with you widowed and me divorced, there could be something between us. Silly me. Silly addicted me. Nothing. Was. Different. You'd met someone new, and I again was your confidant.

In the past weeks, you had confided a lot. For the first time, you were unsure of yourself with a woman. Lillian, as you referred to her (*never* Lilly), was so completely self-assured, she had you worried. You learned that much of the social life of town revolved around Lillian and her shop. It showed how very isolated you'd been, caring for Meredith, that you'd not met her until that day you walked into her gallery. Every party, art event, and interesting person in town was involved with Lillian. Why would she want you? you wondered.

Why, Elliot? I thought, as you spoke. *Because you are warm and lovely. You stupid ass, because you are gorgeous and your hair does this careless thing on your forehead that makes every woman alive want to brush it back out of your eyes.* I said none of this out loud, of course, but just listened as you worried over every word you and Lillian had exchanged. You sounded like a lovesick adolescent. You sounded like me.

"Did I tell you she's been sculpted by a very famous artist who lives in town?" You mentioned a name that I did, indeed, recognize. "It's a life-sized bronze nude. Right in the town square. Public art. You definitely know it's her, though, after you've met her. Everyone knows it's her—even though the face isn't really defined. Her body is so distinctive, with that tiny frame and those big breasts. The way she holds her shoulders back and tilts her head up. The pose is like a Degas ballerina, but you know it's Lillian. That first day, when she walked away from me with my coffee, I realized she must be the woman in the sculpture. I've seen that statue thousands of times—every time I come to town for coffee or the paper. And now, there she was, alive and walking in front of me, her head tilted up in just that way, her behind round and so full."

You actually said these things to me. Oh, Elliot, could you enjoy torturing me this way? Always it was someone else you rhapsodized about. Someone with perfect features. Or someone who made less trouble for you and laughed more and demanded less. Someone fragile who needed you in a desperate way, as Meredith had. Now, it was Lillian, a woman whose body was so extraordinary it inspired public art. Did you assume it didn't hurt?

"Come visit us, Judith," you were saying now on the phone. "Why are you in a hotel? There's lots of space in the house and the train ride is only an hour. We can go tobogganing with the children. Remember how much fun we had sledding in Chicago when we were kids?"

"I don't know, Elliot. We've got so few days in the city. And they've never been to New York. There's so much I want to show them. Museums and shows. Tomorrow I thought we'd go to Central Park. And then ice-skating at Rockefeller Center. They've never been ice-skating, can you believe it?"

"God, remember how we skated at River Park?" you said. "When they'd freeze over the swimming pool in the winter? There was always a fire in the potbellied stove. We'd go every Sunday in the winter, didn't we?" you asked. "You were such a good skater, Judith. We'd clear a little space behind you so that you could skate backward. I never could do that. I'd skate facing front, like we were dancing, holding your hands while you were going backward, and we'd go all the way around the rink. You never fell. You were amazing."

"I'd forgotten that. I wonder if I can still stay upright now." I laughed. "We'll see tomorrow, won't we? But I might be too busy holding up the kids to find out." It was a surprise to hear you say how I danced so gracefully on the ice. That you remembered it.

"Let's all go to dinner after you skate," you said. "We'll come into the city. You'll need somewhere warm after being out in the cold all day. I'll ask Lillian where we should go. She raised three kids in New York. She'll know where to take you." I heard you shout the question.

"How old are the twins?" she asked from the depths of the house.

"Ten," you shouted back. "Or are they eleven already?" you asked.

"Eleven," I said.

"Well, there's only one place to go, of course," I heard her reply. "Serendipity."

"Of course," you said cheerfully into the phone. Had I ever heard you sound so jolly? "Lillian picked the perfect place. Serendipity. They make this thing called frozen hot chocolate. It's delicious. They've even got peanut butter frozen hot chocolate."

"They'll love it," I said. "I'm sure of it. But can we get something solid into them first? Do they serve real food?"

"The best hamburgers in New York. Seriously, the best," you answered.

The following days in New York were as perfect as the first. Blue skies, but still cold enough so the snow remained clean and white, piled high where the snowplows had pushed it. The kids bounded out of bed, chattering about the horses and ice rink they were going to see. We dressed in our warmest clothes and boots. I was pleased I'd splurged on a soft red cashmere coat. I loved its black velvet collar and the way the coat flowed around me prettily. I checked the twins for gloves and hats and scarves. Getting dressed back home was easy compared to this.

First, we went to the stables in Central Park, and Miriam got permission from the barn manager to pet as many horses as she liked. I watched her touch the horses' thick, elegant necks and put her face up to their long noses, feeling the manes brush against her skin as she breathed in their smell. It was an elixir to Miriam. I understood that even the odor of fresh horse excrement becomes sweet when you're an equine lover. The horses were gentle, charmed by Miriam, as horses always were. She spoke to every single one, about forty, each boarded in a clean, well-kept stall, covered with immaculate winter blankets that fit perfectly over their backs and buckled nicely under their bellies. Miriam inhaled deeply, the barn odors filling her and transporting her, as they always did.

Evan was calm and kind to his sister that day, showing none of his usual impatience and frustration. He also liked horses, but with nowhere near the passion of Miriam. He busied himself examining the brass name plates attached to each stall's door—on them was engraved the horse's name as well as its owner's information. Below the name plate was a small chalkboard with special instructions written in Spanish. Evan liked pronouncing the elegant names, reciting each in what he imagined was a lordly English accent. These Central Park horses weren't called Charlie or Dolly or Gordon, as were the comfortable quarter horses we knew back home. Instead, the well-bred East Coast thoroughbreds had names like Medina and Chatham of Hudson Valley. The chalkboards said, "Alfalfa solamente por favor." And Evan recited this out loud, too, rolling his *r*'s. He liked speaking Spanish, all languages, really, and his teachers at school said he had an excellent accent. He was a born mimic, that boy. When I wasn't wanting to strangle him because of all the trouble he got into, he could make me laugh like no one else in the world.

We went to the skating rink next. I gave the children a lesson and, using choppy little steps, they each made it all the way around the rink a few times. Then, the California children they were, retreated inside to warm up with the large crowd gathered near the stove. I stayed out on the ice and went around and round, losing myself in the music, and, with my red velvet trimmed coat softly flaring behind me, was pleasantly surprised that I could still skate with such ease. My blades cut into the ice with long, gliding strokes and I felt young and healthy. When I looked up, I saw that Evan and Miriam had come back outside and were standing behind the barrier, watching me.

"Want to go around with me one more time?" I called, as I skated by.

They both shook their heads, but solemnly kept following me with their eyes. I went a bit faster, showing off for my children, and every once in a while, I looked over and saw that their small heads were tethered to me as if with a string. Finally, the music stopped and an announcement came over the speaker saying it was time to clear the ice. The Zamboni, decorated like a turkey with big feathers attached to its back end, was ready to roll onto the ice in order to smooth the nicked surface. I made my way off the rink with the others. Evan and Miriam were waiting for me. They had already returned their skates and put their winter boots back on.

"Wow, Mom," Evan said. "You're good. You looked pretty dancing on the ice."

"Thanks, hon. When I was growing up in Chicago, we skated all the time. It's even colder in Chicago than here, so there's lots of places to skate. If we lived in a cold climate, you'd probably be playing ice hockey now, Evan," I said. "I think you'd like ice hockey." I sat on a bench and started unlacing my skates.

Miriam stood in front of me and stared down at me with a puzzled look. "What's up, sweetie? What are you thinking about?" I asked her.

She shrugged, then said, "I thought I already knew everything you could do, Mom. Like your job and cooking and reading tons of books and driving us where we have to go. Stuff like that. I didn't know you could ice-skate."

It almost seemed to upset Miriam that she had to move the images in her mind in order to make room for a new picture of her mother.

I shrugged. "I'd forgotten about it, too. But Miriam, there's lots about me you don't know. I had a whole life, don't forget, before you and your brother were born." I reached up and smoothed a thick brown braid.

"Like what?" she asked, leaning away from my hand fussing over her hair. "What else about you don't we know?"

Here was a dilemma. Of a lifetime of thoughts and feelings and experiences and joys and sorrows, what would I tell my dear daughter?

"Well," I said and stood to return my skates to the rental counter, "I'm also a pretty kick-ass roller skater."

We went down into the subway and got off at East Fifty-Eighth, then walked in the dusk to the address Elliot had given me. There was a long line of people waiting outside Serendipity, and I knew that Miriam and Evan were cold and tired and hungry. I hoped I hadn't pushed the twins beyond their limit. Then I noticed you, waiting in front of the restaurant, stamping your feet against the frigid weather. You were wearing a handsome black leather jacket with a long scarf wrapped around your neck.

"Over here," you shouted when you spied us. I grabbed a child's gloved hand with each of my own and ran toward you. You bent and enveloped both the twins in a huge bear hug. "You found it! Good job, guys. Wait, let me get a picture." You took your camera from your pocket and snapped a shot of the kids and me in front of the Serendipity sign. "Okay, let's go inside. You must be freezing." Then you hugged me as well, squeezing me against the buttery smooth leather of your jacket. "Lillian's already there, holding a table." We moved ahead of all the people in line, and as you held the door open for us, I looked back and gave those people an apologetic smile.

It was dark inside, the antique tables were oak and the chairs curly, bent wood. The only light came from the old-fashioned Tiffany glass lamps, which sent rainbows of color onto the tables and walls. You led us through the crowded restaurant to a back room.

"Lillian," you called out, "they're here."

I saw a woman sitting alone at a big table. I couldn't take my eyes off her. Several inches of thin gold bangles encircled both arms and large gold hoops were in her ears. She wore a leopard print jacket, obviously but boldly fake. When she stood, I saw that the plush jacket ended mid-thigh and that she appeared to have nothing on under it other than sparkly black tights and boots that ended a bit above her knee. On me, the outfit would have seemed a trashy ensemble fit only for Halloween. Yet, with her long, thick hair cascading down her shoulders, and her tiny frame, Lilly looked fabulously put together, someone who turned heads.

Before we left on our trip to New York, I had explained to the children that Elliot's wife, Meredith, who was still his girlfriend when they'd met her on the visit to the redwoods, had died. They'd known Meredith was sick and I think I gave them a rudimentary explanation of cancer. Then, on the subway that afternoon, I had told them that we'd be meeting Elliot's new friend Lillian. They hadn't asked many questions, so I'd left it at that.

As soon as we sat down, Evan looked between you and Lillian and then asked, "Where's Matthew?"

You picked up a glass of water.

"The boy whose mother died?" Evan persisted. "How come your little boy didn't come today?"

There was silence. How could I have neglected to explain to the children that Matthew didn't live with Elliot anymore? To children, other children are the main story. The adults are there only to provide the children with an escort. Elliot, even Lillian, was of little interest to Evan, but the little boy, Matthew, whose hand he'd held through the redwoods and sat next to on the narrow-gage railroad, was who he was anticipating seeing. I think my son was especially interested in seeing a child whose mother had died. Evan was very concerned about death. Up until then, I don't believe Evan had known anyone whose mother had died. There had been a child in his class at school whose much older father had had a fatal heart attack. But losing one's mother seemed more catastrophic, and sensitive Evan had obviously given it a fair amount of thought. Perhaps he wanted to see how Matthew was surviving this loss.

Miriam sat next to Lillian. She had politely asked permission first, and was now stroking Lillian's fluffy leopard jacket and staring longingly at her numerous bracelets. But when she heard her brother's question, her hand paused in midair and she looked over to you, the wrinkle between her brows appearing again.

After a too-long silence, all three adults at the table spoke.

"Matthew's having a little visit with his aunt now. Right, Elliot?" I blurted out.

Lillian looked at Miriam and said, as if she hadn't heard Evan's question, "Would you like a few of these bangles? I've got far too many on, don't you think? I never seem to remember that less is more." She started to remove a few bracelets from her arm. "You're a sensible girl, aren't you, Miriam? You'll remember, I'm sure."

You slowly unwrapped the scarf from your neck, carefully folding it, and then said, "Evan, I'm so sorry Matthew's not here. This is actually one of his favorite restaurants. But before his mom died, she decided he should live with his aunt Renata, his mom's big sister. She has kids and a lot more time to take care of him. But seeing you here today, I really wish I'd brought him." You put your hand on Evan's shoulder and you two looked at each other sadly.

"Yeah," Evan said to you and nodded, "that sucks. I bet you miss him. How come she didn't want him to live with you?"

There was again silence at the table. Lillian was still methodically sliding bracelets onto Miriam's small wrist.

"Lillian," I said, "you don't have to do that. They'll probably slip off and get lost. And Evan, I think that's enough questions."

"No, Evan," you replied, "you ask really good questions. I've asked that same question myself. More than once. But, I finally decided that moms know best, and so I had to accept her decision."

Evan continued to stare up at you while Lillian kept adding bracelets to Miriam's arm. My daughter looked down at them, mesmerized.

"Really, Lillian, that's enough," I said, too firmly, and put my hand over Miriam's. Lillian stopped the bracelet transfer, but not before she'd taken three or four more gold bangles from her arm.

"You're great with children, Lillian," I said, hoping for a friendlier tone. "Elliot told me you have kids."

"Oh, yes," she said and shook her head. "All off on their own now. I'm through with all that, thank goodness. And, dear souls that they are, I must say it's a relief to have the quiet house we have." She cocked her head and looked at you. "Right, darling?"

"You don't think about more?" I asked.

"God, no," Lilly answered. "I'm much too old. *We're* much too old."

"Old?" I said, looking from one to the other, but of course the question was for you, Elliot. "I don't think any of us would be considered old, by today's standards. People our age have children all the time."

"So," you said and picked up a menu. "Enough of this discussion. Lillian, you have to understand that Judith thinks no one can be truly happy unless they have a pack of kids running around."

Lilly looked over at me and said, "Then I suppose we'll just have to enjoy the grandchildren when they come along, won't we, darling?" She shifted her gaze to you again.

"Yep," you said, right on cue. "But now I see some very hungry Californians. How about some burgers? Your mom said she wants you to have something healthy before we get to the specialty here. The Frozen Hot Chocolate."

"Oh, what the hell," I said and put down my own menu. "Let's get dessert first. Then, if we have room, we'll order something healthy."

The twins' eyes widened. This was definitely new behavior for their mother. "Dessert first?" Miriam asked dubiously.

Lillian looked up at me and smiled. "What a clever idea," she said and called the waiter over, ordering the special Frozen Hot Chocolates for the adults and two peanut butter–flavored ones for the kids.

After the desserts arrived, you and I began talking about travel. Earlier that year, I'd gone to an international child welfare conference in London. I'd been selected to represent my state organization of social workers. Since you knew London so well from your Fulbright days, we chatted about what I'd seen and which neighborhoods I'd explored. The children were engrossed in their wide mugs of the sticky, sweet drink, which was just about the best thing I'd ever tasted. The kids obviously agreed. But I noticed how restless and bored Lilly looked. She didn't touch her cup, but stared off in the distance while you and I spoke about London.

"Lillian," I said, anxious to include her, "you must know London as well. Did you visit often from France?"

"France?" she said, tossing back her hair. "I've never been to France. Or London. Or anywhere, really, besides New York."

I was confused. "But your accent. I assumed you were from France."

"Certainly not," she said. "I'm from Canada. From Montreal. I suppose my accent sounds French to some people."

To stupid people, was she saying?

"No," she repeated, "I have never been to Europe. We were very poor growing up. There were nine children in our family. Sometimes in the winter we had to choose between food or firewood. There was no money for trips or luxuries like that. I went to work when I was sixteen—I didn't even finish high school. New York is the farthest I've been from Montreal. Maybe someday, I'll take a vacation. See Europe. Who knows?" She waved her hand, making the remaining bracelets jingle.

"You will, sweetheart," you said and took her hand. "We'll go to London and Paris together. You'll see those places. When both of us stop working so hard."

"Perhaps," Lilly said, and shrugged her shoulders, as if travel was frivolous and silly and didn't matter at all to her.

Then you said, as if you hadn't noticed her shrug, "Lillian, you would not believe how many places Judith has traveled to. Kids, did your mother ever tell you about taking a ferry between islands in Indonesia? Or, how she lived in a grass shack on a river in Fiji?"

The children barely looked up from their frozen peanut butter hot chocolate treats. Those places Elliot mentioned, Indonesia and Fiji, I'm sure the twins had no concept of what he was talking about. They could have been suburbs of Chicago.

"Really," you persisted. "Judith's been all over the world. Evan, Miriam, get your mom to tell you some travel stories. She's had amazing adventures. She was really something." You looked at me with admiration, but the twins barely lifted their heads. It had been a long day and besides the sugar overload, their minds were overloaded as well, unwilling to take in much more. I felt embarrassed, like a kid whose parents are boasting about her, but no one wants to hear the stories. Yet, the parents insist and keep bragging, even though no one is listening and everyone's boredom is apparent.

"It's okay, Elliot. To them, I'm just Mom. Someday, I'll tell them travel stories. Today they saw me ice-skate. That was shocking enough. I'll tell them about my hippie life only when they're too old to do those things themselves. I'd worry if they did half the things I did."

You laughed. Lilly looked at me with one brow raised, as if I were an item on the menu she'd overlooked.

"So you were a hippie," Lilly said. "You were a hippie, too, Elliot?"

"Not really," you answered. "I only rebelled for a year or two at Brown. Then I thought I had to be more responsible. Be important and achieve things. I missed out on most of that. No fun for me once I became a lawyer. Judith is the one who had fun in those days."

"Well, Elliot," Lilly said. "Perhaps you and I will be hippies together someday." She smiled and moved closer to Elliot, then looked into his eyes, speaking softly, her sexy French accent, even if it was Canadian, more pronounced than before. "We will learn to be irresponsible together. We will teach each other, my dear."

I took a sip of my frozen hot chocolate, then carefully wiped my lips with the napkin. Cold food on a cold night. Who'd thought of such a ridiculous thing?

8
Sensory Fulfillment

I saw your infatuation at Serendipity that night, the look in your eyes as you drank in Lillian. Once again, I had to accept that not only was my timing lousy, but that you had not chosen me. A widower, you were neither alone nor bereft. I was tired of my Elliot addiction. Any junkie has to hit rock bottom before recovery. And, that night at Serendipity, I did. While I could not understand your infatuations, either with Meredith or Lilly, I do not remember being asked for my approval. Instead, at forty, there was the discouraging sense that life was passing me by. My future, I told myself firmly, did not involve Elliot Pine. I would stop waiting for you.

The children and I lived on Milvia, a street near the UC Berkeley campus brimming with children and their conscientious parents. I saw couples everywhere I looked—walking dogs, packing their children into cars, even bickering in the park. Although I loved my cozy, family neighborhood, it was like being at a dance without a partner. But what were my options? I couldn't be a hot, single woman going to the latest club. I was not hot, for one thing, and that was not what I wanted. I was a mom. Marnie, my neighbor and closest friend, who was always politically correct, said, "Judith, of course, you're a family—you and your kids are every bit a family." She played that popular album for her children and mine, *Free to Be . . . You and Me*, which contained cute ditties about families coming in all sizes and compositions. But this seemed like crap. I did not feel like a real family, no matter what Marnie, or even Gloria Steinem, might say. I thought about that antique three-legged table I'd spotted in a window of the resale shop on Shattuck. Sure it was lovely, and it appeared stable; but when touched, it wobbled precariously on its delicate tripod base. I ached for a conventional table—one standing solid on four legs: Mom, Dad, two kids. We, Evan, Miriam, and I, were a three-legged table. Keeping this table from wobbling was exhausting.

Well-meaning as my parents were, their weekly calls from Chicago did not help. "What will become of them?" my mother asked in one form or another. "Children of a broken home? Twins, besides. They need a father, Judith."

"Don't be so dramatic, Mom, my home is not broken. We have a fine family," I'd firmly answer, wishing I could echo my friend Marnie's eloquence on the subject. Yet, inside, I felt my mother was right.

"How are you managing?" my father asked as soon as my mother finally passed him the phone. He always worried that we were on the brink of starvation. "We could send you a little money each month."

"We're fine." I reassured them both, knowing they didn't have a lot left over to send me. I put on a brave front, never admitting to them my sadness or fear and that since the divorce from Seth, I often lay sleepless at night.

I hated single motherhood from the inside out—from the loneliness in my bed at night, to the way I imagined the children and I looked when we ate out at restaurants on Saturday evenings. I was sorely aware that there was no man either to bed me or to get the check. I was always in a state of heightened alertness, fearing that something was left undone. Had I checked the car's tire pressure? Were Miriam's forms for summer camp complete? Did I change the batteries in the smoke detector? So much to do and no safety net if

I forgot. My few forays into dating had been brutal, leaving me even more discouraged afterward. My insomnia got worse.

Then, one afternoon outside the co-op market, I met Walter Kahn, a man also longing to put a family together. A late bloomer, he was a man who'd had his head down, concentrating only on achieving great things in his field, physics. He'd been so single-minded and passionate about physics, he forgot anything else. First school, then more school, and then work. Suddenly, at forty, he lifted his head and noticed that everyone around him—his few friends, his colleagues, his cousins—was married or getting married. He'd received seven invitations to weddings that year. Walter wanted a home, a wife and children, but realized he had no idea how to make that happen.

He began with the easiest task and purchased his first house. It was on Milvia, not far from my own. I'd noticed him a few times before at the food co-op, the slow, deliberate way he shopped, picking up items and carefully reading the backs of packages. One day, we went through checkout and reached the exit at the same time.

"You look as overloaded as me," I said as he held the door open for me with his body.

"Yeah," Walt said. "As usual, I probably bought too much for one person. Do you live close by?"

"About three blocks down," I said, juggling the weight of my bags. "You?"

"Just one block over. Listen, what if we walk to my place and unload the groceries? Then I'll help you carry your bags to your house."

I hesitated just a second. "Sure. Sounds brilliant. But you're not a serial killer, are you? I always tell my kids not to talk to strangers."

"No, just a boring physicist. At Lawrence Livermore. My name is Walt Kahn and if you're worried, you can wait outside my house while I unload my bags."

He had a nice smile, and as we walked, I told him about the twins, but made sure he knew I was single. He told me about buying his house just the previous month and how much he liked the neigh-borhood—especially the food co-op that he'd discovered stocked his favorite things from back east.

"Like what?"

"U-bet chocolate syrup, for one," he said. "Can't live without it."

When we got to his place, he asked if I wanted something to drink, and I left my bags in the entryway and followed him inside. On the way to the kitchen, I looked around curiously. The house was furnished entirely in shades of brown. The carpeting was a medium brown, the sofa, a massive corduroy monstrosity, was upholstered in a deeper brown, and through an open door, I could see that his bed was covered in a brown tweed spread that looked scratchy to the touch.

"Wow. That sofa is huge," I said, smiling.

"Yeah," Walt agreed amiably. "They just delivered it. It looks bigger here than it did in the store."

"Must have taken a lot of brown fabric to cover it."

"My theory of decorating is to stay monochromatic," Walt said. "I'm not very good with colors, so I figure it's better to stick with just one. Less chance of screwing up."

Using the same reasoning, he told me he dressed entirely in brown—avoiding sartorial accidents. He was, indeed, wearing brown from head to toe. Shirt, belt, pants, socks, and shoes. Later, when I knew him better, I opened his closet door to see nothing but rows of brown polyester trousers and a collection of brown polyester shirts. He owned a single sports coat, camel hair with brown leather elbow patches. The jacket would have been quite lovely, had it been tailored and not hung so loosely on Walt's narrow frame.

Very soon after we began dating, I found myself itching to remodel: to re-carpet in a lighter shade, to reupholster the clunky corduroy couch, and to shop for a soft, but masculine bedspread (I finally settled on a paisley—much later, of course). I also dreamed of making a big bonfire with all the browns in his closet—imagining the satisfying curl and then sizzle as the polyester burned.

"I hate to shave," he told me one night, rubbing his hand along the tight curls on his cheeks. "My skin is sensitive. Such a waste of time—there are so many more important things to think about. It just grows back again and then you have to do it all over."

"Mmm," I said sympathetically, thinking how I would research electric razors and present Walt with a top-of-the-line model that would not irritate his skin. A nicely trimmed goatee, preferable to his current unruly, reddish-colored beard. Despite all these renovation and remodeling plans, from the beginning, I found I enjoyed kissing Walt quite a lot, even when he still had the bristly beard.

And after three months of seeing him regularly, I appreciated even more. I liked his quirky humor. He made witty puns and jokes. He knew the words to every Gilbert and Sullivan operetta, which were favorites of mine as well, and would loudly sing the lyrics in a deep, round voice, as he got ready for work in the morning. I also realized how much I had grown to enjoy the patient, methodical way he made love to me, reminding me of the way he carefully examined groceries in the co-op, although perhaps more tentatively. He seemed to find it a gift to be allowed to merely examine my naked body, let alone have sex with it. I began to imagine a future. At first the twins found Walt's quietness awkward—it was such a contrast to their noisy and exuberant father—but soon they got on well together. The bond between Walt and Evan grew first—when he began to teach my son chess.

"You're gifted, you know? You have a real talent for the game. You've caught on quicker than anyone else I've taught," Walt told Evan, folding his arms across his chest as he pondered the board between them.

Evan looked pleased; the chance to excel at something apart from his sister was intoxicating. There was soon a permanent game in my living room, and both considered their moves on days when they didn't see one another. As soon as Walt arrived, Evan would steer him toward the chessboard, excitedly ready to resume their play. For Evan's enthusiasm alone, I would have married Walt.

He also won over Miriam. Although Walt had never been on a horse, and said he had no plans, ever, to sit astride one, he stood patiently at my side and watched Miriam at horse shows, never complaining as the competing riders went up and over the same jumps, again and again. There is a lot of repetition at jumping shows. At these events, Walt even found a comfortable way to banter with Seth, who was often there watching Miriam as well. Walt would slyly poke fun at my ex-husband's insufferable bragging (the new Corvette, the expensive wristwatch), without Seth even comprehending he was being teased.

"Those are some boots you're wearing, Seth. Do you think you could tell me where I might find a pair?" lanky Walt would ask with deadpan sincerity.

I choked back laughter. I could no more see Walt in cowboy boots than in a Stetson cowboy hat.

"Oh, these," Seth answered and stood a bit taller. "I get these custom-made in Houston. You've got to get custom-made boots if you want a decent fit."

Walt nodded and, with a serious face, borrowed a pen from me and wrote down the name of the boot maker.

We began seeing each other most nights, and when Walt worked late, he'd call from the labs to say good night. I got used to the routine, to his quiet and considerate ways.

One Sunday we were, as usual, standing at a fence watching Miriam compete. This horse show was at the Alameda County Fairgrounds, a dusty, treeless place. Walt cleared his throat. "So, have I mentioned that my parents are coming for a visit?" He looked distinctly uncomfortable as he spoke.

I turned to him. "No, you haven't said a thing. When?"

"Tomorrow," he answered and looked down, tinkering with the long telephoto lens he always carried to Miriam's shows.

"Tomorrow?" I repeated. Then an unpleasant intuition flickered across my consciousness. "Walt, you've told them about us, right?"

Instead of answering, Walt began following the girl who was in the ring. She was jumping her small brown thoroughbred. Miriam had taught him that the number of strides a horse took between jumps was crucial. Too many, and the horse would come up short, too close to clear the jump cleanly—usually knocking down one of the rails. Too few, and the horse would end up dangerously far from the jump and have to awkwardly catapult itself forward to get over. Walt was a good student and he began counting, just as Miriam had taught him, nodding his head with each of the horse's strides.

"You haven't, have you?" I persisted. "I bet you haven't mentioned there's a woman in your life. Do they even know my name?"

Walt sighed and stopped his absurd counting. He turned his head toward me. "Judith, I'm not sure how they're going to accept you."

"Why? What's wrong with me?" I asked. "I'm a nice girl, right? Won't they be pleased you've found someone you're happy with? Jewish, even."

"Yeah," Walt said, looking more miserable. "To me, you're perfect. But I worry about how they'll react."

"To what?" I asked, indignantly.

At this moment, Miriam appeared in the ring and began to jump her horse over fences. We stopped speaking and watched as she had a perfect round, clearing every hurdle. We both applauded enthusiastically as she left the ring with a big smile on her face.

"React to what?" I repeated.

"To you being divorced. To the twins."

"Jesus, Walt. You're forty years old. Did they expect you to be dating a virgin?"

He laughed, but I saw the beads of sweat on his forehead. "Judith,

I'm sure they think *I'm* a virgin. I know my parents and, though I hate to admit it, a divorcée with two kids is probably not what they imagined for me."

"God, that's an ugly word. Divorcée."

"You're right, it is," he said. "You're much more than that. A wonderful mother and a talented social worker. You help people every day. There're so many things to admire in you. But frankly, I'm worried about their reaction. Maybe we should wait until the next time they come out here for you to meet them. I'll begin to drop a few hints this time."

I glared at him, my eyes widening.

"No? Bad idea?" Walt muttered. "Okay, let me think about the best way to do this." And he brought the camera to his face again.

An only child like myself, Walt had told me about his adoring parents—perhaps too adoring. The Kahns didn't find it odd that their son was forty and had never had a serious relationship. He'd gotten his doctorate, then become a well-respected academician. He traveled frequently, presenting at conferences all over the world: Istanbul, Calcutta, Rome. By the time I met him, Walt had authored over fifty papers and was already receiving awards from his colleagues. Mr. and Mrs. Kahn, an older couple from New Jersey, were Holocaust survivors who worshipped their son as a miracle of the new world's triumph over Europe's desire to snuff out their life—a belief shared by my own immigrant mother about me, her only daughter. But unlike my Russian mother, they were German-Jewish snobs. I suspect they thought there was plenty of time for Walt to have a woman's admiration. What was the hurry? They weren't through admiring him themselves. And could there possibly be a woman adequate for this task?

Eventually, I convinced him to bring his parents around the following Saturday evening. They could come for dessert and coffee and see my house and the children. They wouldn't fail to be impressed with the charm of my cozy California bungalow, I assured him.

Everyone loved its cheery warmth: the bright colors I'd painted the walls, the old pieces of furniture I'd rescued and sanded. Miriam and Evan had lovely manners. I knew I could be proud of how they'd behave to Mr. and Mrs. Kahn. I'd make my famous rum cake. It drew rave reviews every time I baked it. Starting with a rich yellow cake, I poked holes with a toothpick up and down its sides and top. Then I drizzled a luscious rum and butterscotch concoction over the whole thing, making each bite a moist and sweet shock to the senses. I was the consummate *balabusta*. Of course the Kahns would approve.

I was overconfident. Besides the coffee and cake on Saturday night, I also persuaded Walt to schedule a Sunday brunch at a nice restaurant in Berkeley. Just the four of us. First, I'd drop the kids off at Sunday school, then we'd meet and chat over bagels and lox. Reluctantly, Walt allowed himself to be swept along with both of these enthusiastic plans.

Poor Joe and Anna Kahn were incapable of joy, let alone the admiration I'd unrealistically expected. The charm of my house, with its brightly colored walls and crafty furniture, was lost on them.

"I don't know how you live with such colors," Mrs. Kahn said, when I gave her a tour that night. "It would give me a headache to live here. Myself, I like neutrals. More restful." She actually shielded her eyes with one hand when she said this.

"Where did you find these chairs?" Mr. Kahn asked, before he sat down.

"Oh, I picked them up at Goodwill," I cheerfully replied. "Then I did a few repairs and, *voilà!*"

"They're strong enough to sit on?" he asked.

Worse, my beautiful twelve-year-old twins seemed to offend Mrs. Kahn. They ran into the living room, then over to Walt, surrounding him, both demanding his attention.

"Walt, you have time for a game, tonight?" Evan asked hopefully. "I got this new chess book from the library. Can I show it to you?"

"Sorry, buddy. We're going to stay in here with my folks, but we'll catch up in the next few days," Walt replied.

"Walt," Miriam said, "that bleach treatment I concocted for the horse seems to be working. His hooves look a lot better."

"Great, Miriam. I knew you'd get it under control," he said.

The fact that there were two—a tall, already maturing girl and her smaller, impatient brother—must have seemed excessive to Anna Kahn, and I saw her recoil from the children. She looked from one to the other: at Evan, hopping from foot to foot, his quick gestures punctuating his long, wordy descriptions, and then up at Miriam, with her somber gray eyes and sleeveless blouse, its shirttails tied rakishly just below her pubescent breasts, leaving her midriff exposed (the latest style at the horse barn).

"They're twins?" Anna asked, her forehead wrinkling, when the children had left the room. "They look nothing alike. They have the same father?"

I was startled at her rudeness. Walt came to my rescue.

"Ma," he said, "of course they have the same father. They're fraternal twins, not identical. I told you Judith was divorced from their father. You know that fraternal twins don't have to look like each other."

"Excuse me," Anna said, looking into her purse for a tissue, "Mr. Fancy Doctorate of Physics. I didn't know. I haven't got all your degrees."

"Anna, please," Joe said, putting his palms up in front of his body, as if to deflect the conversation. Incorrectly, I interpreted this as Walt's father's defense of me and the children.

"Would you like some more cake?" I asked Mrs. Kahn and tried to smile.

"No," she said and held out her cup. "Too sweet. But maybe you could add some boiling water to my coffee. It's very strong."

This began many years of Anna Kahn correcting the flavors of my food. Too strong. Too sweet. Too salty. Too much. One Passover, I came up behind her in my kitchen and, horrified, saw her sprinkle a generous tablespoon of sugar over the tray of gefilte fish I'd prepared for the Seder. She watered down most things, from the finest coffee to expensive cabernets from Napa. Don't get me started on the topic of my mother-in-law and watering down. To me, her taste buds were illustrative of her reluctance to experience strong flavors in life. Tepidness, not just moderation, this was her preference. I wished myself to be more charitable toward the woman. Perhaps this was due to Anna's experiences during the Holocaust. What could I know of that? Yet, Anna's ways irritated me, and I could not help blaming both Anna and Joe for Walt's taciturn personality. In the end, Anna and I made peace, but there were many years of hell before that happened.

Brunch the next day was even worse than the evening before. I had mistakenly thought Joe was my ally. He'd seemed to enjoy the yellow rum cake and had complimented the kids on the trophies in their rooms. But I was wrong. After dropping the children at Sunday school, I drove to the restaurant and dashed over to the Kahns' table. I beamed at Walt's parents as I slipped into the semicircular booth.

"Sorry I'm late. The twins' bar and bat mitzvahs are coming up," I said, and leaned over to Walt, giving him a peck on the cheek, but getting no kiss in return. "It's getting intense," I chattered on. "I had to arrange for tutoring with the rabbi. They can't miss a single class now, there's so much to learn. They're fairly motivated, but it's hard to keep up, with all their sports and homework. I hope you'll come out here for their big day." I stopped, finally, and took a breath. I looked around at the faces at the table. "It's going to be a great party," I added, my good cheer slowly evaporating.

Walt and his parents were sitting in silence. No one was looking at anyone else.

"Everything okay?" I asked Walt, then turned to Mrs. Kahn. "Getting used to the time difference?"

She didn't answer, but said, "They go to Sunday school? Like the *goyem*? What's wrong with Shabbat? That's when Jewish children in New Jersey study."

"Soccer," I said, feeling the chill at the table. "Kids out here have soccer on Saturday. They all play. Most temples have school on Sunday to accommodate sports."

Mrs. Kahn sniffed and all three, Walt and his parents, picked up and studied their menus.

Finally, Joe broke the tension and put his menu down. He waved the waitress over to our table.

"Give me an omelet," he said. "A Denver omelet. Firm. Hold the ham. How about you, Anna?" he asked.

She shrugged, as if she had no interest in what she ate.

I began several conversations at the table that morning. None worked. Finally, I gave up and ate in silence, as everyone else was doing, but I grew increasingly furious with Walt. How could he hang me out to dry like this? Couldn't he rescue me and find *something* for us to talk about? But Walt offered nothing. He ate a few bites, chewed each one thoroughly, then after swallowing a sip of coffee, put his cup down with a clatter.

"Okay, Judith. Let's go pick up the kids. I don't want to get stuck in the carpool line." He stood.

I turned to him with confusion. I had just spread cream cheese on my bagel and was about to take a bite. But I put it down and wiped my lips with the napkin. "Okay, sounds good. Bye, Mrs. Kahn. Mr. Kahn. Thanks for breakfast. I'm sure I'll see you again before you leave." I gathered my coat and stiffly walked out to the parking lot, following Walt.

When we got to my car, I turned to him and glared. "What the hell? Why didn't you talk? You let me chatter like an idiot and never said a word."

"Just get in, Judith. Let's get out of here. I'll drive," he said, and grabbed the keys from my hand. Walt drove in a way I had never seen him do before—angrily speeding and changing lanes and accelerating crazily after a light turned from red to green. I may look tough, everyone says I do. But I become very frightened in the face of such male rage. I can't explain it—my father was gentle and soft-spoken. Yet, when I am in the presence of the kind of seething, boiling rage that Walt was showing, I fold. Could I be the cause of Walt's fury? I wondered.

When we got close to the synagogue building, there was still an hour until the kids were dismissed. Walt pulled into a spot and dropped his forehead to the wheel.

"I'm so sorry, Judith," he finally said, the anger gone, his voice discouraged. "They've been on me since last night. For hours and hours. They started in again this morning as soon as we got to the restaurant and kept going until you walked in. I couldn't take any more of it."

"About me?" I asked in a small voice. "They've been on you about me? They don't like me?"

He nodded. "My father was brutal. He's really a bully, Judith. You haven't seen that yet. It's why I've always been so quiet. When I was a kid, he yelled so much, he scared the hell out of me. Later, he wanted me to be a doctor, a real doctor, not a PhD. He couldn't understand why I wanted to go to Berkeley. Wasn't NYU good enough? Why not a doctor? A *medical* doctor? He'd shout and slam doors and stomp through the house. I hope never to be like him. The opposite. He starts to rant and eventually everyone around him has to shut up and listen. He expects to always get his way. Even with my mother. When he gets like that, she tries to calm him down, but almost nothing works. It's as if every slight he ever received, every humiliation he suffered back in Germany, all of it boils over and he can't stuff it back in."

"What did he say?" I began rubbing the back of his head. I felt I could actually see a headache erupting within his skull—like in a cartoon bubble.

"He says he doesn't trust you. That you'll leave me. You're never going to have kids with me. The twins are already too old and they'll resent me. I'll never be Evan and Miriam's real father. I won't be anyone's father. My mother says you're after my money. She called you a gold digger. It was vile."

I swallowed. "Do you have a lot of money I should be after?" I asked.

Walt looked at me, then barked a short laugh. "That's what you want to know? You don't care about any of the other things they said?"

"Well, I'm not leaving you any time soon. I'm really happy. Why would I leave such a good man? I already had one bastard of a husband who constantly made me wonder why he didn't come home at night. I know a good thing when I see one. You'll come home at night. I knew that as soon as we met. And, babies. You've never mentioned having kids. I actually wouldn't mind having another baby." I stopped rubbing his head and looked out the window, my heart beating. Walt had not asked me to marry him, let alone have a child with him.

When I finally turned back to him, I saw a shocked look on his face. "You wouldn't mind having more kids? I assumed that with the twins so old, you wouldn't want to start again," he said.

"I love kids," I said. "But only one more, I'd think. Three kids are enough. Four is excessive. Unless I had twins again. But the likelihood of that is small. Right? I mean statistically." I stopped rambling and licked my dry lips. Walt hadn't spoken. I went on. "So, that just leaves us with the fortune hunter question. *Do* you have a lot of money I don't know about?"

He looked at me a long few minutes, and when he finally answered, there was a big smile on his face. "As a matter of fact, I do. My father invented a few things. He sold some patents to Dow. One was an antifreeze which worked really well. It's left me with a big trust fund. I'll probably inherit a bit of a fortune when they're gone. Not that I'd know what to do with a fortune." He shrugged. "You see how I live. All in brown. And I never buy anything I don't absolutely need."

"Poor baby. You obviously need someone to help you with that," I said and pulled him toward me in the front seat and kissed him deeply, which is how the kids found us when they rapped on the passenger-side window.

"Mom. Walt. Stop it," Miriam hissed, her mouth barely moving. "Someone will see you."

"Yuck," Evan said, a look of horrified disgust on his face, as if he might vomit right there on the street.

We married less than a year later. It was a lovely Jewish ceremony, more modern than my in-laws were used to, but, to their credit, Joseph and Anna smiled throughout. Gratitude was among the panoply of emotions both Walt and I felt on our wedding day. As we were pronounced husband and wife, we joyfully clasped hands and smiled at one another, finally brought out of the cold and into the warmth of coupledom.

My own parents flew in from Chicago, taking their first airplane journey. I was embarrassed at how much their relief showed. They fawned over Walt, barely letting him out of their sight.

"Such a wonderful son you have," I overheard my mother saying to Anna Kahn.

"Yes, we're extremely proud of him," Anna answered, not bothering to return the compliment by saying something nice about me.

Who could blame my parents for their relief? They'd had such concern about me and their grandchildren. Now, they had a son-in-law with a doctorate. Okay, he was not a *real* doctor, but he was Jewish and gainfully employed. Most importantly, he seemed so genuinely fond of Miriam and Evan and they of him. My mother and father watched with approval all during the party, held in a private room of

Walt's and my favorite restaurant in Berkeley. Walt had even agreed to spend part of our honeymoon at a family dude ranch, not the one in central California that you, Elliot, had paid for a few years earlier, but one in Wyoming. Miriam glowed with anticipation, even though we'd told her that we were going to the ranch not only for horses, but also because of the excellent hiking and mountain biking trails. Walt was an avid bicycle rider and hoped to get Evan interested in the sport.

"Don't even think about putting me on a horse, Miriam," Walt warned her. Miriam swore a solemn pledge that she wouldn't dream of it.

But as we left the wedding reception, I overheard Miriam whispering with one of her friends. "I talked to the head wrangler and he said they have a perfect horse for Walt. A mare. Super calm. She won't give him any trouble at all."

I shook my head, knowing Walt adored Miriam and would probably be unable to resist her. She was a zealot, having a firm conviction that everyone would be happier on a horse. And, of course, my new husband, the bearded city boy, did join her several times for breakfast horse rides in the crisp early morning Wyoming mist. "Miriam," he said, rubbing his seat, "you owe me. I expect you to be ready this afternoon, on your bike, when Evan and I go out before dinner."

I was officially excused from all rides, either two-wheeled or four-legged, because I was in my first trimester. This pregnancy was lovely. My doctor had given me permission to lie in the sun reading through the stack of books I'd packed. Walt pampered me and I felt very queenly relaxing on the chair in front of our cabin. I was still and centered despite the noise and activity all around me.

I wore a beautiful silver maternity dress to the twins' bar and bat mitzvah celebration, which had been postponed for a few months because Walt's father, Joseph, died shortly after that Wyoming honeymoon. He had a massive stroke at home in New Jersey, and Walt and I and the twins arrived only two days before his death. As we stood by his hospital bed, I studied Joseph's face. He was in a deep coma, but there was a serenity in his expression that I'd never before seen. All the anger and belligerence was gone.

"Now I'll get wrinkles," Anna said softly.

"What do you mean, Ma? You have nice skin," Walt said, putting an arm around his mother.

"Joseph always told me that sex keeps away wrinkles. Now, I'll get them," she explained and turned away, a single tear slipping down her admittedly smooth cheek.

I could not have been more surprised. I had never before heard stiff Anna utter the word sex. I could not imagine those two locked in a carnal embrace. But then, what do we know of other people's bedrooms?

We named the baby Joseph, of course, after his grandfather. Anna doted on him, showing a tenderness I'd not seen in her before. She visited us often from New Jersey and, to my surprise, grew proud and fond of the twins as they got older. On her visits, I'd sometimes arrive home from work to find Anna in the kitchen with Miriam and Evan, all three having tea and talking comfortably. The twins actually seemed to like their step-grandmother and, to my amazement, told me how funny she was.

"Funny?" I repeated, never having found my mother-in-law in the least bit funny.

"Yeah. Like today. You should have heard her when she was talking about Joey's pre-school teacher. She called him a *fagele*," Evan said, getting the Yiddish just right, as usual his mimicry of accents flawless. "She's hysterical," Miriam said. "She did an imitation of his walk." Miriam demonstrated Grandma Anna's impersonation of Joey's sweet, but effeminate teacher—swaying hips, bent wrist. I was appalled, but didn't make an issue of it then, relieved that my mother-in-law and the twins were getting along. I'd have to have a talk with the twins later.

Some things never changed, though. Once I interrupted Anna as she was preparing Joey's oatmeal—she was vigorously shaking salt onto it. From the beginning, we had never understood each other's flavor preferences. It seemed we had been born with wildly different sensory wiring—never agreeing on what was too loud or soft, what was sweet or sour and what was bright or pale. When she realized that I was staring at her as she shook salt into the oatmeal for Joey's breakfast, she stopped, scraped the mess into the sink, and shrugged.

"Sorry," my mother-in-law said. "It seemed like it needed something."

So much about that too-short marriage to Walt was right. We lived together in a bubble of safety, imagining it would go on forever. I look back with such fondness on those untroubled years when Miriam and Evan were young teenagers and Joey, the child Walt and I had together, was still small. We sold our houses on Milvia in Berkeley and bought a beautiful old house in the hills with a glorious view across the bay to San Francisco. We kept the house's large stone fireplaces and high ceilings, but modernized the kitchen and baths. Those were busy years; we both worked hard and the children kept us exhausted, but there was nothing real to worry about. Walt and I finally had the family we wanted. The table no longer listed to one side. It was a sturdy four-legged table, and then when Joey was born, thirteen years younger than his older brother and sister, it added only more stability. No wobbling at all.

But there were only to be those six brief years with Walt. I remember our marriage as the idyllic island Walt rowed me out to after the turbulent storms of my younger years: Seth's infidelity, our subsequent divorce, the scrimping and saving. The loneliness of being a single mother on a street full of families. Dining alone. Sleeping alone. Then, the respite was gone. For Walt was diagnosed with cancer in his mid-forties, already metastatic when discovered. This illness left few survivors, and the oncologist could not look us in the eye as he delivered the bad news.

"The expectation is one to five years," the doctor said. He hadn't wanted to tell us this, but Walt insisted. He thought he wanted all the information laid out before him and would not stop asking the doctor questions.

"One to five years in what percent of people?" asked my husband, a man of numbers. He had always found consolation in facts and figures, and I suppose he thought it would be true with this as well. But this was his own body he was asking about. Not some theoretical problem. I wanted to run out of that room and search out a bathroom somewhere in this medical complex. I wanted to find a bathroom and lock its door, then pound the tile walls and howl. But I forced myself to stay at Walt's side, expressionless, while he forced the grim reaper oncologist to recite the horrifying statistics.

"Ninety-five percent of those people with your diagnosis live one to five years. A few live even less, months. Some, even fewer, have been recorded to live longer than five years."

Walt finally stopped asking for numbers. They were brutal and provided no consolation at all. When we returned from the oncologist's office, he silently climbed the stairs to our room and began to get his affairs in order. Methodically, Walt went through papers, made sure all was as it should be. He wanted to organize his files, make our finances easier for me to understand, before he got too sick. He wouldn't talk about his anger or sorrow or fear. Except for one night, when tears rolled down his cheeks and he said, "Too short, it's been too short." The survival statistics revealed that Walt was in the minority—the people who did not make it one year. In a matter of just five months, he was gone. He'd organized his papers with meticulous care, but there was so much I did not and would never understand.

I remember how loved and completely accepted by Walt I was. There was nothing he wanted to change about me, while I was forever trying to fix things about him: his brown wardrobe, his bushy beard, his quietness. Why wasn't I more content with what we had? I had my moods, strong emotions both high and low, while Walt was so calm. At times, his calm maddened me, yet provided a safety net I took for granted. When he was gone, I desperately wished I hadn't always been trying to redo him, as if he were a home renovation project.

For example, there was the way he smelled. I have always had this inordinately powerful sense of smell, like that of an animal. I walk into a room and can tell you what was cooked two days before. I can sniff out a child's damp bathing suit shoved under the bed where it is about to get moldy. And, I am drawn to some people's smells, but not to others. Unfortunately, I just wasn't drawn to Walt's smell. I wasn't attracted to it. Don't get me wrong, I loved him. I really did. It wasn't a marriage of convenience; it wasn't the money. I really loved Walt and I loved our life and I wanted to love Walt's smell.

I tried. It wasn't a bad smell, not at all. Walt was a clean, almost fastidious person. I told myself that it was an interesting smell, complex and perhaps possessing a lingering hint of the science labs he worked in. I even concluded that this was the smell of intelligence. Intelligence is quite sexy, isn't it? Why else do they say the brain is the most sexual part of our body? Walt's IQ was off the charts. But Walt's smell never caused the seismic shudder I craved.

Eventually, I thought of a solution. A renovation of sorts. I went to the men's section of a large department store in San Francisco. There, I tested as many men's colognes as the patient salesman allowed me to sample. I tried to describe what it was I was after. Woodsy, but not herbaceous. Citrus, but not sweet. The salesman sprayed cologne after cologne on thin balsa wood sticks and waved them under my nose. He sprayed his own wrists—back and then front. He sprayed my wrists. I sniffed coffee beans after sniffing every few brands, the salesman saying this would act as a cleanser for my sense of smell. After two hours in the men's fragrance department, I chose a very expensive brand from a famous designer. It had a musky, woodsy smell. I kept a bottle in Walt's and my bathroom and replaced it every year so that it would always be fresh. I encouraged Walt to use it liberally, but not excessively, whenever we went out. I packed it when we traveled. I let Walt know that when I sniffed that cologne, it put me in a very good mood—an obliging mood. And though I could lean into his neck and say, objectively, that I found it a sexy smell, never did I become dizzy with desire.

Do I mean that it didn't attract me as your smell did, Elliot? Because from the time we were children, I'd always loved your smell. When I was with you and inhaled deeply, that smell went right through me and intoxicated me. Honestly, it made me dizzy. It didn't matter if we were in the dark, whether we were indoors or out. Your smell filled me with desire—even before I knew to call it desire. In particular, if I smelled your neck, the crook of your neck right under the jawline, I became weak and started to tremble inside. Damn you, Elliot. After Walt died, I never wanted to smell your smell again. Was I being punished? I wondered. Because I had not appreciated Walt, had wanted more, had wanted you, was that why he was taken away? I know now that there is no reason these things happen, at least nothing that makes any sense. But in the weeks and months after Walt died, lacking any other explanation, I decided that when we do not appreciate a gift, it is taken from us.

9

Being Seen

One night, in the early 1980s, a few years before I'd married Walt, I hired a sitter for the twins and drove over the Bay Bridge at dusk. I arrived early at the Herbst, the beautiful beaux-arts hall on Van Ness, so I'd get a good seat. Two of my favorite writers, a husband and wife, were appearing as part of a series sponsored by the Friends of the Library. The lights dimmed and a host of a local public-radio show enthusiastically introduced the writers. The audience applauded wildly. The married couple were attractive, even more appealing in person than in their respective book jacket photos—two of which I held on my lap. The man sat down, crossed his long legs, then raked his fingers through his thick blond hair. His jeans, faded, but with a carefully ironed crease, were sexy and tight. His shoes looked expensive and stylish. The wife, tall and willowy as her husband, wore a demure jersey dress that covered her knees and, while proper, showed off an excellent figure—full breasts and slim hips. She was dressed as any number of the women in the audience were, many of whom were surely librarians or teachers. However, the writer, with her long, brown hair and flashy gold hoops in her ears, was much prettier than anyone I saw in the audience. She was the picture of serenity, not in the least self-conscious in front of the overflowing crowd.

During the couple's prepared talks, and even more so in the

question and answer period, a nasty taste of jealousy began boiling up within me. This ugly emotion was visceral—I felt it rise through my body, from my gut and then spilling into my throat. As I watched those two on the stage, I saw their beauty and imagined their marriage. They were perfection—this husband and wife—both successful writers. Before they answered questions, they glanced meaningfully into the other's eyes. Each time one spoke, they leaned toward the other, her posture ramrod straight, his a careless slouch. As they decided who would take the next audience question, a small nod was exchanged, followed by an ironic smile. Their smiles reflected a private world, unspoken words. *What are we doing here, on this stage, in front of these hundreds of people?* the look seemed to ask. *So silly. A colossal waste of time.* They made me think that despite their full household of children (for they had six between them) and the astonishing literary output of both, they would still prefer to be alone, in their bedroom, where really hot sex and an endless riff of scintillating conversation awaited them.

It was just too much. Christ, they finished each other's sentences. They even confessed that they passed their work back and forth, sometimes adding or deleting words as they read from each other's novels or stories.

How I wished to be looked at in such a way. I was still alone, divorced for some years and had not yet met Walt. True, Seth had sometimes finished my sentences, but, unfortunately, only with his own opinions. If he did see me, it was at the beginning, when I was still his groupie. I had hung on his stories back then, watched as he mesmerized people, recounting adventures one after another. When I'd tired of these stories, we drifted apart and he looked for new admirers. Being married to Seth was a young woman's game. It was exhausting providing the admiration he needed, even more so after the twins were born. The fish he speared scuba diving were bigger than anyone else's, the cars he drove faster. When, God help me, he became enamored with guns, he boasted that, in a disaster, he'd be safe at home, where he kept an arsenal and food to last a year. Seth certainly did not see me in the way I craved, the way that famous writer had gazed at his wife.

Although most, including me, would agree that my second marriage was happy, still no one finished my sentences. Walt adored me, but often I could tell he was pondering a problem from work. At times, he was so distracted by his thoughts, he neglected to even finish his own sentences, let alone mine. We were so different. I know that many things contribute to making a good and satisfying marriage, and that Walt and I had most of them. Still there was that longing I felt to be seen: to have my innermost thoughts and emotions affirmed.

When we went to bed, Walt fell asleep almost immediately. He was a sound sleeper, light snores coming within seconds of his head hitting the pillow. Although I understood his tiredness, for he left for his job at the lab in early morning, and worked very long hours, I was aching for companionship. One night, after we made love, I was again left lying awake in the dark. How could this man fall asleep so quickly, truly as soon as his head hit the pillow? Frustrated, I punched and repunched my pillow. I switched on the light atop my bedside table, for nothing woke Walt once he was asleep, and read until my eyes burned, but was still unable to find sleep. It was not that Walt was a selfish lover. Just the opposite, he was a careful and considerate man, in bed as in every other aspect of his life. Yet his lovemaking was tentative and he was unwilling to experiment. I blamed his fastidiousness, as I usually blamed all our differences, on Anna and Joseph. He'd been utterly controlled as a child, not allowed to get dirty or make a mess. It had been a childhood of inviolable rules. If he lay down on the couch, Anna was immediately there to put a towel under his feet. (He'd already removed his shoes, but even socks were not allowed to touch the furniture.) Sex, like everything else for Walt, had a protocol. It drove me crazy. After a couple of hours of this restlessness, I switched off the light, threw the covers back, and got up, my thoughts as dark as the stairway I descended.

The rooms below were lit by moonlight as well as the twinkling lights from San Francisco in the distance. I was barefoot, wearing only a thin cotton nightgown, and could not stop shivering. In the dark, cold house, for the thermostat was set low at this time of night, I made my way to the sofa and wrapped myself in the knitted blanket I kept in the living room. I stared out the big windows, still shivering uncontrollably. Usually, the lights of San Francisco seemed beautiful, but that night, the view in the distance increased my loneliness. The world seemed too far away, human companionship unreachable. I so desperately wanted to talk, but Walt was usually tired and not interested in going over the day. The concept of pillow talk was foreign to him. I wanted to lie in bed, telling long, slow stories, voices hushed, until, later, much later, perhaps after sweaty sex, we drifted off to sleep—our awake selves gradually melding into our dreaming selves. But, alas, Walt sometimes fell asleep as I was still speaking. Remember that joke? About men having only two speeds: on and off. Walt was just such a man.

When we did talk, it was invariably about the kids—Evan and Miriam, and later Joseph, the child of our early middle age. The twins still visited Seth on alternate weekends, but then the baby was born and Walt and I rarely had time alone. Even when we did steal moments away by ourselves, it was usually the kids' needs we discussed. Sometimes we considered household purchases and occasionally we talked about our jobs, mine at Alameda County Social Services and Walt's at the lab. But my unscientific brain only skimmed the surface of understanding Walt's research, while he admitted it was hard to keep the stories of the many children in my caseload straight.

We were partners, to be sure, and I am positive that I loved Walt, but I did not feel the understanding at my core that I craved. The real me was not seen or heard. Was I unhappy? Fortunately, those moments in the dark in the middle of the night did not come often, and I'd been single for so long before meeting Walt, I knew what being alone really meant. I'd learned by then that the quiet comfort of companionship in bed and at the table is worth quite a lot.

But that night in the dark, I had treacherous thoughts. I could not explain the way I saw the world to Walt. When I shared my most intimate ideas and passions, he often looked at me, puzzled. I wanted to discuss the latest award in literature, or the music that inspired me, or to analyze the people we'd invited to our house for a dinner party. I wanted to take apart, scene by scene, the movie we had just watched. Walt's world was simpler; he saved complexity for the knotty problems he solved at work.

Did Walt feel misunderstood? Unseen? To all appearances, he did not. My husband seemed genuinely delighted with our union. I'd asked if he felt frustrated because he could not share his life's work with me. After all, he was an important scientist who regularly published in journals and presented papers—papers I did not hear or read, knowing how little I would absorb. We had friends of a scientific bent, and with them I heard him speaking animatedly. I'd smile at the excitement in his voice. I was pleased to hear my normally sedate husband speak with such passion, yet disappointed that I rarely heard it in our own conversations. Certainly he could not tell me about the research questions he was currently investigating. After the first sentences, I'd feel my eyes glaze over. I couldn't even formulate a question worth asking about his research. It was people who interested me. I asked questions about the people he worked with, but rarely about the work itself.

"Marlene, the biochemist, is she married?" I wondered one day after he told me about a meeting at the lab. I always asked who'd been at the meetings, not what the meetings were about.

"Marlene? Married?" I saw Walt puzzling over my question while he continued to carry dishes to the sink. "I'm not really sure. Wait. Yes, I think she said 'we' when she came back from vacation this week."

"Oh, she's been on vacation?" I asked enthusiastically and stopped rinsing the dishes. Marlene was Walt's colleague, a brilliant woman who'd gone to MIT before she'd begun working at the labs. Walt mentioned her frequently through the years, although I'd never met her. "Where did 'they' go on vacation?"

"Hmmm," Walt said. He stopped clearing the table and stared out the window, pondering this question. "I don't believe she said. I'll ask her tomorrow if you like," he added agreeably.

"No, it's not important," I answered, all the while thinking that I could not imagine working with a colleague for five years, as Walt had with Marlene, and not know whether she was married. Or where she had just taken her vacation. But then, I had no idea what my husband and Marlene *had* been talking about in the meeting that afternoon. For all I knew, their meeting could have consisted of fucking on the conference table. I turned around and studied Walt as he methodically sponged off the counter, covering each inch, not missing a spot. No, they had not been doing that. One of the reasons I had married Walt was precisely because I knew he would not be making love to other women in covert places, as Seth had done more than a few times during our marriage.

I cannot proceed without revealing the dénouement of the story about the literary couple I envied at the San Francisco lecture. Some years later, I read shocking news about these writers. The paper reported that the husband had checked into a cheap motel near their bucolic home in New England. There, he had placed the barrel of a shotgun into his mouth and pulled the trigger. This suicide occurred the night before the very day the district attorney was to charge the writer with heinous crimes: sexually abusing his own and his wife's female children. The couple had been separated for some time before his death, yet even after his suicide, the still-beautiful wife refused to speak publicly about these events. She had reportedly been the one to accuse the writer of abusing their daughters, but after his death, she never spoke of it again. She was the real deal: the same elegant, imperturbable woman I'd seen on the stage nearly two decades before. But the marriage was definitely not what it seemed.

Despite this unfortunate evidence that we cannot understand nor truly know what goes on in other people's marriages, my hunger persisted. Does anyone get seen? Is this desire for understanding a fantasy? Like Goldilocks, I'd whined—too hot, too cold. Had I ever come close to this recognition? Who does, anyway?

As a girl, I had felt truly seen by my father. Not surprisingly, I'd worshipped the man. I'd come down the hallway late at night when I was a teenager—knowing he'd probably be awake, reading his newspapers. As he talked about the state of the world, I'd stare at his handsome profile, illuminated by the light of the table lamp next to him. He'd hold his unlit pipe and poke the upraised paper with it while he read one story or another aloud to me, exasperated at the stupidity of our country's leaders—Eisenhower, then Nixon (how venomously he hated the Republicans. The only time I saw him weep was when Stevenson was defeated the first time by Eisenhower).

I'd listen to his ranting, until, eventually, he'd finish with politics. Then he would ask, more gently now, "And you, Judith? How are those *momzers* treating you at school?"

"School's okay, I guess," I said one night when I was fifteen, troubled, but not knowing how to begin. I didn't realize then that *momzer* was a curse. It meant bastards. My father never swore in English, but both my parents sprinkled colorful Yiddish phrases into their speech. Even if I didn't know their meaning, the words always seemed completely appropriate.

"Your teachers?" he asked.

"My teachers are good this semester," I answered, looking down at my hands. "We're reading *A Tale of Two Cities*. I like Dickens."

"Good." He nodded from behind the paper. "Dickens was a great writer. He exposed truth. Made people see what they wanted to keep hidden." Even though he kept turning the pages of the paper, I knew, somehow, that I had his complete attention. He was waiting, always knowing when I had something on my mind.

"Dad, a lot of my friends joined this club," I slowly began. "They're called the Devlons. They have weekly meetings at different houses, in the girls' basements."

"Their basements?" my father asked, puzzled. He was clearly thinking of our own apartment building, where the dank basement housed spider webs as well as the furnace and my mother's old wringer washing machine.

"They're the rich girls," I said, "from the houses on Virginia Avenue or Mozart. They have finished basements with knotty pine paneling and thick carpeting. Not like our basement. The basements in their houses have bars and barstools that swivel."

"I see," he said and sighed. Although my father had managed to move us to this affluent community, ours was a street of undistinguished brick apartment houses on the perimeter of the avenues with big, luxurious Georgians and Colonials—those single family homes where most of my friends lived. Compared to our two-bedroom apartment with its single bathroom, these houses were mansions.

"What's so wonderful about the Devlons?" he asked.

I didn't know how I could explain these clubs, the high school versions of elitist college sororities, to my father. "They have leather club jackets, Dad," I started. "Black leather. With Devlons written in a pretty turquoise script on the back. The girls wear their jackets to school. Every single day. They never take them off. Even when they're inside, in classes." As soon as I'd seen them, I had coveted one of those black and turquoise Devlons jackets. I had been surreptitiously writing the word *Devlons*, copying that flowing script into my spiral-bound notebooks for a year.

"The teachers allow this?" my father asked. "Children are allowed to wear leather club jackets in the classrooms?"

I nodded miserably.

He shook his head in disapproval. "So these princesses, your so-called friends, did not ask you to join the club with the leather jackets? The Devlons?" he asked, saying Devlons in the same tone he'd earlier used when he said *momzers*.

"No, they haven't," I said and looked down. It had been a terrible humiliation when so many of my friends had been invited to join the Devlons. I'd wanted to stay home from school rather than admit I'd received no envelope. "The invitations went out last week and the new members got their jackets yesterday," I admitted to my father. I had not told my mother, knowing she would overreact, perhaps make humiliating calls to some of her friends, and I would be further embarrassed. "But there is this other club, the Ravens. They asked me to join. I got their invitation in the mail."

"But you don't want to be a Raven," he guessed and poked the newspaper with his unlit pipe. "What color are their jackets?"

"Red and black," I said. "But wool, or something. Scratchy. Not leather," I added.

"What's the problem, Judith?" His voice was soft, tender. "It isn't just the jacket, I'm sure."

"Those girls, the Ravens, they aren't really my friends," I said and looked over at him, his luxurious, dark hair just beginning to be shot with silver at the temples. "They're kind of the leftovers. The friends I hang out with have all joined the Devlons." For not the first time,

I wondered how my mother, a somewhat plain woman with frizzy, unruly hair, and only an eighth-grade education, had managed to marry such a handsome and bookish man as my father. I just didn't understand it. It wasn't until many years later, after they were both gone, that the pictures were brought to mind of how often I had seen them kissing on the back porch, my father's hand slipping onto her round bottom, which she moved pliantly under his touch.

"I don't want to be in the Ravens," I said.

"So why do you need to be in any club?" my father asked and shrugged. "You're so busy. The honors English class, your temple youth group, the school newspaper. These are important things, Judith. Every Saturday, you get up early and volunteer at the Swedish Hospital. Didn't you say they'll hire you when you turn sixteen? With all that you do, how can you make room for a club? Sounds like a waste of time to me," he said, and picked up his newspaper again, shaking his head.

"Do you think so?" I asked him behind the paper. I stood up and I think that what I felt was relief. Suddenly, everything about the Devlons looked and felt different.

"Of course I do. And I think you do, too. What do these clubs do, anyway?" he asked.

"I don't think they actually *do* anything. You're right, it probably is a waste of time." I started down the hall to my bedroom at the back of the apartment. "Night, Dad," I said. "Thanks."

It was on that green brocade couch that he answered so many questions about my future, and tried to help me make sense of my adolescence. He rarely put down his paper, as if the questions I asked about high school loyalties, my Jewish north side world, could be found in its pages. He answered as thoughtfully as he knew how. He failed just that once, when I tried to ask him about sex, but on that subject, I'd expected too much of him. He tried as honestly as he could with everything else. He was not a physically demonstrative man, he rarely kissed me, but as I left him reading in the living room that long-ago night, the street outside our apartment building dark and still, my dad lowered the paper to give me a small nod and smile of encouragement.

"You need a new jacket?" he asked, calling after me. "I'll buy you a jacket."

The last time I saw him alive was on a visit to Chicago. It was winter. Walt had been gone just over a year, dead from the cancer that caught us all by surprise. I was still in shock, not quite believing I was a widow after only six years of marriage. I wasn't ready to lose my father, certainly not so closely on the heels of Walt's death. How could I bear this second loss? But in a lengthy phone call the week before, a Chicago doctor made it clear that my father was suffering from congestive heart failure and did not have a lot more time.

I brought Joseph, who was nearly eight, to Chicago with me. His teachers said he was already so far ahead of his class, the time away from school was no problem. The twins were away at college and anyway, they'd had more time with their grandfather through the years. But Joseph had so few memories of my dad. I also thought, foolishly, that having us both there, Joseph and me, might convince my father to stay alive a bit longer. What I remember most acutely from that visit was how much, this time, it was my father who wanted to be seen. And I, the beloved only daughter, who'd always had such communion with her intellectual and book-loving father, denied him this. What a stupid woman I was. I rationalized my behavior because Walt had died only the year before and that other grief was so fresh. I was not ready to say an honest goodbye to my father. Perhaps that was true, but I think now it was weakness of character. Immaturity. Nearly fifty, despite having lost Walt, I was still too young, not comprehending what my father needed. My father was the one who had always given me what I needed.

We'd come the evening before, Joseph and myself, arriving during a freezing cold spell. I saw immediately how feeble my father had grown. The night before, as I'd unpacked our suitcase while Joseph was having a bath, my mother stood in the doorway of my old room. She told me that Dad moved little now. Breathing was difficult and he spent his days looking out the front window to the street below or reading on the old green brocade sofa, faded, but lovelier and more comfortable now that its clear plastic covers had finally been discarded.

"I'm glad you're here. I know it hasn't been easy for you, either," my mother told me. "We're so happy you brought Joseph. What a beautiful child he is." She reached into the sleeve of her cardigan for a tissue, wiping her reddened eyes. "So smart." I wondered what my mother would do, how she would survive when my father was gone. I don't think she'd ever used a checkbook. I would have to teach her this week.

After breakfast the next morning, I told my mother to go back to bed, take a rest. Her best hours for sleep had always been in the mornings, and she was spent from caring for my father. My dad sat reading in the living room of the same flat on Chicago's north side that I'd grown up in. I still remember the put-upon noises my mother made as she packed up her old, familiar kitchen, banging one pot against another in protest. After that, my father was unable to persuade her to move ever again. While the Jews of Chicago continued their march north, almost to Milwaukee, my mother, an immigrant who had been displaced once too often in Russia, insisted on staying put.

"Want more coffee, Dad? There's still some left from breakfast." I called from the kitchen as I put away our few dishes.

"No, no coffee," he answered, his voice now raspy and weak. He'd always had such a strong voice, it broke my heart to hear him now. His once athletic arms were stringy. His big, barrel chest had been replaced by a torso that looked shrunken. "Bring some of your mother's cookies for Joseph," Dad said. "She spent all day yesterday making him those chocolate chip cookies."

At the mention of his grandmother's chocolate chip cookies, his favorite, Joseph looked up happily. He was on the floor with the pirate figures he'd brought in his suitcase from California, contentedly marching them up and down the gangplank of their plastic pirate ship, creating an involved story with many characters and subplots.

I brought in a plate piled high with cookies, as well as a glass of cold milk, and placed them both on the low table in front of the sofa.

"Don't spill, honey," I said. "You know Grandma doesn't like people eating in the living room."

Joseph continued playing on the floor, but reached behind from time to time for a cookie, devouring nearly the whole plate. My father nodded his head with satisfaction each time Joseph took another. I sat on the couch. The childhood memories of sitting beside my father on that couch were powerful. It was where our most important talks had taken place—sitting next to one another on the sofa. He wore the same slippers he'd had since I was a girl, the brown leather now crackled and peeling. He seemed more comfortable when we sat side by side, not looking into each other's faces. He always listened intently, but held the paper up in front of him.

On this last visit of my father's life, however, I could tell that this time he had something on his mind. Uncharacteristically, he looked directly at me, his eyes tired and watery, but not wavering.

"Sure I can't get you anything, Dad?" I asked, uncomfortable under his gaze.

"No," he said. "I'm fine. Look. Your mother already brought me four glasses of juice this morning." He pointed to the end table beside him where tumblers of orange, yellow, pink, and purple liquids were lined up, untouched.

"How're you feeling? The doctor says you're having more trouble breathing."

"Not so bad," he answered. "You don't get to be my age without aches and pains."

I heard the rattling in his chest and remembered the once-constant pipe he'd held in his mouth, the sweet, yet deadly, smell of his tobacco that I'd loved so much.

"You're not so old," I said with dishonest cheer.

He continued to stare at me. I was awkward and embarrassed and couldn't meet his eye. Instead, I folded the paper beside us.

"Judith, how about we face facts? It's almost the end, even if you and your mother don't want to talk about it," he began, waving me quiet when I started to protest. "I want to tell you, before it's too late, that I've tried," he said. "I've tried to be a good father to you. I know it wasn't always enough. I wish I'd given you more. Especially since you were all we had. Your mother wanted more children, but we didn't have any luck. She lost the two babies before we had you. Both of them with heart trouble."

"Mom lost two babies? When?" I asked. "You never told me there were other children. Why didn't either of you tell me about them?"

"Because then we had you. It was enough. You were healthy and you can't imagine how happy you made us. You should have seen your mother after you were born. Every single day, she wrapped you up until you almost couldn't move. Rain or shine, she walked the neighborhood with you. She said you had to have lots of fresh air— and it made her so happy showing you off in the neighborhood. 'Such a beautiful baby,' everyone said. She loved it. We lived up on the third floor then, and she'd drag the baby carriage down three flights, then run upstairs and carry you down wrapped like you were a piece of bone china."

I smiled, but I couldn't stop thinking about those other babies, those lost babies. Growing up, I'd detested being an only child. The house always seemed so quiet and lonely. I could never escape my mother's scrutiny. Her eyes followed me everywhere. She hovered over me when I coughed or sneezed. I had fervently wished, even though my parents seemed so old, that there had been other kids at the dinner table, kids to fight with, to play with, someone else for my parents to worry about.

"Taking care of you, being a good father, that's been the most important thing in my life. But I don't know how successful I've been at it. You had such struggles, Judith. I wished I could have protected you more. I should have done more for you after you got divorced, but you always seemed so independent. We should have tried harder to get you to move closer to us here in Chicago. We could have helped you more with the twins if you were nearer. When you met Walter, we were so happy. Relieved. Such a good man. But, may he rest in peace, now you're alone again. I worry about how you'll manage when I'm dead. How you'll take care of everything with the boy." He looked down at Joseph, who'd gotten very quiet as he played, no longer making pirate noises.

I tried to argue, but he waved me quiet again.

"Here, have a look at my savings account," he said, and pulled a worn bank passbook from his pants pocket. When he tried to show it to me, I refused to take it, embarrassed. The wrinkled green passbook taken from his pocket seemed so intimate. We'd spoken little of money in our household, but I knew that my father had simple finances. There were no investments or hidden assets, only a worn passbook from a savings account at a local bank. He paid cash for even large purchases, including his cars. My father was terrified of all debt, even a mortgage. He and my mother rented, never owned their own home.

"There isn't a fortune," he said in his rasping voice and put the little book down on the couch beside him, defeated that I wouldn't take it from him and look at it. "I never made much money," he said and shrugged. "But there should be enough for your mother, and some for you and the kids."

I worried again about my mother. Would she stay alone in the apartment?

"I know it's been hard since Walter died. He was a good husband and father. Your mother and I liked him very much." My father grew breathless and stopped speaking. Silently, he stared at me for a few seconds before he went on. "I'll be gone myself, soon. I only hope I helped you enough. I regret that I did so little."

His eyes were so watery. It was clear that what he wanted most of all was to be heard. He was dying soon and he knew it. Desperately, he wanted this last meaningful talk with me, his only child. He wanted me to reassure him. I saw he wanted honesty between us. But I couldn't do it. I was too scared and too sad about losing him. I looked away and denied him this one time when he wanted so much to be heard and seen by me.

"Dad, don't tire yourself," I said. "You've done great." I spoke brusquely, not meeting his gaze. "I'm fine. We've got everything we need. Joseph and me. Walt had good insurance, even a trust fund. The twins are doing great. Seth helps them. Their father pays for their college."

Instead of listening to what else my dad had to say, his fears and hopes at the end of his life, I stood up from the couch and kneeled on the floor and played with Joseph. I began to move my son's plastic people around and make silly pirate talk. "Okay, matie, let's get this rig off to sea. Do you blokes think we have all day? Grrrr."

Behind me I heard my father pick up the newspaper again, and crack out the folds. Not ten days later, just after Joseph and I returned to California, he was gone.

10
Being Seen
Part 2

I recently asked my daughter, Miriam, now in her early forties, about her marriage. Sensible Miriam has been married to Gray, the sweetest man (excepting my sons) on this earth, since she was twenty-five. He regularly cooks dinner for the children, always calls Miriam "honey" or "sweetheart," and pulls my chair out for me when I visit. They seem happy, the household seems happy, but still I wondered. Women are so different now. Miriam says she is one of the younger mothers in her children's school classes. Most of her friends are closer to fifty, and have toddlers in tow. With advances in fertility medicine, some are even older. All these women, my daughter included, are so frightfully busy. Do they ever take time to ask themselves whether they are truly seen by their husbands? They don't seem very introspective at all; perhaps they left all that behind them as they got older and busier. Or perhaps it is a generational difference. Miriam and her friends laugh at women my age when they hear we had consciousness-raising evenings when we were young. "Didn't they have anything better to do?" I heard one say.

But I really wanted to know, so I persisted. "Do you feel Gray understands you?" I was visiting Miriam and her husband and kids in Los Angeles and had been washing the breakfast dishes, but turned off the water to hear her answer. Miriam shared little with me and we rarely found time for real conversation.

"Understands what?" she asked distractedly while packing the children's lunch boxes. A juice box in each, turkey sandwiches with mayo for Dylan, a dash of mustard spread on Shane's bread. Carrot sticks for both. She wrinkled her forehead, already wary that this might be yet another tedious conversation her mother was going to engage her in for way too long and that it was going to make her late for her job at the film studio in Hollywood, where she lugs seventy-five-pound cameras up into high and dangerous places.

"You know, the important things," I answered. "The things that make you who you are."

"Shit, Mom. I'm happy if Gray understands we need milk and remembers to buy it on his way home from work."

"Come on, Miriam, you know what I mean. The things that make you unique. Your essence. Do you feel he sees you in that way?" What I was really wondering was, had my daughter found this thing that I'd been searching for?

She stared at me, rubbing her lower back, which has given Miriam trouble since her youthful horse-riding days and makes her concerned about how long she'll be able to continue her well-paying, but physically demanding studio job. "Mom, I really hope he *doesn't* see me. Mostly, when I'm not working or doing laundry or paying bills, I want to be left alone. I hope he doesn't see that I need to shave my legs or that I'm falling asleep while he talks to me at dinner. My essence? Jesus, I'm a cranky middle-aged woman with stretch marks, and I hope his eyes are so bad he can't see me. Or, God forbid, want to have sex with me."

"Oh, sweetie," I said. I took the SpongeBob lunch pail from her hands and put my arms around her. "I know how tired you are. But you are so beautiful. And smart. And definitely not middle-aged." As usual, Miriam allowed only the briefest of hugs between us.

She said, "It's okay, Mom. Gray and I are happy together. There's nothing for you to worry about. But the kids and I have to leave now. I'll see you tonight. Don't let the boys watch TV until they finish their homework." My two grandsons, Dylan, aged four, and Shane, six, each gave me a quick kiss before Miriam shepherded them out the door to the minivan parked under the palm tree in front of their house. She dropped them at school on her way to work. When I visited Los Angeles, I picked them up, so they didn't have to go to after-school day care. It felt good that I could help Miriam in this small way.

"Bye, darlings," I called to Dylan and Shane.

Miriam's twin brother Evan still lives in New York, where he works in the admissions department of Fordham Law School. Evan is gay, a fact that surprised me very little when he came out at the beginning of college (although I heard he had some issues with his father, a man on the macho side of the gender spectrum. Seth probably thinks I caused Evan's homosexuality by being an overbearing mother). When it became legal in New York, Evan married Ira. He and Ira seem to have real chemistry, but it is hard to make out what is underneath all that flirty, bantering humor between them. Ira is almost never serious and Evan seems to work hard to keep up. Does Ira get my dear, sensitive boy? Or is it just banter and wit? Who knows? Certainly not me.

The one who I had great hope for in the Being Seen department was my younger son, Joseph. After Walt died and Miriam and Evan went away to college, it was just the two of us in that big house. While he was growing up, we would sit at the dinner table and discuss life and books and music and, I suppose you'd call it, the soul. He had inherited his father's excellent mind. He was also a fine communicator, which I like to think he got from me. I'd always hoped that he'd find someone who appreciated what he offered, his depth. And yet, who is Joseph engaged to? After all these years of my waiting and meeting several wonderful young women he brought home, he recently became engaged to Dr. Heidi Mortensen—in my opinion, a surprising choice. She is a resident at Johns Hopkins in ophthalmology, where Joseph is in the middle of his own residency in emergency medicine. They also live a life that seems to leave little time for introspection or examination of each other's feelings. When they aren't working, they are usually tuning up their fancy road bikes and, heads down, riding ungodly amounts of miles through the Maryland countryside.

Who sees my son Joseph these days? I wonder and think back to when he was growing up, the two of us talking until all hours about life and death and what makes us who we are. He was full of questions about his father, who died when he was so young. Friends and colleagues from the lab told Joseph how brilliant his father had been, how Walt was a luminary in his field of physics. Where, Joseph wondered, did all that knowledge go after his father died? Are particles of his intelligence still floating around the atmosphere somewhere? Have these particles of knowledge been converted into other living matter? We used to speak about those things when he was a boy.

I wonder if he asks those kinds of questions now. I've watched Heidi, the flawless Scandinavian girl he is to marry next year, lean and muscular as a greyhound. She doesn't seem the type to ponder the afterlife or to spend much time on introspection. She's too busy with her work and riding that damn bicycle. Even though she is to be a doctor for the eyes, I doubt that she sees my son Joseph.

But this is my story: not Miriam's nor Evan's nor Joseph's. Not my father's, either. As I got older, all I could do was wonder when, or if, I would experience this great communion with a man. I liked men, you see, and, though independent in most things, felt incomplete without one. Of course, I have always had dear women friends, like

Marnie and Rachel, good friends with whom I share my story. Yet even after two marriages, and more men sharing my bed than I care to admit to, I still hungered to be seen.

Of course there was still you, Elliot. And, even in my fifties, with Evan and Miriam in their mid-twenties and already well launched, and Joseph getting close to high school, you were on my mind—with greater frequency and urgency than ever. Despite earlier vows, I had not exorcised you. I was feeling on the downward slope of life, watching the months and days hurtle by at an ever more shocking speed. That, and Walt's early death, made me anxiously wonder whether I'd ever find this connection. As usual, as soon as February rolled around, I waited for the annual package from you, which year after year you sent from New York. A book, a bracelet, a decoration for the house—your gifts made me feel seen and bless you, you never forgot. I imagined you thinking about me every year as my birthday drew near, putting in time and effort as from the cornucopia of Manhattan shops, you selected just the right thing. For you always did. When the parcel arrived, it would contain something that showed how well you knew me.

"Have you read the latest Philip Roth?" you asked, the year you sent *Sabbath's Theater*. "I hope you haven't already bought it. You are going to love it. I can't wait to talk about it with you."

"I haven't," I said. "But it's on fire in my hands, I can't wait to start it. What's it about?" We had discovered Philip Roth together when we were in college. We felt we'd grown up with him.

"It's brilliant," you said. "You'll hate the guy, Mickey Sabbath. He's a real schmuck, but what a riveting schmuck. I don't know how Roth does what he does. I think it's his best so far. And," you added conspiratorially, "it's filthy. Soooo dirty. You know, Drenka, the female character in this book? She actually reminds me of you."

"Me? How?" I asked.

"She's really sexy. Yeah, the more I think about it, Rocket, the more I see you in naughty Drenka. She fucks four men in one day!"

"Yeah, right," I said. "That happens to me a lot." Each evening, as I tore through the book, I was delighted and shocked that you saw me as sexy, maybe even filthy, Drenka. I read and reread the scandalous scenes, remembering how sex between us, years ago in the hotel in San Francisco, had also been filthy. Once I'd got over you hiding me in the closet that first night, and you got over whatever it was that kept you from getting a hard-on, we'd grown wanton, willing to try anything that occurred to either of us. How delicious to remember those nights and to know you remembered our desire as well. When I closed the Roth book, I placed it on the shelf where I kept your gifts, not filing it among my other volumes. Since college, we'd had our secret Roth code, telling each other that someone was a Portnoy or a Nathan. Now we'd added to that private language. I was a Drenka, a licentious woman, who would try anything in bed.

Then a new phase of our relationship began, based on this very love of literature. You wrote a long, emotion-packed letter to me. When either of us was hashing out a dilemma, we still wrote one another longhand letters, four or five pages laying out the problem. As it happened, I'd been thinking of you especially pensively that day, so when I got your emotional letter, I took it as an omen.

Joseph and I still lived in the house in the Oakland Hills, looking out at the view that had brought Walt such happiness. It was too big for the two of us, but we both loved the place. I worked part-time after Walt's death, as well as spending many hours volunteering at Joseph's school. I took trips, often with Marnie, who also loved travel and adventure, but whose husband had grown afraid of flying. I didn't resist when friends occasionally introduced me to men they or their husbands knew, but there had been no one who interested me. Joseph became the center of my emotional life. I was uncomfortably aware of this and tried not to smother my son, to give him freedom to rebel, but he never did. Joseph was far too easy a teenager, I feared, trying too hard to please me. On that autumn afternoon when I snatched your long letter from my mailbox, I made tea for myself and sat in my sunny kitchen to read it. I still drink that same tea, a sweet bergamot I love; its scent fills the air wherever I am.

Writing in that fountain pen and dark blue ink you'd always used, you began by saying you'd come to a weighty decision. Although you were still relatively young, you no longer wanted to practice law. You were going to retire. Your practice, beginning with the massive anti-trust suit in San Francisco, had been followed by a series of even more illustrious achievements. Although you did not say this immodestly, you wanted me to know that you had handled many important cases for your New York firm, and brought in an increasing amount of new business. This meant you'd generated a progressively large share of the firm's revenue. You were the youngest lawyer to be made partner in the firm's over one-hundred-year history. As a vested partner in this very successful firm, money seemed to flow endlessly your way. Unfortunately, you wrote, little satisfaction remained in either the money or the success.

You said you'd had an epiphany. You'd come to realize that the activities which had led to you being made partner at such a young age, had been largely immoral. Looking back at your twenty-five-year law career, you did not feel proud of some of the cases you'd fought and won. This gnawed at your gut. Your desire to be a good, no, a great, lawyer, had led you into ethically murky territory. Although the time spent clerking for the Supreme Court justice had been intellectually exhilarating, a consequence of that experience had been the outsized respect for the law you'd imbibed. Law had become your religion, just as it had been of the athlete-scholar who'd been your hero. You looked back at your ambitious career at the firm in New York. Your successes had made you a rising star, and you were counsel for important cases with precedent-setting verdicts. Attracting clients of national and international importance had eventually clouded your moral clarity. Devotion to this Religion of the Law had caused you to lose your way.

I put down the letter. There had been no indication that this was coming. You'd always seemed confident of your professional decisions. My heart pounded with pride for you. I felt as if you were rediscovering that boy you had been, the boy with a social conscience. But there was more.

Your greatest regret had been serving as lead counsel for the international conglomerate that made, among its many products, baby formula. I remembered that case and that I'd read, in one of my liberal magazines, how poor African women unknowingly mixed the powdered formula with contaminated water, usually the only water available to them. At the time, you defended your client's right to market their product. You claimed women had a choice and they chose not to breastfeed. Now, as you reread the court documents, you were sickened at thinking about the preventable deaths of babies drinking contaminated milk, when it was clear that breast milk was the safer option. You knew that you'd been partially culpable. In the past, you'd maintained that because your big wins generated huge profits, your firm had been able to take on pro bono work of great social import. But now, you admitted that you'd closed your eyes to certain ugly facts.

You wrote that you were finished with it. There was no need to work as a lawyer ever again. At fifty-five, you'd still be receiving a handsome check every year. Your firm generously provided fully vested partners with this profit sharing, even after their retirement. You had enough money to live comfortably, and you wanted out. You were through practicing law. To the surprise of the firm and everyone else you knew, you'd quit. In the next few months, you'd tie up loose ends, but that was all. You wanted to change your life, to explore a dream neglected since boyhood.

You outlined a book you wanted to write. It was to be a novel exploring guilt, influenced by the very questions you'd been asking yourself. Instead of the present, however, the setting would be the 1960s—soon after the McCarthy era. The narrator would be a lawyer (much like yourself). This fictional lawyer found himself regretting the work he had done for the government—hunting down and prosecuting communists and communist sympathizers. Concurrently, the novel would tell the story of a doomed love affair between the lawyer and a young woman sick with cancer. You wanted to weave together themes of this ambitious lawyer's professional guilt with his personal guilt toward the lover and his inability to fully commit.

Well. Here I smiled a bit. I'd always thought you were meant for a creative life, not grubbing away in an office representing business conglomerates. Since your boyhood, I'd seen this in you. Hadn't we grown up wanting to change the world? I was surprised, but admired your decision to chuck your successful career and follow your passion. I completely believed in you. I thought there was not a thing on earth that Elliot Pine could not do. But the subject matter made me queasy, especially the love affair part. After all, hadn't I been part of your betrayal of Meredith? Then, at the very end of your letter, you said there was a favor you wanted to ask of me. You hoped I would help you. Could we discuss this in a phone call? I folded the thick letter, stuffing it back into the envelope, and picked up my now lukewarm tea. What on earth could I do to help you?

I called the next afternoon. I knew Lilly would be at her gallery.

"Well, this is exciting," I began. "A whole new life."

"Do you like it?" you asked immediately. "Can you see it as a novel?"

"Elliot, I think you can tell a great story. And lawyers are good writers. But what you're doing takes courage. Not many people would walk away from a law practice like yours."

"I'm serious about this book. I don't plan to write it as a therapy project."

"Okay, I believe you. But what can I do?"

"I want you to read it. We've discussed literature our whole lives. I want to send you chapters and have you comment on them. But I want you to be honest. Don't spare me."

I told you I would think about it, but I wasn't really sure how I could help you. That night, I lay in bed and wondered why you wanted my opinion so much. It would be tricky to read about your deception to Meredith. What if I showed up as one of the characters? Maybe you were trying to expiate your guilt toward me as well. Could I be a dispassionate reader? I wasn't sure, Elliot. Still, I found my excitement for the project growing. This would be something we shared. You and me. I phoned you and said I'd give it a try.

"That's wonderful, Judith. Everything is falling in place. Thank you. I hope you're ready, because I'm going to be sending you some work really soon."

"You've started writing?" I asked.

"Not exactly. But I rented a cottage. Lillian helped me find some great carpenters, electricians, painters. They're doing a fantastic job. It's going to be a beautiful studio." I shook my head at the other end of the line. Just like Elliot, I thought, nothing but the best. Not one word published, but still a writer's studio, and from the sound of it, a charming place in the woods near his village on the Hudson.

"I'd be honored to read what you've written," I said. "But I'm not an expert. I'm no professional editor or anything."

"I know, I understand," you replied, "but you're the reader I want. If you like what I write, I'll know it's okay." Then there was a pause. "You know, it's exciting, but I'm actually terrified to begin and have you read it."

"Elliot, I'll take this seriously, but there's no reason to be terrified. I'm on your side, remember?"

"Yeah, I know. But you can't imagine how much this means to me. The writing." Then you changed the subject. "I've put a telephone in the studio. You can call me here any time. When we're just catching up, I think we should talk by phone. Not write letters. I don't want you to edit my letters," you said and laughed. "Mail for the work and phone calls for everything else. Is that okay?"

"Sure," I said and wrote down the number at the studio, thinking how serious this really was for you, giving up everything familiar. You'd practiced law for over twenty-five years, always been successful at it. Of course you were nervous. "Tell me more about what you need from me," I said, trying to be a good social worker, as well as a friend.

"I feel like I need to write for someone, one specific reader," you answered. "It came to me that it's you—you're that person. No one is as sharp a reader as you. I knew that back in sixth grade, when you beat my ass in the reading competition. You're fast and you remember every word."

How could I resist such praise from you? I laughed and said, "Okay. And I'm proud of you. I know you're going to write a great book."

But before we hung up the phone that day, I had one more question, something I'd been wondering ever since your letter first arrived. "Is Lilly reading your work as well?" I asked, in what I hoped was an offhand way. Of course I was flattered to be asked to read your work, but I wanted the honor to be mine alone, not one I shared with Lilly.

"Ah, Lilly. You know, Lilly is not one for fiction. She's more of a visual person," you answered. "She has a great eye for art, but words are simply not her thing. You're my only reader for now."

A visual person? Maybe a better description would be that she was an inarticulate person. Okay, perhaps a bit harsh, but when I learned she would not be reading your work, I was delighted, pleased to come out ahead in any comparison with Lilly. The honor was truly to be mine alone.

And so, for several years, the manila envelopes flew back and forth between Beacon, New York, and my house in the Oakland Hills. My joy at seeing them was no different than when we'd been at colleges in different parts of the country. And, the envelopes containing your latest work were always fat, like college acceptance letters. It must be said that Elliot Pine was always productive. You had an excellent work ethic and didn't stop writing until you had produced eight new pages a day—every day, including Sunday. You'd edit what you'd done the day before, rewrite, then go on to produce eight new pages before locking the door of your studio and heading home. You said you barely stopped for lunch, but kept the refrigerator in the studio stocked with cheeses and cold meats purchased from the gourmet grocer in town. You kept a fancy coffee maker there as well. I took those pages and chapters very seriously, reading them late into the night. I'd ponder every word sent in those manila envelopes, editing in the margins and writing a cover sheet of questions and comments, but still always cheering you on. I probably knew your novel more thoroughly than you did yourself.

Unfortunately, very early, I began to have qualms about the work. This was just a first draft, I kept reminding myself, and I continued to be your cheerleader. The history of the period you wrote about was thorough and seemed accurate. The politics were all there, the social milieu felt right. You were, after all, an excellent researcher and had been a history major at Brown. But the story never took fire. It read more like a graduate student paper about the 1950s, smart and meticulously documented, but with no life. Even more worrying, the characters never became real. I just couldn't lose myself in the story. The lawyer was stiff and I couldn't see how the cases he worked on were compelling. Was this the way a legal brief read? How could you have written this? I wondered again and again. You were good, no excellent, at everything you'd ever attempted. And so I kept reading.

And remaining hopeful. There was promise, I kept telling myself. The life would be breathed into it later.

Then, one summer, I found myself alone in the big, empty house. Joseph was working as a junior counselor at a camp near the Russian River. Miriam had started her new job with the studios in LA, but Evan was living in Manhattan, interning with a City College adminis-trator, while he looked for permanent work. I missed Evan. He'd never lived so far away before. I could take some time off and visit him. We could go to some shows—the theater was a passion we both shared.

Evan seemed glad when I told him I was coming to visit, but he said that the place he'd sublet on the west side was tiny.

"I don't want you to be uncomfortable, Mom," he said. "There's only a crappy sofa bed."

"That's okay," I said to my older son. "I'll stay in a hotel. I want to. Somewhere near your place, so I can see you often, but not get in your hair."

"You're sure, Mom?" he asked, sounding protective. "It's not a great neighborhood." When had this happened? When had I stopped worrying about Evan and he started worrying about me? "You're okay by yourself in a hotel?"

"Absolutely, sweetheart," I said. "Remember, I'm the one who traveled around the world with a backpack. It'll be fun. Tell me which shows you think we'd like. I'll get us tickets. We'll go to good restau-rants." I planned the week carefully. Visit my son. Stay in a hotel. Go to some shows. Oh, and I could have a meeting with Elliot. We could talk about the book face-to-face. It all made sense.

I phoned you at your cottage so I could tell you about the upcom-ing trip. "I'll bring your latest chapter with me," I said. "We can talk about it over a lunch. How does that sound?"

"Terrific," you agreed. "Great idea. But, listen, as you were talking, I had another thought. You said you were coming next month. In July? How about a mini high school reunion?"

"A reunion?" I asked, puzzled.

"It's a crazy coincidence, but two of our friends from elementary school are here in New York. They've been after me to meet in the city for dinner. You won't believe who. But if you were here as well, I wouldn't mind it so much. It'd actually be fun."

"From our class?" I asked. "Who?"

"Yeah. From Pratt Elementary. Roberta Feingold is one," you said. "Remember Roberta?"

"God yes, of course," I answered. "What ever happened to Roberta? I haven't thought about her in years. Remember how she'd jump up and down, waving her hand frantically in the air, answering questions before she got called on? She drove horrible Miss Schaffer nuts. In high school, she was a really good athlete, remember?" I'd always thought of Roberta with gratitude. She was the first girl to welcome me to the new school when we were ten years old.

"Yeah, right," you said. "She had those really long legs. Now she lives upstate in Albany, but comes into the city for her job. She phoned me out of the blue and wants to get together. I've been busy, so I put her off. But since you're coming to New York, a group dinner would be perfect. You were friends, right? What do you suppose Roberta's doing these days?"

"Something requiring unlimited energy," I said. "Remember she did track and field? She went to meets all over Chicago."

"I don't know," you said. "She didn't sound bubbly when she phoned, not like I remembered. She sounded serious. Maybe even a little down."

"Really? You said there were two people. Who else?"

"Jordan Orelove, believe it or not. He keeps phoning, too," you replied. "You know, the guy from temple youth group who played the accordion. Didn't you used to date Jordan?"

I groaned. "Jordan? God, yes. I'm embarrassed thinking about it. Remember how everyone would sing the spiritual, 'I looked over Jordan and what did I see?'"

Without missing a beat, you finished the song. "They'd say Judith! Everyone would chime in and sing your name. We thought that was the wittiest thing in the world. It cracked us up because you were always all over him." You laughed. "And his accordion."

"Very funny. You shouldn't talk. Weren't you all over your girl-friend Rochelle? You couldn't take your hands off her and her big breasts. So, what's happened to Jordan?" I asked.

"He's a doctor. Kind of prominent. He works for the City Health Department. An AIDS prevention advocate in charge of all the safe-sex ads in the subways and the education campaigns in the schools."

"AIDS?" I asked. "Do you think Jordan's gay?"

"Yeah," you answered. "I'm pretty sure he is. In fact, when he called me, I said something stupid. I'd seen his name in *New York Magazine* a couple of years ago, but I thought I read that he'd died. When I heard from him, I actually said, 'Jordie, I thought you were dead!'"

"You didn't? Elliot, that's terrible."

"I know. It just slipped out. It was an article about the AIDS crisis in New York, crediting Jordan as one of the first to openly talk about it as an epidemic. All the deaths. I swear to God, I remember reading his name and thinking it said, 'the late Dr. Jordan Orelove.' I recognized the name, though, knew it was the same guy from high school and youth group, but I thought it said he'd died."

"That's just awful, Elliot," I repeated. "Because the article linked him with AIDS, you thought he was dead?"

"I know. Really stupid," you admitted. "I'm an asshole. But Jordan didn't seem upset. He laughed and said, 'No, Elliot, I'm not dead. Want to have dinner sometime so you can take my pulse?' I'm not surprised he became a doctor. He was really smart, remember? Maybe he *did* seem gay in high school. At least a little gay, anyway. Did that cross your mind when you dated him?"

"That he was gay? I don't think so," I said. "My mother always liked Jordan. He had beautiful manners. She thought he was a real gentleman."

"Right. A gentleman. Not a barbarian, like me?"

"She never thought you were a barbarian, Elliot. Just driven. But when Jordan came over, he'd sit and talk to her. He paid attention to her, complimented her, and ate her cookies. It took us forever to get out of the house, but she loved him. And that accordion of his."

"When do you think he knew that he was gay?" you wondered. "In high school? Before that?"

"He sure was a good kisser in high school," I said. "He taught me how to kiss. When we were making out, he seemed really into it."

"Oh, kissing, who isn't into kissing? Men, women. Gays, straights. Everyone likes to kiss. But when he kissed you, maybe he was imagining me."

That would make two of us, I thought. *The whole time I was kissing Jordan, I was imagining you, Elliot.* Of course, I didn't say that out loud. I just said, "It would be fun to see them again. Go ahead. Set it up. Roberta and Jordan. You and me. You're right. A mini Chicago reunion."

"Welcome to Une Nork, Mom," Evan said when he met my plane, and we laughed at the old joke. We went to several plays and my handsome son showed me his favorite haunts—bars and restaurants and galleries in the city. I got to know Evan as a grown-up and it was wonderful.

I met you for lunch. You'd made a reservation at the Russian Tea Room, a place whose opulence intoxicated me before I had a single drink. We talked about your book. You had a title you favored, something like *Acts of Ascendance*. I had no idea what that meant and you spent a very long time explaining it, trying to convince me how the title worked. I kept sipping wine and tried to pay attention. You were wearing a linen shirt, a pale, natural color, and the more I drank, the more I wanted to touch your arm, to stroke the finely woven material, which practically shimmered under the chandelier above us. I'd never seen a shirt like that—it made you look as if you were from another place and century. You belonged in that elegant tearoom, yet looked like no one else in the restaurant.

You glanced around the room. The lunch crowd had emptied out and we still had several hours until it was time to meet Roberta and Jordan. "I guess we should go," you said and reached for your wallet. "God, the time flew by, but there's still so much to talk about," and you smiled at me. "It was great seeing you. It's always great to see you." You leaned over and gave me a small kiss on the cheek.

"Why don't you come to my hotel?" I suggested, shocking myself when I heard the words tumbling from my mouth. I'd clearly had too much to drink and too many hours sitting close to you in the red velvet booth. "We haven't gotten through the last pages of the manuscript," I said. "Let's get through that chapter, at least." I emptied the last of the wine from my glass and turned brightly to you.

Let it be stated here, for the record, that I have never had sex with a married, or even sort-of-married man, other than you, Elliot Pine. I have consistently advised friends, coworkers, and relatives as to the lack of wisdom of having sex with a married man. I do not think that having sex with a married, or even sort-of-married man, is a good idea for either sexual partner. Yet, on that afternoon, there I was suggesting that we go back to my small hotel room on West Eighty-Seventh, knowing that under my sedate blue dress I was wearing a new lace bra that lifted the sag of gravity and three children from my breasts. I wanted you and I could think of little else. I wanted to watch you unbutton that fine linen shirt and then feel your naked body against mine. I cannot say what I thought would happen after we slept together, but I am sure it involved some variation of you realizing the inadequacy of your relationship with Lilly, followed by the suggestion that I move to Beacon, New York, or you to Oakland, California, and we stop wasting the remainder of our days on separate coasts, away from one another.

In the booth of the Russian Tea Room, after I spoke and smiled up at you brightly, you stared at me a long time. You looked at me the way I have many times looked when a waiter has offered dessert. The look which says, "I know I shouldn't. I've already eaten quite enough, thank you, but, still, that flourless chocolate cake sounds too entirely delicious to refuse."

You grabbed the check and threw quite a lot of cash onto the table. You'd obviously considered the offer of dessert and decided you could not pass it up. You rose, walked quickly around the table, and slid me out of the booth, pulling me to my feet as if I might change my mind. Then you took my hand and led me out of the restaurant, flagging down a cab and telling the driver the address of my hotel on West Eighty-Seventh.

So glad, I thought. So glad that under this nice navy wool dress, I wore black lacy underpants and bought the kind of bra I hadn't worn in many years. This was a bra that would satisfy any man's desires, my breasts a full, rich feast for the eyes. We weren't young, you and I, but my theory is that once you've had sex with a man, the possibility and the desire are always there. You remember that person as how they were when they were young. After the first shock, the added years and pounds and wrinkles disappear, and you see only the woman or man of your memory. At least, I hoped that was true. I knew it was true for me of you. You still looked glorious, still resembling the El Greco painting of Fray Paravicino I'd seen so many years before hanging in a museum in Boston. Now the good Fray was in middle age, a few gray hairs interspersed with the dark. Yet you, Elliot, like the man in the painting, still had the full lips of a poet. I longed to kiss those lips. That had not changed.

"Oh, Judith," you said, your voice husky as you undressed me, "I want always to have you in my life. Even when we're in an old people's home, I'll crawl to see you."

Crawl to see me. Elliot, I cherished those words. For years to come, I took them out and heard them again and again. You'll see, I never forgot them.

That afternoon, our lovemaking was just right. So many things could have gone wrong. Maybe, you're saying, my standards were low. Wasn't I filled with loneliness, frightened of facing an empty nest as Joey was nearly off to college? No, that afternoon in Manhattan was different from our time in San Francisco, different from any other time we'd been together. And it was not just a result of my loneliness. Certainly in our fifties, we were not crazed as we'd been in our thirties. You were slow and generous. I saw that the years had served you well as a lover. You listened to my body and sensed my every reaction. Some of my girlfriends, Rachel in particular, had begun to say that in their fifties they were losing interest in sex. Rachel, the once-fiery hot redhead, said she was now perfectly happy, relieved even, that her husband didn't chase after her as he used to. Not me. I was still desperately interested in the physical; I still craved touch and passion. It was what made me feel most alive. But then, for my whole life, not just that day, I had craved your touch in particular.

That afternoon was perfect. "Whoa," I teasingly asked you, "did you have some Viagra with lunch at the Russian Tea Room? A little blue pill you swallowed with your borscht?"

"No pill," you replied. "That black bra you're wearing is quite enough of a stimulant."

I remembered back to all the times we'd pressed our bodies together, in the woods in Wisconsin, the hours on your narrow bed in the apartment where your mother died, the steamy cars parked near Lake Michigan, and then, that year of hotel rooms on Union Square. I softly touched the line of soft, dark hair snaking down your belly and now, as always, it drove me crazy. I leaned down to kiss your belly. Perhaps it was not as tight as it had once been, but you still remained a lean man.

Actually, it never mattered whether you and I actually had intercourse; everything we ever did was foreplay. Your touch, eyes, the fact that those eyes were so close to mine, made me happy. I loved the creases that were now at the corners of your eyes. I also had crow's-feet and I was glad that we were the same age, both battle-scarred by life and death. I let you touch the cesarean scar from Joseph's birth. I ran my hands over your feet, no longer soft and narrow, but calloused and knobby. When we were kids and had lain together in your room, rubbing up and down against each other's bodies, it had been consoling sex. After years of frustration, we'd finally had those crazy, wild San Francisco weekends. We were daring and athletic. We can do this. We can try that. After all the teenaged restraint, we were finally adults; we could do what we wanted. It was like the first time some kids can drink booze legally. On the night of their twenty-first birthday, they might go out and binge, showing no restraint. Now, in our fifties, it was different. Everything was slow and intentional. I don't mean to say it wasn't exciting. That afternoon was take-your-breath-away sex for both of us. We were left moaning and shaking. Afterward, I wrapped myself around you from behind, then slowly stroked your back, feeling the rivulets of sweat. We belonged together, I thought. This was what it was like when you'd loved someone all of your life and he was your other half.

Finally, you opened your eyes and reached for the clock beside the bed, turning it toward your face.

"Oh shit," you said. "Look at the time. We're supposed to meet Roberta and Jordan in forty-five minutes."

"Mmm, do we have to go?" I asked sleepily. "I mean, what if we made some excuse?"

You laughed. "Oh no you don't. I'd just have to reschedule and see them both on my own. Come on, you, we've got to get dressed. We're meeting them in the East Village and we're all the way uptown now." You pried yourself from my arms and sat up, your feet hitting the floor with a thud.

In the taxi to the restaurant, I reached for your hand. I was still smiling, but instead of returning my smile, you turned and looked out the window at the darkening streets, barking directions to the cab driver. I felt queasy when you didn't turn to me. The remains of the Russian Tea Room lunch and wine rose from my stomach. Why did your hand feel limp in mine? Why didn't you return my smile? Like every New Yorker, you knew a better route, a way to avoid the traffic we were stuck in. I saw that you were nervous, but then you'd always detested being late. I didn't care what time we arrived. I wanted never to get there. I sat back in the seat and closed my eyes, fighting down the nausea.

When we finally arrived at the restaurant, a dimly lit Italian place, we found Roberta and Jordan at the table together, heads behind menus.

"Finally, you two," Jordan said. "We've already filled up on bread. Which is delicious, by the way."

Did it show that you and I had been holed up in a hotel room having sex all afternoon? I wondered. My lips felt bruised and swollen from all the delicious kisses. Was the bruising obvious to the others? Embarrassed, I hugged Roberta, then put my arm around Jordan, asking them both questions at once, chattering nonsense about the traffic.

I wouldn't have recognized Roberta. She'd become a frumpy woman in a business suit. Her body was still long and athletic, but the feminine blouse with ruffles was jarring and all wrong. She used to spend hours with her hair rolled around large plastic cylinders, which resulted in a smooth hairdo we called a bubble. Apparently, she no longer bothered with these. Instead, her once-shiny brown hair had reverted to its more natural state of wild curls, more gray than brown. I remembered that at the end of high school, Roberta, like so many of the other girls, had her nose shortened by a plastic surgeon. I found myself studying the small upturned knob. It seemed out of proportion, not belonging on that long face at all.

The years had been kinder to my old boyfriend, Jordan, though I doubted I would have recognized him on the street, either. He was dressed beautifully, a gray velvet jacket over jeans, and he was leaner than he'd been as a boy, a trim beard flattering his face, making it seem more defined. He jumped up, looking delighted to see both you and me.

"Jordie!" you exclaimed. "You're looking great. I need a jacket like that. Everyone needs a jacket like that. And, Roberta, wow!" you lied. "You haven't changed a bit."

"Sure, buddy," Jordan said, pumping your arm. "We'll have to go shopping sometime. That is, if you ever leave your office. You got to quit working so hard. Come on down here to the Village more often," said Jordan, obviously not knowing of your retirement.

There was a lot to take in at the table: Roberta, who seemed to have had all the fun extracted from her, and Jordan, once so shy and awkward, now poised with charm and bonhomie. Besides studying them and trying to absorb all the changes I saw, I was conscious of your every word and gesture, every time you did or did not look at me or touch me.

As we made our way through the dinner, I became aware of an odd dynamic: all three of us, Jordan, Roberta, and myself, were flirting with you. And you were performing for the three of us—recounting amusing tales about people in the small town of Beacon, getting us to groan about how those Cubs disappointed us Chicagoans year after year, but how we never, ever gave up hope. Perhaps your performance was more for Jordan and Roberta, for I was the home crowd, already won over. Roberta *did* seem depressed, just as you'd said, not at all the irrepressible girl I remembered from grade school. But slowly, the evening revived her. I learned that her life was a hard one. She worked for a government transportation agency in Albany, was a single mother, and had had to piece together coverage for her two kids whenever she came down to New York for committee meetings. I certainly understood her life, but I'm afraid I was in too much of a postcoital swoon to feel much empathy. She told earnest, complicated stories about state government, stories that made me stifle yawns. But she didn't notice me at all—her interest was directed solely at you, Elliot. She asked you question after question.

"Everyone thinks rapid trains are the answer. But buses are more flexible, don't you agree? Buses can be rerouted, but you can't move train tracks when the population moves. What do you think, Elliot? Why are people so enamored with trains?" Roberta asked. She also wanted your ideas about several legal briefs she was preparing at the Transportation Department. You tried to look interested. Perhaps you were.

Jordan was the greatest surprise, though. He'd come into his own. He was confident and articulate, although he, too, deferred to your opinions. He told you that he'd followed your career, been so proud when he heard that you'd been appointed clerk to a Supreme Court justice.

"And your judge, my God, what a hero," Jordan said. "All of America loved him back when he played basketball, and even more, later, when he was appointed to the Supreme Court. That guy could have been president if he'd wanted to. What an experience it must have been to actually work for him."

"Yeah," you agreed. "An exceptional legal mind. But you should have seen him when he was shooting hoops. He never even broke a sweat, even when he was over sixty! Absolutely the greatest man I've ever known. I loved him."

"I always knew you were going places, buddy." Jordan smiled sweetly and leaned toward you. "You were the smartest guy in the whole school. And there were a lot of smart Jews in our school. Right?" Jordan looked to Roberta and me for confirmation. "Right, ladies?"

"Shit, Jordan, you're no slouch. A doctor, for Christ's sake. And, those programs you've set up to fight AIDS. You've done ground-breaking work." You patted Jordan on the back.

"Hell, I'm just a bureaucrat, like our friends Roberta and Judith here," Jordan said, modestly. "But you, you're something. It wasn't hard to come out in my line of work. Lots of gay doctors, especially in public health. But you, it's not so easy to be gay in corporate law. That's a very homophobic world over on Wall Street."

There was a long silence. I broke off a piece of the crispy bread, scattering crumbs on the table. You looked long and hard at Jordan. "Jordie, I'm not gay," you finally said. "Where did you get that idea?" You reached for a napkin and wiped the corners of your mouth.

Jordan looked down into his plate of risotto. "Jeez, man. I, uh, just assumed. Sorry, no offense. I mean, look at me. I'm as queer as they come. No offense intended at all."

Roberta's eyes met mine. I think we were both remembering the story that went around the halls of school and at our pajama parties. Something about Jordan and Elliot giving each other oral sex when they were in junior high. At the time, when the story was repeated to me, I was so innocent, I couldn't even imagine how such an act was done, but hadn't wanted to ask. Now I wondered if perhaps there had been something to that rumor about them in junior high. Could the story have been true?

The silence persisted, then Jordan uncomfortably continued, "I can't believe I just said that. Really, Elliot, it came out of nowhere."

You returned the thick cloth napkin to your lap. "Hey, Jordan, no offense taken. Remember? I thought you were dead. Can you believe that, Judith? When he called me out of the blue, I said, 'Hey, man, I thought you were dead.'"

I laughed on cue. "Yeah, you told me. You guys. None of us should believe anything we hear or read in the papers. All of us reading and believing gossip. Like the way my mother and her cronies used to gossip. The stories got juicier each time they told them."

"It's obvious," Roberta said. "We've become our mothers. In so many ways. I even play mah-jongg, just like my mother did."

I smiled, but the thought of Roberta playing mah-jongg depressed me. I wanted to picture those long legs of hers sprinting and leaping over jumps, as she'd done in high school. Where had Roberta's energy gone?

"Seriously, Elliot," Jordan said, "forget about it. Tell us about that fancy law firm of yours. What's the latest on Wall Street? I heard Spielberg wanted to make a movie about that big antitrust case you did in Silicon Valley."

"Well, actually," you said, "I'm not in that world anymore. I took early retirement. I made partner, so they still send me shares of the firm's annual profits. But I'm a writer now. My dream-come-true life." You shrugged and smiled pleasantly at Jordan.

"Retired? You're kidding," Roberta said. "You're so young." She rubbed the back of her neck tiredly. "I'd love to retire. Get out of my office. Use my body again. Get back in shape."

"Yup," you said. "I've rented a little studio up in Beacon, fireplace and a view of the woods. It's nice. I'm working on a novel. Judith edits for me. That's what we were meeting about this afternoon." You nodded in my direction. "No one knows a colon from a semicolon like Judith," you said and patted my hand. "Right?"

Just like that, my role reduced from muse to grammarian.

"I sure can believe that," Jordan said. "Judith was always the grammar police. Matching those subjects with those verbs. And her vocabulary." He looked at me. "You must have known every word they threw at you on the SATs. You didn't even need to take a prep course like the rest of us did."

I smiled humbly. Grammar police. Wasn't that sexy? I thought.

"But, really, Elliot," Jordan said. "How great that you're out of the grind. It's beautiful where you live. So unspoiled. I've been up there a few times."

"Yeah, it sure is. And the wonderful part is doing what I've always wanted to do. Every time I get one of the distribution checks from the firm, I open the envelope and look at it with amazement. 'There it is,' I say, 'my fuck-you money.'"

"God, I'd love that," Roberta said. "I hate my job." She picked up her glass of water and took a big swallow. "Fuck-you money. Do you know where I might get some of that? You sure know how to live." Then she gave him a big smile. "Anyone special in your life, Elliot?" she asked, flirtatiously.

I'd expected the question, and was sure you would mention Lilly, but in an offhand way. But you answered, "Yeah, I've been living with Lilly for a long time. She owns a terrific gallery in the Hudson Valley. It's pretty well known. People come up from the city for openings. And, we just refinished remodeling the house—making it more comfortable for the two of us. Lilly designed the whole remodel. Fewer bedrooms, more open space. It's spectacular." You didn't look at me when you said this.

"No kids?" Jordan asked. He looked less bright, more tired than he had when the dinner began.

"No kids," you answered firmly. "I'm not really a kid person. Lilly has three, already grown when we got together. Two married now. No, I've never really wanted kids. Judith's always after me about kids." You chuckled and finally looked at me. "But I don't think I'd be any good at it."

I stared back at you, then checked my watch. "Speaking of kids," I said, "I'm visiting my son Evan, and I'm sure he's waiting up for me. That's the way it goes, Roberta. Eventually kids and parents reverse roles. Now he worries about me and gives me boring lectures about my eating and sleeping habits." I stood and went around the table, brushing my lips across everyone's cheeks, giving each the barest of kisses. "Great to see you, Roberta, Jordan. Please let me know if either of you get to San Francisco. I'd love to see you. Show you around. I'm a good tour guide, aren't I, Elliot?" I smiled down at you. "And don't forget, I'll be waiting for that next chapter." I left the restaurant and walked into the chilly evening, angry more at myself than Elliot. He'd never lied about Lillian. I just hadn't listened.

We continued to exchange manila envelopes for a few more years. I couldn't bear to completely stop reading your work, even after that disastrous visit to New York. I carefully read and edited as best as I could, but we spoke more honestly about it as time went on. You'd worked hard at your manuscript, struggling mightily with it. No one could deny that. Yet, as I'd suspected almost from the book's first chapter, you were not a novelist. The book never felt real to me, the characters never took on life. That was the reaction you got, I fear, when you sent it out into the world. You received rejection after rejection. This was probably the only endeavor at which you found no success. Although you kept the studio for a while, eventually you gave up working on the story about the guilty attorney.

"Someday I'll get back to it," you told me. "But it's feeling stale now. Maybe I ought to try nonfiction. A book about antitrust law. But not now. Now I need a break from living in my head so much. Lilly and I are going to travel. She finally sold her gallery. I promised her we'd go to Europe together. Remember?" you asked me.

Once you gave up your dream of writing, you attacked world travel with the same gusto and ambition you'd shown toward every-thing else in your life. With Lilly, you visited country after country, logging in more frequent flyer miles than you could use in a lifetime. Every few months, you were off to another magical place. Lilly must have given up her stern practicality and begun to enjoy the good life. You sent postcards from exotic locations, first Europe and then beyond: Africa, South America—even the Arctic. Because they were signed, "Elliot and Lillian," the cards were unimportant to me. I'd read them quickly, then toss them aside. How many ecstatic descriptions of ancient hill towns or wide beaches or nearly extinct animal species could one care about? Was it the same as when Seth and I had been traveling the world so many years before? It was difficult then to interest people in our adventures. No one really wanted to hear about it. In your sixties, you and Lillian were finally seeing the world (though the upscale hotels you sent the cards from hardly resembled the youth hostels and shacks of Seth's and my youthful travels). I just couldn't muster any interest.

While you and Lillian were traveling around the globe, I increased my hours at County Social Services, becoming a full-time employee again. I worked hard and my job continued to be satisfying. After Joseph went to college, I often stayed late at the office. Why not? It was a novelty to work without guilt, to have no responsibilities waiting for me at home. No soccer games to go to, no one else's dinner to think of. I became a supervisor of fifty caseworkers, all working toward the Herculean task of placing children in foster homes. Sometimes, though rarely, the placements even led to adoption. Seeing a child finally finding a permanent home, living with people they could call their family, was the best part of the job. I liked mentoring new social workers, too, watching them gain confidence. As I got older, I watched with satisfaction, but from afar, my own three children launching their lives. In college, Joseph made the decision he wanted to be a doctor, as his father had been. He studied conscientiously, preparing for medical school. Miriam surprised me by her marriage in her twenties to Gray, a man neither as charismatic as her father, Seth, nor as bookish as Walt. He was a good, kind husband and they made a happy home, certainly one with less drama than the example

Seth and I had provided. She'd always been easier than her twin brother, Evan, who with his high-strung temperament and difficulty in focusing, had floundered in school. But along with the freedom of no longer needing to hide that he was gay, other parts of his life began to fall into place. He liked his job as an admissions counselor, one he seemed very well suited for. Eventually, Evan found a partner, Ira—and, as far as I could determine, they seemed happy.

I had a large circle of friends. I joined book clubs. I took up yoga. I was busy. Occasionally, I went on dates—but these had become less frequent and there had not been anyone special since Walt. In my sixties, I supposed there never would be, although my tech-savvy friend Rachel had persuaded me to try the online method of meeting people, a phenomena that only seemed to lead to disappointment. Men my own age seemed to fall into two categories: those interested in meeting women decades younger than themselves, or those wanting, as another friend said, "a nurse with a purse." After a few dispiriting coffee dates, I could barely bother to turn on the computer to see who had looked at my so-called "profile." I took vacations. Marnie and I went on a tour of the Galapagos. We loved the animals, especially the penguins, as well as the pristine beauty. When we returned, her seasick-prone husband thanked me profusely for accompanying his wife, again getting him off the hook.

Being seen. It was what I'd always wanted from a man, yet it eluded me. Sure, I'd had moments with you, Elliot, the sexual connections we'd had, those presents you sent me which no one else could have selected, the letters and phone calls. We shared many things: impressions of art and music, the literature we were engaged with, politics. We talked over our respective dilemmas at work, you with your writing, me supervising the other social workers. Importantly, our shared past, the knowledge of our youth and families, remained a bond.

However, there were everyday details of my life which I felt were not lofty enough for our correspondence. Importantly, Elliot, you never understood the place my three children held in my life.

I didn't mention to you, for example, my worries about Evan and, later, Joseph. Could I have helped Evan more in his struggles to find his identity? Seth and I never saw eye to eye on Evan. I felt helpless when I discovered pot, and then cocaine, in his room in high school. And Joseph. He never rebelled, desperately wanting not to be a worry to me. But he was such a perfectionist, so hard on himself. I ached to know what Walt would have said, and wished I had help guiding him. Did Joseph really want to be a doctor, or was he fulfilling generational expectations of his family? Might I have done more, or was that hovering? I lay awake nights and thought and worried about my children, always wishing I could talk over these concerns with someone. Yet I never brought them up to you, Elliot. I knew my concerns about the kids weren't things you could help me with.

Children change your life irrevocably. I'd spent countless hours planning birthday parties, the themes never duplicated—constructing cakes in the shape of whales, witches, princesses. There had been nights when I'd nursed one of the kids, frightened by a flushed face or a loud, croupy cough coming from deep within a tiny chest. There were frantic afternoons trying to get the endless paperwork done at my office, knowing I had to be at a sports field for a game at four, worried I might miss the pivotal play of the season. The twins and Joseph were the heart of my life. Motherhood, though often a burden, was more a joy, but why bother to say any of those things to you, Elliot? You couldn't have related to them.

I began to see a preciousness to the way you spent your days— beholden to no one, having almost no responsibilities. Without kids, people can do completely as they please. I must confess, I saw a sort of shallowness to it. You needed to have had a child, children. In moments of melancholy, as my youngest, Joseph, was leaving for college, I thought sadly how you'd not experienced having a baby, had not taken care of a child, watched this child develop into unique personhood. Your time with Meredith's son had been brief. You even admitted that you had lost contact with Matthew. I was shocked. Imagine, you didn't know where the boy was. Children are the most satisfying experience a human being can have. Walt knew this. It was what made him saddest about dying young—leaving us behind. In his last months, he'd agonized about not being there for the children.

At one point, I said what was on my mind, honestly spoke about what I felt you were missing by not having kids. Isn't truthfulness what good friends give each other? Unfortunately, I learned this is not always the case, for it did not go well and resulted in an almost irreparable rent in our relationship. After you and Lilly came back from Southeast Asia, you rhapsodized about the beautiful children you'd seen in Viet Nam. It had been great being silly with the kids, you said, telling me how you blew soap bubbles from containers you'd brought as cheap gifts. "Language was no barrier," you said. "We just played and played."

"Oh, Elliot, you should have a child, of your own," I responded. It came out without thinking. "You're missing out on the greatest adventure of life."

"What?" you practically shouted into the phone. "Again? Are you out of your mind, Judith? That's the last thing I needed. You're like an old *bubbe* from a shtetl in Europe. Always asking when I'm going to have kids. Since when does a person have to have kids to be satisfied? When will you let up on the subject of kids?"

"I'm sorry," I said. "You're right. It's none of my business." But then, because I often don't know when to stop, I added, "It's because I've always felt you'd have been a wonderful father."

"Ha," you snorted. "After Meredith died, her family couldn't wait to pry Matthew out of my house. Her sister, Renata, swooped down and whisked him away just days after the funeral. They didn't think I'd make such a wonderful father."

"Oh, Elliot," I said, remembering how this had hurt him. "That was completely different. You were working so hard—how could you have been a single father? You'd only known Matthew a short time and he was so needy, so devastated by his mother's death. But a baby of your own. That's what I always wished for you."

"Matthew was better off without me," you said. "Everyone saw that. And a baby?" I heard a short, bitter laugh on the other end of the line. "Have you thought about my wonderful genes? Are you forgetting that my mother had a mental illness that killed her? A baby? Why would I want to pass on my genes? Shit, Judith, listen to what you're saying."

"Maybe," I said. "But your mom, when she could, was a wonderful mother."

"Why are we having this conversation again? How many times do we have to talk about this?"

"I know, I know," I said, again going too far and knowing it. My heart was pounding. "But I've always wished you were with someone younger. Someone who you could have a family with."

What I really wished, of course, was that we'd had children together. That had been my dream. When we were in San Francisco, you yourself had said as much. Hadn't you whispered in my ear how we would make beautiful children together? Why had you said those things to me? I'd actually listened and believed every word.

"It's Lilly I'm with!" you were shouting. "Not someone younger. Not anyone else. Lilly. Do you think I don't notice how you keep putting her down, ignoring her? Why don't you accept that I have the life I want? I don't want anything else."

I was chastened and apologized. I vowed never to bring up kids again. I promised I'd try to be more positive about Lilly. And I meant it. I really tried. I swore to myself that I would bury my decades-long disappointment that you'd chosen other women, especially Lilly, and not me. But you had had enough of my scolding and meddling. After that argument in our sixties, sadly you and I were estranged for years.

Perhaps this was a good thing. With you, Elliot, not occupying center stage, I realized something important. Who I really wished for was Walt. Poor, dead Walt. He was who I wanted to see and who I wanted to see me. Walt had been interested in everything about me, *especially* the children—all three of them. It took more than a decade after he died for me to begin the real process of grieving for him. Busy raising the kids, fantasizing over Elliot, and whatever else I filled my life with, I had deferred the pain for so long, I thought I could avoid it. Finally, I ran from it no longer. All the grief books say that this is the way it happens—unexpectedly and piercingly. Sometimes there was a dream in which Walt was suddenly alive. He'd look at me with his warm brown eyes and say with a kind smile, "You thought I was dead? Ha, don't be silly, I was just away for a while. Why did you think I was dead?" That dream was so real, I'd wake happy. But the dream was evanescent, Walt's lanky form fading before the relieved smile left my face. Awake fully, I felt the loss anew.

Sometimes, it even happened when I was awake. I'd be returning home from visiting one of the children and walk through the door with my suitcase, replaying in my head, for example, the latest interesting thing Joseph had told me. I'd start to formulate the words of how I'd ask Walt what he thought, knowing how interested he'd be in the conversation. But instead there was the quiet house, cold because the thermostat was set low and Walt is forever in the ground, never again to offer his seasoned, sage opinions. Never again to see me.

11

Moving

As the moving crew unloaded the last of my drastically reduced possessions, there was a knock at the partially opened front door. I finished writing the check, tore it from the checkbook, and handed it over to one of the heavily tattooed fellows who had carted and grunted my stuff up from the street into the elevator and down the hall to my apartment. "Thanks, guys," I said, before turning to the woman waiting in my doorway.

"Dolores Levine, MSW, Loma Alta Social Director," her badge read. Curly hair, harried, no makeup, but with good eye contact, why, she looked like . . . me. More accurately, she looked like the former me, the social worker who'd only recently retired. I was probably just five or six years older than this woman, but as we faced one another in the doorway of the two-bedroom apartment I'd now call home, Dolores and I stood at opposite sides of the professional divide. She was a staff member at Loma Alta, while I was a resident. This made me one of Dolores's clients, someone to be ministered to. Shockingly, it also made me officially an old person. I had retired from my job at Child Protective Services and sold my comfortable three-thousand-square-foot home in the Oakland Hills. In doing this, I'd created a new Judith—one who was not a social worker, but *had* a social worker.

I was not in the habit of needing or asking for anything, had certainly never before had a social worker, so I was curious to see what

Dolores would be offering. She looked confident in her role as Judith Sherman's social director. Dolores provided services, but she served those at the other end of the life cycle from my own previous case-load of foster children. In that life, Dolores might have been one of my girlfriends. If she wasn't now standing in my doorway in a professional capacity, wearing an employee badge, we could have been going off to dinner somewhere.

"Come in," I said. "Sorry I can't offer you a seat."

"Not a problem," Dolores said, surveying the mountain of boxes and bubble-wrapped furniture that filled the living room. "I don't envy you, putting all this away, but you'll have plenty of time to deal with it later. Now, you need sustenance. They serve dinner from five until six in the dining room and, trust me, you don't want to be late. The dieticians take no pity on latecomers and they won't give you a morsel after six. Come, I'll show you downstairs and introduce you around."

Yes, I was weary. Moving had been exhausting. The huge house in the Oakland Hills had sold so quickly that the past month was a blur of packing, trying to persuade my children to take belongings it turned out that only I thought were special, carting boxes to Goodwill, and then, finally, hauling the remainder to the dump. Those three children of mine should be on their knees with gratitude that I'd saved them the trouble of sorting through a lifetime of possessions after I kicked the bucket. But they weren't. They were furious with me and wanted no part of this move.

I'd promised myself that this new apartment would contain little nostalgia. Previously, I had been a woman who favored colorful chaos in home decorating—collections of art glass, vintage clothing, tapestries and textiles, unmatched crockery from around the world. "Hippie shit," I overheard my son Evan describe my collections to Ira, his once boyfriend, and now husband, who was an interior decorator. In the new place, I vowed I'd go for a whole different look:

sparse, clean, and clutter-free. I'd visited Evan and Ira's immaculate loft in Soho. They'd undoubtedly approve of the new place—even though they, along with everyone else, were aghast that I'd chosen to move into a retirement community at the relatively young age of seventy-one.

I obediently followed Dolores downstairs and into the dining room.

"We've assigned you to Mrs. Rosen's table," she said.

That said a lot, didn't it? Mrs. Rosen's table. It told you immediately who was the alpha old lady.

"I think you'll like it there," Dolores continued. "At least I hope you will. The table needs a fourth. They aren't always an easy bunch, that group, but they're interesting. I suspect you're up to the task. Not everyone has been." She turned to eye me. "But once a social worker, always a social worker, right?"

"I appreciate your honesty," I said to Dolores, pleased she, at least, recognized my former professional self. "And you're right, after forty years, I'm sure the old habits will still be there."

"Anyway, give it a try," said Dolores. "If it doesn't work out, we'll find other options."

I had been informed that at dinner we were always to sit at the same table—like on a cruise ship. Moving around provided too many complications, and besides, the staff needed to know who had not come out of their apartments that day. That way, they could check on the residents—see if they were still breathing, I suppose. Breakfast, for those who made it downstairs before noon, was open seating. Lunch was a buffet (with waiters assigned to carry residents' trays to any available table). But now it was dinner and as I walked behind Dolores toward my table, I looked around at the people already seated. Old, sad, proud. You didn't need to be a social worker to see that. The dining room was a formal space resembling not quite a hospital cafeteria and not quite a hotel restaurant, but a magazine ad for either. The décor was created to neither offend nor please.

When I decided to move into Loma Alta, every single one of my friends thought I was crazy, and told me so. You would not believe the anxiety it stirred up in people. If I was old, then they were old. My action worried not only my friends, but also my three grown children. There wasn't one person who supported the idea—not even my younger son, Joseph, who was almost finished with his training to be an emergency medicine doctor and usually on the same page as me. You'd have thought I suggested they put me on an ice floe and shove me out to sea.

"These days, seventy isn't so old." Over and over, I heard that one.

My daughter, Miriam, in her mid-forties, seemed the most appalled. As soon as she heard my plans, she phoned each and every day from Los Angeles, trying to talk me out of it.

"Why, for God's sake," she asked furiously, "are you treating yourself like an old lady? It's ridiculous. You just finished a bicycle trip through Vermont. You're *not* ready for an old people's home."

"It's not an old people's home," I said. "Not like in the old days. It's an active adults' community."

I didn't feel as if I needed to explain myself to Miriam, or to anyone. For starters, the house in the Oakland Hills was getting me down. I ate too many dinners alone. Hadn't I counseled people not to wait to move until they were too old to create a new life for themselves? I'd seen plenty of elderly neighbors and relatives delay moving into senior living facilities, or whatever euphemism was currently in vogue, only to end up on the tail end of some debilitating decline. They'd moved too late, when they were already feeble and could no longer take care of their homes or even themselves. Often someone else made the decision for them. And then what happened? Their supposed golden years immediately became empty and bleak. They could barely leave their rooms or apartments. They never made new friends and sunk deeper and deeper into isolation and depression. Then, senility set in. When that happened, what good was the pristine swimming pool or the billiard table in the lobby? Once senile, did it matter that there was a bulletin board full of announcements of activities and concerts and bus trips to the outlet mall?

I had my own reasons for moving. But for now, I'd keep them to myself. It was no one else's business—including my family's. The story I put out and stuck to was that I planned to take every trip to every damned opera, concert, or ballet offered by the old folks'/ active adults' community. I wouldn't have to pay a cent for parking or gas. I'd lean back on the plush seat in the souped-up bus from Loma Alta. At Davies Symphony Hall in San Francisco, or at the War Memorial Opera House across the street, I'd listen to all the Wagner and Mozart I wanted—from prime seats, even. Then I'd get back on the bus and close my eyes for the thirty-five-minute drive back to Belmont, replaying the glorious music in my head, undisturbed by traffic.

I'd made a bundle from selling the house in the hills. Of late, there always seemed to be high-tech millionaires who wanted to enroll their children in the fantastic Piedmont school district and to live in my family-friendly Oakland neighborhood only a half hour from all that was available in San Francisco. The community even offered "diversity," and so these young masters of the universe could tell themselves that although they might be obscenely rich, they still exposed their precious kids to real life: to black or brown or Asian families. When these young millionaires arrived to look at my house, realtors and spouses in tow, I tried looking as feeble as possible. I'd slowly lead them upstairs and then direct their gaze toward the magnificent view from the bank of windows in the bedroom. Then I'd hang back, pretending to straighten towels in the bathroom. When those thirtysomethings looked out at the Golden Gate Bridge and at the skyline of the city, I could hear a collective intake of breaths.

It was, indeed, a splendid view, and, admittedly, the single thing I'd miss most about the house when I sold it.

The realtor would shush her clients, whispering a warning, "Don't act so excited. We'll talk back at the office. Do you want the owner to get you into a bidding war?"

Which is precisely what I did. I waited until there were four people who'd fallen in love with the place, swooning about the tree house (built for my own three kids and still left standing), and the original stained-glass windows. Then I slowed down, pretending that I was having second thoughts about selling and giving up all those memories. You know, "I raised three kids in this house. I have such fond memories. Honestly, I don't know if I can go through with it." This got the buyers really nervous, and they coveted the house even more than they had originally. They'd already been imagining their first Thanksgiving, sitting in the charming dining room with its four-inch crown moldings and now, damn it, they wanted this house. They were prepared to fight for it. Finally, my realtor and I set a date by which we said we'd consider all offers. Bids could be submitted on that date only, not before. As I sat back and waited for the envelopes to arrive, I thought about how much I hated scrambling to find someone to clean the gutters every year, what a fortune it had been to heat the huge, poorly insulated place. I thought with relief about getting rid of the shelves of books and collections I'd once loved, but now felt anchored down by. As those buyers submitted their bids, one by one, it was obvious they had gotten into precisely the feeding frenzy we'd hoped for. Eventually, I accepted an offer which was half a million more than my realtor and I had previously agreed would be acceptable. And, believe me, this original amount was criminal.

"Ladies, look who I've brought you," Dolores said with great good cheer, as if she was delivering an extravagant present to the three women sitting before us. "A fourth. Now your table has a fourth."

She was the only person smiling. The group did not appear to feel the need for a fourth.

A woman dressed in a St. John knit suit, gold braiding along the jacket collar, patted down her perfect blond bob and looked up from the half glasses perched on her nose. She'd been reading the printed menu. There she was—Mrs. Adelle Rosen—trim and neat and Republican.

"Dolores," the alpha old lady said, looking at her watch, "I did not think it possible, but the service in the dining room seems to have gotten even slower. Do you know how long we have been waiting? Fifteen minutes. They hire a new batch of servers and it only gets worse. And why, I wish you'd explain, do they have us order our dinner for tomorrow, when today's has not yet arrived? How do I know what I will feel like eating for dinner tomorrow?" She waved the menu indignantly.

"I know, I know, Adelle," Dolores said soothingly. "You've been terribly patient about the new help and the new rules. But now I want you to welcome someone. Mrs. Sherman. Judith moved into Loma Alta only this afternoon."

Mrs. Rosen looked me up and down, noting my jeans and faded black turtleneck. Clearly, not appropriate dinner attire. *Too bad*, I snarled in my mind. It was moving attire.

"And fish. Again. The third time this week," Mrs. Rosen continued, ignoring me and pointing at the printed sheet. "We'll all die of mercury poisoning."

I sat down. Dolores and I exchanged a look, then the social worker pointed to the clock. "Got to go, ladies," she said. "Meeting. I'm so sorry. Mrs. Block, Mrs. Saperstein, Mrs. Rosen, introduce yourselves. Remember, each of you were once new here. Be nice, ladies, please. Bye for now, Mrs. Sherman. I'll come up and check on you before I leave tonight. Keep a list. Tell me what you need."

This might take some getting used to, I thought. Having a social director look in on me. Especially one, who despite a facelift that raised her eyebrows into a permanent arch of surprise, was practically my own age. I smiled and nodded at Mrs. Rosen across the table. Bitches. They're everywhere. At the playground in grade school. In high school. College. Even in the old people's home. Whoever says that little old ladies are sweet, obviously has not dined at Loma Alta. Young bitches grow up to be old lady bitches. Why wouldn't they?

I turned to the two women at either side of me, who had not yet spoken. "Call me Judith," I said. "Tell me about yourselves," I added in my best social worker voice and smiled.

"Vera Saperstein," said the woman on my right, a woman who appeared well into her nineties. "I practically opened the place. But I'm not the oldest resident here—that one is ninety-nine. However, I'm the oldest resident here who still has all her marbles." She tapped the side of her head. Mrs. Saperstein was wearing a muted brown pantsuit, but the color was in her jewelry, an amazing display of gems. There were rubies and emeralds and sapphires on her fingers, and she had a pendant around her neck that contained the largest amber I had ever seen. I couldn't take my eyes off that stone, the deep honeyed brown of it. Now I'd always know what the color amber should look like.

Mrs. Saperstein noticed me staring. She said, "You're admiring my jewels? Everyone notices my rings and pins and necklaces." She wiggled her fingers gaily toward me.

"That amber is beautiful," I said. "Its color. The perfect shape. It belongs in a museum. It's fabulous."

"Thank you, my dear. My late husband was a jeweler. Whenever he came across a particularly beautiful stone, wherever we were in the world, he had to have it. He'd buy it and make it into a piece for me. This one we picked up in Russia. I wear them all. In rotation. Why not? What am I saving them for?"

"Enough about your jewelry, Vera." Mrs. Rosen broke in. "There will be plenty of time for her to admire your baubles." She looked over at me. "Let me warn you," Mrs. Rosen said, "everyone here repeats the same stories. And, the food. For what they charge, you think we'd get quality, not this substandard rubbish. Someone ought to investigate. Maybe you. You seem like you've still got the energy. Or, are you sick? You look young, but perhaps you signed yourself into this place because you've got an incurable illness? Never mind. Don't tell me." She waved her hand, as if warding me and my germs away. "I do not want to know. But if you do get bored and need a project, I wish you'd look into the buying practices. I assure you, someone in the kitchen is on the take." She sniffed, then dismissed me and went back to studying her menu.

I sighed and looked at the woman on my left, who was different in every way possible from the other two. She was a shadow, faded and pale, no makeup, no decoration, her downy white hair cropped so close to her head that bits of pink showed through. I extended my hand to this shadow woman. "You're Mrs. Block?" I asked.

The small woman nodded. What probably had been deep blue eyes were now pale, watery, and red rimmed.

Vera Saperstein spoke for her. "You won't get too far with Louise. She's not much of a talker. And, Her Highness, over there." She tilted her head toward Mrs. Rosen. "Unless she wants to interrupt someone else, she rations her words. Very stingy. I figure about forty-five per meal. She might have reached her quota already. And, don't expect a smile. She rations those, too. One a week, at most."

Mrs. Rosen ignored Mrs. Saperstein and reached for a yellow golf pencil from the shallow crystal dish at the center of the table. She began circling items on her menu.

Dinner, seven days a week, with this bunch. I gazed at Mrs. Saperstein. A walking jewelry store, but a probable source of amusement. And Mrs. Rosen. Or perhaps it was Ms.? She looked as if she had been a professional woman, not a bleeding heart liberal social worker like me, who'd worn jeans to work and been overwhelmed by the child welfare system that only rarely allowed me to do my job. No, Mrs. Rosen looked like someone who'd had a significant career in which she made important decisions. She was crisp, ironed, and smelled of expensive perfume. I would have to get to know this woman. Charm her, or maybe shock her out of her bitchiness. She looked as if she was in the same virginal condition in which she'd entered this life. No men to rumple her. But who knew? There were always surprises when you learn about other women's lives.

A waiter approached the table bearing a tray with four steaming bowls on it.

"Hello, sweethearts," he said in Spanish-accented English, using the mock-flirtatious tone reserved for old ladies by young, good-looking men. "I've got some nice chicken rice soup for you. Very, very hot. *Muy caliente*, just like you girls. Nobody burn themselves and sue me, okay?" His biceps flashed in front of me as he put the soup bowls down. I wasn't dead. Not yet. I could see the body he honed in the gym—even under the unflattering scrubs that made him look like an orderly.

I lifted my spoon and looked around the table, remembering the children I used to visit, placed in foster homes by Alameda County Child Protective Services. These children had already been scarred by events that should not befall any child. When I visited them, I'd wonder to myself about their future—what they'd look like when they grew up. Would the little dark-skinned girl with the delicate nose and full lips remain a beauty? Or would years of cheap food and street drugs turn her lumpy and gray? Would the stuttering, fearful boy I saw in a group home gain some confidence and be able to look down future tormentors? Or would the gangs of Oakland enfold him in false security?

Now, at dinner, I did the same wondering with my three dining companions. However, instead of imagining the children as grown-ups, I went backward, wondering what these three old ladies had looked like in their prime, when their lives had been at their fullest. Which were the stunners? Who had driven men wild? Jeweled Mrs. Saperstein's voice was now so deep, it sounded as if it came from the throat of a man. Yet, I could picture her sixty years earlier—a raven-haired knockout. I bet there was a cigarette between her sultry, dark lips, lips that blew expert smoke rings. I imagined this feisty Vera frequenting Las Vegas with Mr. Saperstein. He'd have worn a whopping diamond tiepin and probably wisecracked with the high rollers.

Mrs. Adelle Rosen, on the other hand, was all elegance and efficiency. With her perfect bones, straight nose, high cheekbones, anyone could see that she'd been beautiful. She had aged well. Her posture was erect, her hair still thick and full. There was no paunch under the silk blouse she tucked neatly into her trousers. I had long ago stopped tucking blouses into my slacks, had given away all my belts. But Mrs. Rosen wore a narrow brown belt at her waist, fastened with the familiar Gucci horse bit. Even now, her elegance and evidence of a still-shapely figure had the power to make me jealous, I'm afraid. I saw her efficiency, the need to tick things off a list, as she was now doing with the dinner menu. No warmth. Had there ever been?

And what was emaciated Mrs. Block's story? This woman emitted an odor as well, but not of expensive perfume. It was a somewhat unpleasant odor, stale and yeasty. This had been my greatest fear— the scent of bodily fluids. Smells bothered me greatly and the old lady odor coming from tiny Mrs. Block made me put down my soup spoon. What had she looked like as a young woman? I wondered, but saw nothing through the haze of her dreariness.

"We're related," Mrs. Saperstein said, watching me study Mrs. Block. I realized nothing was going to escape Vera Saperstein.

"Related?" I said, surprised. "You and Mrs. Block?" Could any two beings look less alike than Vera Saperstein, a large peacock of a woman, and Mrs. Block, so tiny and pale?

"We're *machatunim*, Louise and me. You're familiar with that word? You're of the Jewish faith?" Mrs. Saperstein asked nonchalantly in her gravelly voice, though I had a feeling she'd been leading up to this particular question ever since I sat down.

"Yes," I said. "I'm Jewish. But I don't know that word."

"You don't know what it means to be *machatunim*? You're a Jew?" She sounded shocked.

"No." I shrugged. "Sorry."

"It means," Mrs. Saperstein explained, "that my son is married to Louise's daughter. There is no translation for the word in English. Our children are married to each other. We share our grandchildren. Isn't that something? Never did we expect to live side by side like this. Louise came from Brooklyn, the same apartment in Borough Park for sixty years. But the snow and ice got to be too much. Especially when, well, you know." She hesitated, then raised her eyebrows meaningfully at me before she went on. "Could she go to Florida? Among strangers? Of course not. My son, who is an angel, wouldn't hear of it. He said to her, 'Ma, you're coming to California. I know just the spot for you.' So here we are, me and Louise Block, the *machatunistas* together. Looking after each other."

The tiny woman answered softly, looking down at her wrinkled hands, "You, Vera. You're the one that looks after me. I'm no good to anyone."

"It's okay, Louise, you'll get on your feet again, darling," Mrs. Saperstein said, and reached across the table to pat Mrs. Block's hands with her own bejeweled ones. Vera lowered her voice. "Louise has had a hard year," she said in her sandpapery whisper. "First her husband. Then her son. One right after the other."

The tears that had been welling up in Mrs. Block's eyes began to fall. She started to sob, quiet little sobs that sounded like the cry of an exotic bird.

The thought went around the table like a child's game of telephone, transmitted silently from ear to ear to ear. What should we do? None of us wanted to get involved. The other two women wanted to finish their meal, perhaps goad each other a bit, talk about the food or the prices. I couldn't wait to eat my early dinner, then go upstairs and unpack. Get settled. I did not want to inquire into the grief of this little woman with the soft white hair. But how could I ignore her? She was now crying brokenheartedly. People at other tables were beginning to notice and turn toward us. *Do something*, said their stern expressions. *She's one of yours.*

"Sha, sha, Louise," Mrs. Saperstein pleaded. "Please eat your soup. I'm sorry I upset you. I promised the kids I'd get you to eat. Now you're not even touching your soup. You can't live on black coffee alone. That's all I ever see you take, coffee. No nourishment at all."

Adelle Rosen straightened her already straight back as she brought dainty spoonfuls to her mouth. "Mrs. Block, have you availed yourself of Dolores's services yet? I, myself, have not done so, but I know some people find it quite useful to speak with her." She reached inside her beautiful black kid bag and removed a carefully folded tissue, then slid it over to Mrs. Block.

"Sorry, sorry," Mrs. Block said as she took the tissue. "Sometimes I don't know when it's coming on. It takes me by surprise. It's not your fault, Vera. And then this." She waved her hand over the bowl in front of her.

The flirting server came up behind Mrs. Block. "What'sa matter, sweetheart? You don't like the soup? Everybody likes the chicken soup. You find it too salty today?"

"No," Mrs. Block said. "It smells lovely. Sorry, I'm just not hungry. May I have some coffee, please, Gabriel? Black."

"For you, honey, I always got coffee," the young man answered.

Gabriel brought the cup and soon after, the main course. "Hope you like this, Mrs. Sherman. Our first night special." He slid a plate of Chinese chicken salad made with miniature canned tangerines and crispy wonton noodles sprinkled over the top before me. I like Chinese chicken salad a great deal, perhaps even more so with tangerines from a can. But it was hard to dive in with Mrs. Block weeping beside me. Gradually, her crying slowed, though her large red-rimmed eyes still watered. The four of us sat in silence, three of us slowly eating our meals.

After dinner, when we stood to go, I swear I couldn't help myself. It was the social worker reflex in me, just as Dolores had predicted. I took tiny Mrs. Block's hand and said, "Let's go sit on the patio outside the atrium. I hear piano music. It sounds pretty."

"No, no," she said. "You've got your unpacking to do. Please, don't bother yourself. I'm sorry. I've ruined your first meal here."

"I have plenty of time to unpack. Now I could use some fresh air— it looks nice out there on the atrium. Come, we'll listen to the piano together."

She nodded slowly. "I like music," she said and kept her hand in mine. The grand piano was a fine one, and the young musician, probably a student from Stanford or San Jose State, played capably, first Schubert, then some Brahms. For a while, we sat and listened. But when the musician slipped into show tunes, Mrs. Block stiffened. She recognized the opening chords of the first song and quickly got to her feet and said, "I can't listen to this one. I'm sorry, I've got to go." She hesitated before asking, "Would you come up to my place? Would that be okay? I'll make us some coffee. Or maybe you're a tea drinker?"

"Of course," I said and sighed, resigned to beginning my unpacking in the morning. How could I not accept the woman's invitation? "Yes, tea," I added.

We got on the elevator and she pressed the button for the floor above mine. I followed shrunken Mrs. Block down the hall, her rounded back making her even smaller than she was. She worked the keys into the lock of her apartment and led me into a room filled with heavy dark furniture, every surface covered with family photographs.

After she started the teakettle, she joined me in the living room. I pointed to a family portrait. It was of a nice-looking bald man, posed with a slender brunette and two teenaged kids sitting on a driftwood log, ocean waves pounding the beach behind them.

"Your daughter and her family?" I asked. "Mrs. Saperstein's son?"

She nodded. "Yes. Marcy and her husband insisted I come out here. They worried that I was starving myself. 'Come,' they said, 'enjoy the sunshine. Let someone do the cooking for you, for a change.'"

"But you are very thin, Mrs. Block," I said. "Very pale. I can understand their worry."

"Who wants to eat? Who wants the sunshine? Of course I'm thin, but I can't eat. Nothing goes down."

"Why?" I asked.

"Because of Artie. My son, Arthur, may he rest in peace."

Mrs. Block's eyes began to water again. I had seen many people cry, but this woman had endless tears—they flowed unceasingly. I wondered if they would ever dry up. Was there a time when a person's tear ducts were empty and could make no more tears? The kettle began to sing and, still crying, Mrs. Block went to the kitchen and returned with our tea.

"Which one was Artie?" I asked. I'd been looking around the room, practically wallpapered with photographs. "Will you show me a picture of him?"

Mrs. Block placed our teacups on a low table and walked to the bookshelf, picking up a photo framed in black wood. "Artie," she said, and held out the picture so that I could study it.

In front of an impressive-looking building, a theater, for it had a marquee, stood a young, very good-looking man. His arm was draped around an older plump, dark-haired woman. This must be Mrs. Block, I thought, though I could see no actual resemblance. The woman in the picture was smiling from ear to ear, blooming with health, her round face framed by the upturned collar of a full-length mink coat. The man was dressed in perfectly fitting clothes—camel blazer, tight-fitting jeans, a scarf tied expertly around his neck. His boyish smile was also bright. He looked down fondly at the older woman, a head shorter than he was.

"He's so good looking. Like an actor. And look at you, you're beaming." I didn't want to look up and trade the image of the healthy woman in the photo for the skeletal one beside me. I tried to make out the words on the marquee above the mother and son. Something short and, I sensed, important. Was it "Cats" or "Gypsy"?

"He created the dances for big shows on Broadway," Mrs. Block answered. "A very well-known choreographer." Mrs. Block wiped her eyes, still sad, but speaking proudly, saying the words distinctly, making sure I heard every syllable.

"You must have seen all his shows."

"Of course. Every show he did—many, many times. There was always a seat for me and my husband—although my husband didn't go as often as I did. At every performance, I waited for the dancers to come out. That was the best part for me. I didn't care what the actors said, sometimes the songs made no sense. I just wanted to see them dance. The steps my Artie thought up in his head and then taught them."

"I love the dancing in shows, too," I said. Mrs. Block's apartment was so tiny, I thought, small like the woman herself. Then I realized that my own place, one floor down, was not much larger. I wondered if after I unpacked, my new home would also feel like a memorial to the past. I was not ready to live only with memories. I still wanted to make new memories. What had I done? What had I consigned myself to? I began to feel claustrophobic. "When did your son die?" I asked, trying to calm myself with social worker questions.

"It's a year this month. On the twelfth is his yahrzeit," she answered and pointed to a little glass filled with wax, a Jewish memorial candle, on a side table.

"What happened?" I asked.

"Cancer," Mrs. Block said in a lowered voice. "My husband went quickly, a heart attack a few months before Artie. He didn't have to be there to bury our son. But Artie went slow." She took a breath. "We watched him suffer a long time. And then, I watched him alone."

The apartment was quiet. "You must have been so proud of him," I finally said, still looking down at the picture. "To be successful like that in New York. It's quite an accomplishment."

"Proud?" Mrs. Block looked at me. She was different than she'd been earlier. She spoke haughtily, as if I was a child, or an unsophisticated rube. "I went to the Tonys every year. The Tonys." She looked at me to make sure I understood. "We'd shop for my gown together. Artie always wanted me in a bright-colored dress, so if he won, he could see me from the stage. And he always won. You know what it's like to see your son get awards like that?" She shook her head, lost in her thoughts. "He always dedicated it to me. When he was on the stage, he'd hold the statue up above his head and look right at me. 'This one's for you, Ma. Always for you!' he'd say. Then he'd blow me a kiss, right there in front of all those people. On television, even, everyone saw him blow me a kiss."

I imagined it and it was exciting. I loved those award shows. I watched them every year, the Emmys, the Oscars, the Tonys. I'd seen the winners give those speeches of thanks to their mothers, their fathers, their wives and husbands. As Mrs. Block told me about her son, Arthur, I felt almost as if I was meeting a celebrity. I was starstruck.

"You had all those experiences with him. He gave you so much," I said.

"But what does it matter now? I'm alive and he's in the ground. If you ever saw Artie move, and then how he was at the end, it would break your heart. Artie never walked anywhere. Always leaping and moving. My husband tried to get him to study something else. He was opposed to the dancing. Marcy, his sister, she was the one who went to business school." Mrs. Block pointed back to the picture of the family at the ocean. "But there was nothing besides dancing for Artie," Mrs. Block said. Then she added, in a smaller voice, "Maybe food. Dancing and food."

"Your son liked to eat?" I asked.

"Oh, yes," Mrs. Block said with a wry smile. "Both of us. He enjoyed food like nobody else. We exchanged recipes. We talked every day about what we were going to eat for dinner that night. He took me to fancy restaurants. And holes in the wall, too. 'Ma,' he'd say, 'you have to try the steamed buns from this place I found in Chinatown. A hole in the wall, but the steamed buns are fluffy, like a cushion. And the sweet bean paste filling. You'll love them, Ma.' Only, as you see in the picture, I didn't dance, so the food went right to my hips. But not Artie, he danced away the calories. Long and graceful. Not a fatso like me."

I smiled and nodded. "Yes. I like to eat, also. Way too much." I reflected on my own lifelong battle with food.

Mrs. Block went on, "But I buried my baby. A mother is not supposed to outlast her child. You're a mother?"

I nodded. "Yes," I said. "I have three."

"Then, you understand, of course. Why is he dead, when he was just beginning? Why am I, an old lady, still here?" Her eyes began to fill with tears again.

"There's no answer to those questions," I said. "You know that."

"But I can't eat his food. That I can't do."

"'His food'?" I asked.

"Everyone thinks I'm crazy, but when I bring a spoonful to my mouth, I think about the food he loved. I can't swallow. It doesn't go down." Tears began to fall again, but more slowly, not like at the dining table. "At the end, he couldn't eat a morsel. He was shrunken, skin and bones."

I had a glimmer of this woman's pain. "Today," I asked, "was there something special about the dinner?"

She nodded. "The soup," she said. "When he worked on a new show, he was nervous. I'd make him my chicken soup. It would calm him. Sometimes, when he worked late, I'd come into town and bring him a Tupperware filled with soup. His friends laughed. They said he did his best work when he had my soup waiting for him. They asked if I would make them some."

I thought I understood. It was a form of survivor's guilt, wasn't it? I remembered when I'd read a book about the Holocaust, about the concentration camps where everyone was starving, I couldn't bring anything to my mouth. In my mind, I'd see pictures of those living skeletons and gag, then push away my plate. How could I eat? I suppose it was the same for Mrs. Block.

This was Mrs. Rosen's table, my new dinner companions. Beautiful Adelle Rosen, who'd probably had her share of losses, and if she did not, then that was loss in itself. Then, Mrs. Saperstein, who'd lost the husband who adored her so much, a man who draped her in jewels. And finally, poor Mrs. Block, who was slowly starving herself to death to avoid eating food her son should be eating. There were no strangers to loss at Mrs. Rosen's table. Somehow, I would make it a foursome. I'd tell Dolores that one of her worries was solved. I'd be the fourth at meals and I'd listen to their stories. There was little that the friendship of women couldn't lighten. I'd learned that long ago. When the time came, and I knew it would not be too far off, that these dining companions discovered the truth of why I had come to Loma Alta, I hoped I'd be able to count on them as well.

I moved to Mrs. Block and sat beside her on the couch. I bent and put my cheek close to hers and inhaled. She smelled good, not stale at all, more like fresh baked bread.

It would be okay here, I decided. Eventually I would make the others in my life understand why I'd moved to Loma Alta, at the age of seventy-one and still healthy. And if they did not, well, I couldn't worry about it.

12
Need

The years are compressed. From childhood to old age, the single constant has been you, Elliot. I have known and loved you more years than I did my parents, my two husbands, or even my children. You have been before, during, and after. When I was in the middle of raising my children, it seemed as if there would never be anything else. But actually, the children were a blink; they were young, they needed me, then they grew up and were gone. Of course, there are vivid memories of each of them: Miriam and Evan and Joseph, bathing them and smelling their exquisite baby smell, watching them reach all the landmarks—sitting, walking, their first words. All three kids were precious, each approaching life so differently. There was Miriam with her no-nonsense competence, Evan in his constant thrum of motion and drama, Joseph carefully watching, making sure everyone's needs were met. There were Halloween costumes, first days of school, trips we took, hours and hours of cooking, then eating meals together around the same bleached oak kitchen table. There was joy and hard work in raising each of the children, and I recognize that it is no small thing to have done it three times—much of it alone. I am proud they've gone out into the world, each doing interesting and useful things. Yet I don't even wonder if they think of me nearly as often as I think of them. Of course they do not. It would be odd if they did. Only now, when I am old, do I have frequent thoughts of my own mother, long gone. I think of her and feel closer to her than I did when I was growing up. We even have imaginary conversations, she and I—the two of us sharing our astonishment at being old. When I was young, she was an annoyance. Now, in my inner conversations, she's more of a friend.

The world is different than when we were growing up back then in Chicago. There are all those gadgets we are supposed to need—those miniature screens that are so difficult to learn and then, just as they've been mastered, get replaced by an upgraded version. But these are mere frustrations, not nearly as challenging as the hurdles my own parents faced. I don't know how they did it—my mother immigrating from a shtetl one couldn't even find on a map today, coming over on a rough crossing from Europe, and my father, fearfully keeping his life savings in a wrinkled green passbook from the neighborhood bank, always checking his balance, fearful of the next disaster. They came from such uncertainty, from such hard circumstances, yet, in spite of being plucked into a world full of differences, they managed rather gracefully. And your parents, Elliot—the way they had to cope with your mother's mental illness, yet not having real tools to do it with.

I've been back, through the years, to our old neighborhood on Chicago's north side. There were family gatherings, weddings and bar mitzvahs and reunions. I don't imagine you went back as often, Elliot. You had fewer good memories. The Jews are still migrating north, living in new suburbs, the towns created out of what used to be considered farmland. Our generation remains huddled together in these enclaves, just as Jews did in our parents' and grandparents' time. Despite horrendously long commutes, they seem comfortable, satisfied. It is surprising how many have married one another. Some got together in high school, others at the University of Illinois, where they met at Jewish sorority and fraternity parties, parties designed to safely connect them to each other, reducing the threat of inter-marriage with the non-Jews. There are few divorces among our old friends. Families remain connected, shoulders cozily pressed against shoulders in suburban dining rooms, a room my own mother would have coveted, gathering for Passovers and birthdays and anniversaries. That could have easily been my fate, I think, perhaps not such a bad one. However, something, Elliot, made us go further afield. We weren't satisfied with what most of our cohort had. We had outsize ambitions, you and I, for achievements and experiences.

When I finally retired from my long career at Children's Protective Services, I was still living in that gracious cedar-shingled place in the Oakland Hills, bought when Walt and I married long ago. No matter how flippant I seemed when I eventually sold it, greedily banking my not inconsiderable profits, I left a big part of me in that house. My personality was stamped in every room. I loved each window sash, scuff on the floor, even the drafts that caused me to shiver in summer's fog. I thought I'd stay there until they carried me out feet first. It wasn't just the memories; I didn't need the house for that. But the house itself was a comfort to me. From the master bedroom, as I fell asleep each night, I'd look out at the lights of the Bay Bridge, which is not as much of a media star as the Golden Gate Bridge, but is a solid and utilitarian structure faithfully connecting me and millions of others from the East Bay to San Francisco and beyond. I liked living where I was. The hills rising above the city felt absolutely correct. Oakland is not a pretentious community, like some of the new money towns of Silicon Valley. Despite Gertrude Stein's denigrating comments, there was most certainly something there. Oakland's charms had embraced me from the time I moved in. Inside the house, there were soft down-filled sofa and chairs that had taken my shape. All the furniture in the large rooms had been arranged exactly the same way for so long that I could wander through the dark on sleepless nights, holding a cup of tea, my body knowing, without thinking, exactly how to navigate around chairs and tables so I never stubbed my toes or spilled a drop from my cup. I knew every inch of that house and could, even to this day, draw a completely accurate blueprint, each room shaped properly, each object in its place, down to the tooth-brush holder on the granite bathroom counter or the order of spices in the wooden spice rack in the pantry. I'd assumed I would remain in this comfortable house for years to come, not foreseeing the events that caused me to leave it. So, it is understandable that when I sold the house and moved into the Loma Alta retirement community, every-one—all of my friends, as well as my three children—was astonished and puzzled. They'd all thought, as I did, that even after I retired, I'd stay in that cedar-shingled house in the hills.

When I looked ahead to life post-retirement, I assumed there would be projects. What were those projects? I can barely remem-ber what I imagined, for they seem so generic now, not really inter-esting at all. Like genealogy—a popular hobby that a lot of people develop a passion for when they get older. But after a few halfhearted stabs at genealogy websites, I found I couldn't get excited about it. Those records from the small villages in Russia, most were burned or destroyed or maybe never kept at all. The Jews were outside of official record keeping, that's the sense my mother gave me. Even if one went looking for birth or death certificates, what were our names before Ellis Island anyway? Certainly not my Sherman or your Pine. How would I ever find my people? Oh, just thinking about it made me weary, and I never got very far on the Sherman family tree.

I considered helping foster kids. I thought I might take the train-ing and become a court-appointed advocate for a child needing a voice in the legal system. Kids got shuffled and lost in the maze of hearings and custody arrangements. I was familiar with this maze and certainly I could be helpful. But wasn't that very much like what I'd been doing for forty years? All that time I'd worked for the county, I'd been advocating for kids. What was the point of retirement, if you did exactly what you'd done in your job, only didn't receive a paycheck for it?

I decided to stop worrying about it. After so many years of raising my own children, as well as solving the problems of children in the foster care system, I craved some time that was unstructured. That was what would come first: freedom to read, to pull a chair out to the backyard and turn my face to the sun. I'd just wait a bit, confident that this next phase of life would appear to me in due time. And, of course, that is exactly what happened. My project appeared.

On my last day at Child Protective Services, the staff threw a big retirement party for me. It was on the patio of a Mexican restaurant near the office, a place we'd been going to ever since I first started working at the dingy county building on Solano. Everyone ate tamales and drank too many margaritas and there were some lovely speeches. Some old-timers even came back for the party, for few people from my era were still working. The younger people, holding glasses with salted rims, stopped by and kept repeating the same question: "Forty years, Judith. My God, how did you do it?" I could only reply that forty years passed by quicker than they could imagine, knowing this must have sounded absurd to the young people. To someone starting out, staying in the same job for forty years seems incomprehensible. I suppose if you'd told me when I was hired at the County that I'd stay there my entire professional life, it would have seemed incomprehensible, too. I don't know how it got to be forty years, I really don't. The young social workers seemed not too interested in my memories, so while I drank my own margaritas and ate chips and salsa, I mentioned my upcoming trip to Hawaii. That was something everyone could talk about. Whether they'd been or hoped to go, visiting the Hawaiian Islands seems to be a goal for everyone.

I did take a retirement trip to Maui and it was, indeed, wonderful. There were luscious hours spent floating in water the same temperature as my own body. How remarkable to stay at the beach as long as

I liked, paddling aimlessly in the ocean, then lying on the soft sand, reading for hours, not compelled by someone else's demands to eat or sleep or be amused. My skin was burnished to a perfect tan (among fatal maladies, I'm sure that skin cancer is not the thing that will get me, and I've been lucky about wrinkles, too, so, wisely or not, I refuse moderation in my intake of sun). I felt renewed and returned happy, quite pleased with my calendar's relative emptiness. But, this was not to last. How could it? I never had the chance to get bored, because soon after I returned to my cedar-shingled house, with little more than holiday cards to connect us, you phoned. It had been nearly a decade.

"My goodness, Elliot. Is that really you? How great to hear your voice. It's been ages."

"Has it?" you asked, acting as if it had been eight weeks since we'd spoken, not eight years.

"It has. What's new? Where have you and Lillian traveled to lately? I can't remember where the last card came from."

"Lillian's gone," you said, no preliminaries or polite chitchat. "She left me."

This news caused such pulsing of blood in my head, that I was almost deafened. I took a deep breath and pressed you for details. Where had she gone? You just repeated the same words, she was gone. You spoke slowly, with some difficulty, as if you yourself had not fully absorbed the news.

It seemed impossible to me that any female would actually leave Elliot Pine. Meredith's death, of course, was a kind of departure, but an unwilling one. If there had been any other woman who'd ended a relationship with you, I hadn't heard about her. You, Elliot, the one who was left? I couldn't imagine it. Why would Lillian go?

"Where did she go?" I tried again. "What happened?"

Finally, in a flat voice, you explained that Lillian was moving back to Quebec. Without you. You spoke with so little inflection, it crossed my mind that you might be taking antidepressants. There were too many long pauses and you seemed to be struggling to recall the details, even correcting yourself a few times on the sequence of events. Serotonin uptake re-inhibitors? I was full of questions, but I didn't push you, just listened. As you told the story, a bit of energy finally seemed to come back into your voice. You said that Lillian's grown son, a chef, was opening a restaurant in Montreal in a neighborhood that was fast becoming a world-class food capital. Lillian was planning to help her son open this restaurant. Her other children were already in Canada, or planning to return there.

"Why?" I asked. "Why would she want to do that?"

Lillian had grown tired of traveling, tired of your whole life together, you said. She claimed she'd been bored for some time and that the two of you no longer shared any of the same goals or interests. Aimless wandering, she called the trips and said she was through with such a foolish waste of time and money.

"Foolish?" I repeated. "She called it that?"

"Actually," you said, with a harsh laugh, "she might have used the word colossal. A colossal waste of time and money." The new restaurant was to be a family business, *her* family's, she'd stressed. Lillian's children were very hardworking; she'd brought them up that way, she said, so she was confident of the restaurant's success.

"You must have told her she didn't need to work," I said.

"Of course, I told her we have enough to live on. We have plenty."

"And what did she say to that?" I asked.

Lillian had replied, "I know all about your fuck-you money, Elliot. But that is your money, not mine." As you spoke, you did a fairly good imitation of her accent. "The restaurant will be my legacy for my children," you said in that distinctive Quebecoise of Lillian's. "I can no longer remain so decadent, doing nothing productive."

I snorted. Legacy? Decadent? Trust Lillian to make such dramatic pronouncements.

"What's that, Judith? What did you say?"

"Nothing, Elliot," I answered. "I'm listening. Go on. How did she seem when she left?"

"Angry, as if I'd done something terrible by providing for her, by giving her a good life. What did I do wrong?" you asked. "I don't understand."

How pathetic you sounded. I couldn't bear it. Besides being puzzled, I was growing furious with Lillian. "But Elliot," I said. "Lillian must be seventy-five years old. Right? People her age don't start businesses as exhausting as restaurants. They slow down. It's a crazy plan."

"I know, I know," you said tiredly. "But that's Lillian. Age has never meant a thing to her. I didn't realize she was bored with our life. I thought she was happy, but she said that ever since she sold the gallery, she's felt useless. Made it seem like it was my fault. She said I took away her, oh, I don't know, took away her something."

Lillian thrived on work, I knew that. That's all she talked about when I'd first met her at Serendipity in New York, her family's poverty and how hard she worked her whole life, implying that Elliot and I knew little about that. Now, as best I understood it, her new plan was to start a restaurant with her son as chef and the rest of the family helping out in some capacity. She'd not only missed work, she'd told you, but she also missed her culture, missed speaking French. The time had come for her to go home. But it appeared that all of it—her boredom, the restaurant, missing Quebec—had been news to you.

As ridiculous as I thought the whole thing sounded, I surprised myself by saying, "Okay, so why don't you go with her? Why not move to Montreal?" I couldn't believe I was making an argument for you to preserve your relationship with Lillian. Yet how could I not? No matter what I thought of the woman, you and she were a couple. You'd built a life around her and you sounded miserable.

There was an especially long pause. "Elliot? Are you still there?"

"What did you say, Judith? Sorry. I got distracted, you can't imagine how crazy this has been."

"I said, why can't you go to Montreal with Lilly?" Why were Elliot's reactions so slowed down, I wondered, so subdued? The whole conversation was strange, especially as we hadn't spoken in so long.

"Sorry, yes, that's right. Join her. I suggested that," you replied. "I said, 'Listen, Lillian, I don't mind selling the house here in Beacon and moving to Canada. There's nothing to keep me here. I can help you with the restaurant.'"

"And?" I asked. "What did she say to that?"

"She laughed at me," you said quietly.

"Laughed at you?"

"Yeah, and then she said I didn't get it. This was her project. Hers and her children's. I forget what she said next. No, I remember now. She asked me what would I do in a restaurant? Wash dishes?"

I could just hear Lillian, see her pursed little French mouth. To her, Elliot's and my lives had seemed privileged. She'd decided we were self-indulgent and soft. Lillian came from a family of nine brothers and sisters. Life was endless effort—they never had enough food, clothing, space. She had mentioned, more than once, that Americans like us had no idea what it was to be poor, really poor. To her, we'd had silver spoons in our mouths. I'd never thought of us as growing up privileged, but it's all relative, I know.

"Apparently she doesn't think I'm a very hard worker," you continued. "At least not by her standards. She laughed and looked at my hands. 'They are soft as a baby's. Those hands were not meant for dish washing.'"

"Jesus, Elliot, you're a lawyer," I said. "What does she expect?"

"Yeah," you answered. "But I thought about my father. Remember? His were the roughest hands imaginable. The way he had to load and unload meat from those refrigerator trucks?"

I did remember. When we were kids, the hugeness of Mr. Pine's forearms and hands had scared me. Besides being big, his hands were always chapped and red from the cold, even in summer, the knuckles knobby and distorted. All these years later, I could still see his sandpapery hands.

"The cold gave my dad terrible arthritis," you said. "At night, he'd massage his fingers, trying to straighten them. He'd say to us, 'You boys get an education. You don't want to be tossing slabs of meat all day. Like me. Work with your brains, not your backs.'"

"You could make a life for yourself in Quebec, Elliot," I said. "You have so many talents. Be their lawyer. Or do the books."

"Judith, you aren't listening. Lillian doesn't want me there." And you sounded completely defeated. "She's very decisive. We're over. Once Lilly is through with something or someone, she's through. Like they never existed. Trust me, I've seen her. There's a grocery shop in Beacon she'd avoid, even if we had nothing in the fridge but spoiled milk, because the owner once slighted her. There are people she hasn't spoken a word to since she sold the gallery because they were once late with a payment."

"I just don't understand it," I said. "Why would she end the relationship now? After all the years you and she have been together."

You didn't answer. There was another long silence.

"Elliot," I finally said, "are you still there?"

"Yeah," you answered after the maddeningly long pause. Then, you delivered your second piece of startling news. "I'm here. But I should tell you that it could be more than the restaurant. There's something else. Something I haven't wanted to admit. But Lilly lived with me and I know she saw. She noticed what was happening."

"What's wrong?" I asked, the pulse in my head getting even louder. "Are you sick, Elliot?"

"Not sick, exactly. But I'm not the same. I'm not me."

Haltingly, you told me that for the past two years you'd been getting more and more forgetful. You could tell that you were processing information much more slowly and could feel Lillian's impatience. More than a few times, you'd had to call her, unable to remember where you'd parked the car in town or even to recall the errand you'd set out on. It was getting worse, you said, and you were frightened, but when you tried to talk to Lilly about it, she changed the subject. She would say you weren't focusing enough. You just needed to concentrate, try harder, instead of daydreaming all the time. Lillian herself had never had even a cold in all their years together. She could not accept whatever was happening. You paused again and said, "You see, Lillian dislikes weakness of any kind."

"That's why she's leaving? Because you're forgetful? It couldn't be that," I said. "We're all getting older. Forgetting things."

I felt myself getting queasy and swallowed hard to keep down the food from breakfast. Elliot was the most brilliant man I knew. Quick, funny, knowledgeable in every area. Could something be wrong with his brain? If there was, then it was a very cruel and ironic joke being played by whoever doled out maladies. Perhaps Elliot was exaggerating the problem. I wanted to believe that.

Everyone I knew was having trouble remembering words. Just last week, I'd gone shopping with two of my girlfriends. We'd met a fourth friend for lunch, Marnie, and were trying to describe to her something we'd just seen in a store.

"It was gorgeous. The softest red leather thing," I said, after we all sat down together.

"What was it?" Marnie asked.

"One of those jacket things. What're they called? You know, we wore them to work all the time?" I answered.

"Yeah," said Vivian, "I can't remember what they're called either. But this was so soft. Like butter. You know what I mean, with a collar and buttons down the front."

"Right," added our friend, Rachel. "We wore them with skirts, like a suit. What're they called again? Damn." She closed her eyes in concentration, trying to remember the word.

Marnie stared at the three of us uncomprehendingly, either because she herself was not able to name the article, or was confused by this game of charades we were inexplicably playing.

Finally, the waitress, who we'd not realized had arrived to take our order and was listening to our desperate fumbling, said, "A blazer," and began tapping her pencil on her pad. "You mean a blazer, right?" She was young, with skinny jeans and thigh-high boots.

"Blazer!" we all shouted at once. "Yeah, that's it. A red blazer."

I looked up at the waitress. *Bitch*, I thought. *Today you may have put us out of our misery and given us the word our minds refused to recollect, but one day, you won't be able to think of some word, either.* "Thanks," I said politely to the young waitress, "just couldn't think of it. Blazer. Of course. That's it. Thanks."

"Sure," the girl said. "Have you decided what you'd like to order?"

Maybe this was all it was with Elliot, the same word-finding problems all of us were experiencing as we began our seventies. Those tricky nouns, or people's names, that sometimes needed special effort to be recalled.

You answered very quietly, "It's bad, Judith. It isn't constant, it comes and goes. But it's happening more often. Not just words. I forget how to do things, stupid things. This morning I couldn't remember how to work the toaster oven. I stood there holding my bagel and stared at the gizmo, but I didn't know what I should do with it."

"Are you alone there?" I asked, my fear increasing. Besides my head pounding, I could feel how hard my heart was beating. "Has Lillian completely moved out?" How could she leave him?

"She's been back and forth a few times. Between here and Canada. She's been packing up her things and shipping them up there, I suppose. I don't think she's coming back anymore, though. She's been gone quite a while this time." You sighed.

"How long?" I asked.

"I don't know exactly. The place looks so empty without her stuff. Her art, her clothes. I go over to our closet and there are all those empty hangers clinking together."

For some reason my mind went to the bronze statue of Lillian, the one you'd described to me so vividly when you first met her. The life-sized nude sculpted by a famous artist who lived in the Hudson Valley. You'd said, with some pride, that even without clear facial features, it was quite recognizable to everyone who knew Lillian. I'd never seen the sculpture, but I'd imagined it many times all these years, could not get the image out of my head. What would it be like to see your naked body as public art in the town where you lived? What would it be like to be the lover of the woman whose firm breasts and formidable ass stood exposed to the elements and all who passed by in the town square? You had seemed so impressed by the sculpture of Lillian when you'd first told me about it. Now, with her gone, how would you feel about it? Unless you made a detour, I suppose you still walked past it on your way to your favorite coffee shop. Did you stop and look at it with longing now? Did you brush off the snow that had accumulated on those breasts? Or did you hurry past? Okay, I had never liked Lillian, but now I felt the woman must be as cold and unfeeling as that bronze statue. Who could leave a man when both of you were in your seventies? When he was obviously having trouble and not as capable as he used to be? Weren't they partners? Even if they had never married, one expected some loyalty from a long-term mate. Her behavior was unforgivable.

"Have you been to a doctor yet, Elliot?" I asked evenly.

"A doctor? For what?" you asked.

I closed my eyes. "About the forgetting."

"Oh. Yeah. My regular guy. Here in town. I can't remember his name right now. He says I need to go for tests. To someone who specializes in de . . . in memory problems."

"Okay, then you need to do that," I said, aching that you couldn't even say the word. Imagining how scared you must be. I knew how frightened I would be. Especially remembering how confused my mother had been at the end. Dementia. It was everyone's greatest fear. "Can you get some names from your doctor, a specialist? A neurologist? It'd be good to get evaluated, to know what you're dealing with," I said. Then, after I took a breath, I added, "Do you want some help with that, Elliot?"

There was no answer. "Elliot?" I repeated.

Then you said, "I'll get back to you, Judith. I think there's something wrong with the washing machine. It's making awful noises. It might be leaking." And abruptly, just like that, you hung up.

For several days, I heard nothing more. I worried about you in the short term. In the best of times, you'd never been a domestic person. What were you eating? Had water flooded that beautiful wood floor of yours, the one you told me you'd had restored when you and Lillian remodeled? I also worried about the long term. What exactly was wrong with you? How bad was it? Was there anyone to help you? With no children, and no relatives nearby, there was just Phillip, your only remaining brother. Your older brother, Jeffrey, had died of an aneurysm some time ago. The last I'd heard, Phil was still living in Chicago, but dealing with his own problems—an alcoholic wife, difficult children. Were there any close friends nearby? I could not fathom how Lilly had just left and not helped you with practical arrangements. It was winter and news of huge snowstorms on the eastern seaboard had been all over the papers.

I couldn't stand it any longer. Several times over the next few days, I picked up the telephone and phoned you. There was never an answer. Finally, on my fourth or fifth try, you picked up, but only after the answering machine had already started its recording, a message made by Lilly in her French Canadian accent.

"Hello," you said, breaking into the message. "Who's there?"

"It's Judith, Elliot. I've been worrying about you. Are you okay?"

"Judith? Sure, I'm okay. Did someone call you? Who told you to call me?" you said, sounding surprisingly suspicious. "What did they let you know?"

"Let me know?" I asked, worried that some new disaster had befallen you over the past few days.

"About Lillian," you said, then paused. "I guess you don't know. Lilly's left me. She went back to Canada."

"Oh?" I spoke in a small voice. "When did she go?" This was like a scary Hitchcock movie. You recounted, once again, how Lilly was in Montreal. How she was going to open a restaurant with her son, the chef. Almost word for word, you repeated the conversation we'd had a few days before, but this time you did not mention your memory problems. You sounded sadder than you had on our previous call, though. Even more beaten down.

"Elliot," I said, "are you alone? Is anyone there in the house helping you?"

"Of course," you answered. "Our housekeeper's here. Uh, you know who I mean. I can't remember her name now. She's been working for us for years. Did you ever meet her? She's here cleaning up now. In the kitchen."

"Elliot," I said. "When we talked a few days ago, you told me you were forgetting things. You told me you were going to get evaluated by a doctor."

"Jesus," you answered, sounding surprised. "I said that? I don't remember that. You and I talked? Shit, are you sure? Or did somebody call you? Lilly phoned you, didn't she?"

"No," I said evenly. "No one called me. You told me yourself, Elliot. Listen, do you suppose I could talk to your housekeeper? Can you put her on?" I heard you put the phone down, then heard your footsteps.

After a long few minutes, a man's voice said, "Hello? Who's this?"

"This is Elliot's friend, Judith. Judith Sherman. I'm phoning from

California. Elliot said he was going to get his housekeeper and put her on the phone. Who is this? You're not the housekeeper, are you?"

"No." The man gave a short laugh. "Trina is here, though. The housekeeper. My name is Julius. Trina cleans for me and my wife, as well as for Elliot and Lilly. Trina called us a little while ago, asked us to come over. When she'd got here, to the house, she saw Elliot wandering out back, where the woods are. It's been terribly cold and icy this week and he was wearing only a flannel shirt and jeans. And slippers, some kind of felt slippers. He'd gone out to get the paper, but he couldn't find his way back into the house. Poor guy was freezing. Thank God Trina came and let him in. She's making him soup right now. I just got here."

This was worse, I thought, worse than I'd imagined. "How long has he been this way? When did Lilly leave?"

"Frankly," Julius said, "we've noticed him changing, little by little, for over a year, though I haven't seen him much since the summer. We heard from Trina that Lilly was leaving. Lilly also told a friend of my wife's, but she didn't come over and tell us. She was back and forth a bit. I saw her car go up and down the road. The last time must have been two weeks ago. We don't actually know what's going on. Friends have been coming over to check on Elliot. We're all trying to figure out what to do. And then Trina, of course, comes every other day. She's terrific. But, as you can imagine, it's kind of awkward. You must know how proud Elliot is. Sometimes, he's quite a bit better. Almost seems like the old Elliot. The problem is, we don't know who should take charge. Someone has to do something, though. It seems as if Lillian has really moved out. The place looks half-empty. Who should we call? Any family around?"

I closed my eyes again. "No, no family to speak of."

"No family. I see." The man, Julius, seemed disappointed. "Well, how good a friend are you?" he asked, hopefully.

"A good friend," I said. "But we've been out of touch for a bit."

And, as has happened too many times in my life, the words tumbled out before I could stop them. "Shall I come?" I asked. "I could help, I guess. I just retired, actually, so I have the time."

Julius exhaled a long breath. "God, yes. That would be excellent. We'd be so relieved. My wife and I. Other people, too. Judith, that's what you said your name is, right? We're neighbors, Judith, we care about Elliot. He has friends. They had friends. People are worried. But this seems bigger than we should be dealing with. You know, something for family to take care of." Then he repeated, as if I might have remembered someone since he last asked, "You're completely certain there's no family in the area?"

"No family," I concurred, then added, "But I'm like family. We've known each other almost our whole lives. I'll come. Of course I'll come." I looked around my comfortable kitchen in the Oakland Hills, wondering where this would all lead. What would I find when I got to Beacon? I couldn't imagine the possibilities. Yet I knew, absolutely, that I had to make the trip to New York. You needed me.

13

Beauty Undiminished

I flew from San Francisco to JFK, then got a train from Grand Central for the ninety-minute trip up the Hudson. Although snow covered everything, the small towns along the way looked pretty, and I wondered why I'd never visited before. By the time I arrived in Beacon, it was dark. I wished I could familiarize myself with your world. I wanted to see the streets of your town: that coffee shop, the bronze statue of Lillian, her gallery, now in the hands of others. I wanted to visit the studio where you wrote and phoned me for those hours-long conversations. But it was cold and dark, so I checked into the Beacon Inn and told myself I'd explore first thing in the morning.

Before I pulled the comfortable, soft duvet around me, I called your neighbor, Julius, to let him know I'd arrived. I'd make my way out to your house the next day. Julius told me the housekeeper, Trina, would be there to let me in.

"How is Elliot?" I asked. "Any change?"

"No, sorry. He seems just as forgetful and confused. I guess it's up and down. I did what you suggested, though and made an appointment with Elliot's doctor in town. For tomorrow. You can go with him—I told Dr. Fagin you'd bring him in."

"Did you tell Elliot I was coming to New York?" I asked, suddenly shy, all the bravado involved with sweeping in and taking charge drained out of me. After all, you might completely reject me, say you didn't even want me around to visit. In my life, I'd made so many assumptions, acted on them quickly, and was left to examine them later—only then seeing the flaws in my plan. I'd impulsively planned to rescue Elliot Pine, a man I hadn't seen in several years and one with whom I'd had a far from simple relationship. Would this be seen as intrusive or a gesture of concern? I was probably wondering this too late.

"The day before yesterday we spoke about you," Julius said. "Elliot seemed pleased about your visit. Spoke of you glowingly. But then," the neighbor continued, "yesterday and today, when we reminded him, he looked surprised. Both days he repeated, 'Judith coming here? In winter? Judith hates the cold. Why would Judith be coming to Beacon? You must mean someone else.'"

I laughed. "Well, he's got that right—I do hate the cold. At least he remembers that."

In the frigid January morning, I stepped outside for my tour of Beacon. But within a block, I scurried back to the hotel, not even making it as far as the coffee shop you'd spoken of for so many years. I had excruciating brain freeze, the front of my head and face aching, my nose dripping. The cold pierced my borrowed puffy coat and stung my eyes. For relief of this alone, Elliot should come with me back to California, I thought. Why would anyone willingly submit to weather like this?

I took a taxi out to your house. The driver went carefully, slowly navigating the roads. The ride surprised me; you lived so much farther from town than I'd expected. There were large open fields, interspersed with forested areas, ice weighing down the tree limbs. The pristine snow emphasized how rural the area was. I saw few signs of other people, no other cars on the road. How could you possibly stay out here alone? The only sound I heard was the taxi's tires covered with chains, slowly crunching over the snow. Trina must have been watching for me. As soon as the cab stopped, she ran out from the house onto the driveway. She was a youngish woman wearing a heavy sweater and fleece jacket over her jeans, clunky men's galoshes on her feet. We both sunk nearly to our knees in the snow as we made our way to the short, shoveled section in front of the house, both of us lugging my suitcase.

"So sorry," she said. "I tried to shovel a bit more, but that was as far as I got. It's been a brutal winter. The snow keeps falling, almost every day, then more again at night. It's impossible to keep up with. Fortunately, the plow came through this morning and cleared the road. Otherwise, I'm not sure your cab would have made it."

When we got inside the house, I tried to stop shivering. The cold was only part of it. I felt the usual tremors of excitement at seeing you, even more nervous than usual because of my mission. The arrogance of my mission.

You came down the stairs and stopped when you saw me. I'd tried to prepare myself for anything, the way you looked, whatever you'd say. Yet I caught my breath, for your beauty was undiminished. I'd anticipated many things about your appearance, aged, disheveled, agitated, but I hadn't expected you to still be so beautiful. You stared at me from the bottom of the stairs for a long moment. Finally, you walked toward me with your arms opened. "What the fuck?" you said. But it was with a smile and the corners of your eyes crinkled the way they always had.

"I heard you might need some help," I said, and shrugged my shoulders. "So I came." I'd decided on the flight to New York that there was no reason to pretend. Honesty was what you deserved.

You bent to hug me, to envelop me in your arms. However, instead of relaxing into the hug, I stiffened. As you'd come near, there was a strong odor I didn't like. Elliot, I am sorry to say, you smelled of piss. Piss and maybe more. I tried not to breathe as you hugged me.

When you straightened, you said, "Help? Help me with what? You look like you're the one needing help. Look at the size of that suitcase.

Trina, leave it. You'll both hurt yourselves. And Trina, could you call Lilly at the shop? Tell her we have company. This is wonderful, Judith, just wonderful. A great surprise."

Trina's eyes and mine met. I looked to her for guidance. What now? Was she going to correct Elliot or let it pass?

She spoke softly, but bless her, she spoke. "Elliot, you remember that Lilly sold her shop? And that she's left? She's gone back up to Canada. So, your friend Judith has come here to give you a hand." And Trina went toward the kitchen, patting your shoulder as she passed, but leaving us alone in the entryway.

I closed my eyes, astounded at how completely the same you looked, yet how different you seemed. Your jeans, your cable-knit wool sweater, maroon and well fitting, all negated by the fact that under those stylish clothes, there was an odor, yes, now rather strong, of someone who'd neglected to clean himself. I was so embarrassed for you.

"See," I said, annoyed at the false cheeriness of my voice, "it took your needing something to get me out here. All these years I said I'd come and now that it's probably sixty degrees warmer in California, and you've had these record snowfalls in New York, I finally made the trip. You'd better be happy to see me." I unbuttoned and then started to slip my arms out of the big puffy coat I was wearing.

You stared at me, then used the same gesture to brush back your hair that you'd used since boyhood. Your hair was also the same, thick and dark, that Kennedy hair, as we used to call it. There was a bit of gray in it now, though not much.

"I need help," you repeated, in a completely flat voice, not a question, nor a statement either.

"You need help," I repeated, more firmly. "You've been forgetting things and I know you, you'll want to get to the bottom of this. See what's going on. We have an appointment later this afternoon with your doctor in Beacon. George Fagin? At two. Remember George?"

"Of course I remember. He's been my doctor for years." You squinted at me. "How do you know George?" you asked suspiciously.

"I don't know him yet," I answered. "But your neighbor Julius made an appointment for us. For you." I hesitated before saying the next thing. For was I to be your friend? Your nurse? Your former lover? I didn't know yet, but there was no avoiding what had to be done. Your body could not be ignored. Your body was part of all this. Not just your mind. So I said what I had to say. "Let's go upstairs, so you can shower and change. I'll help you." I gave you my best smile. "Maybe we'll have time for you to take me out to lunch afterward, before your appointment. Show me the best Beacon has to offer." I started up the stairs, lugging my suitcase with two hands, willing you to follow me and willing myself to be brave.

It must have been the suitcase that jarred you into action. "Say," you said, and rushed forward, "let me get that. It's enormous. You can't take that. You don't even know where to put it."

We walked around the second floor, touring the space, you seeming unsure which of the rooms to leave my suitcase in. There were three bedrooms, all oriented toward the back of the property, with beautiful views of the trees and the sun shining on glistening snowy mounds. The master bedroom, your room, was large and comfortable. I could see places on the wall which were less faded, where paintings must have hung before Lillian took them. The bed was neatly made with an Amish quilt and the door to the master bath was open, a large room with green and blue glass tiles surrounding a deep tub and separate shower stall. It resembled a bathroom in an expensive spa.

The entire upstairs had a pleasantly worn pine floor, the planks wide and honey colored. The remaining two bedrooms were also tidily made up, but I could see that the smaller one had been used as an office. I took the third, the room farthest from your bedroom, decorated in bright yellow and blue, like the Swedish flag. There were new-looking yellow towels folded on the bed.

"It's a beautiful house, Elliot," I said. "I love this room. Can you leave my suitcase in here?" I dropped my puffy coat on the bed, next to the towels.

"Here?" you said and stared at me with surprise. "You're staying?"

"I am." I answered. "I'm staying until we have whatever is wrong with you sorted out. Then, we'll see."

I walked you back toward your bedroom. Shower or tub? I wondered. If it was shower, I might have to remove my clothes and get in with him. That would be too much after I'd just arrived. We'd start with a quick shower, you alone—after I first adjusted the spray so that the lower half of your body was thoroughly rinsed. I'd wait outside the stall, hand you a towel when you finished. Then a bath. I'd sit on the floor while you soaked, talk nonchalantly, try to make the situation less awkward, but help if needed. I doubted that Trina had come into the bathroom with you.

It took a long time, but the plan worked fairly well. It surprised me how passive you had become, how little you resisted. You seemed to have no inhibitions about either the shower or bath. I sat next to the tub in my jeans, after rolling up the sleeves of my black turtleneck so I could wash your back and neck with a thick white washrag. It reminded me of bathing my own children. Letting the warm water drip down your back, I thought of how, in other circumstances, this might have been a sensual moment. You and I had bathed together in many hotels. Then, I might have lit a candle and leaned back in the tub with you. Now, I washed you in a utilitarian, but gentle way. I didn't rush, but there was no lingering, just a thorough cleaning, round careful movements, so that the acrid, unpleasant smell I'd noticed when I arrived was replaced by the clean, fresh smell of the goat's milk soap I found in a dish near the tub. I remembered a game I'd played with my children when they were in the bath. I'd draw some letter on their back so that letter by letter, a word would be spelled out. Then they would try to guess the word. Would I play this game with you someday? Elliot Pine, the wordsmith. I became filled with sadness at the thought.

When you stood, I glanced at your shriveled balls and penis, the parts of your body that had sometimes given me pleasure, and sometimes, when I thought of you being with the other women in your life, caused me such painful jealousy. I handed you the thick towel, then turned away and went back to your room to get clothes.

"Thanks, Judith," you called, quite cheerful now and not the least embarrassed. "Wow, that felt great."

Everything in your room was neat and tidy. I found boxers and a T-shirt in your chest of drawers, corduroy pants and another ribbed sweater in the closet. Everything matched, there were no bad choices. All of your clothes were made of the natural fabrics you favored, silks and linens and wools, all in colors that worked together. I returned to the bathroom and handed you the pile of clothing. You'd obviously been managing to get dressed just fine.

"I'll go change now," I said. "Get some dry stuff. Maybe unpack a little. Then we can have lunch before your doctor's appointment. Remember? Dr. Fagin?"

"I remember, Judith," you said. And you tilted your head toward me reprovingly. "I remember."

Okay, I said to myself as I opened my suitcase to get fresh clothes. *Sometimes he remembers. Sometimes he doesn't.* How the hell was I going to figure this out? When to intervene? When to step back? Well, I'd managed to raise three kids, hadn't I? It was the same with raising kids. Sometimes they shot you withering looks which implied you should shut the fuck up, get out of their way. Other times, their need was desperate. They clung to you when you least expected it—perhaps only an hour after insulting you and telling you to back off. I intuited that it was going to be similar with you. I'd have to navigate carefully, know when to get out of the way, when to move closer. And, I'd have to do it while maintaining your dignity, all the while hearing from you the same kind of teenaged annoyance that I'd experienced with Miriam and Evan and Joseph. With my kids, especially the twins, I'd given and given, even when the recipient was rude and unappreciative. One moment, an outstretched hand would be slapped away and the next, grabbed frantically—the child terrified to be left alone. It wasn't just when they were kids or teenagers, either. Children did this at every stage, when they were toddlers and at every point along the way. Even in her forties, one day Miriam would call to frantically ask advice about one of her children, then, the very next day, rudely put me in my place when I offered what I'd thought was well-meaning advice. "Please, mother," she'd say, her voice dripping with condescension, "that's not the way it's done now." How had I overstepped? I wondered. No longer a kid, she was so prickly—still.

I knew how to do this, I told myself. It was a dance with steps I was familiar with, knowing my partner would sometimes be leaning in and at other times fleeing, abandoning me on the dance floor with barely a backward look. And I realized, also, that just as a parent could never do the abandoning, once I started this with you, I was going to have to stay for the duration. I was going to have to commit in a way you had never committed to me. I could do this, I told myself. All it took was love.

I left that first appointment with your internist, Dr. Fagin, carrying a sheaf of papers. He'd given us referrals for CT scans, blood tests, and MRIs. In addition, there were names of doctors in New York: neurologists, gerontologists, endocrinologists. It took nearly two months to make our way through these referrals. All the while I stayed in the blue and yellow room down the hall from you and kept track of our progress toward a diagnosis. Some days you were patient and easygoing about our many errands. We'd start out for the city early in the morning, discussing where we'd have lunch, thinking about a museum we'd like to visit, if there was time after our appointments. In a museum, you might unexpectedly put your arm around me, or tenderly take my hand as we stood in front of a painting. At long last, after six decades, we were a couple. Of sorts. Of course I realized the situation was not one you had fully chosen. You needed me. Yet, I cherished our time together and it seemed to me you felt the same way.

Some days did not go so well. Your normally good disposition would disappear and you'd be full of irritation. I couldn't get you out of bed, let alone out of the house. There was no use rushing you or trying to change your mood, so I'd cancel whatever appointments were scheduled for that day. I discovered that the best way to approach your obstinacy was intellectually. I sat on the bed next to you, and with markers and a sheaf of papers, I drew a differential diagnosis tree. It reminded me of the trees I'd drawn on placards during your campaign in American Zionist Youth, when we were sixteen. But this tree explained just what conditions we needed to rule out—metabolic, neurologic, autoimmune—and which tests or specialists we needed to see in order to do that, not why teenaged boys and girls should vote for you. You listened and eventually you would become interested and the next day would go better. Fortunately, you seemed untroubled by the long-term problems you might be facing. You left that to me, never seeming curious about the inevitable diagnosis, nor asking questions about your prognosis and what it would mean in terms of function in the future. Instead, I helped you focus on what tasks we still had to accomplish, and what aspect of your condition we were presently exploring. Your intellect would approach its formerly sharp state and you'd think of questions to ask the doctor during our next appointment. I would write down these questions in a notebook I kept for that purpose. This lack of concern for the eventual outcome made it easier for us both, of course. We didn't have to face a bleak future or talk about plans for such a future. We focused instead on what train to catch or the restaurant we'd chosen or what to buy for dinner that night.

We were together day in and day out. In that time, we discovered many things about one another, things that despite the long years of our friendship, we'd never had the opportunity or close proximity to learn. I found out that you had an insatiable appetite for junk food, couldn't pass a fast-food restaurant without demanding we stop for some greasy treat. I learned that you'd again become a Zionist. As when you were the regional president of AZY, the national Jewish youth organization, you idealized the State of Israel, and, judging by the daily volume of mail you received at the house in Beacon, were a large contributor to Israeli causes. These organizations were left-leaning ones, groups promoting peace within the Middle East and with the Palestinians, rather than the more right-wing, hardline factions, but still, your renewed connection with Israel somehow surprised me. I also discovered that you'd been well-respected in town, serving on any number of committees in Beacon: Friends of the Library, the Art Guild, the Commission to Keep the Hudson River Clean. But you no longer had any interest in these groups and would wave me away impatiently when I conveyed a message from a committee member reminding you of a meeting. "Not now." You'd shake your head. "Too busy." Yet the breadth and scope of your involvement in local issues was impressive.

We developed a comfortable rhythm. Besides accompanying you to your tests with doctors and therapists, we had appointments with lawyers and estate planners, even meetings with real estate agents. Slowly, the weather turned warmer, and I saw patches of green appear as the snow drifts near your house began to melt. I ate more McDonald's hamburgers and Taco Bell variations on cheese and tortillas in those weeks and months than I'd eaten during the previous twenty-five years. I rediscovered soft drinks, remembering the root beers and orange sodas of our Chicago childhood, enjoying how thirst quenching a fizzy soda could be. We both hated diet drinks, found artificial sugar distasteful. We laughed at how back then we called the drinks "pop," that word a dead giveaway of midwestern roots. I asked myself: What had I made such a fuss over? Why had I been so rigid about my eating habits? These foods I consumed with Elliot were very, very tasty. I would just have to visit a dentist as soon as I returned to California.

Eventually, we reached the top of our differential diagnostic tree. Your forgetfulness and confusion was not due to a brain tumor or a metabolic disturbance or an allergy of any type. The CT scans revealed no seizure disorder. We could find no other branches to explore which would explain your symptoms. You had dementia, pure and simple, probably Alzheimer's, and your condition seemed to be declining at a fairly rapid rate. The doctors showed us charts and graphs. Although no one could predict the precise rate of decline in months or years, it was certain that you could not continue to live alone. Someone must supervise your care, preferably, I thought, someone who loved you.

In whatever time was left, you and I would be together.

14
Elliot's Table

It was never a choice to love you, Elliot. On that long-ago September day, with Miss Schaffer humiliating and haranguing you in front of our fifth-grade class and blood seeping from the gash on your leg onto your white trousers, my heart ran out the door with you. I have tried to examine it from all sides, to explain it here, yet still I cannot. My love for you persisted, became a part of me and proved impossible to get rid of, no easier than amputating a hand or foot. Now, nearing the end, the question I need to ask and answer is, what space did loving you take up in my life? For I do realize there was a cost. Economists call this an opportunity cost, what we lose when we choose one thing over another. The answer, one I am ashamed to admit, is that because of my love for you, I loved everyone else inadequately. If my whole life, I thought of one boy, one man, loving this phantom of perfection single-mindedly, wasn't everyone else bound to come up short? No one could be as brilliant, as beautiful, as articulate. With no one else did I have the magic, the sensory attraction, the insanity. No one else saw into my soul, then gave and was given such consolation.

I am not blind. I knew, even before the Alzheimer's, how forgetful and tepid your love for me could be, how your passion for me never ignited in quite the way I dreamed. But I did not care. Sadly, my obsessive love for you made me reckless and careless with all the other men in my life: Jordan, Seth, others I wisely or unwisely invited into my bed, and even my dear, late husband, Walt. None stood a chance. God help me, perhaps even the children, Miriam and Evan and Joe, may also have suffered from my love for you. Always a little lonely, a little dissatisfied without you, could I have loved the others better?

So, this is the explanation of why, at the relatively young age of seventy-one, I moved into the Loma Alta Retirement Community. It is why I began dining at Mrs. Rosen's table, rather than in my own dining room in my own house in the Oakland Hills. I needed to find shelter for you and your shrinking mental capacities. Years earlier, making love to me in a hotel room in Manhattan, you'd said it yourself. "We must be connected for our whole lives," you declared, and then added a powerful image: "I'll crawl to see you in the old people's home." Those were your words, Elliot, and I did not forget them.

After I returned from the Hudson Valley early that spring, I spent weeks visiting retirement communities (no longer called old people's homes) throughout Northern California. I went only to the most highly recommended establishments—those limited to people with fat retirement accounts, long-term care insurance policies, or wealthy offspring. These tours were exhausting, but after a while, I realized there was a sameness to all the places, and it was pointless to keep looking. The first stop on all the visits was the office of the marketing director. Their offices are designed to project a homey warmth, with tall vases of fresh flowers and family photos placed strategically on the furniture. The salespeople wear nice suits and ask if you'd like a cup of coffee or tea. Their main job is to reassure guilty families that they are making a correct decision.

"You are doing the very best for your parents," they tell daughters and sons. Mom or Dad will certainly prefer living among people their own age and partaking in full and stimulating programs. This, adult children are told, is preferable to living with their own kin where they would be tucked away in a suburban house, empty and quiet by day and confusing and chaotic in the evening. Life at Loma Alta (or Hidden Hills or Rio Vista) will be far superior.

I was one of the few people who arrived in those marketing offices alone, sans family. I sat before the well-coiffed saleswomen or men and scanned what seemed to be the same shiny sales packet they handed me. All the communities had an art instructor or two, live music after dinner, and buses which ferried residents to grocery stores, cultural events, and even the local outlet mall. You will love the outlet's bargains, I was told. The retirees, both men and women, shown in the brochures looked healthy, vibrant, and well dressed. I was sure this perfect balance of genders belied the actuarial facts of male and female life expectancy. In truth, few men are actually in the mix. Oh well, none of it mattered. I was bored to death by the brochures and the presentations. My single question for these marketing directors was: Did they have a comprehensive program on-site for those with a diagnosis of dementia?

Frankly, I've always found outlet malls exhausting and avoid them despite any bargains to be had. Instead, I could hardly wait to investigate, with you, all the fast-food establishments in the area. My time in New York had reawakened a fondness for bacon-wrapped cheeseburgers, chocolate milk shakes, and potatoes cooked in God-knows what animal fat. Before each appointment with the marketing directors, I did a quick Google search to locate how many Jack in the Boxes, In and Outs, and McDonald's were in the immediate vicinity. You did not yet know about In and Out, Elliot. It thrilled me to think what pleasure that particular chain would give you.

The living spaces I toured also had a sameness to them. There were pedestals outside many of the doors on which residents could place some knickknack reflecting their previous interests: cross-stitched samplers embroidered with the grandchildren's names, watercolors of tropical islands visited, even Hummel figurines depicting doctors or lawyers, or whatever profession represented the life's work of the inhabitant inside the apartment. These small objects on display seemed sad to me. I had no interest in advertising my identity to those passing through the corridors. I'd already decided that I wanted few memorabilia in this new apartment, only minimalist simplicity, no statues or bric-a-brac. The flats all had a boxy layout; sentimental tchotchkes could not camouflage uninteresting design. Most importantly, both of us would be starting out with a clean slate; our apartment would contain few memories, neither yours nor mine.

Any two-bedroom apartment would suffice, I told the salespeople. I told them that in a few months, a friend would be arriving from his home in New York. I explained your diagnosis and said you'd live with me for as long as possible. I hoped to be a buffer between you and any tasks that were problematic for you. But I needed to know that eventually, whenever your cognitive and physical function began to worsen to the degree that I could no longer manage to care for you, that you could receive excellent care by experienced staff in a first-rate unit that was part of the same facility in which I lived. So I insisted that the marketing people tour me through the areas that most people preferred not to see—the places housing people in wheelchairs, people who stared vacantly at blank walls, and even the rooms occupied by elderly people in mismatched clothing who were sometimes tethered to their beds with straps. Of course, these were the areas the sales associates would rather *not* show me.

I'd done my homework, not to mention that I'd been a social worker for forty years. I knew what a good Alzheimer's program should include. I had read so much, I could design such a program myself. More importantly, I was in possession of firsthand knowledge of you and what would and would not make you comfortable. The visits went something like this:

"You wish to look at our Memory Care Unit, Mrs. Sherman?

This is for"—and they'd pause and look down uncomfortably at the paperwork I'd completed—"your husband?"

"No, he's not my husband. It's for my friend. A bit down the road."

The expected conversation about finances and legal matters would ensue. And then, obvious relief when the administrator learned that we both, you and I, had had the foresight to purchase generous long-term care policies, and that I also had the necessary legal documents to authorize me to make decisions involving your care. How happy they were that these unpleasant matters were so easily resolved. With practiced cheerfulness, they first showed me the billiard tables, the swimming pools, the residents' art exhibits, and the dining rooms cum restaurants.

"Would you like to join us for lunch?" one asked. "I'd be glad to order us a meal. We could go the restaurant. Maybe you'd like to meet our dietician."

"That's okay. I'm sure your food is delicious," I replied and thought that whenever we tired of the dietician's meals, we could pop out for a quick bacon cheeseburger.

I barely glanced around on the tours. The endless hallways blurred together. Finally, the administrator would lead me either to the elevator, or on a walk through well-manicured lawns to see a unit separated from the others. One community I toured was so huge, that we hopped on a conveniently placed golf cart to make the trip. At the entrances to these Memory Care Units, there were always keys to turn or numbers on a keypad to press. There would be apologies and fumbling embarrassment about the locks.

"We don't want anyone wandering away, getting lost," the administrator would explain. "That's everyone's worst nightmare."

"I imagine," I would say. "Perfectly understandable." Then I'd ask, "But when exactly was the last time someone wandered off?" I'd fix the administrator with a hard look, waiting for an answer.

Beyond the usual programs of occupational therapy and mental and physical stimulation, I had three unwritten criteria. First, I had to be able to visit any time, any day, and stay for as long as I liked, as well as to take you for outings as you were able. Second, the place must be clean and smell good. There could be no odors of urine, feces, or stale food lingering in the air. Finally, there could be no piglets or puppies on the wallpaper, no pastel clown decals, or anything else about the décor that smacked of the nursery and infantilizing the residents. I scrutinized the staff to see if there were any overtly sadistic-looking types—a muscular fellow who looked like a capo in a concentration camp, or a frizzy-haired harridan who could have worked on the psychiatric ward of *One Flew Over the Cuckoo's Nest*. I knew all about elder abuse and that employees in the low-paying and difficult Alzheimer's units were generally not Mother Teresas. I looked for compassionate caregivers and, to my relief, found many. My worst fear was bullies who preyed on the confused elderly when no one was watching. And I'd be watching. "Don't mess with me," I hoped my eyes said. "I'll be checking for unexplained bruises or missing valuables."

As soon as the house in Oakland was sold, I moved into Loma Alta. I won't deny it, Elliot, there were sleepless nights. When I did sleep, the dreams invariably featured my house in the hills. I never went back to visit or spy on the new occupants. I didn't need to—I went there at night in my dreams. The dreams took place in rooms I'd lovingly remodeled and included the bay windows and light refracted by the stained glass. These amazingly specific dreams continue to this day. The characters vary, but not the setting. Someone is always trudging up and down the scuffed wooden staircase, or putting mason jars on pantry shelves, or letting down the folding ladder going up to the attic. Sometimes, the tone is pleasant: I am tucking a child into bed, usually Joseph. My youngest is still small and I see his shiny brown hair, cut in a bowl cut as it used to be, his dark eyes peering out from a thick quilt as I kiss his damp forehead. Sometimes, the dreams are frightening—I've forgotten to lock the front door and I hear an intruder's heavy step as he walks through the hallway toward my bedroom. I wake up with my heart pounding and I wonder if I have shouted out. Always, my dreams occur in that house I loved so much, now occupied by others. I wonder if my dreams will ever take place in this boxy two-bedroom apartment, spare and clean and decorated in black, white, and beige. Will I ever have enough life here to provide fodder for my dreams?

I'd hired capable Trina to organize closing the house in Beacon. She became much more than a housekeeper, helping with all aspects of your care, including hiring caretakers to come in at night in case you began to wander. Bless that dear woman, she patiently went through every item in the house, helping you decide what to ship out west, what to give away, which objects to sell. I talked to both of you almost every evening, getting efficient updates from Trina and halting, rambling conversations from you. Sometimes you relayed local news from the Beacon paper, sometimes you gave annoyed reports of workmen who were readying the house for sale.

"Too much noise," you said one night when I phoned. "Who hired a roofer? My roof is perfectly solid."

"The inspector found several places that need to be reshingled," I answered. "This past winter was so harsh, everybody had roof damage. Remember those snowfalls? But, no more. You won't have to deal with anything like that out here. No roof repairs ever again. And, the weather. It's already warm and sunny. No snow to shovel in California."

"California?" you sputtered. "Oh, I haven't got time for a visit to California now. Too busy. Besides, Lillian hates California. She'll never come out there."

I forced myself to breathe slowly, not to take anything personally.

"Elliot," I said. "You're moving out here. Remember? To California. To an apartment I got us. That's why you're fixing up the house. You want to get a good price when you sell it. And Lillian's up in Canada. Running her restaurant."

You didn't answer at first. I'd said too much and I could imagine you were puzzling over my words. "Do you think that's a good idea?" you finally asked. "All the way to California? That's a pretty long trip."

"I do, Elliot," I said, relieved you had understood. "I think you'll like it. I think we'll enjoy it together. It's nice here." I realized that what might be worrying you was the actual trip. I reminded myself to slow down, take one step at a time, as the doctors had recommended. Elliot would be thinking very concretely, making short-term rather than long-term plans.

"Trina will fly out here with you when it's time," I said. "She'll take you to the airport and be on the plane with you. I'll pick you up. You won't get lost. You don't need to worry. Besides," I said, "you are going to love the garlic fries I've found."

Two months after I'd moved into Loma Alta, Trina phoned to say that the Beacon house was ready for the realtors. She also thought Elliot was ready to make the trip west. I booked a flight to San Jose, its smaller airport easier to navigate than the massive one in San Francisco. I had longed for this news, fearing your condition would worsen before you could leave and that something terrible might happen while you were still there in New York, a fall, perhaps, or an accidental fire. But now that a date was set for your departure, I felt a new anxiety. I could keep my secret no more. I still had not told anyone, other than the management at Loma Alta, that you would be joining me. It was time. Where would I start? I made an appointment with Dolores. I sat in the comfortable rocking chair she kept in her office. She smiled slyly at me. She'd received an email from the sales office that morning that someone was arriving to join Judith Sherman in her apartment.

"I knew something was going on when you moved in. I just

couldn't understand what you were doing here. So, who is he, Judith? The sales office says he isn't a relative."

"A friend, Dolores. Just a friend. We've known each other since we were kids." I couldn't look at her, but rocked back and forth nervously in her chair. In the past few months, Dolores and I had become friends. She hadn't seen the divide between us being quite as insurmountable as I had when we first met. Now she frequently joined me in my apartment for tea at the end of a long day. I kept her favorite ginger biscuits there for her.

"I see," she said. "Just a friend. Seems like you've gone through a great deal of upheaval for this friend. He must mean a lot to you."

"Dolores, I'll admit this may be difficult. We're going to need help. He's going to need help. He's forgetting things. It's progressing."

"Dementia?" Dolores asked, completely professional now, but caring, too. "How far is he into it?"

I told her what the doctors had said, how the symptoms were inconsistent, but that there was noticeable decline each month.

She sighed. "What can I do for you both?"

"It'll be such a radical change in our relationship," I said, rocking more slowly. "You can't imagine what he was like before. So brilliant. A real powerhouse of a man. It will be awful to see his decline. I visited him in New York earlier this year. But now it's more than a visit. He's moving here and won't be leaving. I know it's going to get bad. I'm terrified."

"Dementia is frightening," she said. "You're right, of course. It will get bad. But you won't be doing it alone. I'll help. The ladies will help. You're strong, Judith. You're a brave woman."

I wanted to tell Dolores that if one more person in my life called me brave, I would have to do them great bodily harm. Instead, I pushed myself out of her comfortable rocking chair and said, "I guess I'll tell them tonight. Mrs. Rosen's table. I have to—he'll be here in a few days."

Dolores nodded. I realized I was glad I had a social worker.

I joined the group that night, conscious that they had changed me more than I'd changed them. Adelle Rosen's pressure to dress appropriately for meals made me glance at the clock each afternoon and go through the ritual of changing for dinner. I no longer allowed myself just a quick swipe of the hairbrush before I went out the door. I never went to the dining room in jeans and whatever shirt I'd started the day in. No flip-flops. Instead, I applied makeup. I rummaged through the closet for clothes that in my former life I would have worn to dinner in a restaurant. I had kept only seven or eight such outfits, a navy pantsuit, several skirts, long and short, a few good dresses. However, worn in rotation with a variety of scarves and pretty pumps, they sufficed. I'd learned the acceptable topics for dinner conversation—the book the community book club was reading, the menu, who was ill, who had recovered and who had not, and the most ubiquitous topic of all—grandchildren. I even started sprinkling my conversation with the occasional Yiddish word I remembered from childhood or learned at the table. I'd grown fond of Adelle and Vera and Louise, and it seemed they liked me as well.

Louise Block had become noticeably brighter, and even found a remnant of her former appetite. Perhaps our friendship was part of that recovery. I'd like to think so, but I think it was due in greater part to the unfortunate decline of our table's fourth member—Mrs. Saperstein. Lately Vera Saperstein was no longer her same sprightly self. It is like that when you age, I'd observed. First you are old, but still mostly yourself and able to do most things. Then, and it can be sudden, people become *older* old, not just old. Vera and her *machatunim*, Mrs. Block, had reversed roles. Mrs. Block was becoming the caretaker, reminding Vera to finish her soup, to brush the crumbs from the front of her dress. This was sad to note, but it seemed to give Mrs. Block purpose. Vera Saperstein had finally begun to look her age and no longer told lively, spicy stories about acquiring her jewelry and the trips to Vegas with Mr. Saperstein. She sat more quietly, looking into each of our faces, speaking less, listening more.

I missed her stories, especially her dirty jokes. "So did you hear about the woman who was getting married for the fourth time? She went to her dressmaker and asked her to make a white bridal gown. 'My dear,' said the dressmaker, 'this is your fourth wedding. Are you sure you ought to wear white?' 'Sure,' said the prospective bride. 'See, my first husband, Al, was a gynecologist. All he wanted to do was look around down there and examine me. My second husband, Harold, was a stamp collector. Well, you can imagine what he wanted to do down there. Boy oh boy, do I miss Harold! My third husband, David, was a psychiatrist. All he wanted to do was talk about it. But my next groom, Jerry, he's a lawyer. So you *know* I'm going to get screwed!'" We all roared with laughter, even Adelle.

Vera still wore her jewelry for dinner, but one night I noticed there was tape wound and rewound around the back of her dazzling lapis lazuli ring, distracting from its magnificent beauty.

I lifted Mrs. Saperstein's hand, the one with the lovely blue ring on it, and stared at the tape with a questioning look.

Her hand remained limp in my own, but Mrs. Block answered for her. "I stopped by Vera's apartment to pick her up for dinner, and I noticed her ring had fallen off. It was lying on the carpet. I'm glad I noticed it before we left. She might have lost it on the elevator or somewhere else on the way. I found masking tape in her kitchen drawer and wound it around the ring. It'll keep it from slipping off her finger again." She turned to Mrs. Saperstein. "Now do you believe me, Vera? You're losing weight. When your rings fall off, you're losing weight. Believe me, I know."

Gabriel cleared the salads, jovial as usual, and I realized I'd have to warn him about our additional diner. I wondered how his flirty comments would change when a man joined us at the table. I picked up my water glass and took a swallow, then began.

"Ladies, I need to speak about something tonight. It's a special favor and very important to me, so I hope you won't object."

I had everyone's attention, although Mrs. Rosen's face had already assumed a critical expression. But I knew what I needed to say to win her over and had rehearsed it.

"Most tables at Loma Alta have four people. But I have a guest arriving next week. An old friend. And, as he'll be here for some time, Dolores says I might have him join us. If you approve, that is, of having five people at the table."

Each woman reacted to a different part of my speech. Vera Saperstein came out of her torpor to smile at me and say with great animation, "He? A *he* is visiting you?"

Mrs. Block replied sweetly, "Judith, if he's a special friend of yours, then he's a friend of ours. Of course he's welcome at the table."

Mrs. Rosen asked, "Just who is this man?" She squinted at me and added, "Where will he be staying?"

"Okay," I said. "I'll tell you everything." Appealing to their desire for exclusivity, I lowered my voice and added, "But please, please don't spread this around. Can we keep this just between us?"

All three nodded. I could sense their excitement building.

"His name is Elliot Pine," I began, and the women leaned forward, closing in, ready for the story. I obliged. I told them how I'd known you since childhood and that I'd cared for you deeply all this time, but we'd always been either in a relationship with someone else or living on different coasts. This was quite a glossing over of the facts, but I thought it was all the information they needed.

"How romantic," Vera Saperstein said, and put her hand over her heart. "An unfulfilled love. Ships passing in the night."

"Wait," I said. "You see, there's more." I explained about your increasing difficulties, that you now had a form of dementia. I told them how there was no one to look after you in New York, where you'd lived for many years. So, I'd invited you to live with me at Loma

Alta for as long as it was practical and then, well, and I trailed off. "Who knows?" I said. "None of us can know." For Mrs. Rosen's benefit, I described how you had been a brilliant lawyer in New York, an important trial lawyer, and for four years had even served in Washington as a clerk to the famous Supreme Court justice known as the scholar-athlete.

"*That* judge?" Mrs. Rosen looked suitably impressed. "You mean from the US *Supreme* Court?"

"Yes, that one. But sadly, my friend is not what he used to be," I said. "He forgets things. He isn't as quick or as funny as before, but I think you'll like him."

Mrs. Saperstein shrugged. "So who's as quick as they used to be?"

Dear Mrs. Saperstein. I reached over and took her hand again. She herself was fading at an alarming rate.

"No wife?" Mrs. Block asked quietly. I had forgotten I might be asked about this and hesitated.

"Actually, the wife"—for what else could I call Lillian?—"bailed out on him. She couldn't accept that he needed help, so she just left."

There was a moment of shocked silence before Mrs. Rosen sniffed and said, "But surely he doesn't need to stay with you. You're implying you'll share your apartment?"

I nodded. "It's better this way. I need to help him. We've known each other really well for practically all of our lives."

"Adelle," Mrs. Block said, looking sternly at Mrs. Rosen, "it's none of our business where Judith's friend stays. We're not children here."

I believe this was the first time I'd heard Mrs. Block disagree with Mrs. Rosen and her opinions.

Mrs. Block turned back to me and, almost with pleading in her voice, asked, "By chance, does your friend Elliot like the theater? Do you think he's seen one of Artie's shows in New York?"

I told her that this was entirely possible as Elliot frequently went to the theater. He loved Broadway.

Mrs. Block smiled happily. "Good," she said. "It will be good to have another New Yorker here."

Vera Saperstein added, more enthusiastically than she'd sounded in weeks, "It'll be good having a man at the table, to hear a man's voice around here. Frankly, I'm very tired of all you ladies. Too many women. Is he a good-looking man?"

I smiled. "Yes, I think we'd all agree that Elliot is good looking. Always was and still is."

"Then Judith, I hope you won't be a dummy, like his bitch of a wife. I expect you to get something going with this Elliot fellow while you still can, and when you do, you'd better tell us all about it. Every detail. God knows, we need some signs of life in this place."

I laughed. "You know, Vera, I'd like that, too. But a romance doesn't seem quite right. Elliot isn't really in full possession of his faculties. Do you know what I mean?"

"No," Mrs. Saperstein said. "I do not know at all what you mean. He's not dead, is he?"

"Vera," Mrs. Rosen admonished. "You are truly lacking in taste."

Gabriel arrived then with our dessert, vanilla ice cream again. Mrs. Rosen, as usual, took charge, and for once I was grateful. "Young man," she said, and looked up at our waiter.

Gabriel stiffened. *What now?* his look seemed to say. What had he done now to displease this impossible woman?

"I want you to know that starting next . . ." She glanced at me questioningly.

"Wednesday," I said.

"Wednesday," Mrs. Rosen continued. "We'll have five at the table. Mrs. Sherman here will be joined by her gentleman friend, Mr. Elliot Pine. He is from New York, so he is used to excellent service. We do not want any sloppiness, nor comments of the vulgar sort you usually greet us with. Is that understood, Gabriel?"

Gabriel stared at her for a moment, then his gaze shifted to me and his face lit up. "You got a boyfriend coming, Mrs. Sherman? Good for you." When he placed the bowl of ice cream in front of me, he winked.

Well, I thought to myself after dinner, that hadn't gone too badly. I hoped it would go as well with my three offspring. And, their spouses, for their practical mates would undoubtedly chime in with more serious matters that I had not, perhaps, even considered. I was on the defensive before I said a word to the children. Since when were things so reversed that I dreaded telling my children my private business? I steeled myself for what lay ahead, dreading their criticism.

They were difficult, those conversations with Evan in New York, Joseph in Baltimore, and worst of all, Miriam down in Los Angeles. The twins remembered you from our long-ago Thanksgiving visit to New York, but I doubt that I'd said more than a few words to Joseph in his entire life about you. Isn't it interesting that these central facts of who we are, we keep hidden from our children? It had been so crucial for me to keep Walt's, his father's, memory alive for the boy, that the name Elliot had barely been uttered.

Miriam, as daughters will, had studied you the few times we'd been together, and she immediately understood what you meant to me and what my announcement was revealing. "Wait a minute, Mom, this is why you sold your gorgeous house and moved to that old people's home? To have a place for this Elliot? Your old boyfriend?" Her indignation jumped at me from the telephone. So disapproving, why did she always have to be so disapproving?

"Miriam," I answered wearily, "this is not an old people's home. I've reminded you of that many times. It is a retirement community and I wish you wouldn't call it an old people's home. I have a comfortable two-bedroom apartment. Plenty of room for an old friend who needs help."

"Friend? Right!" She wasn't buying it and she quickly shared her views with her brothers. Mom was clearly nuts, she told Evan and

Joseph. She'd given up her freedom, the beautiful house in the hills, and sentenced herself to living in an old people's home for this, this . . . and Miriam apparently did not know what to call you. Miriam had always thought my having boyfriends was unseemly. She thought I had been flighty, irresponsible when her father and I had divorced, both before I'd married Walter and after his death. Perhaps she was right. Miriam was a devoted wife and mother, her marriage to Gray had been wonderfully stable and happy. I could not deny that she'd provided a much more stable life for her two sons than I had for my children.

Joseph called me soon after speaking to his older sister. I could almost see the small, amused smile on his face. "Well, Mom. You've certainly got Miriam's panties in a twist. I don't even know the guy, but Miriam thinks you ought to be in another type of institution, one for lunatics. I'm working thirty-six hours out of every forty-eight here at the hospital. So, please give me a nice, easy way to defend you. I don't have time to come out there and get you committed."

I was thankful for Joseph's sense of humor. He was the only one who could diffuse his older sister Miriam's righteous indignation. "Joseph, the last I heard, your specialty was emergency medicine, not psychiatry. So, you can't commit me. And I don't need you to defend me. Miriam, generally speaking, is outraged by everything about me. I'll handle Miriam. You're going to have to trust me on this. I've known Elliot since childhood. It's going to be okay. I actually like it here at Loma Alta. So, don't take time off work on my account. Just take care of yourself and Heidi. Okay?"

"Okay, Mom," Joseph said. "You know, I'm glad you've still got some surprises up your sleeve. We need you to stir things up. My life is pretty dull. All Heidi and I do is work."

"Thanks, Joseph," I said. "For not judging. You're your father's son. Thank God. He was so good about not finding fault with people. You're the same."

Evan also found humor in my plans. Ira had worked on him, and they both got on the phone when they called me. Ira started, "Now, Judith, I want you to be careful."

"Careful?" I asked, expecting a lecture on finances.

"Yeah," Evan said. "We hope you'll practice safe sex. Getting pregnant or an STD might be embarrassing at your age."

It was going to be okay. Or, as okay as living with a man with severe dementia could be. I'd run the gauntlets of my three children and my three table mates. Of course, there were others in my life and their reactions would be unpredictable. But, I'd found that in the last few years, even the most opinionated of my friends was mellowing. Everyone now had burdens: their own health, or their husbands', even a few who still had needy parents, now in their nineties. Everyone had suffered losses and it seemed a terrible waste of energy to be worrying about other people. Ah, how much easier it seemed not to expend energy on deciding whether we approved of the choices our friends had made.

You arrived on Wednesday, as expected. Before she left, Trina spent that day and the next sorting out your few possessions and helping me make the second bedroom and bath comfortable for you. When she said goodbye, I was surprised to see tears in her eyes. You were on the couch, immersed in a Cubs' game. I'd recorded their game with the Giants from the week before. An advantage of the dementia was that you didn't realize it was an old game, with an outcome you'd already read about in the newspaper.

"How can I thank you, Trina?" I asked. "You made it all work."

"Elliot and I have gotten close these past few months," she said. "He's different than he used to be. When Lillian was still here." She looked at me apologetically. "Sorry."

"No, it's okay to talk about her. But different how?"

"Softer. Not as driven as he used to be. I know it's the illness, but I never had the chance to get to know him before. He's been grateful.

Too grateful. I've been embarrassed by his gratitude. He never used to say thank you before, now he says it often, all the time."

"Has Lillian called?" I asked. "Does she know about the move?"

"That's a funny thing," Trina said and wrinkled her brow. "She did call, just this week. She said she'd spoken to Julius and his wife. The other people I work for. They'd told Lillian that the house was for sale and that Elliot was leaving for California. When I talked to her, I said there were a few things she'd left behind. Some clothes in trunks. Books in the attic. Did she want anything? She said, no, I could give everything away. Then I asked her how the restaurant was going. You know, to be polite."

"What did she say?" I asked. Knowing Lillian, it was already probably the most popular eatery in Montreal.

Trina looked at me, a small smile on her face, one I could see she was trying to hold back. "She said that it was very hard, because she was doing it alone."

"Alone?" I asked, puzzled.

"Yup," Trina replied. "Her son, the big-time chef, her other kids, they found it wasn't to their liking. They've all left, gone on to other things. Lillian's stuck there, running the whole restaurant by herself, with just a small staff. She sounded pretty tired."

I looked at her, then I snorted and, forgive me, I just could not help myself, I began to laugh. When I composed myself, I asked Trina if you had spoken to Lillian.

She nodded. "I passed him the phone, but he wasn't on very long. He's pretty much stopped talking on the phone. Loses his train of thought."

I shook my head, then hugged Trina and said goodbye. I handed her an envelope. "Here's something extra. I hope you'll be able to take some time off. I know how hard you've worked. When the house in Beacon sells, we'll want to give you more. You did so much to get it ready."

Trina walked over to you, watching the game. She kneeled on the floor to say she was leaving. You looked confused. Then you did something odd, odd and upsetting. You whacked yourself in the head. It wasn't a light tap—you hit yourself hard on the temple with an open hand. "I'm so stupid," you said. "Where did I leave the car? Damn. I can't remember."

"It's okay, Elliot," Trina answered in a calm voice. "Everything is fine. I'll be taking the rental car back to the airport. You stay here with Judith. Don't worry about a thing."

The hitting yourself on the head became a gesture I began to dread. When you couldn't remember where you'd left something, or a name, or even words, you took it out on yourself. You never blamed me, never spoke a sharp word to me or anyone else. But you became easily frustrated with yourself, and this frustration was always accompanied by that hitting motion with the flat of your hand to the side of your head. I hated it, and tried to put my own hand between your palm and temple, but rarely succeeded. "You are not stupid, Elliot," I'd say. "That's the last thing you are."

We took our first meals in the apartment, me cooking in the small galley kitchen or bringing in fast food. By your fourth day in California, I decided we were ready to face the dining room. We took care with dressing. I encouraged you to pick out something special from your closet. When we went to the elevator, I saw our reflection and thought we made a handsome couple, edging toward elderly, but still current and fashionable. I took your arm and tried to prepare you for the routine and the people, knowing that this was probably useless and that instead we'd rely on your native charm and the remnants of your excellent conversational skills.

There was actually a hush when we entered the dining room. Conversation stopped and people watched us as we came in. I tried first to see it through your eyes. Was the gilded fountain at the center of the room impossibly tacky, or did it have just a touch of old-world elegance? Did the servers look like real waitresses and waiters, or did they look like what they were: staff at a senior citizens' dining room, who worked not for tips, but for just a smidgeon above minimum wage? Then, I tried to imagine what we looked like to the room of assembled diners. Although there were a few other couples living at Loma Alta, I'm sure we were the youngest and, I thought proudly, certainly, the most presentable. I put my arm through yours, reached up and whispered in your ear that we'd walk straight through the room to a table near the rear. With your height, and still rakish dark hair, you had such presence. The blue sports jacket you wore seemed jaunty, yet not new or as if you were trying too hard. You wore no tie, for we'd discovered that you'd forgotten how to tie one and when I tried, I made a mess of it, but your pale blue shirt, open at the neck, was crisp and the monogram at your cuff showed to advantage. I also wore blue, a navy wraparound dress and high heels—higher than I'd worn since moving to Loma Alta. I loved leaning on your shoulder and, I must admit, making such an entrance.

The table, set for five, held a vase of fresh flowers. Who had thought of flowers? Dolores? The management? I couldn't guess. My three dinner companions assumed poise I hadn't imagined they possessed. It is amazing what a good-looking man will do to a table of women, even a table of elderly women. Mrs. Rosen sat straighter in her chair. She wore a particularly nice suit, black with red braided trim, from her closet of St. John knits. And, I believe her hair had been freshly done, not a platinum wisp out of place. Vera Saperstein had raided her jewelry boxes, and in the dim light of our table toward the rear, she glittered with several sparkling rings and the same amber pendant that had stunned me the night I'd first met her. Her eyes widened when she saw you, and she pulled at the neckline of her dress, exposing a bit more of her sun-freckled skin, as well as her generous cleavage. Even Louise Block had made an effort, replacing her usual drab cardigan and skirt with a nice gray silk dress. She smiled up at you and said, "Welcome, welcome, we're so glad you're here." As the tiny woman half rose to reach your extended hand, her dress made a very satisfactory swishing sound.

"Please, please sit down," you said.

I introduced you to each woman and you bent and looked into their eyes, with the deep penetrating look that had won women over all your life. It was how you had made people feel so noticed, so individually regarded. So seen. Of course, I knew your memory had declined to the extent that you might not remember anything from this meal to the next, but still, you made an awfully good facsimile of your old ways. You pulled my chair out for me, then sat and brought the folded linen napkin to your lap. You looked up at the table and laughed merrily, admitting, "Forgive me, ladies, I'm terrible with names. Judith will have to remind me all the time, I'm sure, but I won't forget how lovely each of you ladies are."

I looked around the table happily, glad that you were having an alert evening, pleased that the stimulation of the new environment hadn't overwhelmed you, but instead had brought out your not inconsiderable charm. You seemed to enjoy the meal and told stories about our Chicago childhood, the old memories still accessible, not yet wiped clean by the ravages of disease.

You spoke of me to the table. "You must know what a brilliant girl Judith was. She tore through books so quickly, I called her Rocket. She read everything she could get her hands on. After she finished the Young Adult section, the librarian gave her special permission to read whatever she wanted from the adult shelves. Judith," you asked, "how old were you when you first read Shakespeare?"

I shrugged. "Oh, who remembers?" I said, picking up my water goblet to cover my smile of pleasure.

"Well, I do, Judith," you said. "You were still in seventh grade.

Julius Caesar. Then, it was *Romeo and Juliet*, as I recollect. Or maybe *Taming of the Shrew*. Judith was impressive. She would tell us the plots in that way she has—acting the parts, pretending to do sword fights. You could see it. I love hearing Judith tell stories, don't you?" you asked the three ladies, who were hanging on your every word. You looked at me, then covered my right hand with your left, adding graciously, "And I want to hear your stories, too. Each of you ladies will have to tell me all about your lives. You have some good stories, I'll bet." Then, to all of our embarrassment, you reached over to Mrs. Rosen's plate with your fork and stabbed a piece of her flank steak, bringing it enthusiastically to your mouth.

"Maybe a bit overcooked," you said as you chewed. Mrs. Rosen stared, but didn't say a word. You went on to finish your own steak as well as what was left on Adelle Rosen's plate.

I knew the day would come when you might not even associate me with these memories, that events would blur together and that our nights of such coherent dinner table conversation were numbered. But I was grateful for this first evening and pleased that Mrs. Rosen's table also seemed happy with your addition.

The women's liberation movement has not changed the way women defer to men, especially handsome men. And it was even more true for these women, who had been born at least a decade or so before me. Within days, I think we could no longer call our table Mrs. Rosen's table. Our table of five became Elliot's table, the women turning to you for your opinion, seeming not to notice when you stared at them vacantly, not being able to recall the topic under discussion. Of course Adelle Rosen was and always would be a force to reckon with, but soon everyone in our little group waited for you, not Adelle, to pronounce on the food, the news, the weather that afternoon. The women asked you how you liked the soup, about your health, about every aspect of your move to California. They were not above chastising me if they felt I'd been remiss in taking care of you.

"Judith," Mrs. Block said. "Don't you think Elliot needs a sweater? They keep the dining room so cold. Perhaps you ought to go up and get one for him."

"Judith," Vera Saperstein said. "You haven't taken Elliot to see our redwoods. Isn't that right, Elliot? You must see the redwoods."

You looked innocently at me, then shrugged. "We haven't, have we, Judith?"

I smiled, knowing the fight I'd have to get you interested in a hike, or even a long ride. Venturing outdoors had become limited to fast-food outings or parks close to our apartment. You had little patience or stamina for day-long outings. These days you wanted your creature comforts, not adventure. But I played along and said, "Of course, Elliot, I ought to take you on a hike to the giant redwoods. We haven't been since you were out here ages ago. It must be over thirty years since we did that walk. Vera's right, the trees are magnificent."

Then I addressed the table. "Once, years ago, when Elliot visited me out here, we took a walk with the kids in the redwoods near Santa Cruz—Scotts Valley—where that narrow-gage railroad goes. You did love it, Elliot. Remember that cathedral grove the trees make?" You made no response, seeming to be considering what I'd said. My mind went back to delicate Meredith, already very sick, and her son, Matthew, still a small child. I wondered how much of this you remembered. So the story became about us, our history. The women accepted us as a couple, and even though the circumstances now were not exactly as I'd once dreamed, I still found happiness in it. Does that seem strange? I suppose it does, but I had waited so long for you.

One day, Vera Saperstein arrived at the table with a brown leather jacket, a man's jacket. "Elliot," she announced, "this belonged to my late husband. I was thinking it would look nice on you. It's practically new. I couldn't bear to give it to Goodwill. Here, why don't you try it on?"

You obligingly put your arms through the sleeves and stood to model it. It fit, but was years out of date, with its shoulder pads and wide lapels, the whole jacket cut miles too large. Today's styles in menswear are fitted and narrow.

"Wow, it's in great condition," you said and pulled the jacket around yourself. "Look at the leather. Practically unworn. I love it." You kept the heavy jacket on all during the meal.

Suddenly, you looked like an old man, one who didn't pay attention to style, not anything like the Elliot I knew, always fashionable, looking like a sophisticated European in your well-tailored suits and handcrafted Italian shoes. I wanted to rip dead Mr. Saperstein's jacket from your shoulders and never see it again. Of course, I didn't, because you loved the damn thing. It became your favorite garment and you kept it draped over the back of a chair in the apartment, reaching for it day after day, which brought great satisfaction to Vera and everyone else at the table, and drove me crazy. Oh, well. A small price to pay for your happiness.

Sometimes, in the apartment at night, we spoke of our parents, your memories of the old days much fresher than those of recent times. "Your mother was always there for you, Judith. Present. She was a real mother," you said. "Served fresh baked cookies whenever I came over."

"Too present," I said, and looked up from my book. "Too involved. That's why I put so many miles between us."

"And your father," you said. "He was a thinking man. Smart. He was so proud of you. You used to love talking to him, didn't you?"

I nodded, my eyes tearing up. No one else alive, except Elliot, knew these things about me and my parents.

We had long glorious car rides, then relaxed in the kitchen over tea, doing the mundane chores of our life. You tried to help me tidy up or gather the laundry, but the apartment was small and you usually got in the way. We laughed about it. Most days were surprisingly full.

One afternoon, it was already dark, you seemed restless and turned off the television.

I was at the computer. "What's that you're working on?" you asked, idly looking at the stack of pages beside the computer.

I picked up a few pages. It was this, the story of my love for you. I'd started it soon after I'd moved into Loma Alta. "Just something I'm working on. A story I've begun to write." We began to sleep in the same bedroom, in the big queen-sized bed. You craved the closeness of me, and now, each night, I read to you aloud from what I'd been working on that day. Although you seemed interested in the story and sometimes asked me to repeat a sentence, you made no comments about it. Usually you'd fall asleep after only a few pages. Many nights I kept reading even while you slept, but soon I'd get drowsy and also fall asleep, listening happily to your breathing. In the mornings, we were often touching. I hadn't slept so well in years. How I wished for this calm and satisfying life to go on and on. But after you'd been at Loma Alta about a year, there were undeniable changes, seen first by me and then, eventually, the other women at the table.

Once, after dinner, you asked the women, "How about some strawberry ice cream? Doesn't that sound good?" We all enthusiastically agreed and you flagged Gabriel and got him to bring us each a hearty bowl of it.

However, as soon as Gabriel had removed the five bowls and we were contentedly sipping our coffees, you looked up with a broad smile. "Say, wouldn't some strawberry ice cream be good?" you asked and seemed genuinely delighted by this idea.

Could you be joking? The question lingered in the air, but none of us wanted to protest. We'd all gotten terrified of the slap to the temple when you realized you'd made a mistake, so we said nothing. You again waved to get Gabriel's attention and said, "Say, do you think you could rustle up five bowls of your delicious strawberry ice cream? For the whole table?"

Gabriel stared down at you with disbelief, but only for a second. This was, after all, a residence for old people, and surely it must have happened before. So Gabriel replied with great jocularity, "Sure, Mr. Pine. Bowls of strawberry ice cream all around."

"You're a fine fellow," you said. "Been working here long? You deserve a promotion."

Louise Block protested feebly, "Could you make mine a small scoop, Gabriel?"

And you replied, "Oh, stop worrying about that girlish figure. You could use some ice cream. You eat like a bird."

Somehow, we all polished off that second bowl, but I got to my feet as soon as I was done, fearing that you might order a third and we'd all be sick.

As they will, things continued to change for the others, as well. One night Mrs. Saperstein did not come down to dinner. Louise Block reported that Vera had had trouble breathing all day. She was worried and finally called her daughter Marcy and Vera's son to check on her. After much discussion, and over Vera's protests, she was taken to the doctor. It was pneumonia and Vera was admitted to the hospital.

A few days later, Dolores came to the table looking stricken. She pulled up a chair and told us dear Mrs. Saperstein had died in the hospital, antibiotics unable to relieve her aged and congested lungs. Although we'd expected the news, we were heartbroken. Every person, staff and residents alike, felt the loss. She had been part of the fabric of the place. On the day of the funeral, Loma Alta provided its largest bus to transport the crowd of old people standing patiently in line, waiting to be taken to the chapel. Almost every seat on the bus was filled. All four of us attended—Louise, Adelle, you, and I sitting together closely in a single row of the packed funeral home. At the door, you had reached into your pocket and put a black satin yarmulke on your head. Dolores was there too, of course, sitting on my other side and holding my hand. With surprise, I realized I had grown to love Vera as if I had known her for decades. I don't think I realized when I moved to Loma Alta that I would form such deep friendships. I had not expected these new people would mean so much to me. But Vera had added such color to our lives with her jokes and her extravagant jewelry. The woman had never heard the phrase, "less is more." As the eulogies went on, Mrs. Rosen kept extracting tissues from her purse and passing them down the aisle to us. A life well lived, everyone agreed.

About a week later, Marcy came to clean out her mother-in-law's apartment. She joined us for dinner that night, and held out a box for each of us.

"Special presents from my mother-in-law," she said. "Something to remember her by. She left instructions in a letter." Louise had given each of the women at the table a lovely piece of jewelry. She'd indicated which pieces were to be given to each of us and, of course, I received the enormous amber pendant. I treasure it, although it is far bigger than any other item of jewelry I'd ever owned. The necklace makes whatever I am wearing more elegant.

"And, you, Mr. Pine," Marcy said, "I'd love it if you'd take this jacket of my father's. Louise said you so like his other one." She handed you a black leather jacket, this one a bomber style, not quite as dated as the brown one.

You replied to Marcy, "Why thank you. It's quite lovely. But I hope your mother-in-law is feeling okay. Isn't Vera joining us for dinner tonight?"

Gradually, the faux pas were not just verbal. You spoke less, staring off into the distance during dinner, no longer part of our conversations. I had to remind you to lift your glass, to wipe your lips. You'd been wearing paper diapers for some time, as you could not reliably remember to get to the bathroom. Depends, they were called. In the apartment, there were other kinds of accidents and they began to get more serious. You burned yourself one night, not wanting to wake me when you wanted tea. You'd long before forgotten how to work the fancy espresso machine, crying with frustration when you bungled the job. But now, even the electric kettle proved too difficult to manage. You also left the tap on in the sink once, causing a flood in the kitchen. The wood floor had to be replaced. After you were found wandering the hallways a few times, I tried staying awake at night to watch you. When I was unsuccessful, I began to lock the apartment door from the inside with a key that I kept hidden.

One afternoon, there was a knock on my door.

"It's me, Judith," Dolores called before I could even ask.

"Be right there, Dolores," I said, getting the key and unlocking the door. "Would you like something to drink?" I had been reading the manuscript out loud and was still holding a few pages in my hand, but you'd put your head down on the couch and were lightly snoring.

"Maybe just some water. What's that you're reading?" Dolores asked.

"Oh, sometimes I write stories."

"Stories? What kind of stories?" Dolores asked.

"About Elliot and me. Our lives. I read them to him. He likes it when I read aloud." I put down the papers and went to the kitchen to get the water.

"Do you think he follows the story?" Dolores called after me, staring at your long torso spread out on the couch.

"Honestly, I don't know," I said when I came back into the living room. "Sometimes I think he does. They're about things he knows. Or used to."

"What are you going to do, Judith?"

Of course I understood what she was talking about. I'd been waiting for her question. "When it's time, I'll know, Dolores. I think we've got more time."

She wrinkled her forehead. "Judith, sometimes it's hard to be objective when it's someone we love."

"I'll know, Dolores," I repeated more firmly. Just then you opened your eyes and looked over at the two of us talking.

"What a wonderful sight to wake up to," you said, more words than you'd spoken all day. "Two such beautiful women."

Dolores and I looked at each other. She smiled. "Elliot, you are such a charmer," she said.

Soon you got clumsier. You'd been such a graceful, elegant man, but now seemed unable to calibrate the distance between pieces of furniture. One day you tripped over an ottoman and fell against the large china cabinet in the living room. Glasses flew everywhere, and before I could get to you, you began to pick up the shards. There was a great deal of blood and you needed stitches. And this was the sign that living in the apartment was no longer working. As I'd said to Dolores, I'd know. But first I had to talk to our table, for I was sure that the other two women would want to be included in the decision.

We came to dinner the night after your tumble with a thick gauze bandage wrapped around your hand. Adelle and Louise looked at both of us with what could only be compassion in their eyes.

"He fell," I explained. "Against the shelves in the living room. There was broken glass everywhere. It was a terrible mess. He tried to pick up the pieces. The nurse took seven stitches to close the cut."

There was no question, Adelle and Louise agreed, it was time.

They helped me pack what you needed to move into your room in the Memory Care Unit. Then the three of us squeezed into the back of the golf cart, while you rode in front with the driver. It was a sunny day, about fifteen months after you had arrived in California. We must have made quite a sight, three old ladies packed onto the back of a golf cart. We laughed at ourselves a little, making dumb golf jokes, each of us clutching something special for you, an orchid, a box of candy, an expensive leather shaving kit (which would have to be kept at the nurses' station). A staff member tapped the numbers onto a keypad and we were let into the locked unit. We found your room easily. Dolores, in her usual competent way, had made all the arrangements. Your name, Elliot Pine, was already stenciled onto a large card and affixed to the door. We'd brought only a few suitcases, so everything was put away into the dresser and bathroom far too quickly. Mrs. Rosen and Mrs. Block and I looked around the room, then watched you, already dozing in the comfortable reclining chair near the window. Sunshine poured in through the glass onto your untroubled face. There was nothing else to put away.

I sniffed the air. It smelled fresh, nothing objectionable to my discerning nose. There were no bunnies or nursery characters on the walls. It was a well-appointed room, even tasteful. Adelle and Louise glanced at one another. They kissed me on the cheek and then, ever tactful, left, linking arms, saying they'd walk back together. It was such a beautiful day. They'd see me at dinner that night.

I wanted to sit on your lap, put my head on your shoulder, but I knew I'd startle you. Lately you'd become distressed and agitated when awakened suddenly. How lonely I would be in the apartment without you. I lay down on the neatly made bed and stared at your handsome profile. Despite the diminishment of your mind, your beauty never faded. Asleep, Elliot, you resembled a dignified college professor, your temples finally graying a bit, your hair a bit thinner. I closed my eyes for a moment, tired to the bone from the nights over the past months when I'd remained sleepless, hypervigilant, listening to you roam the apartment. When I awoke, the sun outside your window was much lower in the sky. I felt you close beside me, curled up against me. It was only a narrow, single bed in this new room of yours. I touched your familiar hand, the one without the bandage, and noticed that there were now a few age spots on your once unblemished skin. I brought your hand to my lips and kissed it gently.

This love for you, Elliot, was a story of my own telling, a tale more monologue than conversation. Perhaps it was not always wise, but I loved you completely. In the end, and probably the end would come soon, there would be no regrets.

"Read to me," you said.

"Of course. I know just the thing."

Acknowledgments

When you begin to get serious about your writing in late middle age, there is the sense that time is precious. But not only time makes a book and a writer; the support of friends and professionals also guides the way.

Thank you first to my supportive family—my four children, Alexis Rains, Gabriel Engle, Hannah Klasson, and David Klasson—who understood my passion and sometimes my distractedness.

To my dear husband, David Wong, and to my late husband Bill Klasson, there are not enough words. Both of you, in your own way, said, "Stick to it."

To my cousin Blair Jackson, who showed me there are many paths to Rome.

To Mary Henry and Veronica Schindler, who read and read and read. And commented with support and love. There will never be another group like our Palo Alto trio.

To the sisterhood that assembled in my living room and listened to chapter after chapter, giving feedback with love and laughter and tears: Eleanor Intrator, Rhonda Lappen, Marie Rector, and Jan Schwartz. Your friendship has kept me upright.

To early readers Kendra Schwartz Poster and Beth Gutcheon, and later ones, Stacey Swann and Jo Ariko. Every note was taken.

To the Villa Montalvo Artists' Residency in Saratoga, California, and Hedgebrook Writer's Colony on Whidbey Island, Washington: your places of refuge nurtured and encouraged me.

To Lynn Stegner and Rusty Dollemann, teachers extraordinaire. And friends as well.

To Pamela Long: I never knew what an editor was until you touched this book.

To the sisterhood at She Writes Press. Not all authors are as fortunate as we are to have the comfort of other women writers at every stage of the process. I especially thank fellow SWP author Lisa Braver Moss.

To the indefatigable Brooke Warner, who created this innovative publishing model and who sustains and is a cheerleader to so many of us.

My deepest gratitude.

Questions for Discussion

1. The author tries to analyze the factors that make us love the people we do: Beauty, Consolation, Magic, Insanity, Being Seen, etc. Do you agree that these qualities make us love the people we do? Can you add others to this list?

2. In what ways do the views of people important to us in childhood and adolescence remain important to us our whole lives?

3. How do the people that surround us during our childhood and adolescence mold the adults we become? Can we ever break free of the roles and identities we were given in these formative years?

4. How are Judith and Elliot right for each other? In what ways are they wrong for each other?

5. At Camp Avodah, when Judith and Elliot are sixteen, she thinks, about Elliot, *This is what love feels like.* For all her life, Judith says, Elliot was "the man by which I measured all other loves." Has there been anyone in your own life who was that person?

6. Judith asks herself what her devotion to Elliot has cost her in terms of her other relationships. What do you see as the price of this loyalty to Elliot?

7. If we do not feel the Sensory Fulfillment (touch, smell, etc.) that Judith describes as important to her, can we still love someone?

8. Why does Elliot, time after time, not choose Judith?

9. In terms of power in relationships, is a relationship possible if the power balance is not equal? Would you like to be the one holding the power? Or the one who is less in control?

10. How and when does the power shift between Elliot and Judith?

About the Author

© Mike Mesikep

Elayne grew up on the Northside of Chicago. She went to university and graduate school in the Midwest—Ohio State University and the University of Michigan where she earned a Masters of Public Health and then a PhD in Psychology. She lived in Barbados, West Indies, working as a health care consultant with Project Hope in the Caribbean; then, several decades later, returning as a writer and columnist for the Barbados Daily Nation. Her professional career has largely been in academia at San Jose State University, with her research and clinical area of expertise being the severely mentally ill. A recent transplant to the Santa Ynez Valley, near Santa Barbara, she is a popular lifestyle newspaper columnist there. Elayne has also appeared on San Francisco public television as a restaurant critic. She's been awarded several writer's residencies, including Hedgebrook Writer's Colony on Whidbey Island, Washington and Villa Montalvo in Saratoga, California. She daily walks her young dachshund and aged fluffy white rescue through nearby vineyards. She is married to David, a scientist. Between them, they have five children, all grown.

SELECTED TITLES FROM SHE WRITES PRESS

She Writes Press is an independent publishing company founded to serve women writers everywhere. Visit us at www.shewritespress.com.

A Drop In The Ocean: A Novel by Jenni Ogden $16.95, 978-1-63152-026-6
When middle-aged Anna Fergusson's research lab is abruptly closed, she flees Boston to an island on Australia's Great Barrier Reef—where, amongst the seabirds, nesting turtles, and eccentric islanders, she finds a family and learns some bittersweet lessons about love.

Center Ring by Nicole Waggoner $17.95, 978-1-63152-034-1
When a startling confession rattles a group of tightly knit women to its core, the friends are left analyzing their own roads not taken and the vastly different choices they've made in life and love.

A Work of Art by Micayla Lally $16.95, 978-1631521683
After their breakup—and different ways of dealing with it—Julene and Samson eventually find their way back to each other, but when she finds out what he did to keep himself busy while they were apart, she wonders: Can she trust him again?

Anchor Out by Barbara Sapienza $16.95, 978-1631521652
Quirky Frances Pia was a feminist Catholic nun, artist, and beloved sister and mother until she fell from grace—but now, done nursing her aching mood swings offshore in a thirty-foot sailboat, she is ready to paint her way toward forgiveness.

Duck Pond Epiphany by Tracey Barnes Priestley $16.95, 978-1-938314-24-7
When a mother of four delivers her last child to college, she has to decide what to do next—and her life takes a surprising turn.

The Geometry of Love by Jessica Levine $16.95, 978-1-938314-62-9
Torn between her need for stability and her desire for independence, an aspiring poet grapples with questions of artistic inspiration, erotic love, and infidelity.